NIGHT WORK

A NOVEL OF VIETNAM

Dennis Foley

OPEN ROAD
INTEGRATED MEDIA
NEW YORK

This book is dedicated to
Staff Sergeant Pellum Bryant, Jr.,
a soldier's soldier.

Copyright © 1995 by Dennis Foley

978-1-5040-7316-5

This edition published in 2021 by Open Road Integrated Media, Inc.
180 Maiden Lane
New York, NY 10038
www.openroadmedia.com

"They all hold swords, being expert in war: every man hath his sword upon his thigh because of fear in the night."

Song of Solomon 3:8

FOREWORD

The fact that Lieutenant James Hollister already had one combat tour in Vietnam behind him was of no consequence when it came to his reassignment. He was as available to return to Vietnam as if he had never been there. But he had been there, and he had survived an impressive yet difficult year—the first half of it as a rifle platoon leader in a separate Airborne brigade, the second half as a platoon leader in the brigade's long-range patrol detachment.

While his military record was solid and showed the kind of experience that the army wanted in its junior leaders, it failed to show the hairline cracks that were left. And Hollister was the last one to admit that he had been hurt more deeply by his experiences than the wounds that had laid him up in a field hospital.

Hollister would soldier on, swallow the pain, and lead by example. That's the way the army had trained him and the way his family had raised him.

We all knew Jim Hollister, admired him, and wished that we could be like him. But we never envied him his burden nor desired his trials. Still, there is a little bit of Jim Hollister in all of us. Most of us wish there were much more.

CHAPTER 1

The air churned up by the chopper blades began to evaporate the sweat on Hollister's face as he leaned back against the fire wall in the cramped compartment of the helicopter, trying to grab for air to fill his burning lungs.

He'd done what he could do. They were all in, he had given the copilot the signal to go. His six-man patrol kept their eyes fixed on the black ribbon of trees that surrounded the landing zone as the pilot sucked in some collective and pushed the cyclic forward to start the chopper up and out of the tiny clearing.

Though focused on the outside of the ship, each man was conscious of the chopper's progress and, to the man, each was still amazed that choppers could even fly. Still, the aging Huey rolled forward and started to reach up, coming off its skids, lifting its tail, straining for the transition from forward to upward motion with a pair of unexplained bumps on the hardened rice paddy.

As the chopper reached the end of the clearing, it had gained just enough altitude to kiss the tops of the nipa palms with the chin bubble. Hollister didn't need to look around to know they were in trouble. The chopper seemed to strain more than it usually did to struggle for airspeed and altitude.

At just under a hundred and fifty feet off the ground, and nearly forty knots, the instrument panel lit up with flashing MASTER CAUTION and RPM LIMIT lights. Instantly, every man in the chopper knew they were in very big trouble.

"We're hit! We're going in! No power! No hydraulics!" the pilot yelled to warn the already alerted crew and passengers.

Hollister looked around to see if his five charges were braced for the worst. He then looked out for the ground to gauge how long, how far, and how fast it was all going to happen.

The chopper was yawing over to the right side and heading toward the ground, nose low, at a very high rate of speed. Hollister unconsciously searched the floor of the chopper for something to hold on to as the ground came up at them—faster and faster and faster until, suddenly . . .

He sat straight up, sweat-soaked and naked in his own bed, and screamed as his own death approached.

"Honey? What? What is it?" Susan asked as she awoke, finding him shielding his eyes with his crossed arms. She knew the answer. He was there again. In his nightmares he was back there—back in Vietnam.

***

The heat and humidity that filled the night were stifling. His uniform, stuck to his six-foot frame, was still wet from the rain that fell just before dark, and though he was still sweating from the heat, Hollister knew he would be wet all night. He considered taking off his boots, one at a time, to massage his waterlogged feet, but knew that it would set a bad example.

He'd learned all too well on his first tour in Vietnam that taking off boots was a luxury that field troops couldn't enjoy until they were back in their base camps. And the last thing he needed that night was to have all the men on the patrol with their boots off when things got tight. Security had to be foremost in everyone's mind. Anything else was foolhardy.

A hand reached out of the blackness and tapped Hollister on the elbow. Without unnecessary movement Hollister looked over at the soldier lying next to him and tried to make out his signal. In the black-on-black he was able to distinguish the vague outline of the soldier's raised hand motioning off to their right.

Following the soldier's pointed finger, Hollister was able to pick out some movement on the narrow trail just below their concealed ambush position. The images were hard to separate from the dark vegetation behind them.

Falling back on a technique he had learned in Ranger School, Hollister moved his gaze to the margins of the images, where they blended into the background, rather than look directly at the indistinct mass. It worked. He could make out the figures. He looked at them long enough to decide that he was seeing an enemy patrol moving in single file carrying weapons and some light cargo in packs. Though they moved quietly, an occasional muted clunk, clack, or thunk sounded as they slipped through the night.

It was a perfect ambush setup—above and parallel to the trail, able to place the maximum amount of firepower down on to and across it. On the far side of the trail an embankment rose at least thirty feet at the lowest point. If the ambush was executed at the right moment, the enemy force would be caught in low-angle plugging fire and be unable to escape it by running away from Hollister's position.

He continued to watch as the patrol moved closer and closer to the leading edge of the killing zone of the ambush. If they waited till the right moment, the entire patrol would get into the killing zone, allowing the maximum amount of fire to be placed on them. Waiting too long or triggering the ambush too early would give the enemy patrol the opportunity to evade the most effective fire. And if the leader of the enemy patrol had the balls, he could maneuver his men around and roll up the flank of the ambushers. Timing was as critical as setup.

The soldiers with Hollister didn't have the experience, and it was his job to train them. It was time. He got up into a crouch and looked around at the others. Were they awake? Alert? Ready to execute the ambush? If they weren't, there would be hell to pay.

The enemy patrol moved even closer to the killing zone, marked on their end by a large gash in the nearby hillside.

Cramping up, Hollister gently moved to a more comfortable position that afforded him a better view of the enemy patrol. He settled and diverted his attention back to his own troops. There were a few muffled sounds of anxious hands adjusting equipment, weapons. There were also breathy grunts as comfortable body positions were exchanged for better firing positions. So far, so good, Hollister thought.

He looked back at the killing zone. The enemy patrol numbered seven men, and all but two were well inside of it. He glanced over to his left and watched the soldier next to him pick up the claymore mine detonator and flip the safety clip to the off position.

To his right he heard one of the other soldiers whispering an almost inaudible mantra of caution to the others. "Hold it . . . steady, hold it . . . hold it." With each word the voice got progressively tighter and higher in pitch.

The last two enemy soldiers entered the killing zone, and the voice of the cautioning soldier leaped in amplitude and force as he yelled, "Now!" punctuating it with a burst of rifle fire on full automatic.

The night wash immediately changed from shades of purple to two colors—absolute black and muzzle flashes.

Hollister's ears popped at the cacophony of gunfire, explosions, and soldiers yelling instructions and support to one another. Much of the yelling was a form of feedback that allowed the soldier to convince himself he was doing the right thing and doing it well.

In the killing zone the enemy soldiers let loose with only a few rounds, which were easy to see by their muzzle flashes, but soon all seven men were lying on the trail within steps of where they had been stopped by the fire raining down onto them.

"Cease fire . . . cease fire!" yelled the soldier next to Hollister. The others picked up the command and passed it on.

Hollister watched as the soldier—the patrol leader—scrambled from man to man to check on each one, ascertain his ammo status, and give instructions for some to go forward to the killing zone to check out their kill.

But before the small party got up and started forward, Hollister stood and raised his voice. "Stop! Hold it right there! Patrol leader?"

"Yessir," the patrol leader replied as the others froze in their tracks.

"Hold what you've got. I want to talk to you all. Lock and clear your weapons and gather round me—all of you," Hollister said forcefully. He then turned toward the killing zone and cupped his hands around his mouth and hollered to the bodies on the trail.

"Aggressors! Hey, down on the trail! Very good job! You can recover, and you are released for the night. Who is your patrol leader?"

The dead men got up, clapped their hands, whistled, shouted, and congratulated themselves—proud of their acting. A voice answered from the trail, "Sergeant Ruis, sir. I'm in charge, sir."

"What unit you with?" Hollister yelled down to him.

"C Company, sir, first of the twenty-ninth," Ruis said proudly.

"Well, good show, Ruis. Thank you. You can head back now."

"Thank you, sir," Ruis said as he assembled his soldiers and began to check to see if each one had cleared any remaining blank ammunition out of the chamber of his weapon.

No one had died. No one would even bleed that night. Training was the most important function of the night. And it was up to Hollister to make it effective and memorable—even if he had to be to critical to make his point.

"Where's the goddamn patrol leader?" Hollister asked of the friendlies assembled in the mottled darkness around him.

"Here, sir," a silhouette to his right front replied.

"I have very few negative comments about your performance, but where in the hell was the early warning? Huh?"

Not giving the Ranger student patrol leader a chance to reply, Hollister stabbed his finger in the direction of the departed enemy patrol. "When did you know that patrol was approaching your killing zone?"

The patrol leader hesitated and then started to waffle about the notification. "I'm not sure if I was notified. I looked up and saw the lead element of the enemy patrol moving toward the killing zone, sir."

"What in the fuck made you think that there was only a seven-man patrol and not a whole goddamn VC battalion behind that lead element? Huh?" Hollister yelled at the rattled soldier.

As he badgered the patrol leader, his mind volunteered images of a night when he had unwisely executed an ambush with too small a patrol against too large a Viet Cong unit. He got away with it that night, but Hollister was sure that his good luck would never extend to the young Ranger student obediently acknowledging each pause in his lecture with clipped "yessirs."

Finally, Hollister paused long enough for the student to feel that he had to justify his actions. "Well, sir, I thought that I—"

"You thought shit, Ranger!"

Hollister yanked his army-issue flashlight off his harness and switched it on, letting the red-filtered light play across the faces of the ten Ranger students standing in front of him in a tight semicircle. "Where's the right-side security?"

A second uncomfortable Ranger student stepped forward. "That's me, sir. I guess I screwed up."

"You guess? You fucking *guess* that you screwed up, Ranger?" Hollister yelled sarcastically.

"I *did* screw up, sir," the young soldier said contritely.

"You screwed up royally, Ranger. You were sleeping out there, weren't you? There is no way you could've been awake and miss that patrol. You let your patrol leader down. You jeopardized your fellow patrol members, and you could have caused this entire patrol to end up in metal boxes," Hollister screamed—genuinely angry

"I'm sorry, sir. I just . . ."

"You're goddamn right you're sorry, Ranger! Get down on your face and start knocking out push-ups till I get tired or until you reach two hundred. Hit it!"

The Ranger student dropped to the front leaning rest position and placed his M14 rifle across his knuckles to keep it out of the dirt as he started to do the punishment push-ups.

Hollister turned his light back from the soldier onto the patrol leader. "I ought to flunk you on this patrol. You know that, don't you, Ranger?"

The student patrol leader paled at the thought of failing another patrol. Failing too many meant washing out of Ranger School. "Yessir. I realize that."

"The only reason that I am not flunking you, Ranger, is that you did everything else by the numbers. But don't count on Charlie cutting you any slack—ever."

Disgusted, Hollister switched off the light and continued to talk to him in the dark. "Knowing what you are firing on is more goddamn important than executing the ambush at all. You want to get dead in Vietnam, just keep that shit up, Ranger. Now that I think about it—you piss me off, anyway. Get on down on your face and catch up with your dickhead security man."

It was late the next afternoon before Hollister was relieved by another Ranger instructor. They exchanged information on the status of the student patrol.

The new instructor made sure that he had a head count and the name of every student he would be responsible for in the coming thirty-six hours.

There were two cardinal sins in the instructor business at Fort Benning, Georgia. The first was losing a student and not knowing it; the second was not recognizing a heat casualty early and preventing it.

As Hollister drove back to Main Post from the Ranger Department area in Harmony Church, he watched soldiers and civilians coming out of offices, barracks, and training areas, their day ended.

He looked at his watch. It was four-thirty-five. One thing about troops, he thought. They came to work on time, and they left on time. Most of them would be heading for the mess halls or off post to their families. He wasn't sure if he was ready to go home just yet. He was still wide-awake, even after two days without sleep. He knew that if he went directly home he would have difficulty getting to sleep and might be just too wired for Susan, his wife of a little over a year.

As he considered his options, he turned off the range road leading to the housing area and headed for the Officers Club and the infamous Infantry Bar.

The Infantry Bar was a tradition for infantrymen at Fort Benning. It had gone through several moves and remodeling drills—still it was the IB, the Infantry Bar. The only stag bar on post, it was located in the basement of the main club and thus was windowless. It was a perfect watering hole, where officers could gather at the end of the day, drink, swear, and tell war stories. And given enough time in the IB, an officer could be part of, or at least witness, a good fistfight.

Another major feature of the IB was that it was one of the few places at Fort Benning where officers could go in fatigues. All these features made it the most popular after-work bar on post.

Careful to remove his patrolling cap before stepping off the top landing, Hollister descended the steep stairs to the bar. Custom was that anyone who entered the bar with his headgear on, or placed his headgear on the bar, was immediately obligated to buy the house a round. Lucky young lieutenants learned the expensive custom at someone else's expense. Unlucky ones paid as much as a month's salary to wet down up to sixty thirsty bar patrons. At $222.30, before taxes, a new lieutenant only made the headgear mistake once in a career.

"Hey, Hollister . . . you worthless bipod for an M16!" a voice yelled from the far end of the L-shaped bar.

Hollister looked over the heads of those seated at the bar, and several others who were standing behind the seated ones and saw a GMT-Master Rolex and a hand waving him over.

As he threaded himself through the others, he finally saw the face behind the mock insult. It was Captain Mike Taylor, an infantry aviator who had flown gunships in support of Hollister's long-range patrol detachment in Vietnam. Taylor's was a friendly face. He and Hollister had seen plenty of shooting together and were fond of teasing each other about their respective jobs. But underneath all the kidding, they were solid friends, each of them confident of the other's reliability and happy to have him as a friend.

"Hey, Cap'n Mike. Any beer left? Or have you been here all afternoon?"

"Yeah . . . but y'er buying."

Pulling out a stool next to Taylor, Hollister waved for the bartender to bring another pitcher of beer and a second glass.

Pointing at the empty pitcher, he asked, "Damn, you celebrating something or what?"

"Got my orders today."

The announcement was not a surprise, but it still caused Hollister a sinking feeling in his gut. He looked at Taylor, expecting him to drop the other shoe.

"Got lucky."

"Where you going?"

"Back."

"Back? I thought you got lucky," Hollister said, a little confused.

"I am lucky. I'm going back to Vietnam to a flying job . . . I was sweating out an advisory job with the little people."

It was too common a worry for Hollister to be surprised. He nodded his head in agreement. "Yeah, word's out, I guess. It's all over the Ranger department. If you served with American units on your first tour, you're going to MACV on the second trip across the pond."

"I'd rather have my eyelid torn off with pliers than pull an advisor tour," Taylor said, pouring himself a glassful from the new pitcher of beer.

"You know where you're going?"

"Not yet. They told me that it was a gunship outfit, and I have to go to Cobra transition school en route."

"Cobras?!"

"Yessir! There'll be no more slow-movin' Huey hogs for me. Soon enough, I'll be a qualified, bona fide, Cong-killing, woman-charming, snake driver."

"I saw a couple of them flying over the other day, going to the mad-minute demonstration at Ruth Range. I'd sure like to see one of those suckers in action."

"They're something else all right. I took a familiarization ride in one last month. What a machine! Cobras make the old gunships look like something out of the Stone Age. So it's good news. U.S. unit and a snake-flying job."

Taylor looked over his glass at Hollister. "You should get so lucky, my friend."

Quiet for a long time, Hollister toyed with the condensation on the bottom of his beer glass. He touched it to the bar top, leaving a drop of water, and then dragged it into a straight line. After a couple of inches he would make another line parallel to the previous one. "I just know I'm going to get nailed with a MACV job."

"Why don't you just get your hat and go out and join the unwashed long-hairs out on the street. You can learn to be worthless and disorganized. You'll fit right in," Taylor said, voicing the commonly held attitude at Benning about the average American civilian.

"Oh . . . sure. Me, a civilian."

"It'd be tough. You'd have to make hard decisions, like what color socks to wear in the morning, and who should be president, and whether you should buy a station wagon. Sure, you could even learn how to whimper and whine and drag your ass around, scratchin' your crabs and demonstratin' against fine, patriotic warriors like me."

Putting the glass down, breaking the pattern of lines, Hollister looked up at Taylor and kicked down to a more serious tone.

"What the hell would I do? Only decent jobs there are need a college degree, and it's gonna take me at least five years to get through it—working part-time."

"If you don't kill some long-hair at some campus demonstration."

"Maybe if I just get the next tour behind me, Susan and I can get enough money put together to pay for college without me having to kill myself to afford it. Anyway, they aren't letting anyone out now."

"You got that right," Taylor said, saluting the fact with his beer glass.

Hollister's stated reasons were not the whole truth. He had spent hours and hours dwelling on his obligations to the army, to Susan, and to the soldiers he had served with and would serve with. He knew it was a foolish idea, but he felt guilty about just trying to cut and run. He felt there was an obligation to be true to those who had followed him into battle and risked their lives for him. Some of them had paid a very high price. He couldn't just turn his back on them. But he didn't want to discuss his arguments in such intimate detail at the IB.

Taylor laughed. "'Member Gratten?"

"Over at the School Brigade?"

"Yeah," Taylor said. "He put in his papers to resign, and he got a pretty quick response out of Infantry Branch."

"What'd they say?"

"Told him that they'd favorably consider his request and would allow him to hang up his green suit just as soon as he got back from his next tour in Vietnam."

Looking up from his glass, Hollister made an uncertain face. "Was he on orders for Vietnam?"

"He is now," Taylor said, then raised his glass and tossed the contents to the back of his throat. "Why don't you just put your papers into bail and take your chances? If you stay, you're going back. If you try to get out—you may be able to pull it off."

"Yeah, Susan would like that shit."

Taylor's tone changed.

"So, how's it going with her?"

"Man, I don't know. She and I are okay, I guess. She's just having trouble getting with the program. This man's army is nothing like she expected. Amherst and Greenwich Village didn't prepare her for this outpost on the nation's frontier. Gotta hand it to her, though. She has been a real trooper. I know that so much of all this is eating her up inside, but she isn't an anchor."

"She's pissed that we're all going back, and she's pissed about the war, huh?"

"No. She's pissed that I might go back, and she's pissed that she's confused about the war," Hollister countered.

"She isn't alone. I'm havin' my own troubles gettin' a handle on it." Taylor kidded him to soften the pain he saw in Hollister's face.

"She's smart. Real smart. She reads everything about the war, and listens to all the crap we throw around, and she still can't nail it. I think she knows what makes us tick. We've been there. And, in her mind, we wouldn't be going back unless there was a reason, even if we can't describe it."

"Hell, I'm going back for the flight pay and the suntan and all the exotica I can suck up."

Refilling his glass and silently signaling for another pitcher of beer, Hollister smiled at his friend, knowing he was trying to raise his spirits.

"If I believed that I'd blow all this off and really join one of those hippie communes."

Raising his beer to the thought, Taylor mused, "Yeah, man, free love and no fuckin' reveille! I could get used to that."

"Thought that's how aviators live normally," Hollister jabbed.

The new pitcher of beer came, and Hollister stole a quick glance at his watch while Taylor poured two more.

"Worryin' about gettin' home late?" Without giving Hollister time to reply, Taylor continued, "Oh, yeah, I remember that shit when I was married. You know, of course, that there are only two kinds of aviators—divorced and gonna be divorced. Lucky you didn't go to flight school."

"Seems to be an epidemic here."

Taylor pushed his glass away and leaned back on his stool. "You're right. My guess is that more than half the married guys in my Advanced Course class have split the blanket with their ol' ladies by now. We still have a couple of weeks for the other half to get their divorce papers in," he added, half kidding.

"Not too reassuring, is it?"

"Well, look at it this way. At least you know that the gut-grindin' Susan's goin' through is goin' around. Not like she's alone or something."

"Doesn't help."

"Well, drink up then—and get your ass on home. Sittin' here shootin' the shit with me will only get you in deeper. You come in shit-faced, late, and scroungy as you are, and she'll put your ass on listenin' silence and short rations for sure."

There was an unwritten code that among the brotherhood of the infantrymen no one would really complain about either their domestic situation or the fear of returning to war. They were each bound by the code that demanded of each of them a loyalty to those who were still serving in Vietnam. To badmouth the war was to malign those who were slogging through endless rice paddies. It was just considered bad form not to take it like a man.

The drive home to the Custer Terrace housing area only took a few minutes, but Hollister kept looking in the rearview mirror for any sign of MPs. To get stopped on any army post with alcohol on your breath was almost certainly the end of whatever promise your career held.

The drinking and driving consequences seemed to Hollister to be in direct conflict with the army's acceptance and even expectation of officers' drinking. Drinking was expected in celebration of promotions, christenings, weddings, retirements, prop blast ceremonies, and endless hail and farewell parties.

Nondrinkers were looked upon with suspicion, as if there were something wrong with them. But let an officer reeking of booze get pulled over by the MPs, and it was a slippery slope to removal from the army for behavioral irregularities.

No one ever got thrown out of the army for just a DWI. But the die had been cast once the first DR came across the offender's commander's desk. In no time there would be a letter of reprimand in the officer's file. That would be followed by a marginal efficiency report, and *that* would be followed with a shitty assignment that would lead to further decline in the officer's promotability. In short order, the offending officer would find himself doing poorly at jobs without status or ones that led to a file that showed little potential for higher responsibilities—and higher responsibilities were the goal of every infantry officer. Reduced potential meant certain recommendations that the officer be passed over for promotion or retention on active duty.

The Custer Terrace housing area was a cluster of fourplex, one-story brick houses for permanent party officers assigned to the garrison. Driving through the winding streets at absolutely no more than fifteen miles an hour was a seldom-broken rule.

Even those officers who might disdain regulations, and who might seek out opportunities to bend regulations to show their bravado and their skills, were loath to speed in a housing area filled with so many little children. Everyone who lived there wanted to feel that it was a sanctuary where his kids could run and play without fear of dangerous drivers.

There was a sparkle to each of the aging sets of quarters in the housing area. The glass in each window reflected sunlight without a trace of dirt or film. The wood trim that accented the traditional brick construction was bright, as if freshly painted. There were no junk cars, discarded sofas, haphazardly placed bicycles, or commercial advertising signs of any kind in the area.

In front of each fourplex a cutout in the sidewalk provided parking space for its tenants. People parked in their assigned parking spaces and expected others to do the same.

Also at each curb were neat, fenced-in setoffs that held just the right number of uncrumpled galvanized garbage cans for the number of tenants they served. Nowhere were there cans without lids or remnants of garbage that had not quite made it into the cans.

The policing of the garbage cans and enclosures was the responsibility of each of the families who used them. To disregard the orderliness of these facilities was to invite DRs for the infraction.

In front of each of the tiny housing units, the lawns were manicured to a uniform height and trimmed on the margins to specifications prescribed by the post engineers, but maintained by the units' tenants. Leaves were all raked and removed. Shrubs and bushes were trimmed and well watered.

And that compulsive neatness was topped off by the straight, trimmed edges where the grass met the sidewalks and curbs. Uniformity was paramount. Individuality didn't exist in Custer Terrace.

As Hollister walked up the short sidewalk from his car to his front door, he glanced up at the wooden nameplate hanging from the near edge of the roof overhanging the front door. It read 1ST LT JAMES A. HOLLISTER in perfectly painted black block letters on a white background. It was the only thing that distinguished his own small quarters from the two that flanked them.

Looking at the sign, Hollister realized he would have to put in a requisition for a new one. He would be making captain soon, and it was expected that he replace the sign with a correct one as soon as possible.

"That you?" Susan called from the kitchen.

"Yeah. Home from the wars, hon," Hollister answered as he dropped his car keys and his patrolling cap on the government-issue dining-room table just inside the front door.

In the kitchen Susan smiled at hearing Hollister's voice. She wiped her hands on a dish towel and ran her fingers over her hair to make sure it was in place as he entered from the dining room-living room.

Susan met him at the side of the refrigerator and embraced him. "Hey, you're home, and it's still light out. Did the president call off the war?"

"Don't you wish," Hollister said as he released her and stepped back to take her in. "No, actually we had a schedule change, and I got caught in the right part of the squeeze. I only had to run half a leg of a patrol before I was replaced."

He pulled Susan to him and reached out with his other hand to open the refrigerator behind her. "How we fixed for cold beer? A Ranger needs his nourishment."

Frowning without letting him see her, Susan moved out of his way to let him get a beer. She turned back around and handed him the bottle opener. "Don't you want to wait for dinner?"

"Sure, I'll have one then, too," he said as he pulled a pair of bottles out and handed one to Susan. "You're off duty. Have one with me."

Susan smiled at his boyish way and took the bottle. He took the opener and popped the tops on both bottles, making the caps snap as he did.

She took her beer and sipped slowly as she watched Jim. He was able to take a long drink of beer while he squatted back onto a dining-room chair and quickly unlaced the top three sets of eyelets on his Corcoran jump boot.

As fast, he switched hands—beer for laces. He did the same to the other boot. It always amazed Susan how Hollister could lace or unlace his boots without ever looking down at what he was doing. He had once explained it to her. That it came from years of night operations where the luxury of seeing what he was doing was not afforded him. He had mastered many more important field skills over the years that she was happy had kept him alive.

He ran his index finger down the center of the tongue on his boots, loosened the remaining rows of crossed laces, and then slipped his feet out. Once out of the boots, he scrunched up his wool-clad toes and enjoyed the relief of being free from their confining dimensions and weight.

His hands and feet free, Hollister reached for his beer and took another long drink. As he did, Susan flinched a bit. "Linda Quinlin's husband . . ."

"Next door? Yeah?"

"Got orders yesterday. She is really bummed out. The baby is due in three months, and he has to be in-country in two," Susan said, as much to give him some news as to fish for some from him.

Hollister knew that Susan had her fingers on the assignments patterns that had been emerging. She had talked to many of the wives and probably had better G-2 than the men did.

"So how long's he been back?"

"Nine months," Susan said, with no note of judgment in her voice.

"Whew! That's not much time. He's hardly got his laundry back," he said.

"That's just too damn little turnaround time, Jimmy."

Hollister took a sip of his beer and didn't answer. Instead, he looked over on the dining-room table and spotted the small stack of mail that Susan had left unopened for him. "Anything but bills?"

"No, just bills. No shortage on bills."

CHAPTER 2

The ground inside the tree line was damp, rocky, and very cold. A low fog was rolling in from all directions and forming a thin layer of smoke-like haze that started about three feet off the open field in front of Bui and cleared at no more than thirty feet above that.

Bui knew that if the fog continued to thicken it would conceal most of his five-foot frame from sight, but not his legs and feet. And when it came

time for him to hug the ground for protection, he would actually be exposing himself more than he would by standing.

He tried to resist the shivering that was seizing control of his body. As
much as he didn't want to go through with the probing attack that lay before
them, he almost wished it would get started so he could enjoy the warmth
that would accompany the action.

He had never wanted to be a soldier, much less a sapper. He knew that the
sapper's was the most dangerous of jobs even before he was sent to the unit. In
the months he had been at it, he had been involved in four probing attacks,
an ambush, and many nighttime mine-emplacing patrols. What made it even
worse for him was that he never even had an important job. He would either
have the duty to watch out for Americans or South Vietnamese while the
others did all the critical work, or he would be used as a pack animal to carry
loads of ammunition, explosives, or crude engineering equipment.

The ground just under his nose smelled like the dirt in his home village
near Dong Ba Tinh. It seemed as if he had been gone for years, but it had
been less than one since the VC cadre had come to his hamlet and yanked
him from the tiny classroom where he had been teaching farmers' children
for two years.

He missed the children. Even the naughty ones. He missed his family and
the warmth of their small home. He even missed his chores. Since he had been
drafted by the Viet Cong, his aging father had had to do more work than one
man could do. A chill went through him as he let himself wonder if his family
was even alive. He had heard stories of battles in his district. He had seen such
battle sites in other places and often wondered how anyone could live through
the hell that took place in what had been peaceful villages.

The tap on his calf gave the signal that they were moving out. He looked up
to see that the fog had thinned a bit and was more wispy than before. It was
the first time he had seen the outpost. It was a small compound on the edge
of Tay Ninh that was supposed to protect the highway that entered the town
on the far side of the camp. It was about a hundred yards wide as he could
see it, and he knew it was shaped like an equilateral triangle from the dirt,
string, and stick model he had seen earlier in the day.

His squad leader had made a scale model of the outpost in the assembly
area where they waited for night. The model allowed each of them to get
familiar with the layout and to understand what was expected of him without having to see the outpost first. Seeing it now, he thought the model had
been remarkably accurate.

His job was to carry two pole charges for the others and to use them if needed. He had practiced with the pole charges in a small training area on the Cambodian border. He had never done it for real. But in theory the pole charge was simply a long bamboo pole with an explosive charge tied to one end of it. In use, a sapper would crawl up to an enemy bunker, ignite the fuse, and spear the charge through the bunker's small firing aperture, hoping to be able to time his actions so it would go off after he got clear of the blast and before the bunker's occupants could react and disarm the explosives.

The pole gave the sapper a greater chance of protecting himself, as he would not have to get as close to the aperture as he would trying to hurl a satchel charge through it.

The gravel and rice stubble hurt the skin on Bui's knees and elbows. Mud was collecting under the waistband of his pajama bottoms, and his grip was slippery on the two pole charges that he tried to lift and slide across the ground. To make matters even worse, the flimsy sling had broken on the antique SKS rifle he carried. Retying the sling made it much shorter so the slung rifle dug into his shoulder blades and the sling cut across his neck and chest with each movement toward the South Vietnamese outpost.

From ground level the corner guard towers were frightening. Bui kept looking up at them through the fog. He could just make out their outline against the white blanket. But it was too dark to tell if the guards were at their machine guns and paying attention to the no-man's-land that Bui and the six others were crossing on their bellies.

As they got closer to the South Vietnamese barbed wire, Bui could hear the sounds of a radio tuned to a Vietnamese station. The voice was high-pitched and excited as it described the current successes of Thieu's forces somewhere that Bui didn't catch over the sound of his own breathing and the muzzle of his rifle clanking against a rock.

He instinctively stopped to try to determine if anyone had heard the noise. It was an unforgivable sin, and he was sure that if he lived through the attack he would be punished for sloppy movement. He looked over to his right and met the angry gaze of his squad leader, who said much with his eyes.

After adjusting his rifle so that it rode farther down on his back, Bui took another grip on the poles and edged forward. In a few more yards he came to the double-apron barbed wire, but it was too close to the ground for him to be able to slip under it. Resigning himself to the task, he reached into his pack and pulled out a small square cut from an American USAID rice bag and a pair of rusted wire cutters. He unslung his rifle and rolled over onto his back.

Before continuing, he looked to his left and right to check on the others' progress. He could only see two comrades on one side and his squad leader in the other direction. They too had encountered the barbed wire, but were able to slip under it at low spots in the ground, and one of them was trying to prop a stick up under the bottom strand to give him room to slip through.

Moving laterally—to one of the other spots—would be more dangerous than cutting his way through, so Bui wrapped the cloth around the wire and slipped the jaws of the wire cutters over it. Careful not to jerk the wire, he squeezed down on the cutters' handles. Nothing happened. His strength had been so drained by the cold he was unable to cut through the wire and the cloth.

He looked at the others to see if they had spotted his failure. They were busy with their own sections of the wire. Bui reached up and tried to sever the wire with the cutters. He finally heard the wire give under the muffling of the cloth covering. But just as quickly he heard a terribly disturbing sound. Somewhere on the length of wire there was an empty tin can with pebbles in it. Shaking the wire caused the can to whip violently, making a loud racket as the rocks rattled in it.

Almost without a pause, the sound of the simple alarm was replaced by that from the converging fires of the two water-cooled .30 caliber machine guns in the towers. Tracers flew from two other points between the towers—the bunkers he and his comrades were to attack with the pole charges.

Bui's initial response was to grab for his rifle and roll into a ball. He clutched the rifle and dragged it to his torso, scooping up large gobs of wet dirt with the rear sights and the muzzle. As he tried to clear the mud from the sights, the machine guns were joined by small-arms fire from more riflemen alerted by the initial firing. A hand flare whooshed out of the camp and arced over the sappers—illuminating them spread out outside the wire, hugging the ground.

The shrill sound of a whistle cut through the din. The signal to retreat! Bui was sure of it. He spun on his stomach, deciding to leave the pole charges, and scrambled back to the tree line they had left only minutes before. The flare went out in seconds, and the only light in the night was from the muzzle flashes of the weapons shooting from the compound and the tracers.

He got to his feet and tried to stay crouched over to avoid the tracers zipping past him on both sides and over his head. His footing was faulty, the ground turned to slime in his path, and his focus was distorted by his panic. His heart pounded as he slipped and fell twice trying to get to the trees.

The firing from the camp picked up, and the ground around Bui began to pop with impacting rifle bullets. He was sure that the hundred more yards to the tree line were beyond his reach as he ran, fell, got up, and ran, only to fall again.

Suddenly, he heard the distinctive thunks of mortar rounds leaving their tubes inside the compound. Before the first round landed there was a frightening white light that filled the night. It was accompanied by a blast of heat on his back and a feeling that someone had shoved him. He was hurled forward, lost his balance, and fell once again as he recognized that someone in the camp had detonated the fougasse that was buried inside the wire. Fougasse was thickened gasoline that was stored underground in drums and fused to detonate in order to break up a ground attack.

As quickly as Bui realized he was outside the effective fan of the fougasse, the first of three mortar rounds landed. Two were far enough away for him not to have to worry about, and the third one he never heard.

His hand shook with pain as he dug at the piece of shrapnel in his calf with a small piece of bamboo. The two-inch piece of metal was imbedded in his lower leg, with only the smallest piece of one end of it visible through the blood-gorged wound it had made on entry.

He knew he had to endure the pain and get the mortar shard out of his leg if he wanted any chance of surviving the wound. There were no alternatives, no medics like the Americans had, no hospitals nearby, and certainly no medevac choppers.

Life in Tay Ninh Province was at once civilized and punishing. Within sight in almost every cardinal direction Bui could see huts, hamlets, motorbikes, pickup trucks, and an endless stream of olive drab military vehicles that belonged to the American and South Vietnamese armies. Still, none of these signs of civilization could be of any help to him unless his squad leader, Sergeant Thanh, wished to approach a farmer, a peddler, or a driver to ask for assistance.

Bui knew he would risk the safety of his squad if they moved out of the thicket that concealed them from view. His wound was serious, but not yet life-threatening. As such, it was up to him to try to treat his own wound and not be a burden or make demands that would compromise his comrades.

The bamboo stick chewed up undamaged flesh as he dug its ragged end deeper in an attempt to get it under the fragment. He hoped to be

able to wedge the stick under the jagged metal and by pressing down on
the other end, using his upper leg as a fulcrum, force the metal out of the
wound in the opposite direction from its entry path.

His leg started to shake violently, the pain causing him to lose control of the
muscles. He knew that he had to work faster or the pain and the loss of control
would cause him to do even more damage and fail at removing the metal.

"What are you doing? You are stupid, Bui! You should have died. Instead
you slow us down, and you leave a trail of blood that any republican recruit
could follow. Move your hand!" Sergeant Thanh said, disgust in his voice.

"But, Comrade Thanh, I must clean this wound and dress it or—"

Thanh waved for Bui to shut up, then slapped his hand and the stick away.

Unsure of what he was about to do, Bui watched Thanh for a sign.
Thanh looked up, jerked his head to summon another soldier, and reached
into the ratty satchel that hung diagonally across his body by a piece of
hemp rope.

"You call out and I will make you wish the mortar had killed you. Now,
look away." Thanh waited for Bui to turn his head and then looked up at
Comrade Anh and nodded for him to restrain Bui. Words were not necessary.

Bui, lying on his stomach, grabbed the base of two small trees with his
hands and gritted his teeth as he supported his weight on his hip and his
elbows—his wounded leg outstretched to his rear.

From the satchel Thanh pulled out an aging straight razor that he
had carried since his father had given it to him. It had been his father's father's. He flipped it open with one thumb and took a grip on the
fractured mother-of-pearl handle. With his other hand he brushed his
leathered thumb across the edge to test it for sharpness. It was anything
but sharp, as Thanh found out. The edge had corroded since he had
dry-shaved the few whiskers he had on his chin before they began the
three-day march.

He quickly unslung his submachine gun and turned the leather sling
out to strop the blade a few times, more for effect than for sharpness. His
eyes wandered from the blade to the wound and to Bui's back. Bui was still,
muscles tensed. A bead of sweat forming between his shoulder blades rolled
down to the waistband of his tattered shorts.

Without warning, Thanh traced the length of the shrapnel imbedded
in Bui's leg and parted the skin above it, revealing the entire shell fragment.

The sounds that came from Bui's throat were breathy and guttural as he
endured the pain—as near to silence as possible.

Thanh deftly folded the razor, cupped it in the palm of his hand, and stuck his index finger into the enlarged slit and under the fragment, popping it out onto the ground in one move.

Bui flinched in pain but remained silent, hearing the metal thunk onto the packed earth below his leg.

Thanh mumbled something about Bui's poor performance and left Anh to finish attending to Bui's leg.

"Why does he single me out?" Bui asked.

Pouring water from his battered tin canteen into the open wound to flush it out, Anh looked up at Bui and shrugged. "You make trouble for him. He says, all the time, that you are a bad soldier and that you are disloyal to the Front."

"But I *am* a bad soldier. I am a teacher, not a warrior. I am a scholar, not a fighter."

"Don't speak. You will make things worse," Anh said as he unwrapped a fishing line stored around the muzzle of his rifle. He poured more water on the rusted fishhook that had been made out of a piece of wire and stretched the line to remove the kinks and curls. "Sit quietly. I have to do this, or you will bleed until you die."

Bui knew that the pain of the hook's point would be very uncomfortable, but nothing compared to the cutting that Thanh had just finished. He took two deep breaths and let the last one out slowly. "Begin. Do a good job. I don't want an ugly scar."

Laughing briefly at the comment, Anh pinched the edges of the wound together and began to sew them closed with the fishing line. "How can you talk of a scar when you could have died from that fragment had it hit you in the stomach or head. You are lucky, but you are a stupid man, Bui."

Taking the opportunity to talk instead of just focusing on the pain of the field suturing, Bui challenged Anh. "Why am I so stupid? Because I don't want to be here? Because I am just now twenty-two and want to go home to teach my students?" He paused and lowered his voice even more. "Because I hate this war?"

"Quiet. You will make trouble for all of us."

Anh was right. Any complaining was taken as a sign of disloyalty and a lack of self-discipline by the political cadre. It could not be overheard and overlooked by them. They would surely find out about his grumbling and punish him. But at that moment, Bui just didn't care.

After two days of walking on the wounded leg, Bui was concerned that the pain was getting worse instead of better and it looked worse, too. The entire area was swollen; the edges of the wound were pressed together by the tightly stretched fishing line, but the margins were still oozing muddy colored fluids that kept the area wet all the time. Bui had decided to quit worrying about the wound since there was little he could do as they tried to move back to their base area in the northern Hau Nghia Province.

Movement was hampered by the increasing presence of the American choppers that had started crisscrossing the skies over the flat paddy fields. Their path was restricted to zigzagging along right-angle dikes that were the only ribbons of vegetation tall and thick enough to conceal the ten-man patrol with which Bui was traveling.

Sergeant Thanh came back to the thicket where the others waited to tell them that their course was clear and that they could move forward without fear of being jumped by a South Viet or American ambush. "We will wait until after dark to move to the tunnels because there is too much open ground to cross in the daylight. We will stay here for now. Eat, get some rest, but stay alert. There are too many republican spies here. If they see us we may never get to the safety of the tunnels."

The announcement was just what Bui wanted to hear. He was eager to get into the tunnels for some rest, some release from the constant vigilance of being on patrol, and to see some of his friends. But he needed to rest his leg. He feared holding up the others if they decided to move in the daylight. It would mean moving quickly to reduce their exposure and the amount of time they were visible to farmers and other civilians who might give away their position and destination to the South Vietnamese forces. Moving like that would mean they would change their course to move as if going in another direction in order not to telegraph the general location of their tunnel entrance—ultimately making the move a longer one.

At night, they would be able to slip across the open paddies under the cover of darkness—with little fear of being discovered or reported. He would rest up and hope to reclaim some of his energy for the night move. When Thanh did not issue any other instructions, Bui assumed he had time to eat and try to tend his wound.

He wasn't sure if it was doing any good medically, but Bui took one of the small stones they had used to support the aluminum pot they cooked their rice in to relieve some of his pain. The rock stayed warm for a long time, and Bui wrapped it in a scrap of dirty cloth he had salvaged from a dead villager whom they had come across that morning.

Bui wasn't exactly sure how the villager had been killed. It could have been from a booby trap or an unlucky artillery round, or he might have been carrying some kind of explosive. But whatever it was, the old man had lost his arms, most of the front of his face, and his upper chest to some violent explosion. He had been carrying a small woven basket with hemp shoulder straps. Inside the basket were some mud-covered bulbs, manioc roots, and the rag he had used to wrap up his small hand hoe to keep it from gouging the contents of the basket.

The others took the bulbs and the manioc, Anh took the basket to haul ammunition in, and Thanh told Bui he could have the cloth. The hoe would be turned in at the tunnel in order to use it to make tools or weapon parts.

The stone's warmth came through the cloth and relieved some of the pain in his leg. Even though it caused some of the ooze to seep from the wound itself, Bui still wanted the relief and tried to convince himself that the fluid needed to come out anyhow.

Nightfall came too soon for Bui. He had been slipping in and out of a dreamlike nap as he leaned up against a sapling, his weapon across his knees, his leg elevated on a nearby stump to relieve the pulsing pain that came when his leg was lowered.

"Come. We are moving now," Thanh said in hushed but disapproving tones.

It was clear to Bui that Thanh had begun to hate everything about him. They had never gotten along, but Bui thought that was only because Thanh had always been a soldier, beginning as a member of the older Viet Minh. He had fought the French as a boy and was mentioned in dispatches for his bravery in battle on three occasions since the French had left. But his bravery could do little to overcome his background.

He was angry that he was still a sergeant after more than eleven years of fighting for the North. But because he was an uneducated farm boy from the South, he would never be anything more than that. He resented Bui for having been born in the North, even though his family had moved to the South when Bui was only two years old. Being from the North still gave him a leg up in the minds of all Communist soldiers. The fact that he had been educated by nuns at a Catholic school in Tay Ninh was another thing that Thanh hated about Bui. He could not read or write and Bui could do both, in Vietnamese and in French. The year they had been together had not warmed Thanh up. Rather, it had caused his resentment of what he considered as special privileges for Bui to grow larger.

But the final blow was that Bui was slowing them down and would clearly be a liability if they made unexpected contact with an enemy unit on the way back to their base.

Deciding not to argue with Thanh, Bui got to his feet and gingerly fell into the stretched-out single file that would be their movement formation.

A small flicker of light was visible on the far side of the last rice paddy they had to cross. Someone stood in the palm grove with a small oil lamp to guide Thanh's men into the clear lane, void of booby traps and mines, that protected the tunnel entrance.

Bui's arms shook from weakness as he tried to lower his legs and body into the opening the guide revealed. Even though it was hidden in a pigsty, it stayed dry and tight under the wash of mud and slop the pigs wallowed in.

Once inside, Bui had to maneuver through the cramped passageway, scarcely an inch wider than his shoulders. And no matter how much he had denied the effects of his wound, he couldn't conceal his loss of strength. He was glad to be at the tunnels finally, even though he would be forced to endure the unpleasantness that came with the security they offered.

After passing through several yards of horizontal corridor only twenty inches high and fifteen wide, Bui followed the man in front of him through an open wooden shaft that took them down several feet into a tube of water that served as an air seal. Once under the water, they each had to feel their way down, then forward, then up to another layer. The water served much like the trap in a sink. It prevented air from getting deeper into the tunnels should the enemy try to force gas or smoke into the complex in an attempt to flush them out.

Bui's head broke the water on the far side of the water trap at the same time he ran out of air. He gasped for a fresh breath and found only stale, smoky air that had been in the tunnel for months without any significant freshening. Still, it was air. It was breathable, and it was what Bui needed after holding his breath long enough to get through the trap.

He pulled himself up onto the mud-greased level above the water. Thanh reached out and slapped Bui on the kidneys. "Move! There are others! Move away!"

Bui tried to stop coughing as he gasped for air. His back arched, his face near the tunnel's muddy floor and spittle stringing from his mouth. "Yes. I am . . . moving. Yes . . ." he said, not really moving, hoping to have a moment to get just one more gulp of air.

Stopping quickly dropped his body temperature. And this, coupled with the fact that he was still wet from the trap, caused Bui to shiver uncontrollably. His skin tightened into goose bumps, and his lower lip trembled as he listened to Thanh speak out loud for the first time in many days.

"First order is to turn in the equipment we have brought back from the attack on the compound. Then we clean our weapons and equipment so that we may fight again on a moment's notice should we be discovered here or have to come to the aid of our comrades aboveground. Next we will eat. But I want it to be quick. We have a meeting scheduled before we sleep, and I have many things to cover. Questions?"

No one spoke. They were all eager to get on with the tasks before them and knew that nothing ever got done when they were talking. Bui tried to control his shivering, but found that the wall of the tunnel behind and underneath him was cold and damp and gave no relief. To make it worse, he felt nauseous and his leg wound pounded with hot pain, which had progressed to shooting pains that flashed up his thigh to a point near his groin. He knew his wound was much worse, and he just wanted to get on with healing and eating and sleeping.

He was unable to stifle the urge to vomit and felt a moment of panic as he realized he had lost control and there was not an inch of open floor space on which to vomit. With no other option available to him, Bui grabbed the bottom of his pajama top, pulled it out and away from his waist, and vomited the rice and fish he had eaten earlier into the pocket formed by his shirt.

"Bui! What is wrong with you? Are you so undisciplined that you can't control yourself? You are a disgrace!" Thanh screamed as Bui rapidly emptied the contents of his stomach and resorted to dry heaving uncontrollably.

There was no way to tell what time of day it was in the tunnel. It was always night down there. Bui awoke in a cutout shelf that had been carved into the side of a passageway near the complex's tiny hospital. He couldn't see much near him, but he could tell from the light at the end of the tunnel that there was a much larger one than the one he had crawled through getting into the tunnel complex beyond the light.

"You have a very high fever, Comrade," a female voice said.

"What?" Bui asked, unsure if he'd really heard a woman's voice or if it was a dream in his delirium.

A spark turned to a flame, and the woman touched the flame to the wick on a small oil lamp. Bui squinted against the lamp flame and the woman behind it. Only her face was visible in the dim light, her black hair and black clothing sucking up the light and reflecting none.

"I am told that your wound is very much infected. We must cut it open and clean it out or you surely will die, Comrade," she said.

"Okay, yes . . . but who are you?" Bui asked, so pleased to see a woman and hear a gentle voice.

"I am Comrade Nguyen Te Tich."

Rolling his shoulders in order to be able to look at her face without straining his neck, Bui saw it behind the straight line of black soot that flowed off the top of the tiny flame and mushroomed against the tunnel ceiling, only a scant inch above her hair.

To Bui she was beautiful. Her small round face was a classic Chinese form, painted with strong black eyebrows and very long eyelashes. Her nose was large for an Asian, as were her lips. They were full and had their own red-brown hue, which almost looked like the lipstick Europeans wore.

"Comrade?"

Her voice was so sweet it made Bui giggle as he answered her. "Yes, Comrade Tich . . ."

"Did you hear what I said?"

"Yes . . . are you a doctor, Comrade?"

"No, I am a soldier. But I work here in the infirmary until I too am well and strong." She dropped her head as if guilty. "I have been ill with tuberculosis. But my strength will come, and I will be able to work to help fighters again."

He heard her words, but he didn't believe a word of them. She was spouting acceptable rhetoric, common with Viet Cong who didn't know each other and were cautious about being candid. He decided not to push her for her real feelings for fear that she would suspect him of being an agent who could cause her much trouble. He decided to go along with her, try to find some reason to keep her near him on the grounds of medical business, and enjoy her company without being too obvious.

"Your wound is not large, Comrade—"

"Bui. My name is Bui."

"—but your wound is very serious—Bui," she said informally, without attaching "Comrade" to it.

He tried to be strong and not show her how much pain he was in while she removed the dressings and tried to soak up some of the thickening fluid that was coming from the wound. He could tell that she was trying not to recoil from the smell. He wasn't nearly as close to it as she was, and it still made him sick to smell it. Knowing it would become more painful as she continued to administer to his needs, Bui tried to distract himself from his wound's repulsive look and smell.

He watched her in the flickering light of the oil lamp she had placed on the tunnel floor near her. Her outline against the flame was exciting to Bui, even though he was in considerable pain.

"I must get some ointment to put on this. It is infected, and if we don't do something to heal it we—*you*—might be in for a very long battle," she said.

"Yes, do what you must."

She picked up the lamp and walked upright down the passageway.

At the moment she turned, Bui reflexively reached out and touched the hem of her fitted blouse. He didn't know what made him do it. Maybe it was because he wanted to make sure she was there and it was not some kind of evil trick his mind was playing on him. It had been so long since he had been able to talk to a young woman so privately. The few other occasions had been strictly business, at political meetings and at field messes.

Once she had moved out of his reach, Bui didn't pass up the chance to watch her walk. The light she carried in front of her outlined her tiny body. He could tell by the little he could see that she had unusually wide shoulders in contrast to her narrow hips. Her arms were slender, graceful, and strong—but feminine. At the turn in the tunnel, she disappeared from sight. Bui closed his eyes to hold the image in his mind for a few seconds before it decayed. He liked it—very much.

The strain of holding his body up to be able to speak to her had drained Bui. He slumped back in the carved-out shelf and tried to muster some strength for her return.

He couldn't gauge how long she had been gone, but she quickly re-entered the passageway carrying the lamp and bandages. This time the light played the length of her body and gave Bui a clearer picture of his underground angel of mercy. Her pajama bottoms stuck to her legs from the tunnel's dampness. Her thighs were long and firm, her stomach flat, and her waist narrow. Bui thought of how long it had been since he had even touched a woman.

He tried not to flinch at the pain she was causing while she tried to pluck the bits of rag and dirt from his wound. The smell of the wound grew more powerful. It embarrassed him, even though she showed no sign of being repulsed by it.

"This is very dirty, Comrade. You must have someone more skilled to look after it."

Tich pulled away and stood up, a blood- and pus-soaked rag in hand.

Bui reached out quickly to stop her from leaving. He grabbed her free hand. It was an unforgettable moment for him. The back of her hand was warm and soft. Her palm was rough, but not objectionable.

"Can't you take care of me?"

"I am not a doctor. I told you, I am only here because I, too, have been sick and they need help down here. Soon I will be sent to work somewhere. Some say it could be back on the great trail, but I don't know where."

"Maybe you can speak with someone. Maybe you are not well enough to go back up," Bui said as he looked up in the direction of the outside world. "Maybe they will find you are better here than laboring to keep the trail open in Cambodia. Can't you ask?"

She was quiet for a long moment, not moving to resist his touch. "I don't know. I have never asked. Maybe they will think I am trying to shirk my duty."

"What did you do before you fell sick?" he asked her.

"I was hauling dirt from the tunnels near here. The earth taken from them had to be carried to the river and dumped there so that the republicans could not discover our digging."

"But it makes your beautiful hands hard, like a man's."

Tich reacted by pulling her hand away from his, as if embarrassed by the intimacy. "It is not my job to question my role."

"But wouldn't it be better to help a soldier return to the battle than to carry dirt?"

She thought over his question and coyly replied, "I must think about that. Now, prepare yourself. I am sure this will hurt."

She was right. The greasy salve that she squeezed from a tube with French markings on it burned as it came in contact with the raw flesh of his inflamed wound.

CHAPTER 3

Driving to the team room before work, Hollister wondered what they could tell him in Washington when he called. He was a little anxious about calling. To call Infantry Officers Assignments Branch at the Department of the Army was fraught with risk. Every infantry officer knew that he would rapidly get a reputation as a whiner if he called OPO every time he wanted an assignment or wanted out of an assignment.

Hollister knew well that a good infantryman would take what the army had for him and operate under the assumption that they were putting him where they needed him and that they were looking out for his career development at the same time. Calling OPO could be considered akin to buttering up the teacher. And no one in the army liked a kiss-ass.

Still, Hollister had to make the call to try to find out more about the army's plans for him and to be able to make some decisions about his own future. Earlier, when he was single, he hadn't been so concerned about unaccompanied short tours. But that was before Susan and before Vietnam. Now if he received an alert notification to go overseas, it most likely meant a year without her in a hostile-fire zone. While he took the risk, she bore the harder strain.

He was not completely against another tour in Vietnam. Somewhere in the back of his head he thought that staying in the army a little longer would let him and Susan get some money saved up so that he could go to college once he did get out. The expenses of getting married and setting up housekeeping had just about wiped out their small nest egg.

But if he was going to stay in for a while longer, it surely meant another tour in Vietnam. And he was sure that he didn't want to spend the year with the Vietnamese Army. His limited and unpleasant experiences with it on his first tour in Vietnam had convinced him that he wanted no part of any advisory job. And the only chance he had of avoiding one was to call OPO and try to strike some sort of deal to avoid it.

Hollister wasn't sure if anyone would be in at OPO at that time of the morning. But calling from his team room at six-thirty would give him the privacy to get through the call without being overheard by the others.

He pulled the scrap of paper on which he had scribbled Lieutenant Colonel Adkins's AUTOVON phone number out of his pocket. He unfolded the paper and reached for the phone. And then he hesitated. Everything about the call was so important, his approach, manner, and tone. He was fully aware of the strongly held belief among the junior officers that notes were taken on the conversations with the assignments officers and kept in a special file that was only seen by other assignments officers. The reason given was that if you were a whiner or a real pain in the ass assignments officers wouldn't spend much time on your request and wouldn't bust their butts for you.

Feeling the anxiety, Hollister got to his feet and went over to the percolator. He filled it with water from the nearby mop sink and scooped coffee grounds from the Maxwell House can into the basket.

Placing the top back on the pot, he plugged it in, looked up at the army-issue clock on the wall, and took a deep breath. He was out of things to do, and the others would be getting in soon. If he was going to call Colonel Adkins, he had better get to it.

The phone rang, hollow and distant. The AUTOVON military communications system was far from perfect and often didn't work. Hollister drummed his fingers on the desktop and tried to run through the things that he wanted to be sure to discuss with Colonel Adkins.

"Officer Assignments Branch, Mrs. Calloway speaking."

The sound of a woman's voice caught Hollister somewhat off guard. He had been so deep in thought about Colonel Adkins that Mrs. Calloway was a surprise.

"Hello? Mrs. Calloway . . . is there anyone there?"

"Ah, yes, ma'am. This is Lieutenant Hollister calling from Fort Benning, ma'am. May I speak with Colonel Adkins?"

"Just a minute," she said as she quickly consulted an alphabetical roster of lieutenants. "Is that Allan, Barton, or James Hollister, sir?"

"James, ma'am. James A."

"Your serial number, Lieutenant?"

"05325085."

"All right. Colonel Adkins will be right with you. Please hold, Lieutenant."

"Yes, ma'am. Thank you," Hollister replied, knowing that she was quickly taking a copy of his Form 66 from her office to Colonel Adkins along with the private notes that might have already been made on him. He knew that Colonel Adkins would take a quick pass at his three efficiency reports, his assignments, and the notes that any other assignments officer had made on him.

A booming voice filled the earpiece on Hollister's phone. "Good mornin', young Ranger! This is Colonel Adkins. What can I do for you?"

Trying to control the sound of his voice and unsure if the words he had rehearsed in his head were going to work, Hollister just jumped in and started talking. "Sir, I'm down here at Benning in the Ranger Department, and I wanted to call and see if I could get some idea about my availability for reassignment and—"

Adkins cut him off and finished the sentence for him. "And you've heard that we are sending young studs like you back to Vietnam even before you've gotten your laundry back at Benning. That right?"

"Ah, well, yessir. I am trying to make some decisions and I—"

"Youngster, let me tell you where it stands. I know enough about you from looking at your file here to tell you that if you haven't signed any serious leases or somethin'—I wouldn't recommend you do so. Ya followin' me?"

"Yessir. So I'm short?"

"Son, you're shorter than short. You're almost next. Here's the deal. We're turning around company-grade infantry officers, chopper pilots, and a few other specialties so fast that some of them are just getting a year back in CONUS. You got a good-lookin' file, and you're ready to go, partner," the colonel explained.

There was a pause while Hollister let it sink in. Everything that Adkins had said confirmed the rumors that he had heard at Benning since he had been back from his first tour in Vietnam. "So I should pack?"

"I wouldn't make any long-term plans," Adkins said, laughing to try to take the sting out of it.

Showing any reluctance to accept an assignment—however unpleasant—was one of those things that all officers assumed would merit a negative remark in the secret notes. That in mind, Hollister tried to sound enthusiastic without sounding like an idiot. "Can I ask what you think I might be slated for, sir?"

"Since you have one tour with U.S. troops under your belt and you are about to make captain, you're real ripe for an advisory assignment."

The words were not a surprise to Hollister, but they didn't sit well, either. "Is there any way I can lobby for a second troop assignment?" he asked.

Colonel Adkins laughed. "Got your fill of the ARVNs?"

Again, Hollister was careful not to complain. "It's just that I'd sure like to have a crack at commanding a rifle company if I'm going to be over there anyway, sir."

"Listen, Hollister, I hear what you're saying. I don't blame you, and I think we should have enough folks that would be just as happy to get a soft MACV job and not have to spend their year humping the boonies. But it doesn't seem to work out that way. We have to try to spread out the workload except in special situations."

"Ah, can I ask what constitutes a *special situation*, sir?"

"Well, hypothetically, you can ask for a choice of assignments if you volunteer to go."

"But I thought you said I was close to getting orders now."

"You are. You've got maybe sixty days before you get alert instructions for a will-proceed date of, say . . . a hundred 'n' twenty days. So, *hypothetically*, if I were to get a 1049 from you asking for voluntary assignment with a request for troop duty with a U.S. unit, I just might be able to fulfill a requirement like that before you get tapped for an advisory assignment. The thing is that you'd have to ask for the job before we give you one. Got it?"

As the colonel talked three of the other Ranger instructors entered the team room talking loud and making a racket with their gear. Hollister waved at them and gave them a motion and expression that he was making a serious call. In a matter of seconds they realized he was talking to OPO. They all quieted down and pulled up folding metal chairs in a silent semicircle around Hollister.

Hollister quickly responded to the colonel, his voice brightened with the promise of avoiding the advisory assignment. "Got it, sir!"

"We straight on that?" the colonel asked.

"Yes, sir. You can expect a 1049 as fast as I can get one typed up," Hollister said.

"Okay, listen, while I've got your file open here I need to give you a couple of pointers. You look like you have got a pretty solid start on a career, but you have got to get that college in, partner."

"I'm taking night courses here at Columbus College, sir."

"Good, good! Now, I know that you aren't going to finish anytime soon, but I want you to get your ass over to the education center on post and make sure that they are carrying you as enrolled and that we get a copy of your grades as soon as we can. It's important that folks see that you are working on it when your file gets reviewed for assignments and promotions—ya hear me?"

"Yes, sir, I'll get right on it."

"And, Hollister, I understand your feelings. I'd be unhappy to hear that you were trying to get out of more duty in Vietnam, but you're not. I have two advisory tours under my belt already—one with the old MAAG and one with MACV down in the Delta. I'm hoping to get a battalion in the Cav next time around. So get me the paperwork, youngster, and I'll do my best to slot you in a U.S. troop billet."

"I sure do appreciate your help, sir."

"All right, Ranger. Keep your ass down, and don't go easy on those kids down there. I'll be looking for your request. Now I have to get to a meeting myself. Nice talking to you."

"Yes sir, thank you for the help and the advice," Hollister said, looking up and making eye contact with one of the lieutenants seated in front of him.

The phone wobbled to a rest on its Bakelite base. Hollister took his hand off the receiver and reached into his upturned patrolling cap for his pack of cigarettes.

"Well? What the hell did he say?" one of the lieutenants asked.

Waiting for the tip of his cigarette to glow, Hollister paused before answering. He snapped the lid closed on his Zippo and threw the cigarette pack and the lighter back into his cap. "Says if I put in a 1049 to go early, he might be able to get me an assignment in an American unit."

"How soon?"

"Gotta get him the 1049 ASAP."

No one responded. They all knew that what Hollister was saying was that the turnaround time was getting shorter and shorter. They wouldn't be at Benning much longer.

After a long silence one of them asked the question they were all thinking, "What are you gonna tell Susan?"

The Custer Terrace Officers Club was one of only two places on post where officers could congregate for a drink in fatigues. The informal attire was befitting for the informal behavior. On any night the large room with a bar running down one wall was packed with the tired, dirty, and often muddy instructors and student officers. The beer flowed freely, and the chance of carrying on a serious conversation was severely hampered by the frequent rock bands that performed against the wall opposite the bar.

"S'your turn to buy, Hollister!" a voice called out from the room filled with fatigue uniforms seated below the layer of cigarette smoke that hugged the ceiling.

A smile crossed Hollister's face at the sight of Lieutenant Morgan Rogers, a fellow Ranger who had served with Hollister in his Long Range Patrol Detachment in Vietnam. He raised his hand, letting Rogers know that he was able to pick him out of the crowd.

"You out on a kitchen pass?" Hollister asked as he pulled a chair away from Rogers's table, spun it around, and straddled it.

Rogers pushed an empty glass toward Hollister, one of two on the table. He then filled it from a half-full pitcher of beer. "No, she's on her way over here. It's a trade-off. I get to knock back a few beers if I buy dinner."

Reminded of the hour, Hollister looked at his watch, wondering if he should pass on the beer.

"Why don't you call Susan, and we can wipe out the burger supply here?"

By the time Susan and Ann Rogers showed up, Hollister and Morgan Rogers had gone through a second and part of a third pitcher of beer. The room was packed with young officers, some with dates and wives—most without. The band had arrived, warmed up, and begun playing. The huge walnut organ on the low stage vibrated two glasses together at the foursome's table as the band pounded out its version of Wilson Pickett's "In the Midnight Hour."

"We never get a chance to see you two," Susan said, pushing a french fry clear of the puddle of ketchup on the corner of her plate.

"You've got to be kidding!" Ann Rogers replied. "This is the earliest I've seen Morgan in over two months. He comes home after walking a lane out at Camp Darby, and he crashes just as fast as he gets out of the shower. The next thing I know, it's quarter of three and he's bent over the foot of the bed lacing his boonie boots on again."

"Hey . . . hey . . . You all complain when we are home and when we are gone. Is it some kind of wife rule?" Rogers asked, kidding Ann and Susan.

"I'd like to see more of Jim. But it seems like if he's home and conscious he is reading, studying, or watching Cronkite."

Just the word "Cronkite" changed the tone at the table. It was almost code for "Vietnam" or "the war." Rogers picked up on the reference and went with the obvious. "So, what is the news today?"

"You want this week's statistics?" Susan said, a trace of sarcasm in her voice.

No one at the table bit on Susan's question. They were all disturbed by the announcements of weekly casualties, and it was a topic rarely discussed at Fort Benning.

"Well, I caught it before Jim called. Seems like the Yippies are converging on Washington and the troop ceiling in Vietnam reached four hundred sixty-four thousand this week," Susan said, matter-of-factly.

"How do you know all this stuff?" Ann asked.

"She's a journalist—even at Benning School for Boys," Hollister said.

"What's a Yippie again? I can't keep 'em all straight anymore," Morgan Rogers asked.

"Youth International Party. Hippies with some college. They hope to shut down the capital for the weekend to end the war," Hollister said.

"Long-haired, no-account—"

"Can't we talk about something else?" Ann asked.

"We could talk about Jim's orders. When is it you have to be in-country?" Morgan asked.

Susan's head snapped up, surprised at the mention of orders. "What orders?"

"How could you do this? How could you make such an important decision without talking to me?" Susan yelled, her face flushing with anger.

"Look, I was going anyway. A little early isn't that big a deal. I just had to do something to get out of a job with the ARVNs," Hollister said, refolding the copy of the alert notification and slipping it back into the envelope.

"What kind of answer is that?"

"Well, what good would it have done to discuss it with you? I didn't know if I could pull it off, and if I couldn't there was no sense in getting you upset."

"I'm not upset. I'm hurt. Am I not part of this whole thing? Am I of no consideration? Jesus, Jimmy, give me some credit . . ."

He knew there would be nothing he could say that would make her feel any better. She was never going to understand. He didn't answer.

Susan gave up and silently threw her hands in the air in desperation. Getting to her feet, she walked toward the only bathroom in their quarters. "So?"

"So what?"

"So when do you have to go?"

"I have to report to Oakland December twenty-second."

She turned, tears in her eyes. "Oh no, Jimmy. No Christmas, either? What other bad news have you got?" She didn't wait for him to answer. Her pain turned to more anger, and she stepped into the bathroom and forcefully slammed the door.

The summer was fading fast in Columbus, Georgia, and the nights out in the kudzu with the Ranger students were becoming more of a chore for Hollister. Since receiving his orders his mind had been occupied with thoughts of going back to Vietnam and the things he expected to be there for him. He tried to focus on the business of training at Fort Benning, but he found himself getting less patient with students, and things between Susan and him were more strained as he got closer to his departure date.

His student patrol was doing an adequate job of land navigation through the cross-compartment, vine-covered terrain near Camp Darby, though the acting patrol leader was not showing signs of leadership—only competence with movement and security. Hollister considered stopping the patrol and having a short talk with the Ranger student about his seeming indifference to the mood and confidence of his charges, but he knew that it would delay the patrol from reaching its rendezvous point and what he had to say could wait.

As the student patrol reached a dirt road, Hollister held them up and walked forward from the concealment of the vegetation to the openness of the red dirt range road. Looking around to get his bearings, he quickly confirmed his location and walked toward a nearby intersection, less than a hundred yards to his left.

After confirming that the patrol had held up in a defensive position to prepare for a dawn raid, he left them to find his replacement. As he approached the intersection, he could make out the dark image of a jeep against the lighter color of the red-clay roadway.

"That you, Hollister?" a voice asked from the jeep.

"Yeah—Scott?"

Lieutenant Scott, Hollister's replacement, stepped out of the jeep. As he did, he turned his GI flashlight up and flicked it on for a second. The light painted his facial features in a ghoulish manner. "Yessir, it's me. Slayer of dragons, virgin converter, and Ranger extraordinaire."

"I hope that your sense of humor stays with you through your leg of this patrol. I had to take this patrol leader's pulse a couple of times to make sure he wasn't dead."

Scott and Hollister entered the rotting, one-room range shack near the intersection where they had met. Scott pumped up the pressure on a Coleman lantern and turned up the wick. The room filled with its yellow-white light and hissing sounds. In the corner bunks two other instructors tried to catch some sleep on top of their army sleeping bags under haphazardly hung mosquito nets.

Without waiting to be asked, Hollister dropped the paperwork on the homemade table that held the lantern: names of the students on his patrol, a copy of the patrol order, some notes for emergency numbers to call and frequencies to use in the event of accident or injury.

No longer worried about not setting the example in front of the students, he pulled out his cigarettes and lit one. He inhaled deeply and dropped heavily onto the empty ammo crate nearby. All he wanted to do was get his jungle boots off and get a few hours' sleep before he would have to link up with Scott and the patrol later that morning to give a critique of the students' performance on his leg of the patrol.

"These fuckin' mosquitoes make me nuts," Scott said as he reached into his parachute kit bag and pulled out a can of GI DDT.

"You won't have to worry about them out there in the boonies tonight. The heat and humidity will drown them before they land on you."

Scott laughed in a hushed tone in order not to wake up the other instructors as he pointed the DDT can up toward the mosquitoes hovering near the ceiling. He waved his arm and sprayed a healthy fan of the bug killer.

The suddenness of the urge to vomit caught Hollister totally unaware. Frightened by the complete loss of control, he instinctively spun toward the open doorway and leaped through it. No sooner had he cleared the doorway than he began to vomit uncontrollably. As he retched on the ground outside the shack, he saw the bodies of soldiers from his long-range patrol unit in Vietnam. They were there—then gone, but nonetheless vivid. The horror of their grotesque wounds was mixed with the awareness of the smell of DDT and the foul smell of burst intestines.

Faces, wounds, smells, names ripped through Hollister's mind at a lightning pace between the violent vomiting eruptions that racked his body and kept him retching even after his stomach was empty of its contents.

Not sure of what was happening, Scott dropped the spray can and ran outside. There he found Hollister racked with convulsive spasms.

"Damn, man. What is it? What happened? A snakebite . . . or what?" Scott asked, frantically searching for some explanation for Hollister's condition.

The calming affect of Hollister's damp jungle fatigues quickly turned to a chill in the back of the cracker-box ambulance. Lieutenant Scott and the other two instructors at the range shack could think of no other way to calm Hollister's convulsions, so they'd drenched him with the five-gallon can of drinking water they had on hand.

The shivering quickly replaced the vomiting and the convulsions, but Hollister was most aware of the foul taste in his mouth and the rawness of his throat from the continuous vomiting. His mind raced from the ambulance to the unreal, dreamlike images that flashed through his mind too quickly to identify, but were nevertheless disturbing.

His mind continued to spin as he heard voices and saw mental images: wooden cargo pallets—Sears window fans—fingers touching small holes in a tiger fatigue shirt—"claymore wounds. Damn!"

Suddenly, Hollister started to feel claustrophobic. He shivered again, and things swam in his head. The images blurred, and he drifted off into a twilight.

"I think you are gonna live," the white-coated doctor said with a little chuckle.

The disorientation faded, and Hollister realized that he was on an examining table in the emergency room of Fort Benning's Martin Army Hospital. The room was floor-to-ceiling aqua tiles, and the table made noise as each move he made crinkled the long strip of paper that covered its leatherette surface.

He lifted his head slightly and scanned his own body. He was naked, save a small green drape that covered his thighs and genitals. The first thing he felt besides the chill was the pinch on his right forearm. An IV needle was taped into a vein, and a clear fluid dripped through a tube.

"I'm sorry—but I have—"

"No idea," the doctor finished the sentence.

Recognizing the captain's bars on the doctor's khaki shirt collar peeking out from under his lab coat, Hollister reverted to automatic military courtesy pounded into him years before, when he was an enlisted man. "Yessir. I mean, no, sir. I wreck my car or what?"

"I really don't have a guess. You came in here puking your guts up in pretty violent convulsions. Could be a lot of things, but we have it cornered right now.

"Can't find any insect bites on you, and your chart doesn't seem to show any indications of allergies. But there are many things that could cause such a violent reaction. Nothing in your stomach seems to be kicking it up. Could be a reaction to something in your history. But I'm not a shrink, and I'm not going to worry about that."

Hollister quickly responded to cover any suspicion that he might be losing it. "Doubt if it's anything like that, sir. I'm just an infantryman with a boring history. I've never even met a shrink."

The memory of the convulsions and the recollections that fired through his brain came back to him. Those moments had really happened to him. And he knew that something had made him relive pieces of those moments. The loss of control over his mind and body was very upsetting. What if someone found out? What if his friends, or Susan, thought he was a head case?

Without any further thought, he knew that the one thing he had to do was keep it to himself. If anyone knew that he had flipped out over remembering how awful it was to have to identify the bodies of fallen comrades, no one would ever treat him the same. He was sure. He would just keep it to himself.

The bag hanging on the IV pole was half empty. The doctor reached up and turned it with his finger to read the label—cross-checking to see if his instructions had been carried out.

"That mean it's over?" Hollister asked.

"For now. We are going to run a few tests. I think you need to get some sleep, and let me refill your tank," the doctor said, taking his hand away from the IV bag.

"This kinda puts me off my game, sir."

"You're lucky. It could have put you out. Good thing we got you in here before you did some damage. Another hour of what you were doing might have busted up some of your plumbing. You are going to be sore in the morning, and I'll have some more to look at from the lab. So we're going to check you in and let you bunk down here. I'll see you in the morning," the doctor said as he turned and simply exited without giving Hollister a chance to ask any other questions.

Even though it was before normal visiting hours, the duty nurse let Susan sit in the room where Jim slept. It was a small favor. The nurse was their next-door neighbor in the housing area.

She stuck her head in and made a questioning face at Susan.

"He's still asleep," Susan whispered.

"No I'm not," Hollister said. "I'm just malingering." He smiled and opened his eyes.

Susan reached out, took his hand in hers, and smiled back. "Mornin', sleepyhead."

"You have to pee?" the nurse asked from the doorway.

Thinking she was kidding, Hollister mocked her question, "Pretty personal thing for a neighbor to ask, isn't it?"

The nurse nodded toward the IV hanging next to the bed. "Well, I'm going to keep pouring that stuff into you until you beg me for a bedpan. That way I'll be sure we've replaced the fluids you lost last night."

The on-call doctor from the night before whisked by the nurse and entered Hollister's room without recognizing Susan's presence. "I've only got a minute, Lieutenant," he said while flipping through some medical test results on an aluminum clipboard. "Looks like you are going to live, and I'm going to discharge you this morning. I want you on light duty for ten days, and then I want you back here for some follow-up lab tests. If you have some time off coming, take it and rest up for a few days. You are weaker than you think, and recovery will come lots faster with a little bit of pampering."

Hollister started to say something, but the doctor hastily took a look at his watch, flipped Hollister's chart shut, and turned toward the door. "Gotta go. Remember, I want to see you again."

Susan, the nurse, and Hollister all exchanged looks of surprise at the speed of the doctor's abrupt departure.

"What the hell was that?" Hollister asked. "Bedside manner," the nurse kidded.

***

Panama City, Florida, wasn't the most beautiful spot in the Southeast, but it did offer a nearby getaway for troops from Fort Benning, and Post Special Services was able to arrange for some discounts on motels and other tourist attractions.

Susan put down the suntan-lotion-stained pages of an article she was writing for *Cosmopolitan* and looked over at her husband, who was stretched out on his stomach soaking up the sun. "You haven't said much all morning."

"I know. I'm on vacation."

"From me?" Susan asked, a note of sarcasm in her voice.

He rolled over and looked up at her, shielding his eyes from the sun. "Hey, am I ever going to get out of trouble with you?"

"Jury's still out. I still haven't decided how angry I am. We hadn't even talked about it when you started trying to turn yourself inside out at Camp Darby the other night."

"Oh, so I got the screaming meemies to avoid talking about putting in a 1049? Hell, I could have just not said something. Other guys have pulled that to avoid the heat from their wives."

She looked at him and realized he was at least sincere. "I just don't understand what we are doing. I thought we had decided not to make any decisions about our future—your career, in or out of the army, for a while."

"We did decide not to decide, but Lyndon Johnson has other plans for my time right now. I didn't have any idea that the turnaround would be that fast. And I just don't want to work for the zips if I do have to go back. I wasn't trying to go back to Vietnam early. I was just trying to avoid something more unpleasant."

"Honey, we haven't had any time to talk. I've been living my life with you in ten-minute slices since I met you. I hardly knew you when we got married, and I hoped I could get to know you after. But it has been longer hours, you on the verge of exhaustion, and all kinds of unwritten rules about what we do and don't talk about at Benning. When are we ever going to start our lives together? It all seems to be on hold until you get out of the army— and now that's put off until you get back from Vietnam."

"What do you want me to say?"

"At least tell me if you are staying in or getting out. I never had any idea you were thinking of staying in."

"I don't have that answer."

Susan pulled off her sunglasses and looked at him, aggravated by his reply. "Well, when the subject comes up let me know, will you?" she said sarcastically.

He sat up, trying to think of some way to explain his indecision. "I just can't quit!"

That was enough for her. She grabbed her things, stood up, and walked back toward the car across the warm sand.

He watched her walk away with a sinking feeling inside. In her floral two-piece suit, she was as pretty walking away as coming toward him. Her anger was evident in the way she threw her hips and the way she carried her head, causing her long, straight hair to whip at the middle of her back. He knew he had to try to explain his feelings to her, but wasn't able to describe them. He was filled with her and the newness of their marriage. Still, he was unable to just quit the army—outright, cold. There was a war on. He felt that quitting would be just that—quitting. It wasn't a word he was comfortable with. He felt stirrings of loyalty to the guys he had served with on his first tour, and he felt a pang of guilt every time he even thought about quitting. Too many good troops, good friends, had died for him just to walk away as if it didn't mean anything.

But Susan would never understand his confusion. He'd have to see it through a second tour, try to get her to stand by him until he could make some more definite plans for them.

The beer tasted flat, but it satisfied his thirst. He sat cross-legged on the tiny concrete patio just outside their living-room window. Putting his cigarette out, he field-stripped it, scattered the remaining tobacco in the grass surrounding the slab, and rolled the remaining paper into a tiny ball that he flicked off into the darkness.

"Honey, it's three-thirty in the morning!" Susan said, opening the screen door.

"I know. I just couldn't sleep. Why don't you just try to get back to sleep."

She came out and sat down on a lawn chair. "You haven't slept one night since I've known you, Jimmy. You work out at that damn Ranger Department until you're a walking zombie and then come home still thinking about work. You haven't missed a late-night newscast about Vietnam or a newspaper article about it. Sometimes I think you know more about what's going on over there than Westmoreland does. You don't eat enough, you drink too much, and you need to quit smoking. I know that you're not here with me, and you won't be till you get this goddamn war out of your system."

He looked at her face outlined in the glow of the horizon as she paused, knowing that he just ought to let her get it out.

"I don't know how much trouble this marriage is in because we haven't had enough time together even to find out what it is like." She paused, took a breath, and steeled herself for more. "You know I hate this war and I have been doing my damndest to keep from saying too much about it here. I understand a lot more than you think I do, and I know we are never going to get going until this is over. So, go back to Vietnam, Jimmy Hollister, and know that I love you and that I will hurt every day you are gone. But when you come back this time, it is our time. No more army, no more Vietnam, and no more distance. I want you all to myself, and you and the army are going to have to figure out how to do that."

He looked at her and marveled at how lucky he was to have met and married her. She was much smarter than he was, but never made him feel it. She was strong, but never pushy. Most of all she was saddened by the war, but she never whined. He searched for something to say.

She didn't give him a chance. "All I know is that I love you, Jimmy. I don't have any more answers than you do. Now, come back to bed," she said as she stood and opened the screen door, giving him no chance to reply.

CHAPTER 4

The fever felt like a heavy blanket pressing down on Bui. Sweat pooled in the hollow of his neck as he lay in the cramped cutout along the tunnel passage. He could not tell how long he had been there or how long he had slept—asleep or awake, it all seemed the same to him.

He was tormented by fever and nightmares that were grotesque amalgams of reality he had lived and children's fables he had heard at the knee of his grandfather when he was a boy. Dragons danced with tiny moorhens that fed in his father's fields. Fire mixed with children's faces. All of this came to him in a state of semiconsciousness that was never real sleep. And when he tried to clear his head and take stock of himself and what was going on around him—the heavy malaise held him down.

There were moments when Bui was sure he heard voices and sensed people standing over him, tending to his wound and feeding him. But he couldn't see their faces or recall their words. Somewhere in the deep haze he felt fatigue and frustration and even a momentary thought of just giving up and letting the fever blanket just take him away . . . to something peaceful and cool.

∗

Water replaced his own perspiration. Bui opened his eyes and saw Tich's face just above his as she leaned over to swab his arm with cooling water dripping from a rag she squeezed.

"Comrade?"

Bui answered, but then was unsure if he actually spoke or if he only thought he spoke.

She asked again. "Comrade Bui, can you hear me? Are you still sleeping?"

He knew that moving a hand was something he could be sure of. He tried to raise his left arm, only to find it was underneath her bent-over torso. The backs of his fingers brushed the thin shirt that covered her soft breasts. He knew instantly what he felt, but he didn't have the strength to keep his hand up, making contact with her. It seemed to fall of its own mind back to the dirt shelf.

Tich did not react to him grazing her breast. She simply spoke to him as if guessing that he could hear her. "Your skin burns. We are going to have you moved to a vat where you can be cooled. I want you not to worry. Just let the others carry you. You must be cooled, or you will suffer more from your wounds."

She paused and listened. Bui said nothing, but tried to lift his hand again. This time she had straightened up. She saw him move his hand and reached out for it. It was filthy from being on the ground for days without anything to keep the sweat and the dirt from mixing and clinging to him.

She dipped the cloth in a small pan outside of his sight and then washed some of the dirt from his fingers.

Bui tried to move, to lift his head, only to find that he didn't even have the strength to raise his matted hair off the ledge.

He didn't remember being moved. But the water took Bui by surprise. The medical assistants in the tunnel complex were anything but gentle. Their days were filled with moving and tending patients in the dark, wet, and foul-smelling tunnels.

He had been stripped of his clothing and roughly dumped into a tub made out of a large teak log that had been hollowed out. The water was dark and smelled from some unseen antiseptic that had a distinctive pine and alcohol smell to it. It was not one that Bui had ever smelled except in Western soaps found on the black market

The shock of the cold water caused Bui's skin to tighten and his stomach muscles to spasm. He began to shiver almost immediately. Within a few minutes he had tired of steeling himself against the cold in an attempt to get his shivering under control.

Tich replaced one of the men, who was called off to tend to another patient, heard wailing from another part of the tunnel.

Bui jumped as Tich reached down between his submerged legs without warning. She filled a cup with water and then poured it over his head. The fluid ran through his hair and down his face, cooling as it went. As quickly as Bui got used to the repeated dousing, he felt somewhat self-conscious about her scooping the water from the space between his thighs. He worried that she might come in contact with his nakedness shriveled between his legs from the cold water. He wanted her not to think of him as any less a man than he was. He thought that if he focused on her, and not on the water, that he might be able to generate enough arousal in his member to at least bring it back to normal size.

But he was unable to focus, the cold water converting his shivers into teeth-chattering shudders just short of convulsions.

If Tich was even aware of his nakedness, she never let on.

The swelling in Bui's leg made his calf and ankle appear larger than the thickest part of his thigh. The doctor seemed angry at Tich for taking him away from more serious wounds in the infirmary.

"He will die. We cannot save him, even if we cut off the leg," the doctor said to Tich as he dropped the leg and walked away—angry.

Tich seemed to be waiting for Bui to react to the frightening pronouncement. But he said nothing. He had heard the doctor, and he wasn't being brave for her benefit. He was just stunned by the words in addition to being groggy from fever and exhausted from the demands of the infected wound. He couldn't even form a response.

Bui seemed to remember seeing Tich from time to time. It was a dream, or it was real. In either case he watched her tend to his wounds. The images of her visits were disgusting. She would put hot compresses on his wound and draw the greenish pus from it. She would then rinse out the emptied pocket with some astringent liquid and lightly rebandage the wound with a dressing she had removed earlier, washed and dried somewhere in the tunnels.

During one fairly coherent visit, she smiled at him and told him not to worry. She would not abandon him. She continued to talk to him as she cleaned the wound, but he fell back into the fog of his feverish state.

The ground rumbled, then dirt and large clumps of roots and clay fell onto

Bui. He wasn't sure if he was awake or dreaming, but he instinctively rolled out of the collapsing pocket that had been his sickbed for weeks.

He hit the tunnel floor facedown and covered his head with his arms. Before the pain in his leg had settled to something manageable, he felt others scrambling over the top of him.

He had never been able to find out just how large the tunnel complex was, or how many of his comrades were in it, or even what level he had been on during his stay. Now he was in a tunnel being bombed, and he had no idea how to get out or even if he could move far enough to escape. His heart started to pound.

The explosions were mostly muffled, but one seemed to have a sharp crack—then the quality of the air and the pressure in the tunnel seemed to change. A bomb had broken open the ground somewhere in the tunnel!

Where was Tich? Bui couldn't see anyone. There were just figures ahead and behind him in his short stretch of tunnel. They were all yelling conflicting instructions to one another. He tried to get up. His knee wouldn't work. One leg worked, but the other wouldn't find purchase in the slime of the floor. He dug his hands into the earth and tried to pull himself forward, as if climbing horizontally. The pain was bearable, but his strength was absent and he had no idea if he was going the right way.

There was a short lull in the bombs, and then one bomb ripped open the earth just above him. He heard the deafening crack, and then he heard a more frightening sound—water! A large volume of water was coming down the narrow tunnel that held him in its path. A river, stream, or flooded paddy was emptying into the tunnel complex and rushing toward him.

Should he brace himself? For what? He couldn't get away from it. Could he get back up into his cutout in the wall? Yes, he thought . . . Get back up. Get above the water!

He spun to his left, reached up to what remained of his shelf, and had begun to pull his weakened body up when the water hit him broadside. His fingers never got a chance to get a solid grip on the few exposed roots he had become intimately familiar with.

The water was a mixture of mud, fine gravel, silt, shrubbery, and the contents of the tunnel. Bui felt water rushing up his nose—burning. Then he felt himself being swept toward the depths of the tunnel levels below him.

He tumbled and thrashed out for some control over his travel through the tunnel, coughing in an attempt to clear the mud and debris from his throat and sinuses. The sensation was much like sinking, even though he knew he was doing more horizontal travel than vertical.

Every few feet he collided with root stubs and hard objects. He couldn't catch his breath, and he was beginning to panic. He knew that if he didn't get at least one breath soon he would surely drown before he ever came to a stop.

The channel narrowed, and the speed of the rushing water increased. It turned quickly, hurling him against a wall. The impact dazed him. Water shot from his nose and mouth, and his head banged against a hardened point in the wall. He gasped, but couldn't get enough air.

His hand came in contact with a length of sunken rope on the floor, and he grabbed onto it as he was caught up in a swirl at a bend in the tunnel. Not knowing what the rope was attached to, he jerked up on it. It was fastened to an empty wooden ammunition box, probably a discarded American or South Vietnamese artillery packing crate. The box came up from its jammed position on the floor of the tunnel and was quickly swept up by the flowing water.

Bui heard at least one, maybe two, more dull explosions on the surface. Then the movement of the box yanked him out of his protected corner. He reached out and hugged the long narrow box to his chest and used it to try to hold his head above the brown current still coursing through the complex. Again and again he hit the tunnel ceiling, stunning himself.

By the time he had hit the ceiling for the third time, he thought he might be better off letting go of the box. Then he remembered being totally submerged on the first part of his travel through the tunnel.

The tunnel narrowed again, and the rushing water made him lose sight of his course once more. He was thankful he'd had enough time to take a breath before he was forced under by the narrow passage.

After Bui had a few more moments of submerged travel at a much faster rate, the water took him into a larger intersection, where he was able to raise his head above water. But just as he did he caught sight of a large root, about as big around as his arm, stretched out in his path at the waterline. Before he could duck his head to get under it, he collided with it. It struck him in the side of the head. And that was the last thing he remembered before going unconscious.

Bui heard music—American rock music from a radio—somewhere. He fought to clear his head. The sunlight stabbed into the large tunnel room through a break in the earth's surface. His body had come to a stop in the corner of what must have once been a hospital ward of sorts. Equipment and bedding materials hung in the corners of the room, and bandages were strung from root pegs that had caught them before they were flushed away by the rushing water.

In the shallow wash of what water still remained in the rapidly dissolving room were also the remains of three of his comrades.

They were comrades he had never seen before, but comrades nonetheless. The buttocks and upper back of one was just breaking the water.

In another part of the room there was a body crumpled up and resting on its side, as if in a childlike sleep. The third could only be seen from the knees down, as they peeked around the corner of a turn in the tunnel.

As Bui became more conscious, he became more aware of his condition. He coughed and tried to clear the mud from his mouth. His ears were filled with water and debris, preventing him from hearing clearly. He put a knuckle against one nostril, closing it, and forced air out of the other one to clear his nose. His ear popped, and he immediately heard voices yelling and canceling each other out.

From a tunnel in front of him he saw the dim circle thrown by a flashlight playing on a wall. Someone was coming down an intersecting tunnel and would soon turn toward him.

It was the Americans. He didn't understand English, but he knew it when he heard it His survival instinct kicked back in, and he tried to scramble out of the light painting him from above. But he was sitting on his good leg, and his bad one didn't have the strength to lift him up enough to flee. He knew he would soon be killed or captured, and for a moment the options seemed to have some appeal.

The intruder, down the tunnel, began firing a pistol at the tunnel intersection to reduce his chance of being ambushed by someone hidden out of his sight but within range.

Bui knew that as soon as the shooter reached the turn, he would more than likely do the same in his direction. He could think of nothing better to do, so he started yelling to the approaching GI. He knew only the words for what the Vietnamese called those who rallied to the other side—"Hoi Chanh!"

Suddenly, he thought the Americans might not understand and think he was calling for them to surrender, so, impulsively, he shouted the only American words he remembered, "John Wayne! Salem!" He knew that it made no sense. He just wanted them to know that he knew who was approaching and that the menthol cigarettes were popular in every city in Vietnam.

Then, as a last resort, he summoned up some of the schoolboy French he had learned from the Catholic missionaries who used to run a school in his district—"Ami!"

The flashlight beam sliced down to the floor and continued to paint a steady, yet incomplete, circle on a tunnel wall. Bui then heard the distinctive sounds of someone popping a sandy magazine out of a .45 caliber pistol, reseating a new one, and jacking a round into the chamber. Then the flashlight's beam came up off the tunnel's muddy floor, grew brighter, and turned into the tunnel that ran directly toward him.

Bui took a deep breath, lifted his chin, and prepared to die as the brightest part of the beam fell squarely on his face. He knew he couldn't even begin any thought, prayer, or movement before the large bullet struck him down.

The blindfold frightened Bui, but he resisted the urge to cry out for mercy. His hands were bound behind him, and his leg pounded from pain. He could tell from the heat in his leg that the infection had flared back up. He guessed that the very uncomfortable swelling in the glands in his crotch was the result of the infection.

The Americans kept talking and yelling at what Bui assumed were other prisoners around him. He had been blindfolded before they pulled him through the hole in the tunnel. He could still hear the portable radio playing American music. He told himself that men who listened to music would certainly not execute him—not blindfolded.

He listened to what he guessed was a love song and felt a sickening feeling in his stomach. He was reminded of Tich. Where had the water caught her? Had she lived through it? Was she a prisoner? Would they hurt her, rape her, kill her?

He had heard many terrible things about the Americans and how they tortured his comrades. He wanted not to think that he would never see Tich again. Then he laughed to himself at the futility of his thoughts. How could he even worry about her? He would either be shot by the Americans or die of his wound very soon.

"Get up, gook!" a voice seemed to say to him.

He wasn't sure it was addressed to him and didn't want to move lest he draw attention to himself.

The voice screamed again—much closer to Bui's face. He still didn't move.

Without warning a boot planted against his shoulder shoved him over onto his side. He could not get up because his hands were tied and his leg was all but worthless to him.

A pair of strong hands reached under Bui's elbow and jerked him up to a shaky standing position. The yelling continued, and all Bui could think to do was drop his head and try not to provoke one of his unseen captors into striking him or shooting him. He did not want to show how frightened he was. But he was sure they could see his body trembling and his heart pounding in his chest.

One of the American soldiers tied a wire to the binding twine that held Bui's hands together and then stretched the line around his waist and away. Bui was able to figure out that they were stringing the POWs together to move them. Bui took that as a sign that if they were going to be killed it would not be right then. As long as they were moving, they would be alive.

The pain in his leg and the loss of strength and control made him hobble and stumble. The third time he fell down he was pulled out of the line and untied from the others. The realization that he had drawn attention to himself frightened Bui. He knew he had angered his captors, and he was sure he would be shot.

He had never been in a helicopter before. Though he could not see it, he could tell by the engine noises that he was being carried to one, and he quickly remembered the stories he had heard in the political meetings in his platoon about VC being thrown from helicopters to force others into talking. He was sure he would be sacrificed to extract information from the others.

He knew he had missed too many chances at being killed to escape death on the chopper. He began to pray, occasionally and unconsciously slipping into his childhood French. Much of his boyhood Catholic training came back to him—bits of prayers and lines of contrition recalled from the rote training. To him it was all a blur of overwhelming sensations—fear of flight, fear of death, fear of eternity.

The urge to vomit came and went. Bui had no idea how high they were or how fast they were flying. But the movement of the chopper was enough to make him unsure he could keep down the rice the Americans had fed him that morning.

Someone patted him on the shoulder, and he flinched.

"Hey, man. Cool it. Here," a voice said. He felt the end of a cigarette being pushed between his lips.

Though Bui didn't understand the words, he did understand that someone was giving him a cigarette to smoke. Did that mean they were about to throw him out of the chopper? His mind whirled in confusion. Were they just being nice? Or were they being nice before killing him?

He took a drag off the cigarette and found it fairly pleasant. It was not like the Vietnamese, French, and Cambodian cigarettes he had smoked. Neither was it like the American menthol cigarettes. He took another drag.

The American allowed him to smoke the entire cigarette. Bui waited for something to happen. But nothing did. There was a change in the altitude of the chopper, and his stomach told him they were descending.

Bui could smell the oily protective treatment that had been sprayed on the canvas stretcher on which they were carrying him. It reminded him of the smells that had clung to Tich when she used to come to tend to him in the tunnels. He would later learn that the smell was that of a standard disinfectant used in hospitals everywhere.

They took him into a building where it was cool, but filled with people all talking at once. The examining table was cold and hard, and Bui felt uncomfortable and vulnerable as he held his head down while the Americans poked around looking at his leg. He didn't want to let anyone know he would just as soon sit up. After all, he thought, they were tending to his leg, and they wouldn't be doing that if there were any plans to kill him. Would they?

"Take that silly fucking blindfold off this man," someone said, but the words were unintelligible to Bui. "What the hell are we worried about? He's gonna run off with the secrets of the Eighty-fourth Evac?"

Others around the table laughed at whatever the voice had said, and feminine hands untied the blindfold.

They were all in American uniforms, and a few had rubber gloves on. The woman who had taken off his blindfold smelled of perfume and wore wire-rimmed glasses. Bui had never seen a woman wearing glasses.

She smiled at him and strapped a blood pressure cuff on his arm. At the other shoulder a uniformed male swabbed his arm with cooling alcohol and stabbed him with a hypodermic needle.

Bui didn't understand the words, but it was clear that the large man who had just adjusted a work light to shine on his leg was talking to him. "Okay, there, pal. You just relax, and let us clean ya up a bit. Then we'll carry you on over to a ward and let you do some healin' up. How's that sound? Huh?"

Even if Bui didn't understand the words, the tone was reassuring.

The man gave instructions to several others in the room, and people fell into a multitude of tasks, all relating to Bui. Bui took some comfort in their attention and began to relax for the first time in days. He wasn't even aware that sleep was overtaking him.

It was late at night when Bui awoke. His first sensation was that of feeling clean and dry. He couldn't remember how long it had been since he'd felt clean and dry. He had been sleeping in an American hospital bed, complete with a thick firm mattress and crisp white sheets.

The ceiling was a regular pattern of extruded aluminum that curved over his head. He had seen Quonset huts from a distance, but had never been in one before. It came down from the peak to a point where the ceiling became the wall and disappeared behind him.

The room was a long rectangle with ten other beds in it. Each bed held one patient—all Vietnamese. At the end of the room the only light was a lamp that washed the desk that supported it and a small margin of flooring below it.

An American woman was seated at the desk talking to an American soldier who was wearing a pistol. Bui didn't recognize him to be an MP, but assumed that security was his responsibility. He decided not to make any noise or motion that would let them know he was awake.

The other patients were sleeping. They all seemed to be in worse shape than he was. Two had stumps of limbs showing—bandaged and peeking out from under the covers.

At the other end of the ward, the door had heavy wire mesh covering the windowed upper half. Near the door a Vietnamese patient thrashed and moaned in low tones, as if suffering some pain that was keeping him from resting.

The scraping of the chair on the dirt that spotted the linoleum floor caught Bui's attention. He tried not to be noticed as he looked back toward the two Americans.

The nurse got up from her desk and walked to the far end to the moaning patient. She made some adjustments to a tube that fed fluids into him. She then checked her watch and made a notation on the clipboard that was hanging from the end of the bed.

On her return trip to her desk, she made an abrupt turn at Bui's bed and stopped near the foot. She seemed to listen to Bui's breathing as he faked being asleep. She then pulled the sheet back and revealed his leg.

Bui couldn't resist taking a look himself. He made a tiny slit in his eyelids and peeked down toward his leg. He could see that while he was unconscious they had done something to his leg and then neatly bandaged him from midthigh to ankle. His foot was exposed, and from what he could see they had cleaned all of the mud and grime off his leg.

The nurse turned his leg from side to side in order to see the underside of the dressings. She next reached for his toes and took them all in her hand. Bui enjoyed the warmth of her soft hand, but wondered what she was doing.

"You're probably going to live. Your leg won't ever work right, but you'll live to complain about it. And I know that you are *not* sleeping," she said as she looked up from his foot to his face and smiled as if she had caught him stealing a cookie.

Bui panicked and slammed his eyes shut. He didn't know what else to do. And it began to anger him that he didn't know what she was saying. He just lay still until she flipped the covers back and walked away.

The antibiotics worked miracles. By the fourth day Bui's fever had cooled. The swelling in his groin and the throbbing pain in his leg were gone. He could feel the disappearance of the pressure that had been his constant companion since just after he was wounded. The general swelling had almost disappeared, and the redness on the edges of the wound was turning to a healthier-looking pink.

He didn't know the nurse's name, but she was his angel of mercy. That an American woman would replace Tich was an irony that he was trying to reconcile in his mind. He had been taught to hate the Americans because they were allies of the republicans. He had never seen an American up close until they found him in the tunnel. And even then he hadn't seen much because of the blindfold.

But she was mesmerizing. She was much taller than he was, and she had blue-green eyes. Her hair was short and brushed back on the sides of her head, but that didn't make a dent in her femininity. Each morning she would come to his bedside and change the dressing on his leg. She would give him pills three times a day and take his temperature and blood pressure morning and afternoon.

Other Americans who worked on the ward used the word "Kathy." Bui didn't know if this was a name, a rank, or a title. He tried to listen to the way they addressed each other to rule out the possibility that "Kathy" might be the American version of "comrade."

After several days of healing and listening and watching, Bui decided that Kathy was a word that identified her. He was most confused when the male doctors came to check on his wounds and addressed her in words he didn't hear very often.

An older Vietnamese woman was frequently brought into the ward to translate for the nurse and the doctors in cases far worse than his. It occurred to Bui that she was well fed, clean, and appeared to be treated well by the Americans. This was in contrast to most older women in Vietnam, who suffered and died from starvation, neglect, disease, and abuse.

As the old woman passed his bed, Bui tried to strike up a conversation with her. She seemed to be in too much of a hurry to do anything more than bid him good day. Still, he kept it up. He wanted to know things, and she could tell him what he needed to know about the Americans, about his future, and about how she found herself working as a translator.

Each day his infection died away some more, but the damage that had been done by the shrapnel and the infection left its mark. Much of the muscle had been lost to the scraping and cutting away of infected tissue. The large tendon that narrowed into his Achilles had been distorted and scarred by the course of healing and the infection, causing his leg to draw up. In bed he could neither fully straighten his knee nor lift his foot to a ninety-degree angle with his lower leg.

By the end of the second week, Bui was being taken from his bed and walked from one end of the ward to the other. The seventy-five-foot trip took him several minutes and made him suffer a great deal of pain from the lack of flexibility and loss of muscle tone. The atrophy was pronounced, and even his good leg had very little strength. Still, he was afraid not to get well. What would they do with him if he became a permanent burden on them?

The nurse made one of her trips to Bui's bed to administer yet another injection. As always, he forced himself not to appear to be bothered by the sight or pain of the hypodermic needle. He felt that showing such fear would make her think he was a coward.

She put the syringe down on a tray table behind her and pulled the light sheet off his legs and lower body. With a minimum of motion she pulled the strange-looking scissors out of her shirt pocket and sliced through the dressing on his leg. The wound was completely closed, save a small scab that topped the remaining break in the skin. The area was pink and clean, and the dead skin around the wound had completely sloughed off. Scar tissue broke the normally smooth profile of the calf, and his leg and ankle were still at an awkward angle.

The sight bothered Bui, but he felt lucky to be alive and still have his leg. He didn't know much about medicine, but he did know that many of his comrades had died from infections and that he could have been one of them.

She wrapped her hand around the back of his knee and seemed to be feeling for heat. Then she reached for the snaps in the side of his trouser legs. He was wearing orthopedic pajama bottoms that could be split open without being taken off.

She had done this to him each day since he had been there, and he had been embarrassed by it, but still he couldn't wait for her to do it. Unfastening all of the snaps, she flipped the trouser leg away from his upper leg and groin. Then she slipped her long, soft fingers down into the space between the top of his leg and his manhood. He knew she was checking the condition of the swelling that had been in his groin since he had had the infection. The swelling no longer bothered him, and he was only slightly aware of the infection's residual effect. His greatest sensation was that of her fingers in his groin.

The nurse finished her palpation of his lymph nodes and withdrew her hand. As she snapped the pajama bottoms closed, Bui couldn't resist the urge to speak to her for the very first time. "Bui," he said, pointing to himself.

"Bui?" she asked. "Is Bui your name?"

He didn't know that she already knew his name, that it had been written on his chart after one of his interrogations that had been interpreted by the old woman. He also didn't understand everything she said, but he liked hearing her say his name. He repeated it again and tapped the tip of his nose, then nodded his head affirmatively.

"Well, Bui. I'm Kathy."

"Kat-te?" Bui said, unsure of his pronunciation.

"No. Kath-ee," she corrected.

"Kath-ee," he repeated.

She smiled, and he knew he had said it right.

She was called to another bed before he could exchange any more words with her. But at that moment he decided his future would be in learning her language.

He had spoken to the old woman and found out that she had learned to speak English working as a laborer while they were building the large base camp for the hospital he was in. She had grown too old to carry the heavy stones and clear the tree roots, so she worked her way into an interpreter's job with the security police and then the hospital.

Bui was sure that learning the language would help him survive. He feared the VC response if they ever caught him. He was also sure they would dispose of him as worthless if they ever got hold of him again. He had resigned himself to the knowledge that he would never walk again without a seriously halting limp. A man who could not run could not be a VC.

CHAPTER 5

The noise level rose and fell as the plane full of Vietnam-bound passengers continued through the sequential steps of what the army called "pipeline." Pipeline was a long series of events, stations, processing phases, and preparation that ended in soldiers finally getting to Vietnam.

It was easy for Hollister to tune out the racket in the jet as it turned toward Hawaii after lifting off at San Francisco International. He thought about Susan. It seemed that there were only two things he ever thought about anymore—Susan and Vietnam.

The last night with Susan was at the Guest House at Fort Mason, near San Francisco's North Beach. Susan wanted to travel west with him to see him off. She had to leave their quarters at Fort Benning because dependents—how she hated that word—were not allowed to stay on post while their husbands were overseas. Since she was moving back to New York to write, there was no need for them to say good-bye in Georgia.

Christmas leave en route to Vietnam had been warm but short. Before they knew it, the visits with his family and hers came to an end and they were on the West Coast.

Fort Mason sits above the bay, barely a few city blocks in size. Over the Officers Club there were two rooms for transient officers. Hollister and Susan checked in for their only night together and decided to go out on the town. After some barhopping, they walked arm in arm along the strip in North Beach. It was the height of the nude and topless bar phenomenon, and the streets were filled with rowdy customers, hippies, and the dregs of life from the Tenderloin district.

Thinking of Susan, Hollister smiled as he recalled how they were enticed into a particularly loud and well-packed bar named the Condor. They both knew it was a topless bar and decided to go in on a lark to see what the fuss was all about.

Hollister followed Susan as they paid the cover charge and stepped through the heavy velvet curtain that blocked the view of the stage from the street. Just inside the smoke-filled room Susan stopped and gasped. "Oh, my God, Jimmy. I don't believe this!"

He stepped up next to her and stopped long enough to peer over the heads of the crowd at what Susan saw.

There, on the elevated stage at the front of the room, was the most famous dancer in San Francisco—Carol Doda. She wore a small bikini bottom and fishnet stockings but was naked to the waist. Unaware of his response, Hollister let out a whistle. "I have *never* seen anything like this before!"

Susan playfully elbowed Hollister, who was staring at the two huge, swaying, naked breasts that held every man in the room transfixed.

Susan and he just stood at the back of the crowd, amazed at the sight of Carol Doda energetically go-go dancing while taking every opportunity to exaggerate the movement of her triple-D breasts for the cheering audience.

Suddenly, Carol stopped, raised her hands to her brows to shield her eyes from the stage lights, and bent forward for a better look, her breasts dangling, pendulumlike, to a stop as inertia and gravity collided. "Hey! You two back there by the door," she yelled.

Susan and Hollister looked around to see to whom she was talking.

"You two." Carol pointed directly at Susan. "You, honey. You and your boyfriend. C'mon down here in front."

Susan looked at Hollister and shrugged. She led, he followed, and they threaded their way through the crowd that had gone quiet trying to figure out what Carol Doda was up to.

As Hollister and Susan reached the front of the room, Carol pointed to a reserved table, then raised her hand for an unseen waitress. "Hey, somebody get these folks something to drink on the best set of tits in San Francisco."

She next bent over even farther and lowered her voice. "You two drink up and enjoy the show. GIs are always welcome in my place. Not all of us are peace pussies."

Hollister, surprised that Carol Doda had recognized him as a service-man by his haircut, felt good when those nearby heard her words and started applauding Susan and him.

They laughed as they walked up the hill from the Condor to their room over the Officers Club. Hollister remembered how with each step they each knew it meant there was that much less time until he had to leave her.

By the time they climbed the narrow, winding stairway over the bar, they had stopped laughing and Susan held his hand tight.

It was well after midnight when Hollister stepped out of the shower. It was small and worked poorly, but he knew enough to appreciate it. It would be a long time before he would see one as good.

He turned off the bathroom light and walked into the small bedroom. To his surprise, Susan still wasn't finished for the evening. She sat, propped up by a stack of pillows, against the headboard of the small double bed. Her long brown hair flowed across the pillows and her bare shoulders as she held the rough white army sheet to her breasts.

A burning sensation stabbed Hollister's midsection. He was taken with her beauty and pained by the thought that he would have to leave her in the morning. He stood near the bed taking her in until she reached out and placed her fingers on his backside and pulled him toward her—as she pulled the sheet away from her nakedness.

Their night was filled with lovemaking and the emotions of his departure. She was so afraid that she would never see him again. Susan was normally very strong. But that night he held her close while she quietly cried, her tears running down his chest.

By dawn they were completely exhausted from trying to pack a year's worth of emotions and lovemaking into one night.

The noisy chatter in the plane had dropped to a hush when the first passenger spotted the coast of Vietnam and pointed it out to the others. Faces were soon pressed against the cracked and discolored windows until the stewardess announced landing instructions. By the time she got to the words "tray tables," the din had picked up again as the men in the cabin, mostly first-timers, started comparing notes on what they had seen out the windows.

As the plane banked to line itself up to land on the tire-marked concrete runway, Hollister could see how the little town of Tan Canh, the only civilization near the natural deepwater port, had exploded into a bustling GI town just outside the protective wire.

He sat back in his seat and wondered how much of Vietnam had seen the same kind of growth as Cam Ranh Bay had. Certainly the business of soldiering in Vietnam hadn't changed as much as the building and expansion of the physical support structures of the war—or had it?

The noise level again dropped as the plane taxied to a stop on the apron of the runway—only to jump up again as the forward compartment door opened up and all got their first smell of Vietnam.

After much confusion getting hand baggage out of the overhead bins and from under seats, the passengers walked down the truck-mounted stairway that had been pulled up to the fuselage of the 707.

Cam Ranh Bay looked nothing like the pristine little South China Sea port that Hollister had first seen almost two years before. The sandy white beaches and unmarked dunes had been covered up or edged out by miles and miles of concrete, piers, runways, warehouses, docks, barracks, endless rows of concertina wire, minefields, and gun towers. He would not have been able to recognize it if he didn't know it was Cam Ranh.

The blast of hot air was every bit as solid as real brick. Although it was nearing sundown, the oppressive heat, coupled with the humid wind coming off the water, painted each of the deplaning soldiers with a wilting welcome blanket.

"All right! Don't just stand around! Get on those buses! I want army on the first two buses and all other services on bus number three. Now let's get this show on the road," yelled a wiry little army staff sergeant with an armband that read: IN PROCESSING.

On the bus the newly arrived servicemen kept up the chatter. Their voices filled the metal cavity as they moved to their seats.

"You been here before? Huh, sir?" asked a young PFC whom Hollister hadn't noticed on the plane earlier.

Realizing that the soldier had taken the cue from the Combat Infantryman's Badge pinned above the ribbons on his wilted khakis, Hollister looked up at the PFC stowing his bag in the overhead rack and getting ready to sit next to him. "Sure have. Where you headed?"

"Don' know, sir. I'm just assigned to the Replacement Battalion for further reassignment," the soldier said, sliding into the aisle side of the bench seat, taking his hat off, and folding it across his lap.

The crossed rifles on the brass disk on the soldier's left collar were immediately evident to Hollister. "With your MOS there's bound to be a vacancy for you somewhere in-country," Hollister said with a smile.

"I'm afraid yer right, Cap'n. I don't mind tellin' you I'm scared shitless."

"That's good."

"Good? What's good about being a giant jellyfish?" the soldier asked, surprised at Hollister's response.

"You don't think that everyone else on this bus is as afraid as you are?"

"No, sir. They all seem to be holdin' it together. I wish I could be that cool about the whole thing," the soldier said.

"If you aren't scared, you won't do your job right, and that's what'll get you and others around you killed. You get too damn casual out there and Charles will have you for lunch. You do what you're told, watch the old-timers, and listen to the NCOs, and you'll be on one of these buses again in a year."

"I sure hope yer right, Cap'n. I'm sure lookin' forward to that bus ride," the soldier said as he self-consciously looked around the bus at the others. He seemed to be satisfied that there were no other officers close enough to hear him, and he turned back to Hollister. "Sir, I appreciate what you're sayin'—you being an ex-enlisted man and all."

Realizing that the soldier had been sharp enough to spot the Good Conduct Medal on Hollister's shirt, he simply nodded. He had forgotten how soldiers look for any sign, any indication of who an officer is and where he has been. The Good Conduct Medal was a dead giveaway since only enlisted men and NCOs are awarded them.

Someone, somewhere in the back of the bus, had a small tape recorder that was pounding out "Magic Carpet Ride" by Steppenwolf. Hollister looked out the side window at the rows of two-story barracks, office buildings, and Quonset huts that had popped up since he was last there. He was amazed at the expansion and the great numbers of Americans walking along the asphalt roads.

The buildup represented all the services, the Red Cross, government agencies, construction contractors, and even commercial vendors. It was not at all what Hollister had expected to find. Sure, he expected to see signs of the escalation of the war, but not to the degree he witnessed in the streets of what had become the largest deepwater port on the South China Sea—Cam Ranh Bay.

They were ushered into a comfortable briefing room that had rows of backless benches on tile floors. Hollister stepped into a row and slid to the end of one bench, dropping his gear at his feet before sitting.

As the others were staking out their own seats, a young Signal Corps second lieutenant wearing stiffly starched and pressed jungle fatigues, spit-shined jungle boots, and full-color metal pin-on collar insignia walked to the front of the room and mounted the foot-high platform.

"Good evening, gentlemen."

There was an indistinguishable meshing of the many grumbling replies that came from the group.

The lieutenant chose to ignore the low-level discontent and launched right into his prepared speech.

"On behalf of the Commanding General, Military Assistance Command, Vietnam, the Commander, U.S. Army, Vietnam, and the Commanding General of Cam Ranh Bay, I am pleased to welcome you to the Republic of Vietnam. I am Lieutenant Fox, and I will be giving you your initial in-country briefing before your in-processing begins."

There was another audible grumble in response to the thought of having to sit through a briefing.

The lieutenant smiled. "Look at it this way, people. Every bit of the briefing and the in-processing counts on your time in-country and gets you that much closer to the exit briefing you will get here or in Saigon."

The remark was met with a cheer and a few wolf whistles. The lieutenant raised his palms to quiet the room. "If you will let me continue, I will get through this and get you all to some hot chow, showers, and some clean sheets."

Clean sheets? Hollister had not expected to hear that. Clean sheets and Vietnam didn't seem to work together in his mind no matter how much he stretched his imagination. There was so much change that he was going to have to get used to. Vietnam had certainly come a long way if the troops could get a chance to sleep in clean sheets. The last clean sheets that Hollister had seen in-country were in the recovery ward after he was wounded on his first tour.

The briefing lieutenant's voice droned on into the uninteresting details that were old hat to Hollister. His mind wandered to what was ahead of him. With orders to a leg infantry division, he had every expectation that he would be commanding a rifle company within hours after his in-processing was over.

He wondered if he was in good enough physical shape to withstand the acclimatization that he remembered from his first time in-country. On his first tour it had taken him two weeks to stop dripping sweat just standing still in the shade. He hoped that this time his body would remember and snap back into being accustomed to the heat.

His mind started to wander down the organized checklists of things he had to remember, get prepared to do, and promise himself to do on the job as CO of a hundred grunts. As soon as he realized he was getting his act together on autopilot, he felt better and even started to get excited about the possibilities and the demands of being a rifle company commander, the most revered job an infantry captain could hold.

He knew the job was filled with endless opportunities to fail, screw up, or even die. Still, it was a challenge. And it was one he was ready to face if someone gave him the chance. As always he found himself making little promises. He promised to go that extra mile, to do those things that all ideal commanders should do.

A touch of reality crossed his thoughts. He knew that no company commander could do everything, so he tried to establish some hasty priorities in his mind. Communication and security within his new company were the first items that he mentally moved to the top of his list.

Remembering his days as an enlisted man and a junior NCO, he promised never to let the troops bed down for the night without making sure that each one of them was told, through the chain of command, what he was doing, what their mission was, and what they had accomplished on that day.

He knew how important it was for the troops to know what was going on. He knew that even if it was bad news, they appreciated being cut into the net, rather than being treated like shit and kept in the dark.

Security. He would personally walk the perimeter every single night, before and after dark, to make sure that he saw each of the troops, that they saw him, and that he knew exactly where the perimeter ran. He knew how easy it was to get overwhelmed with last-minute details before dark and not get around to checking the perimeter laid in by the platoon leaders and the platoon sergeants. He also knew that if he didn't check the perimeter in the daylight, it was foolish to try to check for the first time just after dark. That was asking to get killed by your own men.

The row in front of him stood, snapping him out of his thoughts. The briefing was over, and they were filing out of the room to get back on the buses to be taken to the billeting area for the night.

Outside, the buses were joined by a smaller, GI version of a community school bus. It held no more than twelve passengers, and the officers were loaded onto it.

Hardly a man on Hollister's bus missed the last sliver of the sun dropping behind the Annamese mountain range, which ran down the center of Vietnam, west of Cam Ranh. As they watched, each wondered what the next year held for him. The level of anxiety and hope was unmistakable, although silent. The silence continued as they weaved through the crowded streets of Cam Ranh's sprawling base.

As dark closed in on them, the bus stopped in front of a two-story transit BOQ and off-loaded most of the officers. Hollister and one other man ended up being driven to still another building, where they were met by a Specialist 4, who took them inside and gave each of them a bunk—one upstairs, one downstairs—and instructions on how to get to the mess hall and the Officers Club. His last remark told them they were expected to remain on the base and report to the orderly room behind the BOQ at zero seven hundred in the morning.

It was too early to sleep and too quiet to sit and do nothing. Hollister looked around the BOQ, disappointed to see that there were no other temporary residents—only other empty army bunks, with their thin mattresses stripped and s-rolled at the foot of each bunk.

He looked at his duffel bag and decided not to bother unpacking anything but his shaving kit, which was crushed under the four-way folding top flap. He guessed that he would be able to take a shower, shave, and brush his teeth with only the contents of his shaving kit and that he would find and put on his jungle fatigues in the morning before he left. In the meantime he felt like he could use a drink.

The tiny Officers Club was a combination snack bar and Officers Club for the Admin Company officers and all the transient officers who came through the processing unit.

As Hollister entered he was quick to pull his cap off his head before crossing the threshold. The enter-covered-buy-a-round custom was widespread in every Officers Club he had ever been in.

And the last thing he wanted to do was buy drinks for a roomful of strangers.

No one looked up as Hollister crossed the concrete slab floor to the makeshift bar that had been thrown together with three-quarter-inch plywood and then covered with split bamboo to give it a Polynesian look. The workmanship was shabby, and the nails used to make the bar were too big for the bamboo. They had splintered the yellowed strips in several places.

"Okay—Cap-i-tan," the little Vietnamese bartender said from the other side of the bar. She wiped rice husks from her forearm after pulling a beer out of a cooler.

"Hi," Hollister said. He looked over her head at the back bar for an idea of the inventory. He was not thrilled to see the old standbys:

> Canadian Club—three-quarters full.
> Old Forester—full.
> Haig & Haig—half full.
> Gilbey's—almost empty.
> Seagram's 7—empty.
> Wild Turkey—half full.

There was also a complete array of Suntory, Japanese offerings generally considered undrinkable by most troops.

"Let me have a Jack Daniel's—up."

"No hab."

"What?" Hollister said, kidding. "That's un-American."

"This is Ve-nam, Dai Uy," she countered.

"Oh, guess you're right at that. What kind of Scotch you got then?"

She reached under the bar, pulled out a new bottle of Black & White, and twisted the screw cap till it popped loose and cracked the paper seal. Before Hollister had a chance to object, she was pouring a few fingers of Scotch into a chipped tumbler.

"That shit any good?"

The voice came from an overweight Transportation Corps captain who had stepped up to the bar next to Hollister.

"Don't know yet. Haven't tried it."

"Gotta watch 'em. They'll fill American booze bottles with that sorry-assed Japanese stuff."

With a mock salute, Hollister knocked back the Scotch and made a face. "Seems to be genuine. Watch me for a while. If I drop dead on the floor, don't drink it."

The captain looked at the barmaid and pointed a stubby finger at the countertop and then toward Hollister. "Honey, come over here and gimme another one, and pour another tall one for my newfound friend here."

"Thanks. You just coming or on your way home?"

"On my way home—one more wake-up. I'm so short, I'm next! How 'bout you?"

"Just got here today," Hollister said.

"Um-hmmm," the portly officer said as he shook his head. "You've been here before. I gotta tell you. Whenever you pulled your last tour, it was the last good deal. This place ain't the same. It's about as rucked up as Hogan's goat."

"How do you mean?"

"I been in this man's army, man an' boy, nearly twenty-two years. And this is the biggest collection of the halt, lame, and stupid I ever seen. We don't know what we're doing, why we're doing it, or how we're gonna get our heads out of our asses to finish up here. Just watch your back, man. Used to be you couldn't count on the Viets—now you can't count on anybody but yerself. The whole war's gotten so big that it is out of control—com-fucking-pletely. It's bad news—just bad news."

The words were not reassuring. The last thing Hollister wanted to hear on his first day back in-country was that things were worse. But he had. He waved to the barmaid for another round and quietly killed the few drops in his glass before she picked it up.

Back in the BOQ it seemed to take forever to drift off to sleep. Hollister's hours of napping on the flight over and the time-zone changes, coupled with the heat of the Vietnam night, kept him from feeling comfortable. After several attempts to sleep, several cigarettes, and a trip outside to the screened-in latrine that serviced two adjacent BOQs he finally fell off into a deep black hole with no dreams or any sensation of the outside world.

He slept soundly for a few hours, oblivious to the jets and prop cargo planes taking off and landing only a quarter mile from his bunk. Somehow his mind knew that it was time for him to start grabbing as much sleep as he could find while it was available to him. He certainly knew that his schedule as a rifle company commander would be barely punctuated by naps and stolen moments of superficial sleep. So he slept and ignored all that was going on around his temporary billet.

Around two in the morning Hollister awoke. His bladder was full again, and his stomach was complaining from the greasy meal he had eaten at the mess hall and the too many drinks at the tiny Officers Club.

He decided against getting dressed, but searched for his shower shoes. He stumbled on the plywood floor as he tried to put them on while he was walking to the doorway. With his index finger he was able to extract the last cigarette from his pack, and he lit it with the matches he had slipped between the pack and the cellophane.

Hollister stopped outside on the steps of the BOQ to get his bearings and take in the night. The planes were still taking off and landing, and the constant whir of distant chopper blades had not stopped since he had arrived.

He looked off in the distance, toward the dark spine of the country—the Highlands. The mountainous terrain was black against the ink-blue sky. Still, the outline was set off by a pair of parachute flares that hung above and behind the first row of mountains west of Cam Ranh.

A tiny shiver went up Hollister's back as he watched the distant flares sliced earthward under their parachutes. Below them a few tracers sliced up into the sky and burned themselves out. He had spent many nights in those same mountains on his first tour, and not one of them had been either forgettable or uneventful. But that night, somewhere out in the dark, there was a company commander who was holding on for all he was worth, trying to turn the night into day by keeping a steady stream of artillery-fired and air-dropped parachute flares over his company's position.

Hollister wondered how long it would be before he was again managing a night contact in the same mountain range. It had been seventeen months since he had last humped the rain forest at night with all his senses screaming for input. He wondered if he would be up to it. His mind asked a question he wouldn't have said out loud: Who would die?

The thought chilled him, but he finally remembered that he was out there to take a piss. He finished his cigarette and walked toward the small latrine.

The inside smelled like all army latrines in spite of the fact that there had been a considerable amount of effort expended during the day by a crew of Vietnamese laborers whose job it was to keep it spotless. He knew they could make it gleam, but they could never remove the smell of urine and burned human waste. It had become the Vietnamese national aroma.

While Hollister stood at the long metal urinal trough, a red-faced, fortyish, pear-shaped major entered the far end of the latrine, selected one of the six side-by-side unoccupied holes on the shitter, and parked his large behind over one.

It quickly became obvious to Hollister that the major was suffering from a fairly serious bout of diarrhea. But then, Hollister thought, any bout of diarrhea was a serious one.

The night sky had picked up a light broken cloud cover when Hollister reached the steps to the BOQ. He looked over his shoulder to see what effect the scattered clouds had on the illumination being fired for the unit in contact, way off on the western horizon.

He was sorry he looked. The flares were igniting just above the clouds, and all the light was being reflected back upward, instead of down to help the unit in contact. Seeing in the rain forest was not impossible in the dark—unless there was a flare above you creating a glare overhead that didn't paint the ground with light. Then the dark was darker and the visibility was nil.

Time was starting to race by for Hollister.

As Hollister reached the end of the barracks where his bunk was, he was met with the business end of a flashlight. "You Captain Hollister?" a voice asked from behind the flashlight.

"Yeah, what's up?"

"Ah, sir—I'm the CQ runner."

"You have a name, CQ runner?"

"Oh, ah, yessir. Lester, sir. Lester Simms," the unsteady voice said.

"Well, Lester, how about getting that light out of my face and telling me why we are having this conversation," Hollister said, a trace of irritation in his tone.

"The duty NCO sent me to get you. They want you at the orderly room in twenty minutes with your gear, ready to go."

"What? I'm not due to fly out of here until tomorrow morning. You sure you got the right Hollister?"

"Sir, I'm just a runner. I don't know nothin' about nothin'—'cept the sergeant told me to come get you. I'm thinkin' that I'm lucky that you are the onlyest officer on this floor or I mighta had to wake up the wrong guy—I mean the wrong captain, Captain."

"Okay, Lester. You did your job. Tell the duty NCO that you've found one grumpy captain and that when I get over there with all my gear he had better be sure that it is me he wants or I'll *really* be pissed."

"Yessir. G'night, sir. I mean, I'm sorry to disturb you."

Hundreds of tiny white flying bugs circled the small desk lamp on the duty NCO's desk. The NCO looked up. "Oh, sorry, Captain. We got a change in plans for you, and you have to be out on the active in ten minutes for transportation."

"Change?" Hollister asked. "What kind of change?"

"Don't know. I just got a call to have you out on runway four-five with all your gear. There'll be a chief minor out there to pick you up."

The change was a little confusing for Hollister, but he could tell that no amount of questioning would help him figure out what the army had in store for him.

"There's a quarter ton outside waitin' for you, sir," the duty NCO added. "Simms, take the captain's gear out to the jeep."

The jeep driver knew even less than the duty NCO. He just had instructions to take Hollister to a certain point on the airfield apron.

As they turned down the flight line, Hollister could see an endless row of fixed- and rotary-wing aircraft tied down for the night. About a quarter mile down the row, the jeep lights illuminated a turboprop with a jumpsuited warrant officer standing by one wing tip.

"Mornin', sir. Might you be one Captain Hollister?"

Captains didn't rate fixed-wing turboprops. Hollister's guess was that some VIP was heading out to the division rear and they wanted to fill up the plane—and that was why he was summoned in the middle of the night.

"Right, Chief," Hollister said as he returned the warrant officer's salute, stepped out of the jeep, and reached for his bags. "So, who else we waiting for, Chief?"

"You're it," the pilot said.

"Me? You might just have the wrong guy." Surprised, Hollister looked around and saw only the copilot and a ground crewman preflighting the airplane. "How the hell do I rate?"

"I never ask any questions. I leave all that up to the commissioned officers and the Secretary of the Army, sir. I'm just a plain ol' airplane driver looking to get as many landings as I make takeoffs. I figure if I worry about that part of the war, then the real warriors will take care of the rest," the pilot said as he made a mock bow and generously waved Hollister toward the open cockpit door of the sparkling, white-over-olive-drab airplane.

Once they reached flight altitude, the pilot trimmed out the aircraft and reduced the engine thrust. The resulting drop in cabin noise allowed them to talk without screaming.

"What's the flight time to division?"

"Division?" the copilot asked. "What division is that, sir?"

"The Americal. That's where we're going, isn't it?"

"No, sir," the pilot said as he banked the plane over to a new heading.

Leaning forward, Hollister glanced at the compass. It was one-eight-o. They were heading south, not north, or even west, which was the general direction of the Americal base camp. "Where the hell we going, anyway?"

The pilot looked over his shoulder at Hollister. "You don't know?"

"Hell, no. The last time I looked at my PCS orders, I was on my way to the Americal Division."

"Well, sir—you're on your way to Long Binh now. The new home of Disneyland East."

"What for?" Hollister asked.

"I have no earthly idea. Ya see, sir, we were mindin' our own business with not a single flight on the board when we were jerked out of *The Singing Nun* and told to take you to Two Field Headquarters."

"Nothing else?"

"No, sir. Nothing else. We're aviators. All we need is a heading, a departure time, and enough avgas, and we'll find a straight piece of real estate to roll this baby to a stop."

Smiling at the pilot, Hollister shook his head and sat back in his seat to try to figure out what it might mean. He had a sudden sinking feeling that he might have been pulled off an assignment to a U.S. unit and diverted to an advisory job. Shit, he thought, after volunteering to come back early and all the hell he had to go through with Susan, to end up as an advisor would really piss him off.

He surmised that it must be his date of rank. He had only pinned on his captain's bars a month earlier, and there had to be a line of more senior captains waiting to command rifle companies in-country.

Deciding that he wasn't going to sort it out during the flight, Hollister settled back and watched Vietnam fly by out the right side of the aircraft. The U-21 had nothing if not terrific visibility.

Outside was a part of Vietnam he had never seen. On his first tour he had spent all of his time in the northern half of South Vietnam. He had never been south of Cam Ranh Bay before.

As he watched the countryside roll by, he could see occasional tracers of green and red scratching across the blackened horizon in lazy arcs. And everywhere over the mountains and along the coastal lowlands, the navigation lights of American and South Vietnamese aircraft dotted the skies.

It was starting to sink in that this was not the Vietnam he had left less than two years before. It had grown from under a hundred thousand Americans to more than four times that—populated by a field army with all of the manpower, equipment, and aircraft it needed to win a war.

He didn't know where he was going, but he knew for sure that this tour would bear little resemblance to his first one.

CHAPTER 6

It was just beginning to glow on the horizon when the pilot put the comfortable turboprop down on the cement runway at Bien Hoa Air Force Base. His mastery of the aircraft was evident in the ease with which he allowed it to sink softly toward the blackened tire marks only to cut the power and kiss the runway with the touch of a surgeon.

As they taxied to a tie-down point, Hollister tried to absorb as much of the area as he could. He had never been to Bien Hoa. He had never seen such a concentration of army, air force, and Vietnamese Air Force planes, jets, choppers, and hangars.

Bien Hoa Air Force Base and the surrounding countryside was completely unlike the Highlands. It was flat as far as he could see in any direction, and there was virtually nothing on the horizon taller than one story, except a lone thirty-four-foot jump tower that was identical to the four that stood on Eubanks Field at Fort Benning.

A sergeant first class wearing a IIFFV shoulder patch stood on the apron waiting for the pilot to shut down the engines. He waved his arms and called out to Hollister as he stepped from the airplane. Normally, a captain in Vietnam wouldn't expect to be picked up by someone, but in his case it was consistent with the treatment he had been getting since he had been diverted to Cam Ranh. Hollister acknowledged the sergeant with a wave and turned back to the cockpit to thank the pilots and wish them a safe trip back.

As Hollister and the sergeant drove out the gate at the sprawling Bien Hoa base camp and started down the road that connected it to the equally spread out Long Binh Headquarters complex, Hollister tried to find out what was going on. "So, what's the deal? You have any idea where I am going?"

"No, sir, I was just getting off duty as the G-1 staff duty NCO when the sergeant major caught me and told me to come over here and pick you up. I haven't got any idea what for or how deep," the sergeant replied. He nodded toward the Combat Infantryman's Badge on Hollister's shirt. "But you know how screwed up this place is—just about anything's liable to happen around here."

They shared a small chuckle, and Hollister resigned himself to sit back and enjoy the short ride to IIFFV, where he was sure to find out something.

In a fraction of a second Hollister knew he wouldn't like to have anything to do with being assigned to the massive headquarters. As he weaved his way through the rows of metal desks and listened to the clacking of typewriters and the nonstop ringing of telephones and field phones, he remembered the First Field Force Headquarters in Nha Trang. It had been primitive by comparison with the chaos of the maze he now found himself in.

The sergeant finally stopped in front of an empty desk and turned to Hollister. He looked at the empty chair and then at his wristwatch. "Sir, the sergeant major must be in the can or something. I'll leave you here, if it's all right with you?"

"Sure," Hollister said as he reached out to take the sergeant's hand to thank him for picking him up after an all-nighter on duty. "I'll be okay. I guess that I can find a place to work for a year here. If they haven't got something for me to do, then none of us belongs here."

Finding a clear spot on the floor next to the sergeant major's desk, Hollister dropped his bags and reached for a cigarette. It wasn't even seven in the morning, and already he was sweating through his undershirt and his shirt. He lit a cigarette and blew out the match with the smoke.

"Oh, good mornin', Captain. You must be Hollister, James A.—that right?"

The voice came from a form standing in the doorway marked DEPUTY CHIEF OF STAFF FOR PERSONNEL G-1. It was the G-1 sergeant major—Norman Carey. He was a medium-height man of fifty with a stack of papers in one hand and a coffee cup in the other. He put the cup and the papers on his desk, then turned back around to close the door behind him.

"That's me, Sergeant Major. Hollister, James A."

The sergeant major stuck out his hand. "Welcome to Two Field."

His hand was frail and without substance, and his grip was weak. Hollister looked down and noticed the scar that ran from the sergeant major's wrist toward the inside of his elbow. It was ragged, deep, and ugly.

The sergeant major was used to people reacting to his scar. "Oh. World's most embarrassing Purple Heart," he explained. "Sniper popped a few over our heads, and my jeep driver turned us over in the ditch. I came to a stop with a piece of the side mirror up my sleeve."

"Sorry to hear that," Hollister said.

The sergeant major's face split into a big grin. "Naw, it gives me a good excuse to talk women into holding my pecker for me while I take a piss. I tell 'em I've lost my grip and go for the sympathy thing."

"Does that line ever work?" Hollister asked.

"Never, but it breaks the ice and gets them off of worrying about how I got the scar."

He could tell by his face that the man had spent many days in the field, which probably accounted for some of his weathering. Hollister also knew that he liked him, but he didn't like his headquarters.

Then, a sobering thought went through his mind. What if he was being assigned to a desk job on the IIFFV Headquarters staff? Is that why he was here? That would really be worse than an advisory job.

"Have a seat, Captain," the sergeant major said, pointing to a folding chair near his desk. "Let me tell the colonel you're here."

He assumed that the sergeant major was talking about the G-1, who was behind the closed door. He took the chair and reached for the ashtray on the desk to dump the ash that was dangling dangerously from his cigarette.

The sergeant major grabbed some papers that Hollister assumed had something to do with him and stepped back to the door. He rapped once in an obligatory manner, with no intention of waiting for the voice behind the door to tell him to come in.

He opened the door and stood in the doorway. "Colonel, Captain Hollister is here."

"Great. But I won't have time to talk to him," Hollister heard him say. "Please apologize for me—the general is on my ass about six other things—no time at all. Just send him on over to Colonel Downing's shop."

The sergeant major nodded and mumbled something acknowledging the colonel's instructions, then closed the door and turned back to Hollister.

He bent at the knees and waist, squinted out the small window over Hollister's shoulder, and pointed. "Sir, you need to go to that wing over there and report to Colonel Downing in the Ops Section."

Getting up from his chair, bent over, Hollister looked at the extension of the building the sergeant major was talking about. "Can you tell me what I'm doing here, Sergeant Major?"

"Sir?" the sergeant major said with a puzzled look.

"I'm supposed to be on orders to the American Division up in I Corps, and you're sending me over there to see someone else."

The sergeant major laughed to himself. "Sir, stateside orders don't mean squat in-country anymore. By the time they fill a requirement from stateside, we've already filled it with a local resource and we have a newer requirement to fill. We have to change orders all the time."

"So?" Hollister asked.

"All I can tell you is that you ain't goin' to the American Division, Captain. I'd tell you more if I could, but I'm only a sergeant major."

"That's a bigger line than the one about the scar," Hollister said, kidding him. "So is it that you don't know or you can't say?"

The sergeant major leaned closer to Hollister and lowered his voice. "I got a pretty good idea. I just put in a RFO to have you reassigned to the Field Force Headquarters—"

Hollister's heart sank. He made a face of disapproval.

The sergeant major stuck his hand back out to shake Hollister's hand good-bye, then finished what he was saying. "But you aren't staying here in the head shed. They're gonna work you hard. You need some help, you come find me, Cap'n. You remember that. Okay?"

Not sure what the sergeant major was saying, Hollister trusted the sincerity of his offer and thanked him. He still didn't know that much, but he felt as if he had just made a friend.

There was something completely different about the bearlike sergeant major who sat behind his desk in the Operations Section of the headquarters. Hollister could read most of his credentials from across the room; he wore a CIB with a star and a 25th Infantry Division combat patch on his right shoulder. It meant he had spent time as an infantryman in Korea or in Vietnam with the 25th, but the star on his CIB meant that he had seen infantry combat time in both wars.

"Good morning, sir," the sergeant major said, getting to his feet and immediately reaching out to shake hands with Hollister.

"Sergeant Major," Hollister said as he took his hand and returned his firm shake. "Hollister—I was sent over here to report to Colonel Downing."

"Goddamn it, Hollister! Where the hell you been?" the tall, balding officer said as he stood and came around from behind his desk to confront Hollister.

Unsure of the colonel, except for the fact that he was clearly angry with him, Hollister snapped to attention and saluted smartly. "Captain Hollister reporting, sir."

He held his salute and stared straight ahead at a rigid position of attention as the colonel kept coming. Within a second the colonel's face jutted into Hollister's, chin forward. "You think we have the whole damn year to wait on you, mister?" the colonel challenged as he quickly dispatched Hollister's salute by returning it with an air of disdain.

Dropping his salute, Hollister looked at the colonel and tried to size up the cause of the challenge. "Sir, I didn't even know I was supposed to be here, much less when."

"Don't be a smart-ass, Captain. We've been waiting for you for a long time," the colonel said as he turned and walked back behind his desk. He picked something up off it and started to read: "Captain, Infantry, Airborne-Ranger, CIB, Silver Star, Purple Heart, one tour under your belt with a LRP outfit, a six-month stint as an Airborne rifle platoon leader, Ranger instructor . . ." The colonel paused and looked up at Hollister. "Son, we need you a whole lot here," he said as he broke into a wide grin. He stuck his hand out to shake with Hollister, then he laughed. "You just don't know how much we need you here. Welcome aboard."

"Sorry, but I'm not sure just *what* I am aboard, Colonel," Hollister said.

The colonel looked at him for a second and realized that in the rush of events someone had actually forgotten to pass the word. He motioned for Hollister to take a seat in the out-of-place leather couch that sat against the wall facing the desk.

He didn't wait for Hollister to sit. Instead, he raised his chin in the direction of the door and asked, "Coffee? Something cold?"

"Coffee'll be fine, sir."

"Sergeant Major! Will you have one of those folks out there round up some coffee?"

The colonel didn't wait for one, and the sergeant major didn't give an answer. He just assumed he was heard and could go on with what he had to tell Hollister.

"L-R-P—that's where we want you, and that's where we need you, young man."

The letters were a relief, an excitement, and a disappointment all at the same time. Hollister knew that if he did decide to stay in the army it was important that he make an effort to get a crack at commanding a rifle company in combat. He had set his mind to it, and the thought of finishing his second tour in Vietnam without getting that ticket punched on his Form 66 would make the future more difficult and reduce some of his options. Of course, he was relieved to find out that he wasn't going to some advisory job or a staff job at the headquarters. And, ultimately, the sound of Long Range Patrol made his heart race a little faster.

"We have figured out that the divisions and a couple of the separate brigades have been getting excellent results from their long-range patrol detachments, and the Field Force commander wants to put one together to see if we can have the same luck. A couple of weeks ago, we put out the word throughout Two and Three Corps that we wanted volunteers, and they're just arriving now. We've put a major in as the company commander, and we have temporarily activated the colors from an infantry company—deactivated since World War II—and given the LRPs that designation. It's Juliet Company . . . J Company, Fifty-first Infantry."

It was customary for Hollister to show some enthusiasm for his new assignment, even though he wasn't sure what it was—completely. "That's great, sir."

"We've stolen a Special Forces major who is already onboard at Juliet Company, but there isn't much more there yet. So I can only offer you lots of work. This is *the* project around here right now. We are trying to get your company up and working soon—but not so soon we get them in over their heads."

"Have you got a mission for the company yet, sir?"

"Hell, we don't have a decent place to put them up yet. You just get on down there, and roll up your sleeves. They need training, organization, and good leadership. You up for that?" the colonel asked.

Hollister didn't think he had to answer the question, so he just nodded.

An awkward, baby-faced PFC tried to move into the office unobtrusively with a wooden in-box filled with coffee mugs, sugar, and a glass with a couple of spoons in it.

"Don't be shy, son. Git yer butt in here, drop off the coffee, and get on with yer business."

The PFC looked at the colonel to see if he had made him angry. The colonel smiled to let him know there was no reason to tiptoe around him.

"You new here?"

The soldier straightened up and spoke mechanically. "Yes, sir."

"Well, you're stuck here. And you're gonna have to stand tall and step out if you don't want to get crushed under the weight of this damned headquarters. So you get used to moving with a purpose around here, and don't worry about whose feathers you ruffle if you got a job to do. You got that?"

The PFC nodded and awkwardly exited.

Hollister put down his coffee and reached into his pocket for a small notepad and pen. He had a feeling there was going to be an avalanche of information coming his way, and he didn't want to miss any of it.

The colonel waited for Hollister to get some notes down, then continued. He picked up his cup, motioning for Hollister to do the same.

"Now, where was I?—oh, okay—the problem is that we're not well suited for the job here in the flat land. We've got four infantry divisions, an armored Cav regiment, and a couple of separate brigades—all of which sound like freight trains moving through the damn bush. The only units that have been doing any good finding VC are the small long-range patrol detachments that they have.

"Well, our conclusion is that we ought to be able to develop better contacts with a top-notch LRP outfit and then pile on with regular units when we find 'em."

As he listened to the colonel, Hollister could feel the pit of his stomach starting to become more relaxed. He was getting into something he understood, and the large unknown about his assignment was finally filling in.

The colonel continued. "We don't really know how to put this outfit together, what it ought to have, how big a territory we should give it, or how complicated a mission to lay on it. I'm guessing that raids, ambushes, prisoner snatches, and any number of other things are going to be your standard missions. But you and your boss are going to have to tell me if that's how we ought to use you."

He got up and stepped to the large wall map that represented the III and IV Corps Tactical Zones.

"We own every piece of dirt and all the mud south of a line from the Lao-Cambode-Viet border in the northwest to the South China Sea." He poked his index finger at Hollister. "And you are going to find, fix, and kill VC for me with that LRP company."

With a nod, Hollister replied, "When do I start?"

"You're already on the clock. You go forward today, and we'll talk again in a week and work out some operations that'll let the little people know you aim to kick ass and take names."

"That sounds good to me, sir." Hollister beamed.

The colonel changed his tone. He sounded less gung-ho and more confidential. "I really am glad to have you. This is a really tricky business, and I just don't need anybody OJTing out there with those teams. They're too light in the ass to take up your slack if you are just feeling your way around.

"You're going to have a big job ahead of you, son. So why don't you go on forward and meet Major Sangean."

Standing, anticipating a good-bye, Hollister waited for the colonel to wrap it up.

"We are very pleased to have found you, Hollister. I know that doing your kind of stuff in this part of the country will be different, but it will nonetheless be important."

He stuck out his hand and shook Hollister's, then looked beyond him toward the outer office. "Sergeant Allen? How about fixing the captain here up with whatever he needs."

Changed into jungle fatigues and trying to digest a heavy meal from the headquarters mess hall, Hollister struck out for his new unit.

The tiny speaker of a transistor radio was scratching out the lyrics to "Hang on Sloopy" as it swayed on the end of a piece of commo wire attached to the jeep's windshield.

"The music bother you, sir?" the PFC from the colonel's office asked as he stopped the jeep at the guard gate.

"No, leave it on if you want to," Hollister answered, detecting the unsteadiness of the soldier's voice.

The two MPs at the gate saluted Hollister and raised the steel pole that crossed the roadway in front of the jeep's bumper.

As Hollister returned the salute, he noticed that one of the MPs gave the driver the approving pump of a closed fist and a smile.

"Friends of yours?"

Startled, the PFC bungled the clutch and pulled ahead with a jerk. "Yessir. I used to be an MP. We were in the same company."

"So how'd you end up in Operations?"

The driver paused at the highway crossing in front of the IIFFV Headquarters compound and looked both ways. "Ya see that? Over there?" he asked as he pointed off in the distance to an isolated group of buildings set off in a large clearing, surrounded by barbed-wire-topped fences with guard towers at the corners.

"Yeah—what is it?"

"It's the POW Compound and Interrogation Center. I was assigned over there, but I got in some trouble and they decided to reclassify me as clerk-typist," the driver said, his voice trailing off in some embarrassment.

"What kind of trouble?"

"My section sergeant said I didn't have enough *presence* or *authority* to be an MP. He was always on my back and finally got pissed off enough at me to get me reassigned out of his section. I ended up here."

There was no doubt that the boy was hurt by the rejection. "Was he right?" Hollister asked.

The driver looked at Hollister, surprised. "Sir, you're the first one who ever asked me."

"Well?"

"I guess so. I just get a little flustered. Seems like everybody in this damn army is so confident and so sure of what they're doing. Hell, sir. All I seem to do is try to find ways of not being noticed so I can just get over and avoid catching hell."

"What do you want to do about it? Anything?"

"Sure, I'd like to be big and bad like so many of the other guys. But the NCOs and the officers—no offense sir—really give me a hard time."

"What scares you about them?"

The soldier cleared his throat, the conversation obviously uncomfortable for him. "Sir, you try being me and have to walk into an office with someone like the colonel and a captain like you being in there. It'd make you feel a little inadequate, too."

"Don't you think I was ever a PFC?"

"No shit? I mean, really?"

"Sure. I remember how intimidated I was as a new Spec 4 going through the Seventh Army NCO Academy in Bad Töolz, Germany. Let me tell you, the Tactical NCOs there were gods. They stood taller, looked sharper, and knew more than any NCOs I have ever met. They prided themselves on looking the part and being completely proficient. They busted our humps on leadership, map reading, military instruction, drill and ceremonies, and PT. I thought I'd never make it through that place. But I owe those NCOs so much, looking back on it."

"I don't know, sir. I'm just not sure I can hack it all."

"Tell you what—when you get ready to try, you find me, and I'll see what I can do to help you. Deal?"

The soldier looked across at Hollister and smiled for the first time. "Deal!"

***

As they entered the main gate going back into the Bien Hoa complex, the driver turned away from the airfield toward what was known as Bien Hoa Army. Hollister was immediately surprised to find it was not just a base camp but a small city.

The jeep bounced along poorly graded and crowned roads that were flanked by drainage ditches and telephone poles that carried miles and miles of phone and power lines to all the buildings, huts, hooches, and shacks that had been built since the war started.

Trying to distinguish what was what, Hollister marveled at the extent to which the area had been organized, sandbagged, painted, roofed, screened, and marked with an array of signs and directional arrows that would confuse even a genius.

Troops of all sizes, colors, and functions crisscrossed in front of the jeep. He had never seen such a hub of activity, both business and personal. Trucks, trailers, tractors, graders, front loaders, choppers, generators, pumps, air conditioners, and fans of all sizes filled the air with a frenzy of noises that would forever change the once quiet and simple rice-paddy farmland. Hollister had expected the Field Force Headquarters to be busy and well appointed, but finding Bien Hoa like this was a real surprise.

"This is your rear area, sir," the driver said, turning off the main road.

Hollister looked up ahead and was confronted with a complete, life-sized copy of one of the thirty-four-foot parachute jump towers used at the Airborne schools in the States. It was the one he had seen earlier when he landed.

At the tower's base stood several tropical huts with blackout doors over windows that were open to allow cross-ventilation. The roofs were all ripple aluminum, and each had screened-in uppers and steps in front of all the doorways. Commo wire was strung from the eaves of each building to a central building that looked very much to Hollister as if it might be an orderly room or commo shack.

The driver pulled into a circular gravel drive and halted the jeep in front of the building that Hollister had spotted as the company headquarters. He stepped out of the jeep and reached into the back for his B-4 bag. The driver had also stepped out to help Hollister, but quickly realized that he would carry his own bags. "Well, good luck, sir."

"You remember our deal now"—Hollister looked at the soldier's name tape above his pocket—"Cathcart?"

"Yessir, I will," Cathcart said, then saluted smartly.

He thought it strange that there was virtually no activity at all in the LRP compound. A few vehicles stood in what looked to him to be a makeshift motor pool, and a pair of chubby puppies played at biting each other's tails on the opposite side of what served as a company street.

He knew he wouldn't find out anything standing outside the orderly room, so he moved his bag out of the roadway and leaned it up against the poured cement steps leading to the doorway. He noticed that the corner of the steps had a soldier's version of a cornerstone, the date scratched into the wet concrete: 23/5/65.

He knew the compound was not new enough to have been built for the new LRP company, and it was certainly too well appointed to have ever held infantrymen. As he reached for the door, he was able to read the unit designation that had been originally painted on the doorway, but recently painted over, unsatisfactorily. It had been the headquarters of an engineer battalion. Hollister smiled. That explained the quality construction and the lavish appointments—by infantry standards.

There was no one inside the orderly room. A Japanese fan whirred in a whisper and rotated on its base, painting the room with invisible warmth. The room itself looked awful. Files stood on the floor as there were no cabinets to put them in, trash was stacked in ammo boxes, and the only lighting came from the screened windows. Rickety desks were topped with aging Remington manuals, and there was not a chair in the room.

Suddenly, footsteps slammed up the wooden steps on the far side of the building and the screen door swung wide. A small soldier with a box of toilet paper in his arms burst through and hollered, "Lookee here what I just got!"

He peered over the top of the large box and came face-to-face with Hollister, just short of plowing him down in his rush. "Oh, shit! I'm sorry, sir. I thought Sergeant Dewey was here."

"He must be in real trouble if he needs that much toilet paper," Hollister said jokingly, trying to relieve the soldier of his awkwardness.

The soldier thought a minute, then got it. "Oh, yessir—I mean, no, sir. He doesn't need it. We all need it. We haven't any real ass-wipe in almost a week. We been stealin' extra copies of the *Stars and Stripes* from the Message Center over at Long Binh and using anything else we can find."

"Well, good. What's your name, and who and where is Sergeant Dewey?"

"Coots, sir. PFC Leonard Coots, and Sergeant Dewey is the company clerk. And I don't know where he is."

"Tell you what, Coots, my name is Hollister, and I'm reporting in. Since there's no one here, why don't you stay here—answer the phones and such— and I'll go try to round someone up?"

"That's all right with me, sir. But I don't think you'll find much of any-body if you don't find Sergeant Dewey."

Outside the Orderly Room the company area was still void of signs of soldiers, except for the two pairs of fatigue trousers that Hollister could see sticking out from under a three-quarter-ton truck in what appeared to the motor pool's maintenance area. He was sure that whatever their skills were, getting him signed in and on the Morning Report were not their responsibilities.

Deciding to look somewhere else, he wandered toward an unmarked building that seemed to have some noises coming from it—scraping sounds.

Inside, Hollister found three soldiers dragging a field range across the concrete floor to what appeared to be a loading-dock arrangement on the back side of the building. It was the mess hall, and the large T-shirted man supervising the positioning of the field stove turned to see who had entered.

The man turned out to be an old friend of Hollister's, Mess Sergeant Kendrick. Kendrick beamed. "Well, I'll be damned! If it ain't—"

"It is," Hollister said. He smiled and reached out his hand to take Kendrick's. "How you doing? I thought you'd be out of the army and running your own gourmet restaurant back in New Orleans by now."

Kendrick laughed at the thought. "Oh, no, sir. I can't be cookin' in no fancy restaurant. I can't find a place in N'Orleans that needs a guy who can only cook gumbo for five hundred at a sitting."

"Good to see you. You the head spoon here?"

"Yessir, and a fine job it is—or will be as soon as I kick a few asses and get it organized. I was in a headquarters mess over at the one hundred ninety-ninth Brigade and heard they were puttin' up a new LRP company—and you know me, sir."

As always, Kendrick had drawn his jump wings and his rank on his paper cook's hat. Hollister took note of the change since he had last seen Kendrick as a cook in his old LRP detachment on his first tour. "You made seven?"

"Yessir, this war must be gettin' to 'em. They be promotin' jus' about anyone nowadays." He then noticed the captain's bars on Hollister's collar. "Oh, ah, sir—I didn't mean—"

Hollister smiled at his old friend. "Forget it. I think you were right, anyhow."

"So you're here with us—like back in the Airborne Brigade?"

"I hear that I am, although I can't seem to find anyone to log me in for duty."

"Oh, sir, there's nobody much here. This is our rear, and the company's forward workin' out of Cu Chi—trying to get some training done. I only came back to pick up some stuff that I need. The Ol' Man, the first sergeant and everybody be up at Cu Chi."

The flight to Cu Chi was at a low-enough altitude to get a feel for the terrain. Though he was wedged between the field range and some mailbags, Hollister worked his way to the chopper's open door to take in as much as he could.

The ground below was as flat as his home in eastern Kansas, but unlike the fields of grain, soybeans, and millet, there were geometric squares, rectangles, and pie-shaped paddies and garden plots that used every square hectare of the precious soil to grow whatever would thrive in the rich delta of the sprawling Mekong River and the two other major rivers north and west of Saigon-Bien Hoa.

As he looked down, he was surprised to find that almost every square mile was teeming with villagers, children, livestock, and military vehicles. There was no unfilled soil and no uncontested, undefended land as far as he could see. As soon as he saw it, he knew that tactics as he remembered them from his first tour in the Highlands would not work well there.

Cu Chi was the base camp for the 25th Infantry Division. Over the course of two years in Vietnam, the division had gained and lost units through what the army called "task organizing." It had also been the landlord for units not under its control, which were given space at the huge base camp and afforded the protection that the division's perimeter could afford.

Tenant units were always a point of friction for divisions. They tended to take advantage of what the division had to offer, giving little back. The troops assigned to the division were always convinced that tenant units were "getting over," dodging guard duty and some of the other more unpleasant duties.

Juliet Company had been given a half-dozen broken-down tropical huts on the eastern side of the base. The area had belonged to a unit once assigned to the 25th and then later reassigned to some other part of Vietnam. The type of unit and its actual function was not apparent by looking at the abandoned barracks, mess hall, supply room, and chopper pad. Over time the area had taken on the name of the large Indian head with full warbonnet that had been painted on the concrete chopper pad: OLD WARRIOR.

As the chopper settled onto the pad, Hollister was only able to catch part of the cracked and weathered insignia that had once been painted in bold primary colors. He thought it was a good sign that as he stepped out his foot first touched the word WARRIOR.

As the blades spun down, a frenzy of activities took place. Soldiers, some obviously LRPs and some probably not, came to pull supplies from the chopper. The crew members went through their shutdown checklists, and Sergeant Kendrick shepherded the movement of his field range to a low, flat-roofed building several dozen meters away.

"Where's the CP?" Hollister yelled over the turbine whine.

One of the soldiers turned to point at a building on the far side of the chopper. "That's it over there, Cap'n."

Looking back through the chopper's cargo compartment, Hollister could see that the building was clearly different from the others in that it was L-shaped, had a fresh set of protective sandbags around it, and four guy wires held a tall, spiked 292 antenna head well above the roof. Anyone could tell that it was a CP of some type.

CHAPTER 7

Inside the CP Hollister found the company headquarters and the operations functions in separate ends of the L. There was no indication as to what the building had originally been designed for, but the waist-high counter that served as a dividing line between the two legs of the L told Hollister that it might have been a supply room of some type. If there had ever been any shelves or bins to hold the equipment, they were long gone.

No one noticed Hollister's entrance. He put his bag down and scanned the room. He stood behind the two radio operators and two NCOs who were bent over the makeshift bench that held radios and a scattering of paperwork, clipboards, and coffee cups.

Above the radio bench a status board covered with a cracked piece of acetate had the numbers of deployed teams scrawled by what appeared to have been a crumbling grease pencil. The word "schedule" had been misspelled. It was obvious from the radio cross talk and the preoccupation of the RTOs and NCOs that something critical was going on in the field.

One of the RTOs turning to reach for a trash can where he could dump a half C ration can filled with cigarette butts, noticed Hollister. "Oh, sir . . .," he said, starting to stand, not sure if Hollister would expect him to.

Raising his hand so the soldier would not stop what he was doing, Hollister shook his head. "Please, carry on. We can all say hello later."

The others, equally busy with radios and a field phone, took a second to look back at Hollister to size him up. They nodded and gestured acknowledgment and a hint of appreciation that he didn't seem to want everything to stop just because an officer had entered.

The radios crackled with cross talk. Hollister decided to find a spot in the back of the room and watch. The two radio operators hunched over the long bench and spoke rapidly to unseen operators on the other ends of their pork-chop mikes.

The Operations sergeant, SFC Kurzikowski, an old Airborne soldier who had seen service in Korea, paced between the two, occasionally turning to Hollister to explain who owned what voice and where they were on the map or in the sky.

A team was being extracted because it had been compromised by a group of children who had walked right into their ambush position about a thousand meters from their village. There was no shooting, but every insert and every extraction was fraught with danger for the LRP teams, the chopper pilots, and the crews. Hollister knew that just about anything could happen, and even the most simple move could get people dead. His heart started pumping enough for him to realize he was back. It was real to him. It was almost as if he had never left Vietnam.

"Coming out," said one of the pilots over the radio set on the chopper frequency. His voice came from the small OD speaker tied up against the wall behind the radio bench.

"We're up," came over the FM radio that the company commander and the team were on.

Hollister immediately liked the cross-communication checking that the Operations personnel could do by having a radio on every frequency being used to conduct the operations. There was even a radio on the air force forward air controller's frequency and another on the artillery fire direction center's frequency.

It gave Hollister confidence that when things were happening someone would be able to pick it up if there was a lack of communication or a miscue on the part of the supporting units. He smiled to himself. He had never had the luxury of so many radios in his old LRP detachment. It was a good sign.

Kurzikowski looked at his watch, made some mental calculations, and looked at Hollister. "Sir, they'll be out on the pad in sixteen mikes."

Hollister nodded. He liked the fact that the operations setup was precise enough to know exactly how long it would take the ships to return to the FOB. He liked the no-nonsense performance of the leathery sergeant who was taking a White Owl out of its cellophane wrap and wetting the end in his mouth before lighting it.

Somehow Hollister had expected Major Sangean to look different from the small man who stepped out of the Command and Control helicopter.

Yelling over the chopper noise, Hollister saluted. "Sir, my name is Hollister. I was told to report—"

Sangean returned the salute and pointed toward the far end of the CP. "Meet me in there in zero five." He didn't give Hollister a chance to respond. He simply broke into a trot and headed for the Operations end of the building.

Hollister stood when Sangean entered from the Operations section. He waved Hollister back to his seat on the edge of a footlocker. "Gimme a sec," he said as he took his pen out of his jungle fatigue pocket and jotted something down in the green army notebook that came out of the other pocket.

While he made notes, Hollister took a second look at his new commander. He was so typical of all the Special Forces officers he had met in his six years in the army. Though his frame was small, he was wiry, almost stringy. The tendons in his face and neck were taut, and they flexed as he thought about what he was writing. He wore a West Point ring on his right hand and a GMT-Master Rolex watch on his left wrist. His eyes were shielded by GI-issue aviator sunglasses, and the skin in front of and below his ears was marked with the impression of a headset that he must have been wearing for hours in the chopper. His uniform was the new camouflage pattern that had come into the inventory for special units since Hollister had last been in-country.

On Sangean's chest were his Combat Infantryman's Badge and Master Parachutist wings. He also wore the hard-hat helmet insignia of a school-trained diver. Below his pocket flap he wore the Jungle Expert patch.

Over his right pocket was sewn subdued cloth Vietnamese jump wings. His right shoulder bore the Special Forces combat patch, and on his left Hollister saw the distinctive tab that he would wear with Juliet Company. It was a simple arc of black on OD that read LONG RANGE PATROL. Sangean wore it beneath his Ranger tab and over the Airborne tab that topped his arrow-shaped IIFFV patch.

The field phone rattled, and Sangean picked it up, answering with only his last name. As the major listened to the caller, occasionally speaking in clipped one-word responses, Hollister noticed outside the window the LRPs who had come in on the second chopper with Sangean. They were different from the fresh-faced young soldiers whom Hollister had been with on his first tour. They weren't as playful, they seemed older than he expected, and they looked as if they were unhappy about something. None of the usual banter was going on as they crossed from what Hollister assumed was a debriefing shack to their billets.

"They're pissed off," Sangean said, interrupting Hollister's thoughts.

"What about, sir?"

"This fucking AO's useless. They're compromised from the moment they step out of a chopper out there."

"Sir?"

"There isn't enough vegetation in all of western III Corps to hide a LRP team. So anytime we insert a team there's a good chance that someone, somewhere out there, spotted them."

Hollister remembered the terrain he had seen on the east side of Cu Chi on the way out. He had to assume that it must have been the same out in the AO—to the west, toward Cambodia.

"It's nothing like what you're used to. The Highlands were a tough hump, but the concealment was your best tool. You could go anywhere up there and not be seen. I was up there with an A Team. I know what you are getting ready to find out. This place wasn't made for LRPs.

"Down here there are VC sympathizers in the damn base camp and out in the AO pointing their fingers toward our teams. I can't believe we haven't lost a team yet in the two weeks we have been shaking out the kinks."

"They any good yet?" Hollister asked.

"The teams are new. Lots of experience scattered around the troops we have been getting, but they're far from teams yet. First team we put together isn't even five weeks old yet, and I've still got twenty bodies going through the Recondo School at Nha Trang. The new ones we get in will follow them. That means it's three weeks of school and a week or so of slack on either side to get 'em there and back.

"We're less than fifty percent strength, even counting the troops in Nha Trang."

The major pulled off his sunglasses and threw them angrily across the top of his field table. "All I want to do is get these guys into shape to operate without losing a team. I'm afraid it's going to happen. We're in the wrong place. And that's why you are here."

"Because we are in the wrong place, sir?" Hollister asked, puzzled.

"Because the only way we can compensate for the lack of security is to make these teams harder than anvils and slicker than snot."

Hollister nodded in agreement, but still hadn't heard the answer to his question.

"There are damn few officers that have any LRP experience, and I bitched and bitched until they diverted you." Sangean's tone changed. "I know you were looking forward to honchoing a rifle company. But this is where the army needs you right now. I'd say I'm sorry, but I'm not. I'm sure that probably pisses you off. But you're a big boy."

There was little Hollister could say. Complaining about being yanked off orders to a division wouldn't accomplish much. It was done. At least he was with LRPs—the only two jobs he wanted were LRPs and commanding a rifle company. So he wasn't as upset as Sangean guessed.

"I got lots of good troops here. And that's all. I got shit for junior officers—not their fault. Second lieutenants don't get much chance to get experience. The NCOs are a mixed bag. Some are great, and others escaped from other jobs to get here. We're going to have to weed 'em out while we're trying to whip this company into shape.

"Topping all that off, there's no Intelligence in the entire Corps area that's any good, and we haven't got a sliver of information on just what we are up against. Put that against the fact that we have a company that is just a few weeks old and in that time we have become a thorn in the butt of everyone on the Field Force staff except Colonel Downing and you have Juliet Company. So welcome aboard, Hollister."

Shaking his head at all the bad news, Hollister replied, "Thank you, sir. I don't know what to say. It's a little much to take all at once."

"Don't say anything. Just know that if I had time, I'd give you more time. But for now you're my Operations officer, and that means Operations *and* training. If we don't train 'em, we'll bury 'em. You up to it, Ranger?"

That was all Hollister needed to hear: that his new boss had a job for him and confidence in him. It was the stuff that made Hollister operate. He stood up. "Yessir. When do I start?"

The next three days were filled with finding his way around, getting his issue gear, meeting people in the company, and trying to figure out just what was going on.

One of the first surprises was that the LRP teams were prisoners. Sangean had explained to him that their operations, which were normally classified as Secret or Top Secret, frequently exceeded the security clearances of the sol-

diers assigned to Juliet Company. Some of the soldiers had minor juvenile records and couldn't get high-enough clearances, and others were waiting for
the lengthy background checks to be completed. But Sangean couldn't wait
and had elected to restrict the movements of the troops when they were off
duty. That meant they weren't allowed out of the compound without an NCO
escort and when they went on leave or R&R they had to be brought in and
debriefed and then warned about discussing classified information. It made for
some grumbling, but most of them went along, understanding the need. After
all, any information they leaked would only come back to haunt them.

A small building next to the CP served as quarters for Hollister, Major Sangean, and Captain Cates, the air force LNO. It was a single room with
four bare walls, topped at waist level by screened and louvered uppers. The
louvers were rotting, and the screening had rips in it the size of small windows. There was just no way to protect the structures from the damage the
elements did to them.

Each man took a corner of the building and treated it as if there were
actual walls separating them. Their furnishings were nonexistent. Metal
army bunks and wooden footlockers made up the complete list of amenities
they could call their own.

By the second night, Hollister realized that Sangean was in the habit
of going to bed very late. He stayed up reading maps, manuals, books on
tactics, and the after-action reports of his LRP and other in-country teams.
He supported his long hours with cup after cup of strong mess-hall coffee
and an occasional shot of George Dickel, a bottle of which he kept on the
top of his footlocker.

Though Sangean was an open nerve ending, it never showed in his
treatment of anyone in the company. He was civil, though not very conversational. His troops were his, and he protected them like a mother bear.
He had little tolerance for outsiders who shorted his troops or failed to give
all their attention to matters concerning his company. He trusted no one
outside Juliet Company and took only slight comfort in not letting anyone
know what his patrols were up to. As a result he was constantly being sniped
at by other units like the 25th Division, whose members often complained
to their common headquarters, IIFFV, about Sangean's lack of cooperation.

Sangean explained to IIFFV that the 25th's problem was that they
didn't like the idea of just supplying food, water, fuel, housing, and perimeter security for Juliet Company without being able to tell them what to do.
He explained it as a power issue. He said Colonel Downing backed him up.

Hollister liked the fact that Sangean's priorities were his troops and getting the job done. He had seen and heard of too many commanders who had all their energies focused on themselves, at the expense of the troops and the mission. In every case it ended in disaster for someone— rarely the commander.

"I'm not going to tell you how to run your patrol," Hollister said, handing Sergeant Harrold a beer from a homemade cooler on the back steps of the mess hall.

"Sir, it's gonna be kinda hard forgettin' I got me a captain taggin'—ah, I mean, observin'."

The beer spewed from the can's rusted top as Hollister opened his beer and passed the church key to Harrold. He smiled at the young redheaded sergeant's habit of tapping the top of the beer can a few times with the opener. It was some myth passed around among teenagers that promised less foam. Hollister had always thought it was crap.

He didn't want to spoil Harrold's ritual, so he said nothing. He was sure he liked Harrold, even though he was a brand-new sergeant with only six months in Vietnam. He had volunteered for Juliet Company after serving as a squad leader in a rifle company of the 173d Airborne Brigade.

"Why J Company?"

Harrold looked up at Hollister and passed back the opener. "Well, sir . . . I don't mean no kinda disrespect or nothin', but the Old Man, I mean the CO of my rifle company, wanted me to come be his RTO and driver. And shoot, sir, I ain't no kinda CP gofer. I'd be feelin' much better to stay in a rifle platoon. The cap'n wasn't happy to hear that, and my platoon leader kinda got a case of the hips at me. So I heard Juliet Company was looking for field troops. And I guess that's how I got here."

Sergeant Harrold looked at Hollister for his reaction.

"Well, that's as good a reason as I had. You see, I was tapped to be a headquarters briefer back on my first tour myself."

Harrold grinned and raised his beer with a slight salute at the top of the arc to his lips. "All right, sir."

"So where do you want me?"

"Sir, I don't rightly know till I find out our next mission. Could make a lotta difference."

Hollister raised his can in recognition. "Good answer. I can see we're going to get along fine. So what do you say we check out what's up next for your team . . . Ah?"

"Three-Three, sir. Team Three of the Third Platoon."
"Right. Three-Three."

There was almost no paperwork. Juliet Company had been formed as if by fiat. The Field Force commander was a lieutenant general and could simply create the unit out of his own resources. No one at Field Force Headquarters had any idea what to do with them.

The southern half of South Vietnam had so many different varieties of enemy forces and problems for the Americans and South Viets that it was just assumed that once organized they would know what to do. It was the first thing Hollister found out about J Company—it was probably the wrong unit for the AO. Not enough terrain features existed to conceal their movements while on the ground or to protect their intentions when being inserted by chopper.

He searched the limited paperwork and found that while the small missions were typical of almost any infantry unit—raids, ambushes, prisoner snatch operations, sensor emplacements, and trail watches—there was a missing big picture. He wondered where they fit into the war. Was there a specific chunk of the war General Westmoreland and the Field Force commander wanted Sangean and Hollister to tackle? If so, no one had told him.

"We don't have a general mission that's any more specific than assuming responsibility of a major piece of Vietnam and saturating it with patrols to develop the situation," Major Sangean said as he pushed a plug of chewing tobacco into the space in his cheek and opened the map case on top of his footlocker.

To get a better look, Hollister took a seat on an M60 ammunition can that had been appropriated for just that purpose. "So, what do we own?"

Major Sangean tapped an area only three miles east of the Cambodian border, between two distinctive bends in the line that separated the two countries. One was called the "Angel's Wing," the other the "Parrot's Beak."

"We own just about everything on this map sheet. West of the Twenty-fifth's AO to—" He looked up to make a point of his next words. "—and *including* the border itself. Most of it is reeds and abandoned rice fields that are too risky to farm. There's hardly a terrain feature higher than a rice-paddy dike, and the ones that are end up being somebody's home."

"Looks like a tabletop with clumps of vegetation but too far apart for our business," Hollister said.

"I'd rather be working in the trees—War Zone D, the Hobo Woods. Anything's better than this," Major Sangean responded.

"So how do we get around it?"

"We have got to be smarter and move faster." Sangean raised his hand. "Now don't say anything. I know, I know. LRPs don't move fast; they move skillfully. Well, here if you aren't fast getting in, getting moved, and getting out, you'll be found and you'll be killed."

"You'll get no argument with me, sir. How about support?"

"We're real weak on that. We get supported by whatever is in the AO they send us to. That means we are never in an area long enough to get to know the guys yanking lanyards and pickling off rockets for us.

"We could be supported by the Twenty-fifth Division, the First Division, the One hundred ninety-ninth Brigade, or the Eleventh Armored Cav on any given day."

"Not good," Hollister said, almost below his breath. "Not good at all. I just don't like the idea of trying to train someone to shoot between the uprights when they don't know the game. Most people don't have any idea what LRPs do, and while you're getting shot at is no time for them to learn."

Sangean kicked the screen door open with his foot and squirted a pencil-thin stream of tobacco juice out into the dirt. "That's why I got you."

Hollister tried to sit in the back of the room and not make the others uncomfortable. It had been different when he was a lieutenant. Troops were quicker to accept lieutenants who tagged along on patrols, but the rank of captain intimidated some of them. His mind wandered to the first day he saw a captain in his basic training company. Hollister knew that a captain was the lowest rank that really had power. A company commander could bust a soldier in rank, fine him, and restrict him to the barracks under Article 15 without even having to buck it up the chain of command.

SFC Kurzikowski, a man easing out of his forties, was competent in his job. His combat patch tagged him as a veteran of earlier service with the 101st Airborne Brigade, whose reputation gave him a leg up with Hollister.

Kurzikowski ignored the fact that his new boss was in the room receiving the patrol order and delivered the information as if he had personally checked out every fact in his notes. After a few days of watching what Kurzikowski had been able to do, Hollister figured he probably *had* checked it all personally.

"Now the information may be sheer bullshit, but if it is right, you guys will bag some bad guys and be back here for heavy beer drinking in a day," Kurzikowski announced.

"Where did you get the report?" Sergeant Harrold asked.

"Some canal digger came into an ARVN outpost and said the VC were kicking the gates out of the irrigation canals he had been digging. Seems that they flood a canal this guy is working on during the early evening and then drag small skiffs loaded with supplies down it. With the water they can cut a chogie and be across what woulda been a hard hump in no time."

Kurzikowski drew an imaginary circle on the map behind him, indicating the huge open area that would have been much more difficult to cross at night on foot carrying heavy loads.

Hollister looked at the same area on the map on his lap. Tree lines, canals, mile-long rice-paddy dikes, rail spurs—it appeared to him that he had to accept a new way of thinking about the linear nature of movement and concealment on his new battlefield.

As Kurzikowski continued, slipping into the details of the upcoming combat patrol, Hollister could feel his gut tightening up. He knew it would get progressively worse as he got closer to the shooting.

Sergeant Harrold tried to look comfortable inspecting Hollister's equipment as they stood in a single line with their gear on and weapons at the ready. Hollister had insisted it was Harrold's patrol, and he wanted to see how things were done in Juliet Company. So Hollister would go along without rank.

With less than a week back in Vietnam, Hollister knew he was *really* back when he leaned forward under the weight of his heavy rucksack and headed for the Huey lift helicopter. His skin started to burn from the camouflage stick he had applied to his face, neck, and hands.

He would be a scout grenadier for Sergeant Harrold's six-man patrol. The deceptively small M79 grenade launcher in his right hand reminded him of the battle-damaged one he had cut down his last time in-country. That one had been shorter, lighter, and less of a nuisance, but he only used it to mark targets and as a signaling device. The one he was carrying would be used to fire high-explosive rounds, shotgun rounds, and fléchette rounds.

Fléchettes were new to him. The round had a tightly packed warhead of bradlike pins sharpened at one end and flattened at the other—like tiny arrows. When fired, the "nails," as they were called by the troops, would straighten out in flight and penetrate softer targets with a tight pattern. A man in its path could expect to be punctured once in every four square inches of body surface exposed to the nails.

Hollister also carried flare rounds. They were a smaller-caliber round originally designed for flare pistols. But some enterprising soldier had figured out that they would fit into the barrel of the M79, and the loss in accuracy was unimportant since flares only needed to be fired aloft to get their job done.

The chopper was showing its age. Hollister guessed it had been in-country since the D Model had been introduced to Vietnam—at least two years. In that time a lift ship could stack up lots of air miles, a frightening number of combat sorties, and could have ferried thousands of soldiers into terrifying landing zones.

Hollister tried to tell himself that the appearance of the body-and-fender work on a Huey was no indicator of the ship's airworthiness. The very strictly applied maintenance schedules required so much periodic inspection and replacement of parts and major components that a chopper could be brand-new—flightwise—but look like something from a demolition derby on the outside.

Still, Hollister would have been happier to see a chopper that looked as if it had just come off the assembly line at Bell Helicopter.

His stomach grew even tighter as the pilot increased the rpm on the main rotor. All the chatter among the troops dropped off to none. Hollister knew that each man was silently preparing himself for the unknown and cutting deals with his own God about his survival.

The first chopper lift that had taken Hollister into enemy territory had been over two years earlier. It had been chaotic and very confusing. When the choppers landed on the beach at Tuy Hoa to pick up his company, they weren't sure how many troops each chopper could lift. Back then the ACL of a chopper was very unpredictable and varied widely from chopper to chopper on any given day. So Hollister's platoon had been broken down into five-man chalks. Even then, some of his soldiers were turned away from choppers that couldn't lift them, only to run frantically to choppers ahead or behind them and find that they, too, could not take them. Once Hollister's platoon was on the ground, he discovered that two of his sergeants and one RTO had been left behind at the pickup zone. Since that day he had been very conscious of the helicopter's few shortcomings. He had learned to respect its vulnerabilities and never trust his soldiers' lives to the choppers.

"Lock and load!" yelled Sergeant Harrold as the chopper lifted off the OLD WARRIOR emblem.

Each man yanked back on his charging handle and chambered a round into his M16. Hollister slipped an HE round into the M79 and put the weapon on safe, still holding the muzzle so that it always faced out the chopper's open door.

He looked around at the others. Each man sat on the edge of the deck with his feet dangling out and down toward the skids. All were looking down as the sprawling red-brown base camp zipped by below the aircraft.

Hollister watched as Harrold picked the radio handset off the lift harness of his radio operator and called Operations for a commo check and to report that they were off and headed for the landing zone.

Major Sangean was somewhere behind the insert ship in his C&C chopper. With him were the artillery liaison officer from the supporting battery and two other team leaders. The two team leaders were along to watch the insert and to conduct a VR of the landing zones for their own upcoming patrols.

A small flutter in Hollister's stomach was his reaction to seeing the arc of barbed wire and neatly spaced perimeter bunkers pass beneath the chopper. They were now in Indian country. While no part of South Vietnam was safe, there was a feeling that the farther away from American units you were, the more danger you were in. In fact, that was not really the case. Any spot in Vietnam was likely to be completely free of enemy activity at any given time—and as hot and hostile as possible at any other time. The war and enemy activity were so dynamic that soldiers had to remind themselves that location didn't imply certain proximity to enemy forces. Hollister knew all this, but his stomach couldn't be convinced.

He absentmindedly traced the outline and the position of the equipment on his harness. He had not been wearing it long enough to be sure where everything was or if it was all secured. He wished he had had time to loosen up some of the stiffness in the pouches, check out his compass, cook some of the protective oils off his canteen cup, zero his M79, adjust his rucksack for his height and the load, and break in his new jungle boots.

With the time he had available, he was able to do a little of each, but not enough to make him completely confident with his equipment.

The countryside below the choppers' flight was a map of commerce and transportation. Tiny hamlets consisting of as few as three thatched-roof houses stood at the end of narrow dirt roads or wide paths. At the other end the paths fed into roadways built by the government. These threaded around the precious farmland and eventually found their way to the two-lane highways, almost all of which led to Saigon.

There were no densely populated areas. The whole area was dots and clusters of hamlet after hamlet, some clumped into common villages, but still separated by even the tiniest garden plots.

The other major features were the waterways that crisscrossed every piece of property, finally feeding the two major rivers—the Saigon and the Dong Ngai.

It was as if he had been sent to a different war than his last one. Hollister had been used to fewer people per hectare, fewer waterways, and more hills. In the Central Highlands there had been so many more hills, tropical rain forest, and tall hardwood trees that had isolated and protected his LRPs from observation and enemy fire.

Of all the things bothering Hollister, his unfamiliarity with the terrain troubled him most. He knew he would have to get used to it fast and take it into account in every decision he made and every plan he put together. To ignore it was to ask for trouble. He was absolutely sure about that.

A few minutes out of the Cu Chi base camp, a pair of gunships joined the flight. It irritated Hollister that no one from the aviation units supporting the patrol insert showed up at the patrol order or the patrol leader's briefback. This was sure to slow things down at a critical moment. He hated the higher headquarters' attitude that choppers were like buses and all they had to do was send one to pick up troops. Coordination was everything, and that only sprang from communication. He pulled his notebook from his pocket and made a note while trying to keep the pages from ripping in the turbulence of the rotor wash.

Sergeant Harrold tapped Hollister on the back and gave him a spread hand—fingers out. They were five minutes from their landing zone.

CHAPTER 8

Five minutes out. It was time to steel himself for the upcoming events. Hollister made one last check of his equipment and re-checked the safety on his weapon while the chopper descended to treetop level.

While frying to avoid the wind's eye-drying blast, Hollister peered out and ahead of the chopper to see if he could pick up the landing zone. It was like looking at a pool table from table height. It gave him a sinking feeling to know that he had no idea where the landing zone was from his vantage point. He knew it meant the patrols had to place plenty of trust in the pilots—pilots who didn't come to briefings, and couldn't call one LRP in Juliet Company by name.

He tried not to be too obvious as he looked at the others inside the chopper. They were the same. The same as every other LRP he had worked with. They were quiet, alert, and anxious. The problem never changed. The uncertainty of the insertion was the first major crunch point for the patrol members.

If they got to the landing zone and found it hot, the choppers would wave off and pull out. Their job would be to return fire from inside the chopper in order to help suppress enemy fire as they pulled up and away.

If they got in and down, then they would have to make sure they moved as fast as possible to the nearest concealment, and hope not to get cut down by enemy fire while they ran. They all knew the frightening reality that they would probably not hear the firing that would slice across the landing zone. Their first indication of being fired at would either be casualties or the return fire from the M60 machine guns manned by the chopper door gunners.

And their crossing of the open area between the chopper and the trees would probably be hampered by the knee-deep rice-paddy water and the mashed-potatolike ground beneath it. Or it would be made very difficult by the boulder-sized clumps of sunbaked mud that often caused ankle sprains in their dash to the trees.

If they made it to the concealment of the tree lines, they would hope they didn't walk into booby traps or find themselves in such an obvious piece of real estate that the VC had it registered and could easily lob mortars into the spot without having to adjust their fire, racking up kills on the first round.

Hollister also knew that if they were lucky enough to get past all that, once they were in the trees they would have to wait for the noise of the choppers to clear before they could even begin to determine if there was any other threat to them. And even that would be a chore, with their breathing labored by the sprint and the heavy load they carried, not to mention the pounding of their hearts and the sounds of water dripping from every crease and bend in their uniforms.

Not worried about taking ground fire from high ground since there was no high ground, the pilots closed on the landing zone at a low altitude. Hollister and the others watched fifteen- to forty-foot-high bamboo and nipa palms flash quickly by. The shadow of the chopper on the paddy fields below was almost life-sized at that altitude, and the feeling of speed was more evident because of their proximity to the ground and the trees.

Normally, Hollister would follow the terrain features—rivers, stream junctions, roads—on his map as they approached a landing zone. But he was not the patrol leader, and he knew that doing so would show a lack of confidence in Sergeant Harrold's ability to get his team to the right spot. So he was pretty much blind to their progress and had to rely on chopper clues.

Hollister still couldn't see the landing zone as he took one more look out and in front of the chopper. He knew it had to be very close because the pilots began to draw back on the cyclics, raising the nose, which slowed the aircraft. Just in front of them was a row of trees that looked like a twenty-foot-high hedge. Hollister assumed from the chopper maneuvers that the LZ had to be just on the other side of the trees.

The door gunners had grabbed the firing handles on their stowed M60 machine guns and pulled them up from the vertical into the firing position. Their eyes and the front-sight blades of the guns were trained on the ribbon of trees rushing by.

"Stand by! Watch your footing! Keep your heads up!" Harrold yelled.

The warning was unnecessary. Each man in the chopper knew what was happening and what was expected of him. The charge to keep their heads up was important. It was human nature to duck their heads, if only symbolically, as they ran out from under the twenty-four-foot rotors that reached out from the rotor shaft. Added to that was the preoccupation with the unsteady footing. That day, they would be knee-deep in paddy water. The combination of the two distractions would keep their heads and eyes down if Harrold didn't remind them to keep their heads up so they could move, shoot, and communicate.

The chopper felt like a roller coaster as it halted its forward momentum and began to sink toward the wet field a split second after skimming the treetops with its skids.

This is it, Hollister thought as he walked the cheeks of his ass closer to the door. His toes reached out for the skid that was just outside his reach. Still, he was looking to miss the skid, not step inside of it as he had once seen a soldier do in the Highlands. The misstep caused the soldier to pitch forward and break his collarbone when the chopper lifted off, upending him.

He already didn't like the spot the pilot had picked. It was much too far from the trees. His guess was that they were easily three rotor disks away from the concealment that the tree line would give them.

He knew each step they had to run across the open area could be that much more exposure to enemy fire and would exact a greater toll on their energy once they stopped inside the trees.

He didn't wait for the chopper to settle before he leaned forward, letting the momentum pull him out and down that half foot to the ground.

Within two strides he felt the power from the downward force of the main rotor blades.

The team was out, and the pilot, not wanting to remain on the ground for a second longer than he had to, was sucking power back into the collective to lift off. Hollister fought the rotor wash as he slopped clumsily through the rice paddy, the water spattering his face and filling his eyes with mud and grit. He was determined not to fall on his face—not in front of five LRPs, four chopper crews, his new commander, and any VC who might be watching him.

Hollister promised himself that he would quit smoking. He felt pain as he attempted to get his heaving chest under control while trying to gulp enough air to put the fire out in his lungs. His head pounded. He spat mud and tried to clear his eyes of the mud and sweat that blurred his vision.

The six LRPs had formed a tight perimeter, each kneeling at the ready, facing out, concealed by the narrow band of trees where they had assembled.

The sounds of the choppers faded. Soon the only one heard was the C&C ship, circling at fifteen hundred feet off to the east of the team so as not to aid the enemy in locating them. It was this chopper that waited for Harrold to call in the status. Hollister turned for a second to see what he was doing.

Sergeant Harrold pulled the handset from the RTO's radio, straightened out the coiled cord, and cupped his hands around the mouthpiece. Hollister couldn't hear him, but he assumed Harrold was calling in a cold LZ and a normal SITREP.

Harrold pitched the handset back to the RTO and pointed directly at Hollister and one other soldier, a small LRP named Miguel Montagna. Once he had their attention, he pointed in the direction he wanted them to go. It would be up to Hollister and Montagna to form a two-man advance element to lead the other four to their lay-up position, only two hundred meters from where they were. They would be able to move more quietly than all six at once. Moving more quietly, they would have a better chance of discovering any threat to the team.

As Hollister and Montagna moved, they stopped periodically and let the main body of the patrol catch up. Then they moved out again.

If they made contact, it would be VC at close range. With this in mind, Hollister broke open the action on his M79 and dropped the high-explosive round out into his hand. He tucked it into an ammo pouch on his pistol belt, which held only three rounds—each one had an HE, shotgun, and fléchette. He pulled out the shotgun round and slipped it into the chamber.

He thought about selecting the fléchette round, but was not sure of the range and dispersion of the nails.

That was another thing bothering Hollister. He had never been able to fire the fléchette round in the States, and before the patrol left they were unable to get permission from the 25th Division Headquarters to test fire weapons. The 25th claimed they could only allow the LRPs to use the small range on Tuesdays and Saturdays because it was overbooked. A notation that this must change was already in Hollister's notebook.

A few meters on, Hollister stopped and knelt next to a sapling not much bigger around than his forearm. He quickly took up a ready firing position, and assumed the overwatch responsibility for Montagna's movement.

Only ten meters in front of Hollister, Montagna moved like a cat, one foot coming straight up, moving forward above the scraps of vegetation that dotted the hedgerow and then back down—toe first. The movement was laughingly referred to as the "Alabama High Step" back at Ranger School.

Comfortable with the footing, Montagna repeated the movement with the other foot. As he did, Hollister watched ahead of Montagna for any flicker of light or change in texture, color, or movement that might indicate the approach or presence of the enemy.

After several meters Montagna stopped and waited for Hollister to move up and pass him, taking up the point for a while. The movement by bounds gave each of them a periodic break and kept them more alert by sharing the pressure.

The feeling of nakedness was what first hit Hollister. He had become so used to moving inside the lush rain forests of the Highlands that moving along the length of a narrow strip of trees that had only been planted to divide property and break up the monsoon winds made him very uncomfortable. He knew that anyone monitoring the team's movement would know they had only three options after entering the tree line—stay put, move in one direction inside the trees, or move in the opposite direction. Those few options gave the enemy a distinct advantage.

Hollister chided himself to keep his mind on what he was doing. There would be time to straighten out all the difficulties when he got back to the launch site at Cu Chi.

The ground had many footprints. Most were from bare feet, but some were shod and still others displayed the characteristic rubber tire pattern of what had become known as "Ho Chi Minh sandals." These sandals were often worn by the VC, but they were not the exclusive property of the enemy. Many farmers wore them to protect their feet from the unseen dangers of ragged metal that was piling up all over Vietnam after years at war.

Scanning the trees immediately in front of him, Hollister edged forward. Something told him to look down sooner than he might have. The sun coming through the channellike break in the trees reflected off a small loop of silver wire. Booby trap!

Hollister raised his hand to let Montagna know that he was stopping and to cover his movements. He then carefully knelt down to get a closer look. Before he made the wrong move, he made sure the booby trap was not just a lure to get his attention while he triggered a less visible one nearby. The movement to a crouch took several seconds—done correctly.

The wire was similar to the wire bands that held army C ration cases together for shipping. Only slightly smaller in diameter than pencil lead, the wire was formed in a loop raised only an inch and a half off the ground to serve as a snare to catch the boot of an approaching soldier.

The loop was connected by a second length of wire to the pin in an old pineapple grenade. The pin had been flattened out so that it would slip easily from the spoon, letting it fly free and allowing the striker to spring around and detonate the grenade.

Disarming the booby trap would have been easy enough for Hollister to do. He could simply bend the pin back and remove the wire from the ring on it. But Hollister knew there was a chance the grenade was old enough to be unstable and that the booby trap just might have been booby-trapped against disarming. So he turned to Montagna, signaled that he had found the trap, and reached into his shirt pocket.

He pulled out a tight roll of GI toilet paper, banded with a piece of brown wrapping paper. Breaking the small bundle open, he pulled off three small squares of tissue and tore each of them halfway through. He then slipped the slit in the tissue over a part of the booby trap, marking the center and the limits of the wire and the grenade.

The paper would stand out vividly against the earth and grass colors around it and allow the others on the patrol to identify the trap and avoid it as they moved forward along the same path that Hollister and Montagna had crossed.

The movement continued for the next forty-five minutes. Finally, Hollister and Montagna reached the site where they would hole up and watch the nearby canal.

They had selected a concealed position where the canal came toward them and then took a slight turn and crossed in front of them. The nearest point was just over one hundred meters from them. Just inside a dense clump of trees, they were in the best location to see the water level, spot any approaching VC early, and be able to fire on them once they made the turn across the team's front. The canal was dry, save a small trickle of water that ran through it.

The other four team members closed on the position, and Sergeant Harrold set up the perimeter they had rehearsed back at Cu Chi. He made some adjustments to account for fields of fire and the relationship of the position to the canal.

Watching, Hollister thought there was a little too much confusion in the perimeter, but kept his opinion to himself. He knew that the disruption of calling attention to it would be more damaging to the integrity of the patrol than the slight confusion itself. Better to let the confusion die down by itself and discuss it with Harrold back at Cu Chi.

The team had touched down just after eight A.M. Four hours later the sun was beating down through the large break in the trees above them. Hollister wasn't even almost used to the climate, and sweat formed on his face and neck, rolled down the center of his chest, and pooled at his navel under his camouflage fatigues. He was still wet from dashing through the rice paddies, and everything he touched was either wet or muddy.

Two years earlier he and others used to complain about the discomfort they felt in the Vietnamese tiger-striped fatigues they used to wear. Things had not improved by changing to the American cammies with the ripstop cotton. Hollister wasn't sure, but he thought they might be even hotter.

Sounds. They were so different in III Corps. When he had been in the Highlands there were rain-forest sounds. But the collective sound there had not been much sound at all.

Now he was listening to a sky full of the complete inventory of American aircraft. He could hear vehicle noises and flocks of mud ducks and cocks. Since he had arrived in Hau Nghia Province, there hadn't been an hour when he hadn't heard a rooster crow.

He didn't like the feeling of being surrounded by things that could compromise his location, his security, and his life. He knew that many of the problems that might make his tour difficult would come from the over-population of his AO.

Now Hollister could feel someone watching him. Turning back toward the perimeter, he saw Harrold staring at him. Harrold put his palms together and raised them to the side of his face. It was the signal for Hollister to try to get some sleep.

In the patrol order, Harrold had insisted that they try to get some rest during the days because he feared they would be out five full days—the length of patrol for which they had supplies. He made a point of explaining how his greatest worry in the AO on this patrol was complacency and fatigue. He knew that if he didn't force patrol members to get some sleep during the day, they would doze off at night—a fast way for a patrol to get overrun.

Hollister would be one of two to sleep at this time. He knew that the other four would be awake and that he would be able to get in at least two hours of sleep if he could ignore the discomforts of lying on the damp ground in the baking tropical heat. He smiled for a second, thinking how good the kudzu and red clay back at Fort Benning would look now.

Harrold reached over and tapped Hollister on the foot. He then handed him a set of binoculars and pointed off toward a point far up the canal, toward the Cambodian border, nine thousand meters west of them.

Clearing the fog from his deep and dreamless sleep, Hollister sat up and wiped the sweat and grime from his face. He took the binos and found the right focal length on the thumbscrew. Using his knees like a tripod, he steadied the binos in the direction Harrold had indicated. There, at a distance of at least two thousand meters, a single Vietnamese boy sat astride the broad back of a water buffalo. Hollister didn't like the sight of either one. He knew how dangerous they both could be.

The boy was pretending to be tending the water buffalo and not paying attention to much else. The thing that made the scene ring with a dull tone was that there was no reason for the boy to be tending the animal there. It was not farmland nor was it a place where the boy might either feed or wash the animal. The kid, who looked about twelve, was a lookout of some sort.

"Think he saw us move in here?" Harrold asked in a voice that was barely audible, though spoken only inches from Hollister's ear.

Shaking his head no, Hollister watched the boy kick the water buffalo with an almost imperceptible flutter of his left heel. The animal responded by clumsily moving closer to the empty canal.

He handed the binoculars back to Harrold and stood up slowly. He pointed his index finger at himself, and then toward the limbs on a nearby tree. He next pointed upward.

Harrold got the message, but didn't speak. He took Hollister's M79 and helped him get out of his web gear.

Hollister took the binoculars back from Harrold and began to climb the small tree. He was only able to get six feet off the ground before he ran out of limbs that would support his weight and branches that would conceal him from the boy—or anyone else who might be watching their position.

A second look through the binoculars confirmed Hollister's suspicions. The boy was maneuvering the water buffalo to a point where he could step down and be right at a small sluice gate that separated the dry canal from a bend in a substantial but wandering stream that went off in another direction—eventually spilling into the Dong Ngai River.

He took the binos from his face and looked around. It was getting late, and farmers were finishing their chores, packing up bundles of produce and hand tools for their walk home at the day's end. Hollister knew the boy could crack the gate and start flooding the canal, and it would be after dark before anyone would discover the flooding. For all Hollister knew, it could take hours for the rising water level to be noticed. That would give the VC a wide window to use the canal.

Hollister saw the boy slide down off the back of the huge water buffalo and stand next to it for a moment, looking around casually while flicking a small bamboo switch to keep the flies away from the animal's eyes and backside.

After a few moments of shepherding the animal, the boy bent over and splashed some river water on its back, as if to cool him from the sun's baking rays. He did it three more times, and the fourth time he reached out and pulled the wooden locking pin from the gate, then raised it slightly. The water squirted through the slot horizontally and began to eat away at the loosely packed earth on the far bank.

The amount of water didn't seem sufficient to fill the canal deeply enough for the VC to float skiffs. But Hollister couldn't be sure.

He watched the boy get back on the water buffalo and head off to the northwest, then he climbed down the tree.

As soon as he was down, Hollister leaned over, took his gear back from Harrold, and whispered what he had just seen.

As if they were both thinking the same thing, Hollister and Harrold looked at their wristwatches. It was just after six, and the sun was sinking quickly into Cambodia. Harrold smiled. They had guessed right, his expression seemed to say. He nodded his head at Hollister as if to say, "Good job."

By the time Hollister had slipped his rucksack straps loosely over his shoulders, settled back into his assigned position, and scanned his sector of fire, Harrold had finished writing a note, a situation report that would be passed to each member of the patrol so that he could understand what Hollister had seen and what it meant. It didn't take them long to read the note and nod affirmatively—they were ready.

By the time the note got back around to Hollister he could almost guess what Harrold had written, but he read it anyway. He wanted to make sure they were in agreement, not just close. The note read: BOY=VC. FILLING CANAL, GOOKS ALMOST SURE TO COME DOWN CANAL AFTER DARK. ACKNOWLEDGE.

Hollister knew that he was going to like the way Harrold did things, and he hoped that the others were as good as Harrold was.

Damn! As Hollister read the note and thought about Harrold's performance, it came to him. The way to get enough water into the canal to use it quickly and delay anyone from discovering it and redraining it was to dam it somewhere before it spilled out.

He hurriedly scribbled a note on the next page in Harrold's notebook: BET THERE ARE A FEW VC AT FAR END DAMMING WATER!

He began to write another sentence telling Harrold to call the guess in to Operations so they would send choppers out to look for the other half of the VC team. But he stopped. He had promised Harrold he would let him run his patrol and not pull rank on him. That meant not thinking for him or being *too* helpful.

He put his pen back in his shirt pocket, returned the notebook to Harrold, and fought the urge to oversupervise the junior sergeant. He knew he would have to trust Harrold to make the right moves.

After reading the note Harrold didn't need to give Hollister the big grin and nod that he gave him. It was obvious from the expression on his face that he knew exactly what to do.

Another page of the notebook was used to compose the most concise message Harrold could write. Hollister watched as he carefully chose his words and then reread them for completeness. He could see that Harrold had written the acronym S-A-L-U-T-E at the top of the page before drafting his message. It would help him make sure to include information on size, activity, location, uniforms, time/troops, and equipment.

In less than two minutes Harrold had drafted and proofed the message and reached for the radio handset. He took off his floppy hat and wrapped it around the mouthpiece to make a kind of cup to surround his mouth as he transmitted the message.

By dark the ground they were lying on was crawling with water leeches that had discovered their presence and traveled the few inches from the surrounding paddy water to the ledge they were on.

Each man knew that for every five of them that they picked up and pitched back out into the water, at least one found its mark and was burrowing into fatigues, under belt lines, and down their boot tops. None of them had any confidence that they would make it through the night without feeding at least a couple of the quiet and slimy vampires.

Night between Saigon and the Cambodian border was nothing like any Vietnam night Hollister had been in before. In every direction he could see lights. Cook fires, lamps, smoldering trash fires, headlights, chopper navigation lights, flares, and tracers—they all interrupted the dark. For no apparent reason, tracers would arc up into the sky. There were no targets for the fires of the South Vietnamese automatic rifle fire. And only on rare occasions would a stream of green Communist tracers whip up trying to hit a passing helicopter.

The noises continued. There were night sounds of insects, plenty of frogs and crickets, but they were almost drowned out by the continuous and irritating high-pitched sputter of Honda motorbikes. Their sounds seemed to come from every direction but Cambodia. It was just another mental note that Hollister made. He was sure the sounds and the lights might be exploited in some way to help teams on the ground. He just didn't know how at that moment.

He pulled the unbuttoned sleeve of his fatigue shirt away from his watch and checked the time. It was after nine. Two things bothered Hollister. There was no sign of movement on the canal. And there had been no indication that any effort had been made to re-con the other end of the canal by chopper to see if the VC were damming it.

The night seemed to drag on. Hollister tried every trick he knew to stay awake and still found himself drifting off with his eyes still open. It made him very angry with himself. It was a sign that he was tired, that the heat and newness of the humidity was getting to him. He looked around to see if the others knew he was having a hard time staying awake. No one seemed to even be looking in his direction. Still, setting the example was very important to him, no matter who was leading the patrol.

Just then, Hollister felt a pebble bounce off his shoulder. It was Harrold trying to get his attention. He was allowing each man to get an hour's sleep before midnight and one before sunrise. It was Hollister's turn. He made an exaggerated nodding gesture to let Harrold know he understood him and was going to follow his instructions.

Harrold then turned to a sleeping body just outside his reach and rolled over so he could gently wake him without startling him.

***

It seemed as if it had only been a matter of seconds since Harrold had told Hollister to get some sleep. But someone was pulling on his trouser leg.

Hollister sat up silently, but with a start. Must be something wrong, he thought. He looked at his watch. It had been just over an hour. He was back on. He turned over and looked back out toward the black where the canal would be, if he could see it. But the moon had set and visibility was severely reduced. As he began to look around the tiny perimeter, he caught something out of the corner of his eye. For a moment he didn't believe he actually saw anything.

He stopped moving and looked once more. There it was again—the glow of a cigarette cupped in a hand but glowing brightly as the smoker dragged on it.

He turned to pass the word and came face-to-face with Harrold. The kid didn't miss a thing. Hollister wondered if he had even taken the time to get some sleep himself.

Without talking they both agreed that what they were watching was at least one person coming down the center of the canal, smoking a cigarette.

CHAPTER 9

The cigarette went out, and the figure in the dark continued down the canal toward the LRP position. Hollister stood up, full-length, his body pressed against a small tree to camouflage his form. With the binoculars he tried to determine if the smoker was alone or if there was someone following him in the canal. The binoculars were a small help in cutting through the dark, but he couldn't be sure of what was in the canal.

This upset him. He knew they couldn't open up on the leading VC unless they were absolutely sure it was VC and that there was no other enemy element nearby that could swing out wide and attack the patrol. If they fired, anyone in the area could nail their location in a matter of minutes and bring accurate fire on them almost immediately. And the patrol would have nowhere to move since the green patch that concealed them was hundreds of meters from the next nearest clump. The flight time of their choppers would be at least twice the time it would take the VC to find, fix, and destroy the small team.

The whole issue could have been avoided if they had their own choppers standing by, available to crank up and stand by for a contact call.

But that wasn't the case. IIFFV told Juliet Company that they would get choppers when they needed them, and that in the event of a contact they would get priority by declaring a tactical emergency to the chopper outfit assigned to support them. Another totally unacceptable feature of Hollister's new company.

Harrold whispered into Hollister's ear, "Called for gunships to roll up the canal and fire up the VC."

And? Hollister shrugged.

Sergeant Harrold turned his palms up, hoping the choppers would arrive on time and at the right location.

Hollister raised the binoculars again and took another look at the approaching figure in the canal. The image had improved with the reduced distance, and Hollister could identify the figure as a Vietnamese carrying a rifle diagonally across his back and wearing a ChiCom ammo pouch on his chest.

He poked the binoculars toward Harrold to let him see the VC, feeling better about considering the man in the canal a target.

As he waited for Harrold, he tried to figure out an alternative to calling gunships or firing their own weapons at the VC. He thought that a single shot from a sniper rifle would do the job. But they didn't have any. He made a mental note to check into it when they got back to Cu Chi.

Harrold returned the binoculars to Hollister, who continued to watch the lone VC haul a small boat loaded with supplies. He again wished he had a scoped rifle with a trained shooter. It would allow them to get just one shot off and drop the VC without advertising their location.

Suddenly, he spotted a second and then a third VC—evenly spaced about three minutes apart—almost out of sight of one another. They, too, were hauling supplies on the calf-deep water in the canal. Hollister looked back toward Harrold, who waved that he, too, had seen them.

The luminous dial on Hollister's watch read just after one A.M. And no choppers. They had waited for over forty minutes, and the first VC had made the turn in the canal in front of the team and was walking out of sight. The second VC was just approaching the turn, and the third was clearly in view behind him.

After ten more minutes the sounds of the choppers grew out of the east. A few minutes later Hollister could make out the rotating beacon on the tail boom of the lead chopper.

Harrold tried to establish commo with the chopper on the air-to-ground frequency and on the company frequency—with no luck. The choppers, two Huey gunships, locked onto the canal a couple of miles east of the team and started following it toward the bend in front of them.

Every few thousand meters one of the choppers would break out of the formation and circle the other one, playing its chin light on the fields on either side of the canal. Every so often one of the choppers would fire a burst of machine-gun fire into clumps of vegetation in order to recon by fire.

The search took over fifteen minutes to reach the LRP team, and Harrold still had not made contact with the choppers, even though he had tried all their frequencies and even called back to Company Operations for help reaching them.

Each man in the patrol was aware that the choppers were unsure of their location and that there was a chance they could stumble onto the patrol and mistake them for the VC. None of them wanted to think of the possible results. They had all seen the damage a pair of gunships could do in a matter of seconds.

"Harrold! Choppers!" the RTO whispered loudly, to be heard over the sounds of the chopper blades and turbines.

Hollister watched the reactions of the other team members as Harrold reached for the handset and spoke with the chopper pilots. Most were splitting their attention between the lost images in the canal and the choppers slowly crawling toward them.

Harrold reached up to the left side of his harness and slipped his strobe light out of its upside-down carrier. He pulled the shield off the body of the strobe and attached it to the glass end that covered the high-intensity-light coil.

By the time he stood up, the choppers were less than two hundred meters from the team and getting closer. Harrold turned on the strobe, and the high-pitched squeal cut the chopper noise. He raised the strobe and pointed it directly at the lead chopper. By the time the strobe had fired the second time, the lead chopper had turned off all its lights and turned them back on again—to let Harrold know he had them located.

He hadn't realized how long he had been holding his breath, but Hollister finally exhaled, releasing some of the tension in his chest.

Harrold came to Hollister's position and explained what had happened. It was a bust. The choppers had found nothing along the canal and had trouble with the communication because they were not given the right frequencies for the LRP team.

Hollister nodded that he understood, but it was obvious he was not happy with the turn of events. To him it was a series of screwups that should not have happened. He was only consoled by the fact that there didn't seem to be any fault on the side of the LRPs. He knew that all the problems would be his to solve as the new Operations officer for the LRP company.

Harrold told him they would be extracted as soon after first light as the morning ground fog would permit since they had to assume the canal would probably not have any activity on it for the next several days. He put the team on two-thirds alert for the rest of the night and rechecked the perimeter before settling back into his position.

Packed up and ready for the pickup, they squatted in the tree line, half facing forward toward the pickup zone, half facing to the rear to cover their backs.

Suddenly, Hollister, who was facing to the rear, spotted the small face of a child no more than seven years old standing nearly a hundred yards out into the rice paddy on the other side of the trees that concealed them. It was a small girl with big black eyes. She was bent at the waist, her little hands on her thighs, peering into the trees—as if she saw or heard something.

There had to be someone else, Hollister thought. The child was too young to be that far out in the rice fields at daybreak without an adult or some older children.

He shifted his position to see around a bush that blocked his view and spotted two adult women wearing laborers' pajamas and traditional conical hats. They were carrying crude hoes and were pecking at a chunk of higher ground, pulling manioc roots from the earth.

Not sure what to do, Hollister remembered that the call was not his to make. He turned and pitched a small stick at Harrold, who was facing away, waiting for the choppers.

Harrold reacted by moving to Hollister's side and looking out on the field behind them. He shook his head, mouthed the words "No sweat," and went back to his position.

As he stopped and knelt down again, the sounds of approaching choppers grew louder than the morning sounds and the slight breeze that rustled the bushes around them. Hollister looked back at the little girl. He saw one of the women drop her hoe and ran out into the field to scoop up her child. The sounds of the choppers meant something completely different to the villagers than it did to the LRPs.

As he sat in the corner of Operations drinking a room-temperature Coke, Sergeant Kurzikowski ran down the debriefing checklist. Hollister read his notes and made some more in order to refresh his memory later. He was angry at how the patrol had turned out. Though he had found little to complain about in the team's performance, his list of coordination and support problems was lengthy.

He was also very disturbed by the nature of his new area of operations. In his opinion it was not for LRPs, it was for larger, conventional units that could defend themselves if compromised by a little girl or by firing at a target of opportunity. With LRPs the minute they were discovered or gave their position away they needed to be yanked out—and fast. The chopper support gave Hollister no confidence in their future response. He knew his work was cut out for him. Tactical support and coordination were his main responsibility. And he would do it right—too many lives depended on it.

"They don't care!" Major Sangean said, anger in his voice as he sat stiffly on the edge of a folding metal chair at the far end of the CP, his eyes fixed on the Patrol After-Action Report on the field table.

"They have to care. They can't just screw around and send a pair of gunships out with no solid frequencies, no locations for the LRP team on the ground, and no air-ground coordination. That's criminal! We're just lucky we weren't splattered all over the province by them—mistaking us for the VC," Hollister said, his own level of frustration clear.

Sangean's expression turned to a scowl. "Don't lecture me, Hollister. You think you are the first one to realize how important support is?"

Hollister said nothing, knowing it would be useless to try to apologize for his feelings.

"This is a goddamn big operation—a whole Field Force that is up to its ass in units and commanders and targets, all competing for the same combat-support assets. Because of that, half the time Long Binh doesn't even know where its gunships, artillery, and air support are. Half the time they have long and elaborate excuses as to why they were late, or in the wrong place, or carrying the wrong ordnance."

"We could get our own."

"Get our own?" Sangean asked.

"Yes, sir, why don't we make a case for getting our own aircraft and our own organic support?"

Sangean laughed. "You will be a fuckin' brigade commander full colonel before that'll happen. I have been bitching for more of everything since I got here. You see what it's got me—zip!"

Hollister noticed that as quickly as Sangean's laugh overtook him it was gone and he was back to the rigid coldness he had first noticed about him.

"I want to try. I can write up the justification and try and push it through Field Force. There's no other way I can feel like I am doing my job if I don't try to beg, borrow, or steal all the support I can get for this company, sir."

"Do it. Don't talk to me about it—just do it."

"Okay, sir. I'm on it, but I have to tell you that I am also going to jump into the supply situation. We need much more equipment than we have. We need Starlights, cameras, and sniper rifles. We need to find out about silenced weapons. We need better—"

Sangean held up the palm of his hand to stop Hollister. "ACTIV. Go see them. They're in Saigon."

"ACTIV? I'm not sure I—"

"Army Concept Team in Vietnam. They're the spooks of the supply business. I heard about them when I was running an A Team up-country. Seems they've been developing some interesting stuff and have been acquiring some off-the-shelf stuff for us to use. They made us some jungle boots that left bare footprints rather than boot tracks. If it can be had—they know where and how."

"Roger that, sir," Hollister replied.

Hollister rubbed his eyes. They burned from hours under the harsh light of the cheap Vietnamese fluorescent light that splashed across the papers he had spread out on top of the wooden footlocker.

"Here, this will keep you from going blind," Major Sangean said as he pushed a mess-hall cup in front of Hollister.

"What is it?"

"George Dickel . . . sour mash whiskey. It will fix whatever ails you."

The booze filled Hollister's nostrils long before it wet his lips. The effect was immediate. He had not had a drink in a couple of days, and the back of his neck was knotted from the strain of trying to find the words to justify the additional resources he thought the company would need to operate.

Hollister turned to thank Sangean only to find that he had walked back to his end of the building and back to the map he had been studying for hours. It was obvious to Hollister that Sangean was in anything but a chatty mood. He decided not to press it.

Operations had no choppers scheduled for a routine trip from Cu Chi back to Long Binh. That meant Hollister would have to get a ride over to the division airfield to try to scrounge a ride with a chopper or fixed-wing aircraft heading to IIFFV or Bien Hoa. A makeshift orderly room had been set up in one of the broken-down barracks. Hollister entered and found Sergeant Dewey scratching a brittle rubber ink eraser against a form in his typewriter.

"Yessir? Can I do something for you?"

"You got a quarter ton around here that could run me over to the airstrip?"

Dewey brightened. "This must be your lucky day, sir. I have to leave in zero five to pick up the new first sergeant. He's s'posed to be over there—in on the mail run."

"It's about time. We sure could use one around here. How long you been without a first shirt?"

Dewey screwed up his face and looked toward the ceiling. "Been at least a month and a half since the old first sergeant—don't guess you ever met him—left. Too bad about his wife dying like that. He sure was a good man. You woulda liked him, sir."

"Well, save me a seat in the jeep when you go to pick up his turtle. I've *got* to get to Long Binh today."

"Can do, easy," Dewey replied as he turned back to his typewriter.

Outside, Hollister walked over to the mess hall to find a cup of coffee. His head hurt from the extra two doubles of George Dickel that Sangean had poured him the night before. He was sure the lightweight hangover was due to his lack of acclimatization and the lack of sleep since arriving at Cu Chi.

The coffee was hot, but it looked very strong. Hollister assumed it had been warming for a few hours and would probably taste stale and burned.

He couldn't get Dewey's words out of his mind. *Can do, easy.* It was a phrase taken from the pidgin English the Vietnamese bar girls spoke. But it reminded Hollister, painfully, of First Sergeant Horace P. Evan-Clark—known widely as "Easy." Easy had risked his life on Hollister's first tour in Vietnam to save his life. He ended up losing half a leg doing it. When Dewey talked about first sergeants, he could never have known of the dedication and loyalty of a soldier like Easy.

The coffee was as bad as Hollister had guessed. He put the cup back down and looked at the date on the paperwork in front of him on the table—January 29. A twinge of guilt and depression went through him. He knew that at the end of the month Easy was scheduled to be released from the Army Hospital in Denver to begin extended convalescence. He had told Hollister, in a letter, that after he had several months of limited duty a medical board would convene to evaluate him for disability and eventual medical discharge.

The army would do all it could to rehabilitate Easy and would let him go with twenty-eight years of service. Hollister knew that if he hadn't pulled a stupid move and ended up on the ground in a hot extraction when he shouldn't have, Easy might still have the leg. A lump came to his throat, and he found it hard to swallow. He missed Easy—he missed him a lot.

He had taken his mind off Easy by scratching out a short letter to Susan while he waited for Dewey to drive over to the airstrip.

The ride was the first time he had seen an American Infantry Division base camp since he had been at the 1st Cav's base in An Khe on his first tour. He remembered that as being big and dirty and loaded with men, machines, and endless fields and buildings filled with all kinds of support gear.

The 25th Division's base was almost as big and dirty, but it also had some other things that caught Hollister's eye. The most noticeable was the troops. They weren't the proud, cocky, competent troops he remembered from the Cav. They were sloppy. They slouched around, displaying very little military bearing or military courtesy, and they clustered by color.

Driving along the road, he would see pairs, bunches, and groups of soldiers—walking, standing around, waiting in lines, or playing ball together. But in almost every case they were segregated by color.

The equipment in the base camp needed a lot of repair and attention. Things were piled haphazardly. The grounds were littered with garbage, pieces of blowing papers, and trash piles. Latrines and mess areas looked dirty from the roadway. Weeds were everywhere, and the buildings needed lots of repairs to keep out mosquitoes and rain.

He didn't like what he saw, but sat back in the jeep and patted himself on the back for being in a unit that had more self-respect and dignity than to live in such shabby conditions. To Hollister it meant a failure in morale—a leadership problem. The symptoms were as clear to Hollister as a child with measles.

"Yessir?" the cocky, mustached Specialist 4 behind the desk asked.

"You got something going to Long Binh?"

The soldier got up from the ammo box he was sitting on and walked two steps to a clipboard that hung from a nail on the wall of the small control shack that had been built off to the side of the taxi strip. He started at the top of the page and ran his stubby finger down the list, then stopped on an entry near the bottom. As if to reward himself, he tapped the entry proudly and announced, "Yessir. We got courier flight—a chopper, headed out of here in about forty minutes. If you'll stand by here, I'll let you know if they can take you."

"How does it look?"

"They hardly ever have a full load, less'n they have some guys going home on emergency leave or something. I think we can do it. You're not goin' AWOL or nothin', are ya', Captain?" he asked, breaking into a big grin that revealed the missing bicuspid on the left side of his mouth.

"No. I just got here. Got almost a whole year left," Hollister said.

"*Choi oi!*" the soldier said in mock surprise, using the Vietnamese exclamation stolen from the bar girls. "You'll be sorry!"

Hollister laughed and filled in his name on the manifest the soldier handed him.

"I'll holler, Cap'n. You can wait here if you like."

Next to the airstrip were a few primitive roadside Vietnamese concessions. The owners of the stands were allowed to sell their services and wares on the large base camp, but had to be gone by early evening.

Hollister rubbed his hand up the back side of his neck and looked down at his boots. His hair was beginning to feel a little prickly. His boots were not much better.

Under a large oak tree two Vietnamese barbers had set up shop with nothing more than a comb, a plastic drape, a folding chair, and a pair of hand clippers.

Their misspelled sign leaned up against the tree trunk and read: HIAR CUT CHEAP 10 PIASTER. Hollister quickly glanced at his watch and figured there was not much chance the chopper would be early and it would only take a few minutes to get his hair cut and his boots shined.

"Listen, I'm going to try to squeeze in a haircut before my ride gets here."

Sergeant Dewey, lighting a cigarette, raised his hand to let him know that he heard him. His cigarette lit, Dewey yelled after Hollister, "Don't let 'em fuck with your ears or pop yer neck, sir."

Without turning back, Hollister waved. "I've been here before, remember?" He knew the Vietnamese thought everyone was fond of having his earwax cleaned out with bamboo brushes and his neck cracked. It only took a soldier one time in a barber's chair to lose any confidence in the cleanliness of the barber's tools or to question the wisdom of having someone grab his head and spin it until the vertebrae popped like large knuckles.

The outdoor setup had no electricity, no running water, and no mirrors. Still, it worked for the barbers and soldiers like Hollister. The two barbers were older Vietnamese, who must have found the sudden influx of American customers a godsend.

Hollister was the first customer of the day, so the old men leaped from their barber chairs and offered Hollister his choice of chairs.

The nearest barber flared the plastic drape for Hollister and flashed a steel-capped grin as if he were a matador luring a bull.

Hollister took off his shirt, hung it over a branch of the large shade tree, and picked a chair. The barber threw the dirty cloth over him and started sizing up his semiarmy crew cut. There was very little a barber could do with it. Either it needed to be cut shorter or left alone completely. There was no doubt what Hollister wanted. The barber reached for the hand clippers that were laid out on a small wooden table in the shade of the tree with the rest of his equipment.

Hollister leaned back and let the barber do his job. The rhythmic clipping was relaxing. Hollister closed his eye and wondered what the day would hold for him at Field Force Headquarters.

A truck stopped along the road, and two soldiers jumped out of the back and walked toward the airfield control office. Then, before the truck pulled away, a Vietnamese boy jumped out and waved thanks to the unseen driver. He straightened up and adjusted the string over his shoulder.

The string was attached to a shoeshine box dangling next to his waist. Like the boy, the box was not very big. It only carried one can of black shoe polish, a brush, and a tattered rag. He might have been all of eight years old, but it was hard to tell from his size. American kids were a lot bigger.

In spite of his size, he showed a lot of self-confidence as he walked toward the hair-cutting tree and sized up the business prospects. Since Hollister was the only one getting a haircut, he was it.

The two barbers and Hollister watched the boy as he walked up to Hollister's chair and looked down at Hollister's jungle boots. They had seen enough time in the field since they last saw shoe polish that parts of the blackened surface appeared to be almost white from the abrasive rice paddies, scuffing in and out of choppers, and general wear.

The boy took his time, studied Hollister's boots, then shook his head as if passing judgment on the size ten and a half combat veterans.

"Hey, kid," Hollister said, "you shine my boots?"

"Can do, easy, GI," he replied as he swung the shoeshine box off his shoulder and maneuvered it next to Hollister's right boot.

"How much?" Hollister opened the customary Vietnamese bargaining ritual.

"For you . . . ten P," the boy said.

Hollister was not worried about spending the ten piasters, which was the equivalent of about a dime in U.S. currency. It was the principle of the haggling that drove the conversation. "Ten P?!" he replied in mock outrage.

"Okay, what you pay, Dai Uy?" the boy responded, showing Hollister that he was fully aware of his rank of captain and his pay rate.

Hollister was impressed by the enterprise that caused the boy to check out his shirt hung over the tree limb for signs of rank. "Two piasters" was Hollister's response.

Calmly, the boy lifted his shoeshine box and started to walk away. "You a cheap Charlie," he said over his shoulder.

"Hold it," Hollister yelled. "How about three P?"

The boy stopped, turned back to Hollister, and studied him for the longest time. Slowly, he walked back, replaced the box, squatted down, and started to shine his right boot. "Okay, GI. Three P number ten. But I do 'cause I like you, GI," the boy said.

Hollister felt as if he had made some minor triumph over the inscrutable Oriental mind—even though that mind was in an eight-year-old head.

Smiling to himself, Hollister sat back smugly as the barber finished his trimming with the ancient hand clippers.

The boy worked very hard on the boot until it shined like new. Soon he had converted the ragged-looking leather to a deep ebony gloss that made the unshined boot look even worse by comparison.

Just when Hollister thought the boy was getting up to get a better angle on the other unshined boot, he shouldered his shoeshine box and started to walk away again.

"Hey," Hollister yelled. "Where are you going? You haven't finished my other boot!"

He looked down to confirm that the job was not complete only to see that the contrast between the two boots looked ridiculous. One was beautifully glossy and black, while the other was scuffed, bleached, and dirty.

Hollister looked back at the boy, who now leaned against the large tree. "You want *two* boots for three P?"

"Well, of course I do!" Hollister said. "I can't walk around with one almost white boot and one black one."

The boy took the shoeshine box sling off his shoulder again and said, "Okay, I do it—ten P."

The barbers and a few soldiers who had gathered burst out in laughter. Everyone delighted in the boy's triumph over the American officer.

Hollister knew he had been had and broke out in laughter. He, too, found it clever of the little shoeshine boy. "Sure," he said. "You make it your best shine, and I'll give you twenty P."

The boy came back, repositioned his shoe box, and started on the remaining boot—smiling smugly.

***

Hollister knew he was stuck with the hair down his back until he could grab his next shower, but he tried to brush it away with his hand by reaching down the back of his shirt.

"Here comes the first sergeant," Dewey said, gesturing toward a large, khaki-clad frame walking out the tail ramp of a C-130 that had stopped only two hundred meters from their jeep.

Hollister wanted not to believe that Dewey was right when he saw the obese first sergeant waddling toward them carrying an equally overstuffed B-4 bag in each hand. Hollister double-checked the large yellow first sergeant's chevrons on each sleeve of the wilted khaki shirt—sweat-stained at the neck, under the arms, and in horizontal bands where his body rippled. He had some kind of pomade on his hair that pasted it to his red and sweaty scalp, his piss cutter was folded up and stuffed under the epaulet of his shirt, and he had a familiar mannerism that had always looked stupid and sloppy to Hollister.

There was nothing about the man that convinced Hollister he was what Juliet Company needed.

"Mornin', Cap'n. I'm First Sergeant Morrison. I'm guessin' from your uniforms that you must be from the Lurps." He dropped his two bags and stuck his hand out.

Hollister shook his hand. "Yep. Sergeant Dewey here is your reception committee, and I'm just waiting for a ride to the rear myself. Welcome aboard, anyhow." He resisted the urge to wipe the sweat from Morrison's fat, clammy hand on his trousers for fear it would embarrass the man.

"I'm looking forward to getting on the job. I'll bet trying to keep track of this company is gonna be a first sergeant's nightmare."

"Oh, not right now, Top. We got most of the teams in for one of them damn cease-fires," Dewey said.

"So the entire company's back from the field?" Morrison asked.

"Yeah, but some of the troops are still in Nha Trang going through Recondo School. 'Cept for them, everyone we got's in Cu Chi."

"Good. I'd like to get a look at the troops as soon as possible."

Hollister knew he wasn't happy with his first impression, but that was no excuse for him to insult the man. He decided to reserve judgment until he had time to find out more about Morrison. Anyway, he thought, it was up to Major Sangean to decide if the first sergeant could cut it.

But tipping the scales at around three hundred pounds, Morrison was not likely to please Sangean. There may have been many things that Hollister didn't yet know about Sangean, but tolerance was not one of his long suits.

As Hollister got into the Huey, he was struck by the way the business of the war in Vietnam had become more and more impersonal. He remembered it as a brotherhood with a common cause, but now he was finding himself getting into a chopper flown by pilots he would probably not exchange five words with and would probably not run into again during his tour. It brought back the gnawing feeling he had about how the increase in numbers of troops, numbers of operations, and numbers of requirements on the combat resources put the life of the LRP at greater risk. He was convinced that he had to make his point at Field Force Headquarters even though he was expecting resistance.

It was his first look at the IIFFV Headquarters complex from the air. The chopper flew the length of the sprawling base, which was many times longer than its half-mile width. He noticed that the major factors influencing the complex's shape were the highway on one side and the farmland on the other. Both were immovable and needed to be avoided if the emplacement of the headquarters and support facilities were not going to cause trouble for the Vietnamese.

The pad had a gaudy-looking South Vietnamese chopper just leaving it. As it took off, Hollister could see the placard on the side near the pilot with three stars painted on it. Inside the chopper were six Vietnamese officers, all wearing clean, crisp fatigues and highly shined boots. Two were wearing lavender scarves around their necks, and sunglasses. The look bothered Hollister.

For a fleeting moment, Hollister let himself be pleased that he was with Americans, not sitting in the far side of the Vietnamese chopper where an American captain sat. Hollister assumed he was in some advisory capacity.

Hollister hopped out of his chopper and grabbed the claymore bag that held his paperwork and some overnight gear he needed to spend the night in Long Binh. He stepped up on the flat spot on the toe of the skid and mouthed the words "Thanks a lot" to the pilot, waved, and walked away.

Out from under the still turning chopper blades, Hollister looked around to try to get his bearings and decide how to find his way to the Operations Section of the Field Force Headquarters.

"Hey, Captain Hollister!"

Turning toward the roadway next to the concrete chopper pad, Hollister spotted PFC Cathcart, the driver from the Ops Section. Hollister waved and walked toward him, not speaking until he was close enough for Cathcart to hear him over the chopper noise. "How ya doin', Cathcart?"

"Pretty good, sir. You going over to Operations?"

"Not unless I can figure out how to get there from here."

They were soon traveling down one of the fairly new asphalt roadways that ran the length of the compound. "So how's life treating you, Cathcart?"

"Well, sir, I been thinking about what you said, and I'm about ready to go in and ask the headquarters company first sergeant to put in a 1049 to come to the LRPs," Cathcart said hesitantly.

Hollister didn't respond right away, and Cathcart turned around to look at him for his reaction.

Pushing his arm out, Hollister pulled back the folded collar on Cathcart's fatigue shirt. It covered a set of cloth jump wings sewn just above his US ARMY tape. "Seems to me you have the qualifications. You put the paperwork in, and I'll see what I can do on my end to get it okayed. How's that?"

Cathcart brightened and put his eyes back on the road. "That's great, sir! I'll do it today."

"Good deal. Now, I'm going to be here at least until tomorrow. How about helping me find my way around?"

"You got it, Captain. I'll switch with another guy and take the duty driver's job this afternoon and tomorrow. That way I'll be around the Ops Section if you need anything."

Hollister entered the headquarters and snaked his way through a maze of desks, chairs, file cabinets, and lockers filled with office supplies.

He was wearing the distinctive camouflage fatigues, and a great deal of attention seemed to be paid to him as he crossed the large room. Some seemed to recognize him as a LRP, and he assumed others just wanted to see what a LRP looked like. He said a little private thank-you that so far he had been able to avoid headquarters duties.

Sergeant Allen saw Hollister approaching, smiled, and stood up. "Well, Captain, how you getting along out at Cu Chi?"

"Don't really know. Been up to my ass in hand-grenade pins since I got there. But I don't guess I need to tell you what I'm back for," Hollister said, smiling.

"Sir, I knew you'd be back right ricky-tick as soon as you checked out the situation forward. My guess is that you might want to be seein' the colonel."

"You got that right. I came with a long list."

"Um-hmmm, I'll bet," Sergeant Allen said. "Lemme see if the boss is free."

***

"Colonel, I know you have lots of conflicting demands for combat and combat-support assets. But I promise you that you'll get the best out of Juliet Company if you give these kids the tools to do the job.

"They need to know that if they get compromised out there on that wet pool table that they can bring in the steel on target and not fall through the crack.

"The company is just not suited for deployment in terrain like Hau Nghia Province without having the confidence that it can have almost immediate support once it makes contact. And by rotating the support units, or waiting for what's available, we never get a chance to smooth out the wrinkles of unfamiliarity that slow down reaction time.

"And Major Sangean and I feel that the terrain isn't the best and that the company can be even more effective at developing situations and collecting intelligence if you would consider moving the patrols to more difficult terrain."

Colonel Downing listened and drew his leathered index finger down the letter of justification that Hollister had drafted. He looked up and raised an eyebrow.

"Son, you know that I am sympathetic to your request. But that doesn't mean I can pull it off. Everyone—four full divisions and five separate brigades—wants his own support package."

Downing waved his arm toward the small window in his office and continued., "There ain't a combat commander worth shit out there who doesn't push higher for more of everything."

The words disappointed Hollister. He was sure Downing was setting him up for a letdown.

"But you are one of the few who really needs it," the colonel said, picking up the papers and tapping their bottoms on his desktop to straighten them. "So here's what we are going to do—you gonna be around?"

"Yes, sir. Don't think there's much chance of getting a ride back tonight. Cathcart's got me set up in the transit BOQ."

"Good, good. I want you to talk to Major Fowler, my Assistant G-3, when he gets back from USARV Headquarters. I'll put him on trying to tag some units to tie up with your people."

A smile crossed Hollister's face. But the colonel raised his hand to stop him. "I can't promise you'll get everything on your wish list there. But we'll give it a shot. That good enough for you?"

"And about the AO, sir?"

The colonel got up and walked to the map on the wall. He waved his spread fingers over the western III Corps area. "We have only put you guys there for the time being to create a little economy-of-force situation. We could use another infantry division, but we don't have one. So while the four we have are tied up other places, we're using Juliet Company to keep from completely abandoning the area we've dropped you in. I know it's not the best. The good thing about it is that it gives you and Sangean time to shake down the teams and get some problems behind you."

He took a step to his left and tapped the map in the vicinity of the Cambodian border. "We're soon going to move you guys into where Charlie lives. The Cambodian border between the Angel's Wing and the Parrot's Beak is the launching area for combat troops and logistical support. Up till now we've been having trouble getting clearance to work that area. I think we're there. Soon as we move you into the area, you can make life miserable for Charlie this side of the Ba Thu Corridor—the end of the Ho Chi Minh Trail. What do you think of that?"

"Sir, that's all I can ask for . . ."

The colonel smiled back at him until Hollister finished his thought.

"For now," Hollister added.

CHAPTER 10

At the end of one row of desks was Major Fowler's. He was on the phone, facing the wall. From the sounds of it, he was trying to communicate over a bad switchboard connection.

"I don't give a shit! You tell those people that if they can't seem to find a fucking way to get . . . Hello? Are you still there? Hello? Operator! Goddamnit, Operator!"

He paused long enough to listen to the explanation the switchboard operator gave for the interruption, then exploded again. "Well, get them back on the goddamn line, and call me back ASAP!

"Goddamnit!" Fowler mumbled to himself. He spun around, slammed the phone down, and tried to reorient himself to the work spread out on his desktop. He had very little working space sandwiched between an in and an out-box. Frustrated, he shoved aside a pile of reports that sat directly in front of him and extracted something from the bottom of the pile. Realizing it was not what he wanted, he dropped it onto the other pile and looked to his in-box, which was starting to hang over the edge of the desktop.

He flipped the classified-document cover back on a file in his in-box and lifted it out. The first page had instructions for him to initial after he had read the attached document. He reached into the breast pocket of his starched fatigue shirt and came out with a GI pen. He pushed the plunger to extend the point only to realize that it didn't catch. He tried it a second time. Still no results. Finally, he slowly pressed the plunger until it locked into place, exposing the point.

Fowler placed the pen on the line next to the abbreviation for his job title listed on the buck slip and began to write his initials. He got as far as his first initial before the pen gave up the stream of ink and left a greasy blob on the paper. He reached over and scribbled on a piece of scrap paper. The pen made a circle, then a second loop, then left only an impression in the paper—no ink.

Angrier, Fowler raised his arm and hurled the pen completely across the room. "Motherfucker! Doesn't any goddamn thing work in this fucking country?"

"I was told you'd be the man to see about some Ops and organization changes, sir," Hollister said, trying not to find Fowler's foul mood funny.

Fowler was startled by Hollister's arrival and question. "Where the hell did you come from, Captain?"

"My CP, sir."

The answer hit him wrong. Fowler bolted to his feet and rested his knuckles on his desk as he leaned forward toward Hollister. "You get smart with me, young captain, and I'll have your ass. You got that?

"You goddamn Lurps come in here acting like you are God's fucking solution to the war and expect everyone else around here to drop what they are doing and jump through hoops for you!"

"Was that a question, sir?" Hollister said with a hint of sarcasm. He wasn't about to take Fowler's unjustified shots at him. Fowler responded with a cold expression that left little doubt about his immediate dislike for Hollister.

Hollister made a snap judgment about Fowler. He was sure that there would be more run-ins with him and that he had better watch his back. He had met officers like Fowler before—ambitious, angry, and worried that the war was passing them by. They were always hard to deal with and often unreliable. They seemed to operate as if the unfortunate turns of events in the war were personal.

He remembered a pair of terms that he had not paid much attention to when he was an officer candidate back at Fort Benning, four years before. The terms were "careerists" and "professionals." It was his Tactical officer who chastised his platoon of officer candidates to avoid the path of the careerist, who makes every decision based upon its impact on his career. He had said that the mark of a professional was one who made the right decision for the men and the mission, not the right decision for himself.

The only other thing Hollister knew about officers like Fowler was that if you butted heads with them, you ended up wasting a lot of time and rarely ended up with your original goal accomplished. He decided to try to sidestep Fowler's behavior and get on with what he was there for.

"Sir, I'm sure you have plenty of very important things that are pressing. But I'm in some trouble and need your help."

Fowler's mood changed immediately. He leaned back in his chair, as if preparing to pass judgment on Hollister's words. "Go on."

"Sir, we need organic support. We're fairly ineffective as combat patrols if support is delayed by tasking units to support us on a rotating basis.

"I brought in some justification. I think that's a copy of it in your in-box," Hollister said.

Fowler plucked it from his in-box and read the routing slip the colonel had attached to it. It simply read: "For your action—Downing."

"And just where do you suppose I get these units?"

"The way I look at it, if you're going to give us support from different gunship platoons on a regular basis you've got one gun platoon gone all the time. Why not just attach one platoon to us permanently and let us take advantage of working as a team?"

Fowler didn't argue with Hollister. Instead he waited for him to continue.

Hollister leaned forward and flipped over several pages of requests and justifications. Fowler took them and spread them out on top of his other work.

As Fowler read them, Hollister took a second look at him. You could tell a lot about an officer by the little things. Fowler had a West Point ring on his hand and no wedding ring. He wore a watch with a leather watchband. That told Hollister he had no orientation toward field operations. A leather band wouldn't last a day in the field. He wondered if Fowler had ever spent much time in the field besides that necessary to earn the Ranger tab on his left shoulder.

The telltale sign of a rear-echelon officer was an infantryman without a CIB. The space over Fowler's shirt pocket was only partially filled, with a small set of novice parachutist's wings. Making it to major without earning a CIB or a higher parachute rating made Hollister suspect that

Fowler might have spent much of his time in headquarters jobs, maybe even graduate school.

Hollister envied him the schooling, but guessed that it probably irritated Fowler to be talking with a junior officer with more combat experience and a Senior Parachutist rating—indicated by the star on top of his own jump wings.

"Quite a shopping list, Captain," Fowler said, dropping the last page back on his desk. "Just how soon would you like all this delivered to your CP?" he added with a trace of sarcasm.

Hollister was determined not to lose sight of his objective and get mired in an argument with Fowler.

"Sir, at this point, I'll take what I can get and come back for more. I really believe that we can do some good work and earn our pay if the troops feel like they can be backed up quickly."

"Oh, so the *troops* are complaining?" Fowler said with more sarcasm.

"No, sir. That's not what I said. I can tell you that just the other night I was out on a patrol and tried to get chopper support to fire up some VC using a canal. By the time the mission was passed to the gunships, the VC had long left the area. It's all a matter of response time, sir. That's all."

"I read the report on that and thought the team leader might have called in the request a bit earlier."

"Sir, our team leaders can do a lot of things, but predicting the future isn't one of them," Hollister said, irritated by the suggestion.

Fowler's tone turned harsh. "Don't get smart with me, Captain. 'Cause I'm the only hope you have of getting a fucking poncho liner!"

Hollister was upset that he had let Fowler get to him. He wondered for a split second how a guy like Fowler could get into a job of so much importance and as quickly remembered others like Fowler, who look great from above, but the folks counting on them know what horses' asses they are.

Fowler waved Hollister's typed request in front of him. "Don't press me," he said. "How the hell can I answer any of your petty requests until I read this? Now, quit wasting my time, and let me get back to work."

Hollister tried to calm his anger on the way out of the complex. He couldn't remember the last time he wanted so badly to drop someone in his tracks. But he knew that popping Fowler would do no good for anyone and would get nothing done for Juliet Company.

Outside the Operations Section, Cathcart, toying with a rolled-up piece of paper, waited for Hollister. "So, how'd it go, sir?"

"Don't know. I'm still empty-handed," Hollister replied.

"Major Fowler, huh?"

"How'd you know?"

"Well, sir, I don't want to say nothing against no officer, but . . ." Cathcart didn't finish the sentence, but Hollister got the message.

"I'm waiting for him now. I have to take him to a meeting at USARV, so I can't be much help to you until later," Cathcart said.

"Don't worry about it. I've got to see him later, then try to wrangle a ride back to Cu Chi. I'll be able to find my way around. You've been lots of help."

Cathcart nervously offered the rolled-up paperwork to Hollister.

"Sir, this is that copy of the 1049 you asked for. I've filled it out and dropped it off at the Orderly Room."

Hollister took the form, opened it, and looked it over quickly. "Okay, I'll take it with me and start pulling from my end."

As Hollister folded the form up and stuck it in his shirt pocket, Cathcart smiled, then frowned. "You think I can really be a LRP, sir?"

"I think so. You'll think so, too, after a little bit of training."

"What I need is your help setting up a recruiting process within the Field Force," Hollister said to Sergeant Major Carey in the G-1 Section.

"I s'pose we can put an ad in the Field Force magazine, and I can put the word out at the next sergeant major's meeting," Carey said, looking over his glasses at Hollister.

"My guess is that'll generate an opportunity for some folks to get rid of deadwood that way."

"Sir, you don't have to take 'em. If they don't look right, just throw 'em back—like fish. I can always find places to put warm bodies, even lukewarm ones."

The remark brought a smile to Hollister's face. "Somehow fish seems like an appropriate term. But is there any way you can prescreen them before they get orders to Juliet Company?"

"Captain, I think your boys got balls bigger'n helmet liners, and I'd be the last guy to send you some lightweight. I can't promise you more than I can do. But count on me to help. I can usually get the G-1's attention on an assignment policy here and there, and right now selling LRPs to him ain't a big problem. So count me in."

"Well, I'm really happy you feel that way. Can you start by keeping an eye on this," Hollister said, handing Carey the copy of Carthcart's 1049.

The sergeant major grinned as if he'd been had and took a quick look at the paperwork. "Shit, sir! Ten seconds, and you're already raiding my headquarters!"

"I think he'll be a better LRP than a gofer. He's a good kid that needs to do something right for a change. I've got plenty of jobs for him."

"Well, I'm going to catch hell from the headquarters company first sergeant, but he owes me one—or two."

The firecrackers started early in the afternoon. Hollister had forgotten the reciprocal agreement the allies had with the North Vietnamese. For American Christmas and the Vietnamese Lunar New Year they would each promise to cease fire and conduct no offensive operations. That was why almost all of the LRP teams were in, back at Cu Chi, and why the mood around the headquarters was a little more casual than he would have expected. He tried to get used to the noise from the little staccato explosions, but found that he couldn't completely block them out.

It was only a little after six o'clock when Hollister walked into the IIFFV Officers Club, his stomach full from a greasy mess-hall meal. He ordered a Scotch as he settled into the barstool's swivel seat.

The false eyelashes and the bouffant hairdo on the tiny Vietnamese barmaid looked out of proportion to her small face and well under five feet of height.

All of it was an amazement to Hollister. When he last left Vietnam, the closest thing he had seen to a club was some building or tent that had an icebox in it and a flat surface to use as a bar. But there he was, on a leatherette barstool, drinking from a real glass, with clear ice-machine-made ice cubes, that was resting on a coaster with the IIFFV insignia printed on it. To top it all off, the drink had a swizzle stick with the letters IIFFV on the round, lollipop-type top.

There were about twenty-five headquarters types in the bar. No one appeared to have dropped into the bar from a field unit except two warrant officer pilots who sat at a table near the jukebox nursing two soft drinks.

The phone behind the bar rang and the Vietnamese barmaid answered it. Her voice became agitated, and she started talking rapidly—in Vietnamese. She finished the call and started talking to someone on the other side of an open door.

Soon the club NCO, an American sergeant wearing a tailor-made walking suit from Bangkok, came out from the office behind the bar. Listening to the conversation between the barmaid and the manager, Hollister was able to gather that the problem was with the band. Somehow they were AWOL. They had been expected earlier in the day to set up and to rehearse.

She and the sergeant exchanged a few more words in a mixture of English and Vietnamese. Finally, the sergeant turned to Hollister and threw up his hands. "I hope that you weren't waiting for the band, 'cause they ain't comin' tonight, Captain."

"I'm just happy to be able to belly up to a bar and knock back a Scotch or two."

The sergeant reached back behind the bar. He pulled down a bottle of Johnnie Walker Black and poured Hollister another drink. "This one's on me, sir."

Hollister raised the glass to the sergeant before taking a sip. "Thanks. I'll have to see what I can do about having the band ambushed more often," Hollister said.

They both laughed.

"Well, sir, I'll see what I can do about getting someone to replace them worthless zip rock and rollers. Shit!" He wandered back into his office, closing the door behind him.

The jukebox kept playing, even though no one in the room was putting any club tokens into it. Hollister had yet another drink and listened to the music, his mind wandering back to Susan. He missed her, but the fact that he had almost a full tour ahead of him made the feeling more depressing. He wondered if he would even make it through the tour without becoming a casualty. Sure, he'd been banged around before and picked up a little shrapnel, but he was sure that every day he survived made the next that much more difficult.

He caught himself getting down about his prospects and immediately told himself to do something about it. He knew if he worked at increasing the survivability of the members of Juliet Company, he would also enjoy some of the benefits. With that he pulled his pen out of his pocket and grabbed a napkin off the stack on the bar rail.

He began to make notes about techniques and procedures that he wanted to effect as soon as he could get back to Cu Chi. He knew he had to make the LRPs more invisible to give them staying power if and when they made contact. That would be his job. If he just got that much done, he'd feel as if he had earned his pay.

After several napkins, two more Scotches, and lots more fireworks outside, Hollister laid out the napkins to look at his random notes. They all had three things in common—equipment, technique, and training. Those were the keys, as far as Hollister was concerned. If he could get the right equipment and support and train the troops in the techniques that would give them an edge in the flat margins of the Mekong Delta, he'd feel much better.

"You making up another list, Hollister?" Colonel Downing's voice boomed behind him.

Spinning reflexively at the colonel's voice, Hollister began to stand.

"No, sit," the colonel said as he waved at the barmaid for a refill for Hollister and added, "How about a beer for me?"

"Well, sir, I'm just trying to get a handle on what we need to do out there."

The colonel leaned against the corner of the bar, standing between two barstools. "You getting what you want from Major Fowler?"

"Well, I have to see him again in the morning. He needed a little time to look over my list, sir," Hollister said.

Colonel Downing took a long sip from the glass of beer the barmaid had poured. "The general would sure like to see you guys do some good work out there on the border. We just can't get close enough to them with conventional units to do any good and not take heat for being inside Cambodia." He took another drink and screwed up his face. "When I was a brigade commander in the Big Red One, I got damn tired of watching Charlie tag us and then run back across the fence to laugh in our faces."

Before Hollister could respond, Major Fowler entered the bar, looking around as if he were trying to find someone.

"Fowler, what's the story? Hollister here tells me you haven't filled his requisition yet," the colonel half kidded.

The remark cut into Fowler. "That's not entirely true, sir. But I need to talk to you about something else right now. Could I see you outside?"

The two left, but not before Fowler shot Hollister an expression of displeasure for complaining to Colonel Downing.

Oh shit! Hollister thought. All he needed was Fowler dragging his feet to punish him for his unintentional gaffe.

The shower in the small transit BOQ was much better than the fifty-five-gallon drum on the roof in Cu Chi. At least the one at Long Binh had a shower head—much like a gardener's watering can. The shower in Cu Chi had only an open pipe, with a knob to turn the flow on and off. And "on" meant a single stream of cold water, about the size of a finger. The Long Binh shower had been heated and appeared to have cleaner water.

The fog from the Scotches dulled Hollister's brain and made him consider just dropping off early and getting a head start on the following day. He lit a cigarette and sat on the edge of the army cot that was snugged up against the wall in the very tiny semiprivate BOQ room he had all to himself.

He stood and crossed the room in one stride and pulled his notes out of the pocket of his wilted shirt. He flipped through his notebook and checked off things he had wanted to accomplish while at IIFFV. The scraps of napkins fell out. He carefully folded them back up and made a promise to himself to consolidate the notes on something sturdier than the cocktail napkins.

He then came across the note to himself about recruiting and remembered Sergeant Major Carey's words. He wondered if he should speak to Carey about the new first sergeant—Morrison. Hollister was sure the guy had almost no chance of working out.

He reminded himself that it wasn't his call and resisted the urge to get involved, knowing it would probably be a problem for him sometime soon.

Hollister lay in the dark with his arm up under his head, smoking his last cigarette. He was not surprised by all the continued fireworks outside the Long Binh compound, but he was bothered by the noise. He took a drag off the cigarette and remembered the first such celebration he had been through. He was on the beach at Tuy Hoa. At the stroke of midnight of the Lunar New Year, the city of Tuy Hoa, just north of his company's position by about six miles, opened up as if under attack. The South Vietnamese outpost there decided to celebrate by firing all of their weapons and many of their flares up into the air.

It was a matter of great concern to many of the Americans, who realized how dangerous it was. The ordnance fired up had to come down somewhere. That year several buildings caught fire in Tuy Hoa.

The soundness of his sleep was shattered by the double rattle of a burst of incoming and one of outgoing small-arms fire on full automatic.

Instinctively, Hollister rolled out of his bunk and flattened himself on the floor. He tried to clear his head of the alcohol and get his bearings. His first discovery was that he was naked save his GI boxer shorts.

He had a fairly good idea of the orientation of the BOQ in respect to the perimeter and concluded that the shooting was coming from the guard posts. But he also became aware of shooting at a distance from the compound. He assumed it was in the direction of Bien Hoa Army Base, just seven thousand meters away.

Rolling across the floor to the chair, where he'd hung his uniform and the pistol belt that held his holstered .45, he cursed himself for being a little drunk and a little rattled. He knew he should have taken the time to find out where the bunkers were and what the emergency plan was within the compound in the event of attack.

"Shit!" Hollister said, pulling the pistol from the holster and jacking a round into the chamber. He was angry with himself for only bringing one magazine. He had only loaded eight rounds and wasn't real proud of his accuracy with a .45 automatic. He laid the pistol on the floor and grabbed his trousers. He rolled over on his back and tried to put them on. He finally gave up, stood at a crouch, and quickly slipped into the camouflage fatigue bottoms. All the while the firing outside continued and the activities escalated to the firing of flares and launching of choppers.

Dressed, Hollister moved to the doorway of the BOQ. The slanted louvers only allowed vision out and down, not straight out or up. His first view was that of fire. The wooden building directly across a small roadway was on fire and would quickly burn to the ground.

Soldiers were running everywhere, and a siren kept wailing. The small-arms fire that had started out as sporadic exchanges was now picking up, and the number of flares floating over Long Binh were soon matched by flares over Bien Hoa.

What to do next was Hollister's immediate problem. He wasn't part of any organization and didn't fit into any kind of reaction force plan. He was sure that much of the firing was just spookiness prompted by hearing firing on one part of the perimeter. He was also sure that some of the firing he had heard was in fact VC fire. After a while even a tin ear could tell an AK47 from an American M16.

Hollister decided to head for the Operations Section to see if he could be any help in resolving the enemy contact or in helping control some of the frightened rear-echelon troops—many of whom were, no doubt, hearing their first incoming fire.

As he crossed the compound, he was careful to move in the few pools of light he could find in order not to be mistaken for a VC and shot by a trigger-spooky REMF. He realized that doing so would expose him to enemy fire, but guessed that the threat to him was greater from his own than from the VC.

The doorway leading into the TOC of the Operations Section was crowded with officers and NCOs, some trying to get in on official business and some who just wanted to find out if they were really under attack.

It was obvious to Hollister that he couldn't be of much use. He considered trying to get a message into the TOC that he was there and available, when Cathcart came hustling by. The boy was a different personality. He forcefully cleared people out of his way, a handful of classified documents in his hand. The chaos outside didn't seem to rattle him. Instead, he took on an official and important manner that convinced senior NCOs and officers that he should be let through the doorway because he had something important that needed to get inside. Hollister smiled at his perceptiveness. He'd known that Cathcart had it in him the first day he met him.

A chair was at the far end of the hallway leading into the TOC. Hollister grabbed it, spun it around, and squatted astride it. He watched the flow of bodies running in and out of the doorway and started to piece together the situation. The scuttlebutt had it that there were several simultaneous ground probes being reported in from all parts of III Corps. Most were attacks on fixed installations. He figured that much of that was due to the standdown in effect throughout the country. Most combat units were in their base camps and enjoying the relief from commitment to combat operations. That meant they were more than likely asleep or up drinking and having parties. In either case that gave the enemy the advantage of surprise.

After several trips in and out of the TOC with messages and documents, Cathcart stepped out into the hallway to get out of the crowded room.

"You earnin' your money?"

Cathcart turned to respond to the question, a freshly lit cigarette hanging from his mouth. "Oh, sir?" He pulled the cigarette from his lips. "You hear the shit's hit the fan?"

"I figured something was up when they started using the second floor of the BOQ for target practice. Some units getting hit, huh?"

"Everywhere! Hell, there have already been thirty-six attacks reported and all kinds of reports of VC units moving from G-2. They been runnin' me crazy getting stuff to the three shop."

"Any word on Juliet Company?"

"I ain't sure I got all of it, but I heard that there is a team in contact and the base at Cu Chi is taking incoming mortar." He snatched a quick look at his wristwatch. "That was about an hour ago. You want me to go in and snoop around?"

"No. I don't think so. I can find out what I need. Little good that it'll do. I'm stuck here. By the time I could get out to Cu Chi, it'd be all over. Wouldn't hurt you to keep an ear out so you can find out what you're getting yourself into," Hollister said with a grin.

"I'm going to slip in and get some coffee. You want some, sir?"

"Yeah, I could use some. Seems they had a bad batch of Scotch at the Officers Club tonight."

While Cathcart went for the coffee, Hollister thought about lying to him. He wanted very much to know everything about what was going on with Juliet Company, but knew he would be in the way in a TOC that was trying to coordinate the support and combat operations of four infantry divisions, five combat brigades, and dozens of outposts, bases, and stations that were under their control. The events of Juliet Company would no doubt be a minor concern. He was as afraid to find that out as he was to hear any bad news about Juliet Company.

Looking around the hallway, Hollister discovered a closed doorway. He peeked in and found that no one was using the office or the desk. He looked around the room. It appeared to be in some sort of transition. Boxes of files were stacked in the corner and marked with some crude code, and half of the office furniture was missing—all except the stuff that was broken or not worth stealing. Then Hollister spotted what he was looking for—a field phone. It was on the floor behind the desk, but seemed to be connected to WD-1 wire that snaked out through a hole in the plywood-paneled wall.

"Here's your coffee, sir. Hope you like it black," Cathcart said, putting the mess-hall cup on the dirty desktop. "Thought you'd left."

"Thanks. No, I figure I can find out what I want without being in the way in the TOC," Hollister said, lifting the phone and base to the desk.

He pulled open a drawer and started rummaging through the papers abandoned by the office's former owner. "Look over in those other drawers, Cathcart," he said.

The PFC walked around to the other end of the desk, put his coffee down, and started with the top drawer. "What am I looking for?"

"Phone book. I want the Admin and Log phone numbers."

"What good will that do, sir?"

"If I want to talk to anyone in Three Corps tonight, I'd better not try to get through on the Operations lines."

Cathcart smiled. "Nifty idea." He slammed the top drawer shut and reached up under the secretary slide that was tucked into the pocket, just under the top lip of the desk. Pulling it open, he found a telephone wiring diagram taped to the surface with yellowed, cracking transparent tape. "Bingo!"

Hollister moved over to the other side of the desk and screwed his neck around in order to read the phone numbers that were taped down so they could be read by someone in the missing chair.

"It isn't the phone book, but it lets me get a handle on the switchboard system here," he explained. Hollister ran his finger down the list and found the Admin switchboard operator's number, picked up the field phone, and cranked the ringer.

Cathcart stuck his head out the door of the abandoned office to see if anyone was looking for him and then turned back in and watched Hollister weave his way through the unpredictable phone system.

He went through a series of switchboard operators and good and bad connections before he got to his destination. Finally reaching the Juliet Company Orderly Room, he had to yell to speak to Dewey.

Meanwhile, the shooting in and around the IIFFV compound heated up again. Small arms were popping sporadically on the back side of the base—near the large ordnance depot

After some frustration and often repeated questions, Hollister finally hung up the phone and let the conversation sink in for a moment.

"Bad news, sir?" Cathcart asked.

"Yeah, Cu Chi has been taking a real beating at the airfield. And some of the mortars that were targeted for the Chinooks on the ground went long and landed in Juliet Company. Sergeant Dewey thinks they have six KIAs and about ten WIAs so far. On top of that, there are two teams in contact out west of Cu Chi, and they're playing hell getting any kind of priorities for Artillery. A third team made contact and is trying to E and E to a PZ."

Cathcart remained silent for a moment. "But I thought everyone was in for the holiday stand-down."

"Juliet Company was tasked to leave a few teams out in *recon only* mission to keep an eye on some sensitive areas. Now they're out there holding on for all they are worth."

Cathcart was silent again.

Hollister looked up at him. "You sure you want to be a LRP?"

Cathcart nodded yes, but said nothing.

"So what other tricks you got up your sleeve? Any chance you have a chopper in your pocket? I've got to get forward."

The question stirred Cathcart out of his deep thought and propelled him to the phone. "If there's one to be had, I'll find it, sir."

"Good. You do what you can. I'm going back to my room and pick up my gear. I'll be back here in zero five."

Outside the air hung heavy with the smell of burning flares and cordite from the small-arms firing that had taken place. In the distance, Hollister could hear the nonstop firing of dozens of artillery pieces. He knew each round was on its way out to help someone who was in the grip of fear and uncertainty. He got a sinking feeling in the pit of his stomach about the months that stood before him, and he wondered again if he would live to make it to his DEROS. He could only guess that he was using up his ration of luck.

Hollister was snapped out of his thoughts by the ripping sounds of a C-130 gunship loaded down with high-speed Gatling guns, spewing out thousands of rounds of tracer ammo. He stopped long enough to look off in the sky at the blacked-out gunship. The mission was being fired south of Long Binh, and the tracer rounds snaked out of the rotating barrels of the machine guns like long red whips. The sounds of the firing were not unlike a heavy version of a deck of cards being shuffled.

He shook his head at the technology that had been brought to the business of war. A twenty-year-old airplane was flying at thirty-five hundred feet and raining accurate death and destruction on a darkened enemy below.

More small-arms fire on the perimeter snapped Hollister out of it He entered the BOQ and ran to his room. On the way he found two other officer residents standing in the hall talking. They were inspecting the row of bullet holes that dotted the wall just above arm's reach.

"Medevac," Cathcart said, beaming with pride.

"Medevac? Good idea. Where?"

"The pad on the south end of the compound is for the medevac chopper that supports the medical detachment there. They are going over to Bien Hoa Army with some medical supplies they needed and say you can hook a ride that far."

Hollister patted Cathcart on the shoulder. "That's good enough. I'll see what I can do from there. There sure are lots more planes and choppers leaving there than here."

Hollister pulled out his notepad and jotted down a message, then handed it to Cathcart. "Will you see that Major Fowler gets this? I want him to know I went forward. And tell Sergeant Allen."

"Yesssir. Can do, easy."

The ride took only a few minutes since the two compounds were so close. Still, flying supplies to Bien Hoa was more reliable than trying to drive them over. As they flew over the road leading directly into Bien Hoa Army, Hollister and the chopper crew could see the firefights going on near the main gate. From the limited amount of flare lights and the exchanges of tracer fire, it seemed as if the ditches on either side of the roadway were littered with dead VC, with an equal number still alive and still attacking.

Bien Hoa proved to be a good start. Hollister found a driver from the Evacuation Hospital who gave him a ride to an aviation company that was shuttling an L-19 Bird Dog to Cu Chi to replace one of the radio-relay aircraft that had just been pulled out of service because of an aging airframe. While he waited at the hangar for the dawn departure, Hollister watched what would come to be known as the Tet Offensive unfold around him. On the far side of the sprawling Bien Hoa Air Force and Army complex, American and South Vietnamese exchanged sporadic fire with real and imagined VC outside the wire.

The operations shack for the aviation company had only air-to-ground radio capability and could only monitor a slice of the war. Nonetheless, it was becoming clear that the North Vietnamese had entered the war in larger numbers and more locations than ever before. From listening to the cross talk, it was hard for Hollister to tell how the Americans were doing, but he couldn't imagine their losses could ever be greater than the North Vietnamese casualties.

After several more cups of coffee cooked in an open coffee can over a squad stove, Hollister started to feel the fog clearing in his brain and the sourness rising in his stomach. He made a little promise to himself to forgo any future opportunities to drink that much Scotch again.

The backseat of the Bird Dog reminded Hollister of a terrible crash site he had once been tagged to evacuate. He strapped himself into the theadbare body harness. That done, he tried to check out the distances he would need to reach if he had to use the emergency tool and the first aid packet attached to the bulkhead above his head. He wanted to make sure that if he needed either item he could reach them. He had seen what it meant to have them out of reach.

The L-19 bumped along the runway, gathering speed as if the fuselage itself was flexing with every deviation in the concrete strip. The engine was the only thing that gave Hollister any confidence. It sounded healthy and well broken in—like a '49 Ford flathead V-8. The plane's cosmetic appeal left a lot to be desired. It had so many air miles on it that there was hardly any paint on the metal surfaces inside. The seats were broken-down, and the Plexiglas in all the windows and in the windscreen was pitted and scratched to the point where every spot of light that tried to pass through them was distorted.

The pilot was a warrant officer who had been in Vietnam for almost three years. He had come over just before the troop buildup began and decided to stay.

As they flew west toward Cu Chi, the sun was just breaking the horizon behind them. The view out the open window was very revealing. From two thousand feet, at ninety knots, they could see the early activities of the farmers and merchants who were not in the path of the offensive. Cook fires dotted the villages and hamlets. Hondas turned onto two-lane blacktops from dirt side roads. Children fed livestock before eating their own breakfasts, and everywhere—even though they couldn't be heard— cocks crowed.

Off their flight path, Hollister could see ARVN, RF/PF, and government outposts under attack by small forces. Where they could, Hollister and the pilot directed artillery and gunships to their targets as an extra set of eyes. Over the headsets, they were listening to the war most important to the pilot—the air war. He had turned the radio to *guard*—a frequency used only by aviators for emergencies. Radio cross talk filled their ears with calls for help, choppers shot up, air force fast movers reporting damage to their aircraft and one pilot reporting his position *on the ground.*

Hollister tried to put it all in perspective and extrapolate the good news he might be able to hear if he were able to listen to the tactical frequencies of the maneuver units and combat-support units. They were surely making progress. Even so, he was feeling the return of that knot that always gripped his lower gut when things got dicey. He thought about Juliet Company. He hoped they had been spared.

Things seemed to be well under control at Cu Chi when they landed. The 25th Division's Chinooks had taken some real hits, and one was still smoldering, although there was little left of the airframe to recognize. Scattered buildings showed evidence of small-arms fire, and there was something beyond Hollister's view that was still burning, sending up plumes of white smoke on the other side of the base camp.

A pleasant boy from Tennessee driving a five-ton diesel truck gave Hollister a lift to the Old Warrior Pad. He thanked the driver and took one last shot at recruiting him to the LRP company, but was pleased to find out that the LRPs' reputation was exaggerated enough to scare him off.

The reputation of a LRP company made lots of difference in whom it could recruit. Hollister had discovered that the more the reputation grew, the larger the number of volunteers. That gave the officers and NCOs a wider choice of new LRPs.

No one said anything when Hollister entered Operations. They were in the middle of handling a medevac of a team member who had suffered a concussion and broken eardrum from a booby trap that had detonated near him.

Sergeant Kurzikowski must have assumed that Hollister was looking for Major Sangean and poked his thumb toward the Orderly Room.

Major Sangean sat in the corner of the room signing forms. Dewey and the new first sergeant were both pounding away on typewriters.

"Sir? I got back quick as I could."

Sangean looked up and nodded coolly. "Glad to have you back. Make any money at Two Field?"

"I'm pretty sure Colonel Downing is behind us, but my bet is that Major Fowler doesn't share his attitude," Hollister said.

Sangean put his pen down and looked out the window at a 25th Division chopper passing nearby.

"What you mean is that Fowler's a shit-eating frog and is angry that you even attempted to divert his attention from his personal priorities."

Hollister decided not to bad-mouth a superior in front of Morrison and Dewey. He had always thought it bad form.

"I've known Fowler since he was a plebe at West Point," said Sangean. "He was a prick then, and he has perfected the affectation."

"Ah, is there some time you can get me up to speed on what happened last night?"

Sangean signed one more document and passed the pile to the first sergeant. He stuffed the pen into his top shirt pocket and automatically checked to see that the pocket flap covered the pen top. He stood, looked at Morrison as if to ask if there was anything else, and then started for the door, catching Hollister's eye. "Let's go talk."

Sangean led Hollister across the company street to an abandoned building that had been used by the supply sergeant for storage. The end of the building that had been empty had now been pressed into service as a temporary morgue.

"Mortars got three of them, and being on their own out there in the reeds got three more," Sangean said, surveying the bodies of the eight dead LRPs.

"And the other two?"

"One took a stray round from somewhere, and the other broke his neck trying to get away from the incoming."

The sight was nothing new for Hollister, but neither was it something he was ever going to get used to. He felt a twinge of guilt because he had never even gotten to know them. It would not happen again. He would brief every patrol and debrief them on return. He would meet some of the new ones when they were being recruited and all of them in training. Of all the things he had learned in the army, training was the thing that kept soldiers alive. He planned on laying it on heavy and making sure no one died from a lack of training.

Timely support was Hollister's job, and he promised himself that he would not see any more body bags filled for lack of support.

"I've been doing this a bit longer than you have, Hollister," said Sangean, "but I don't need to tell you that we are traveling light around here, and if we can't get this operation working right we might as well shut it down. You are the only officer I have that has enough experience to back me up. I don't have time to waste. I don't have time to double back. I have to guess that you know what needs to be done as well as I do.

"Your 201 file reads the way I wanted it to when I went looking for an operations officer. I've got a crack Admin guy coming in to be XO, and I want you guys to work like a Swiss watch. But his business is Admin and Logistics, and yours"—he raised his hand and pointed toward Cambodia—"is out there."

Hollister kept looking at the bodies. "Count on me, sir. You just give me my marching orders, and that'll be all I need."

"I want you to act right and do good stuff . . . That's all I expect."

He finally turned to Sangean and saw the pain in his eyes. He had thought that Sangean was just cold and aloof. That wasn't it at all. It was pain. Hollister knew then that Sangean had seen his share of filled body bags. "Yes, sir" was all Hollister could get out without choking up himself.

CHAPTER 11

Hollister spent the rest of the day trying to get up to date on the tactical situation and the developments of the Tet invasion. His best guess was that the stand-down cease-fire was called off, even though there had been no official statement. And he knew that it could be a matter of hours before the company could receive orders from IIFFV to resume full combat patrols in the AO. He didn't want to avoid being committed if they were needed. But training was what they needed. And he was worried that the company was very short of manpower from the combat losses and that the company hadn't completely filled out its MTO&E.

The combat readiness of the teams was of major concern to Hollister. The field and base camp casualties had cut across four of the teams, reducing each of them by one man. Another entire team had been zeroed out by wounds and KIAs. That left him with only five of the ten teams they had filled out before the casualties. Even the ten teams were far short of the twenty they were authorized. He had to recommend to Major Sangean that they either consolidate to make full-strength teams or stand down the short teams until they could be filled and get some training in. His experience told him to avoid mixing up team members and moving them to fill out short teams.

The decisions and the planning were going to take all Hollister's concentration and energy to make the right moves for the company. He decided to pick up all his notes and the manning roster Dewey had provided him and head to the mess hall, where he could get a cup of coffee and spread out his work.

Crossing the company street again, Hollister passed Major Sangean. They exchanged salutes, and Sangean said, "I'm on my way over to the Division TOC to piss on the assistant G-3's desk."

Hollister made a face, not bothering to ask.

"They just called down and issued orders for us to provide forty-five warm bodies to serve as perimeter security tonight. They're expecting more ground probes, and it seems that having an entire fucking infantry division at their disposal isn't enough."

"Seems like they could put them shoulder to shoulder on the berm and hold off Ho's entire army," Hollister said.

"It'd seem so to me. Anyway, you take over in case we have any more trouble around here. I'll try to be back in a couple of hours. I've got a shit pot full of bones to pick with those dickheads at division."

Sangean didn't give Hollister a second chance to respond. He simply walked away. Hollister was beginning to understand two things about Sangean. One, he didn't have time for anything but business. Two, there was nothing more important to him than his troops. Hollister was sure they would never be close, but they thought a lot alike when it came to the troops and the mission. And that made Hollister feel better about the tasks before him.

***

"Here you go, Cap'n. This is just brewed," Sergeant Kendrick said, placing a steaming coffee mug in front of him on the picnic table that had been made out of the decking from an abandoned building. The telltale boot marks on the plywood created an unusual pattern on the dining table.

"Thanks. I won't be in your way, will I?"

"Sir, you never been in *my* way. You want to use my mess hall—you just let me know, and I'll make room for you."

"Thanks," Hollister said, remembering the time they had spent together in his first LRP detachment. "I'm looking forward to your cooking on this tour, too."

"Well, I just happen to have some sweet rolls coming out of the oven in a minute here. Would you like one, sir?"

"No thanks. Maybe later. I've got to earn my pay before I fill my face."

"Roger that, sir," Kendrick said, touching the lower edge of his paper cook's hat. He then smiled, turned, and hollered to the unseen cooks and helpers in the kitchen end of the building. "Hey! I don't hear no pans bein' washed or silverware bein' dried back there!"

Kendrick's manner amused Hollister and gave him a good feeling about the type of soldiers he had served with in LRPs and Airborne units. Kendrick was one of the unique ones who preferred to do a very unheralded job in a unit that had a big reputation. He liked being around the soldiers and NCOs he cooked for, and he liked being a LRP. He had never been out on a patrol, but there was never a man in any unit Kendrick was with who ever lacked for plenty of good food and hot coffee in the wee hours. He took lots of pride in what he did, and even though most of the troops forgot to tell him, they appreciated him.

Hollister wondered what the future held for Kendrick. He would not be able to get too many more promotions. The top of the NCO Corps pyramid becomes very pointed. For him to advance, he would have to work for a much larger organization and take on jobs like being mess steward for a ten-thousand-man mess hall or an even larger one. Doing that meant Kendrick would have to leave units like the LRPs and move to an Airborne division or a separate brigade.

As the afternoon gave way to dusk, Major Sangean returned and called a meeting of the officers and senior NCOs in the unit. Kendrick's mess hall was the only place that could hold everyone and offer work light.

Hollister took the chance to say hello to a few of the platoon sergeants, a platoon leader, and the supply officer—none of whom he had met earlier because of schedules.

Sangean held up a handful of papers that were stapled together. Several blue lines had been drawn under the typed entries with a ballpoint. "These are holes in our TO and E. We haven't even filled out yet, and we are hurting for replacements. On top of that, the division is trying to squeeze us to beef up their security."

Knowing looks were exchanged by some of the NCOs.

"I told 'em to go fuck themselves," Sangean said angrily.

The room erupted in whistles and applause and catcalls.

"Okay, okay. Let's not get too crazy. I won the argument, but we have to be busy with our mission or the division is going to tap us for sure. Before we can get back out in the bush, we have to sharpen up some skills. Captain Hollister will be tagging each patrol platoon and some of the old-timers for instructors. Don't give him any shit."

"Anything's better than fucking guard mount with the legs," someone said from the back of the room, spurring on more catcalls.

"All I want to see is training. I don't want any reports that any of our people are seen up in the division area. Anyone that needs to go there on business *will* wear leg fatigues—no cammies," Sangean said, looking toward Morrison. "You got that, First Sergeant?"

"Yessir," Morrison said from his place near the back door.

Sangean popped the catch holding the metal wristband on his Rolex and absentmindedly rubbed the inside of his wrist. Hollister had noticed that it was a thing Sangean did when he was tired.

"Gentlemen, we shipped off eight bodies in rubber bags today. There is no excuse for any of it. I want the sandbagging to speed up around here, and God help the man I catch sleeping with his head above parapet level. The other losses could have been avoided with more training and better support. Captain Hollister and I will take care of the support problem, but the rest is up to you-all. Do I make myself clear?"

"Clear, sir! Airborne!" many of the assembled NCOs and officers yelled, reminiscent of their days at the Airborne School.

They stood at attention as Sangean grabbed his floppy hat, placed it on his near shaven head, and exited the building saying only: "Carry on."

That night the probes on the perimeter continued. The division command post took three rockets that damaged some of the buildings, but caused no additional casualties. On the bunker line there were ten more 25th Division KIAs. The rumor was that more than half of them were from friendly fire.

The most effective damage happened to the airfield, which was pockmarked with mortar rounds. Several of the aircraft that had been dispersed around the base camp had been damaged by small arms, and a Chinook was knocked out of action by a truck driver who panicked during one of the mortar attacks and backed a deuce and a half into the fuselage.

By first light on the third day of the Tet Offensive, the single remaining LRP patrol had to return to Cu Chi after having been held up at the ARVN outpost at Hiep Hoa.

That same night the VC made one last, feeble attempt at attacking Cu Chi and only succeeded in hitting one of the ammunition storage pits that were spotted throughout the base. The ordnance detonated and continued to cook off from the flames of the burning wooden packing cases and the spilled contents of some of the artillery powder bags. The glow on the horizon and the muffled explosions could be heard all over the base camp, keeping many of the newer and more timid soldiers awake.

"Basics first!" Hollister said to Sergeant Kurzikowski. "Before we put any of these folks out of a chopper on string, or try some elaborate demolitions training, I want every man—officers and NCOs—to review basic patrolling techniques, radio procedure, map and compass reading, hand-and-arm signals, and immediate-action drills. When they aren't doing that, I want every weapon zeroed and plenty of practice on the range. Tell division that if they can't accommodate us with range time, we want to build our own."

"Whoa, Captain. I can't write that fast."

Hollister stopped long enough for Kurzikowski to catch up, then asked, "You think it's too much?"

"Only the writing part, sir." He tapped his pen on the pad. "You do all this training, and we'll have lots more LRPs making it to DEROS," Kurzikowski said, looking up and giving Hollister an approving smile.

"Good. Now, I think that we also ought to spend time working on identification—civilians and VC, like that."

"What do you mean?" Kurzikowski asked.

"I want someone who can tell more about a Viet from looking at him to teach us what to look for. My first tour it was pretty easy to spot a bad guy." Hollister waved his arm in the direction of the Cambodian border. "But out there they all look alike to us round-eyes. Out there in the paddies, they're all likely to be VC. But you can't make me believe that the Vietnamese don't know more about it than we do. We need to find that person."

Kurzikowski put his pen to his lip and rolled his eyes. "Makes sense, but I'm not rightly sure I know who that is. Give me time to sleep on it."

* * *

The training started almost immediately. Hollister assigned himself to teach patrol-leading techniques to the Specialist 4s and sergeants who were assigned as team leaders. He insisted that the two platoon leaders—both second lieutenants—take all the training as if they were LRP team members.

The decision wasn't popular with the lieutenants, but they didn't complain too much. They knew they had to win the confidence of the patrol members by showing they could—and would—do everything the members of their platoons were expected to do.

It didn't take very long for the lieutenants to find out that Hollister himself had been a platoon leader of a LRP platoon. They also knew they were not going to be able to put anything over on him. Of the four lieutenants in the company—two platoon leaders, a commo officer, and the supply officer—two had been Ranger students while Hollister was an instructor at Ranger School.

So there was no getting out of anything with Hollister. To most of them, he was consistent with Sangean's approach to hard training and serious business in the field. But unlike Sangean, they found that Hollister had a sense of humor and they could talk to him.

It didn't take them long to acquire a carcass from a Huey, minus the tail boom and the rotor assembly, by way of what the Airborne called "midnight requisition." With it the LRPs practiced loading, unloading, firing, and supporting the fires of onboard door gunners.

Their progress was easy to measure with a stopwatch. The time on the ground getting into or out of a chopper was the most vulnerable time for every LRP.

The troops started each day early and ended very late, with a critique of the day's training. After that, the playfulness that normally took place before training gave way to more practical things—like sleep.

The platoon leaders and the patrol leaders had extra training beyond that of the patrol members. Hollister and Kurzikowski gave classes on the use of gunships, medevac procedures, calling and adjusting artillery, and close air support. And Major Sangean drilled Hollister and Kurzikowski on company operations, planning, coordination, communications, and reporting.

Hollister found himself grabbing an hour of sleep here and there, but never anything near a full night's sleep. He was only able to get a letter out to Susan about every third day and then only by writing in five-minute snatches, when he could. He knew his words would make little sense and paragraphs would be completely disconnected in subject matter and mood. Still, he wanted to get them off to her to let her know that he was thinking about her and that he missed her.

***

There was no avoiding the special complications that working in western III Corps brought to Juliet Company. As a result Hollister took every opportunity to get out over the AO in a chopper or fixed-wing aircraft. He studied the patterns that civilians used to get to places and took note of what they avoided. He felt that the local guerrillas were certainly being used to guide North Vietnamese and Main Force units through the area. He also suspected that the patterns the locals had developed growing up would not change much in their selection of routes and places to hide from U.S. and South Vietnamese observation. He hoped he was right.

The patterns seemed to break down into very practical matters. Civilians wove easily recognizable trails into the countryside as they avoided the farmland, which was near to being sacred. Paths were along dikes and on the margins of dirt roads and highways. The waterways were followed extensively because of their convenience and the lack of damage using them caused. Often, paths ran just under the overhang of trees planted to mark property and break monsoon winds.

Hollister's first instinct was to suspect this was a way to avoid aerial observation. But then he realized that the paths had been carved there long before the skies were patrolled by aircraft, and he remembered that Vietnamese didn't value a suntan the way Americans did. Everywhere, in the field and in the cities, he saw Vietnamese women holding hats, books, or parcels between their faces and the sun to prevent the rays from darkening their skin. Dark skin was the mark of field hands, not the mark of aristocracy. The paths under the trees were simply to avoid the sun where possible.

Hollister took Lieutenants Osborne and Seeley along on the terrain flights. Osborne was a VMI grad who had a slow Southern drawl and an unshakable personality. Hollister liked his stability and thought that all he needed to work on was Osborne's awareness of the troops and their needs.

Hollister didn't envy any officer who had not been an enlisted man. In his mind the experience was invaluable in understanding the point of view and the perceptions of soldiers who rarely have the big picture and often mistake the motives of the officers in charge.

Seeley was another West Pointer, but unlike most of his classmates, he was a former enlisted man who had taken competitive exams to get accepted into the Military Academy Prep School at Fort Belvoir. After a year at the prep school, he'd been accepted by West Point with the other plebes, who were there by congressional appointment.

Seeley had a handle on his relationship with the troops, but needed work on decision making under pressure. He had only been out of the academy for a year, and during that time he had been a general's aide at Fort Leonard Wood in Missouri. Fort Leonard Wood was an engineer post that had a small training brigade to teach infantry basic training. The deputy post commander was an infantryman. So Seeley's development as a platoon leader had been put on hold until he arrived in Vietnam and was able to convince the assignments officer at the Replacement Battalion that he should be assigned to the newly forming LRP company.

On their flights Hollister called out situations to the officers to test their reactions and to critique their performances. Hollister was fond of picking out terrain features like road junctions, or even a grazing water buffalo, and charging one of the officers with determining the grid coordinates, as if he were preparing to call for artillery or air support. He pressed them to do it rapidly, reminding them that time was half of effective fire support.

He would develop scenarios where imaginary patrols were holed up in patches of green and in need of medevac, emergency equipment, or gunship support, then let the lieutenants explain how they would handle the situation—who they would contact, what frequencies they needed to monitor, what considerations they would make concerning the immediate situation near the patrol. The hardest part for them was sizing up the intentions and the threat presented by the civilians working and wandering near the simulated patrol locations.

At the end of each flight, Hollister would come back with his map case covered with grease-pencil notes on the terrain, so hoarse he could hardly speak.

"I've got some good news for you, Hollister," Major Sangean said.

"What's that, sir? I could use a lift," Hollister said as he entered Operations.

"Meet Captain Jack Stanton. He's from the One hundred forty-fifth Aviation Battalion and will be honchoing our new gunship support."

Stanton stood, put down the cold drink he was sipping, wiped the can's condensation from his hand, and stuck it out for Hollister to shake.

Taking Stanton's hand, Hollister looked from him back to Sangean. "Permanentlike?"

"You got it," Stanton said. "We've been attached for operational control. The One hundred forty-fifth is going to provide maintenance, Log support, and Admin. All you have to do is fly us, feed us, and bunk us down."

"Hot shit!" Hollister yelled. "Man, are we glad to see you. So, what can we expect?"

Stanton looked to Sangean, as if they had a secret.

"How do you feel about Cobras?" Sangean asked, cracking a smile for the first time in days.

"Holy fuck!" Hollister said. "I can't believe it! I just can't believe it! Cobras!"

"Believe it. I've got six snakes and crews to go with them. Only problem is that only 'bout half my crews are checked out in snakes. And they all need more in-country transition and check rides. But they're wetting their pants to get to it," Jack Stanton said.

"I gotta sit down," Hollister said, half kidding. He dropped his map case and hat on the field desk he had set up in Operations and flopped onto the folding chair next to it.

"This Major Fowler's doing?" Hollister asked Sangean.

Sangean shrugged.

"I don't know who Major Fowler is," said Stanton, "but I got my marching orders through channels from USARV. They wanted to tie up the first Cobras in-country with a larger Log base to support any maintenance needs and test us with small units. There are a bunch of 'em going to the Cav, but they're working on a different concept. So we belong to you, and we're ready to move forward from Bien Hoa in the next couple of days. You got room for us?"

Sangean looked at Hollister, and they both replied together, "You bet!"

After his excitement over the good news started to wane, Hollister sat down and drafted another letter to Major Fowler about his request for additional support. He still hadn't seen anything that looked like artillery, air force, or communications support—or evidence that something was ongoing. He finished the letter and let Kurzikowski read it.

"You're just gonna piss him off with this, Captain. Seems to me I remember something about officers needing tact," he said, attaching a smile to his words.

"A little too pointed, huh?"

"Pointed? Naw, it's not pointed for a real soldier. But for a REMF it's a stick in the eye."

Kurzikowski was growing on Hollister. He was an old-hand Airborne NCO who had seen his share of special operations and unconventional units. He wore a tiny Bronze Star on his Master Parachutist wings for the combat blast he had made in the 187th Regimental Combat Team in Korea. His right-shoulder patch gave away a combat assignment with Special Forces on an earlier tour in Vietnam.

Kurzikowski didn't remember him, but Hollister remembered Kurzikowski as a tough and no-nonsense instructor at the Airborne School at Fort

Benning when he was a student. Since there were over three hundred in Hollister's class, he didn't take offense at Kurzikowski's not remembering him.

The Fowler letter behind them, they went over training schedules. Kurzikowski discussed his ideas about training the teams after training the individuals. As he spoke Hollister realized how much of his life had taken place in the company of, under the scrutiny of, and being protected by NCOs like Kurzikowski. He made a mental note to try to get a letter off to First Sergeant Easy before he crapped out that night. He had tried to do it three nights in a row without success.

Kurzikowski came up with a variation that Hollister didn't particularly like, but he decided not to make an issue out of it. He had learned as a young sergeant himself that it was worse to win every argument than to lose a few privately. It kept things on a professional plane and reduced the likelihood of things becoming personal due to continued wins and losses going to the same parties. When that happened it always seemed to ruin the relationship and become bitter. He didn't want that to happen between him and Kurzikowski. He needed him, he trusted him, and he wanted his respect.

Hollister allowed himself two beers before he fell into his bunk. He had moved into another building that was across the company street from Operations and next to the Orderly Room. It had been a dispensary of sorts in its first life and was partitioned by plywood walls that had been fitted with several shallow shelves that must have once held medical supplies.

Hollister used the few hours he had free to clean out the rat-infested shack and patch the tear in the tin roof with a panel off a nearby shack that had burned in some long-forgotten fire. His end of the hooch was ten feet by twelve and had a single lightbulb hanging in the center. The other half of the shack would be claimed by the XO, who was already in-country and due at Cu Chi within the week. Hollister had taped a map of the area west of Cu Chi, which included the first ten kilometers inside the farthest part of the Cambodian border, on the wall just above his bunk.

He was finishing his beer while reading the Intelligence Summary that came to them every three days from IIFFV. The INTSUM gave a recap of all reports of enemy activities, sightings, intelligence-gathering efforts, and PW (prisoner of war) interrogations. As far as Hollister was concerned, much of it was pure crap. He was quickly able to determine the level of accuracy in the details by reading the entry that summarized the short patrol he had been on with Sergeant Harrold's team. It read: AT 0200 HRS, JANUARY 25, 1968, A IIFFV LRP TEAM ENCOUNTERED ENEMY ELEMENTS AT XT516798 ESTIMATED

SIZE 10 VC. ARMY GUNSHIP FIRED IN SUPPORT OF THE GROUND ELEMENT. RE-
SULTS: ESTIMATED 4 ENEMY KIA, 4 WIA. NO FRIENDLY CASUALTIES.

Three years into the U.S. ground war, numbers had become the standard.
Body count was everything. No progress or success could be claimed or an-
nounced without comparative estimates of friendly versus enemy body counts.
And as fast as the system was instituted, it became inflated and suspect.

It started when he was with the Airborne Brigade. Hollister remembered being involved in a firefight in the Highlands and knew firsthand that
they had only killed fifteen VC. But a week later the *Stars and Stripes* had
a headline that read: AIRBORNE TROOPS CLASH WITH VC IN HIGHLAND BASE
CAMP—50 ENEMY SOLDIERS LOSE LIVES.

He was confident that he had never exaggerated any body counts, but
he could never seem to control what happened to the information that started on his end of a radio handset. It always grew in numbers as it went higher
and higher up the chain of command.

But the numbers and the slight inaccuracies in the INTSUM were not
as important to Hollister as the trends and the bigger picture. He knew
that most of the information had come from individual reports by RF/PF
outposts, patrols, pilots, infantrymen, and a long list of other sources that
didn't coordinate their input. So most of the reports were worth reading and
comparing to the map.

As he made the ground-report relationship, Hollister was able to see
that there had been a steady flow of very small groups of VC moving from
Cambodia toward Saigon prior to the Tet Offensive. He wondered if he
could see it in the reports, why couldn't the people who specialized in analysis see it?

Still, that was nothing he could do anything about. He shook off the
pre-Tet reports and looked at the reports since the offensive. He was careful
not to try to find a solid pattern in activities that were only a few days old. He
would watch for trends and changes and patterns. his early assessment was
that there was a considerable amount of movement at night coming across
the border heading toward the small villages and hamlets close to it. To him
the reason was obvious. The distance from the safety of Cambodia to major
American and South Vietnamese bases was too far for infiltrators to make
in one night. They had to hole up somewhere, and blending in with the
villagers in the daytime was the best way to do that.

He started to make little marks on the map for activities—no special
distinctions, which would take too much time to do and clutter the map up
too much—just marks. He had a hunch that if he kept putting a mark on the

map each time he read a report, he would find a pattern and a flow in his AO. He knew that if he could make an educated guess as to where they were moving at night, he could place teams in their path and do some damage.

He placed over two-dozen marks on the map and then gave up. His eyes burned, and he wasn't able to make much sense out of some of the interrogation reports that were extracted from poor translations. Even he knew that a paragraph that read 2 VC WERE REPORTED BY AGENT TO HAVE CARRIED 600 KILOS OF RICE TO SUSPECTED TUNNELS LOCATED AT XT 620102 was just not credible. He knew there were many "super-soldier" claims attributed to the VC, but carrying three hundred kilos of rice was one for the books.

After a cold shower and another cigarette, Hollister walked to Operations for one final check before he called it a night. Lieutenant Seeley was the duty officer. Since all the teams were in and the company was not on alert for anything but a full ground assault of the base camp, there was little to worry about. The radios hummed with the cross talk from other units out on operations trying to track down the few remaining NVA units left after the militarily unsuccessful Tet Offensive.

"Evening, sir," Seeley said, looking up from what looked like a letter to someone at home.

"How's it going? Anything shaking?" Hollister asked.

"No, sir. There's an ARVN unit north of the Sugar Mill that seems to think the entire North Vietnamese Army is getting ready to attack it, but the gunships prowling the area for them can't find anything but dark out there."

"I'm not surprised," Hollister said. "You going with me tomorrow?"

"On the practice inserts?"

"Yep."

"Yessir. I'm ready," Seeley said, obviously trying to sound gung-ho.

"Well, try and get some sleep. We don't need a platoon leader falling asleep in the door of a chopper."

Seeley smiled and nodded. Hollister waved and stepped back out the door.

As he walked across the company street to his hooch, he remembered the nights he had pulled the duty officer's watch only to get up and head out into the operations of the day. It seemed so long ago, and he seemed to have had more staying power then. At his age he should feel stronger—he promised to make the run in the morning with the troops.

He entered his hooch, turned on the light, and looked at his watch.

"Oh shit!" he mumbled to himself. It was just after one A.M. He didn't even bother to take off his fatigue trousers. He just flopped on his bunk and fell off the edge of the war.

Someone banged on the door to Hollister's hooch. "Cap'n Hollister? You asked me to tell you when it's zero four hundred. Well, it's zero four hundred, sir." Then there was a pause and the soldier added, "Ah . . . Airborne!"

Hollister's head hurt from the tension he had been carrying. It was the first thing he felt when he raised it to get up. He reached for a cigarette, coughed up the night's congestion, and lit up. The smoke burned all the way down, and he remembered that he had every intention of making the PT run. He considered putting out the cigarette and then figured, what the hell, he'd already had the first drag.

He had been too lazy to shave the night before. He regretted the decision after splashing cold canteen water on his face, lathering up with a can of Foamy, and dragging the razor down from his sideburn. The shave was painful and short of Airborne School standards.

Hollister stumbled out into the darkness. He knew where the troops were, even without looking. He could hear the drone of the mumbling that always took place while everyone was waiting for the formation to be called to attention and the coughing that punctuated the drone.

He bumped into Lieutenant Osborne, who was heading in the same direction. "Good morning, sir," Osborne said cheerfully.

"Matter of opinion. You in charge of this mob this morning?" Hollister asked.

"Yessir, unless you'd like to lead the run."

"Nope. I'm real sure you'll do a good job and bring almost as many of us home as you take out. How far you going this morning?"

"Well, I thought I'd . . .," Osborne began.

"No. Never mind. I'll find out when it happens. Don't tell me."

"Company! Attench-hut!" a voice hollered in the dark.

Hollister got closer and realized it was First Sergeant Morrison standing in front of the formation of fewer than a hundred soldiers, divided up into two platoons and a headquarters section. Morrison did an awkward about-face and waited for Lieutenant Osborne to step in front of him.

"Sir, the company is formed," Morrison said, rendering a fairly snappy salute for a fat man.

Osborne returned the salute and in a more moderate tone replied, "Thank you, First Sergeant. Take your post."

Morrison did another about-face and marched to the end of the formation, where Hollister had positioned himself. Recognizing Hollister, he whispered, "Good morning, sir."

"How come I'm the only one that isn't sure about that, Top?"

Morrison stifled a laugh, then followed Osborne's instructions to the company to face right, forward-march, and double-time.

As they passed the last building in the area belonging to the LRPs, another figure came out of the dark and fell in on the other side of the first sergeant. It was Major Sangean, who simply said, "Morning," and fell into step.

As they left the company street and turned onto a laterite road that headed toward the 25th Division commanding general's quarters, Osborne started singing Jody cadence—loud, arrogant, and very Airborne.

Hollister couldn't help but be impressed with the first sergeant. With all his bulk, and already breathing heavily, he was keeping up and making no excuses. After a couple of weeks together, Hollister was changing his attitude about Morrison. He was turning out to be a terrific senior NCO and adapted to the ways and the needs of the LRP company as if he had spent years in one.

It bothered Hollister that he had misjudged Morrison based on his looks. But he was happy to find out that the man was worth keeping. He had never mentioned his weight to Morrison, although he had the feeling that Sangean had.

The column of fours snaked its way through the streets and roadways that crisscrossed the Tropic Lightning base camp. About a mile into the run, Lieutenant Osborne turned the column toward the flagpole that marked the 25th Division Headquarters complex and the nearby division commander's quarters.

Recognizing the direction of the running company, Hollister took a quick look at his watch. It was only five A.M. and the glow of the dawn was turning a peach color on the horizon. He was sure the general was still tucked into the clean sheets of his rack, sleeping to the hum of the air conditioner that made his house trailer the envy of every man in the base camp.

As they approached the general's trailer, Osborne raised the volume of his voice and sang out the Jody cadence challenges. The troops quickly caught on and raised their voices in the responses. The small company could be heard at least a thousand yards away yelling, AIRBORNE, RANGER and LONG RANGE PATROL. There could be no doubt in anyone's mind that the LRPs were up, doing their PT, and cutting themselves no slack. It was the kind of stuff they lived for—to be LRPs and to rub it in to those who weren't.

Hollister was sure that Sangean recognized the potential for an ass-chewing coming down to him through channels. But if he cared, he didn't show it, and he certainly didn't try to stop Osborne from spurring on the troops.

They went through it on the ground first. Hollister had the slick pilots park two Hueys in trail, and the gunship pilots stood out to the flanks representing the gunships they would be flying. Hollister felt it was more dangerous than useful to park loaded gunships in a field where fifty-odd LRPs were walking through the choreography of a LRP insert. He also knew that the Cobras were such a novelty that the troops would be tempted to investigate them and risk injury should one of the rockets malfunction and launch or detonate.

But even though the men were restricted to the practice area, the Cobras would distract much of their attention while Hollister was trying to perfect the routine of loading, getting out on a landing zone, and moving to a rally point. He wanted all the distractions eliminated so the pilots would see what the troops would be doing and the troops would see where the gunships would be flying by using the pilots to simulate their own Cobras.

The morning went by quickly. Hollister made every man in the company pose as a LRP team member and go through the loading, landing, unloading routine more than once. Even the headquarters personnel.

He then did the same for all of the pilots. He insisted they pose as LRPs to see what problems LRPs faced as they went into potentially hot landing zones knowing they would be getting off in the crosshairs of every VC within effective range of his weapon.

At first the pilots balked at the idea, and then they started to taunt each other into going through the drill. By noon the resistance had turned into competitive practice teams pitting the gunship pilots against the slick pilots. All wanted to get out fast and get to the designated rally point without tripping or falling. It was hard work for everyone, but they quickly got into the spirit of it when it turned completely competitive within the LRP teams.

CHAPTER 12

The letter from Susan was the first in a pile of six that had arrived at once. It had taken almost three weeks for the mail to be forwarded from his old unit—the one he was originally assigned to but never saw. He had received three letters written after the packet of six that had come directly to Juliet Company once Susan had received his new address.

He didn't care that they were out of order or that he was reading about things she had planned after he had already read how the plans came out. Her words, her handwriting, and the feel of the paper she had handled gave him a feeling of belonging to something permanent, something hopeful, and something safe. There was nothing that fit that description in Vietnam—nothing but Susan's letters.

It was late, he was tired, his head ached, and he had a sour knot in his stomach. Still, he was going to read each letter at least once before he slept.

He poured himself a couple of fingers of Scotch from a bottle he had brought back from the Long Binh Class VI Store. The liquid burned his throat and made him feel flushed as quickly as it hit bottom.

Her words were at once warming and a little disturbing. She had always had a problem with him being in the army. Her upbringing in an all-civilian family, her education at Amherst College, and working as a journalist for five years couldn't help but leave her that way.

Even though they had lived at Fort Benning between tours, it had done little to take some of the edge off her opposition to the war. She was becoming more and more uncomfortable with the American involvement in Vietnam. Her letters told Hollister about the news slant, the nightly body counts, the antiwar demonstrations, the division within Congress, and the sinking feeling that the war would drag on and on until tens of thousands of American boys died in Southeast Asia.

He understood her concerns, but was bothered by the fact that while he was in Vietnam she was doubly distressed by having a husband in Vietnam and by her growing doubts about the purpose and the wisdom of the involvement in the first place.

She told him she was going to continue her involvement in the antiwar movement as a journalist, but was also feeling a need to do something about convincing the administration that the war must be brought to a quick and decisive end.

Her words didn't bother him as much as he knew she thought they would. He didn't want the war to continue. He wasn't one of the stereotypical military men who the newspapers and TV commentators suggested were thrilled to have their lovely little war. He was sure there were people like that. He was equally sure the description didn't apply to him or anyone he had served with. He couldn't understand how anyone who had ever been under fire could want to put himself or others in that situation again.

She summarized much of the news that he never got. The press had been having a field day with their interpretations of the successes of the North Vietnamese Tet Offensive.

Hollister's understanding was that while there were considerable successes politically and a great body of world public opinion had been swayed, the numbers of dead VC and North Vietnamese spoke to him as a huge failure.

He tried to remember the difference he often saw between what was happening before his eyes and how it was reported and colored in the American press. That factor considered, he could quickly see how it would upset Susan. He started drafting a reply in his head, cautioning himself not to start defending the actions in Vietnam to his own wife and further polarize what was now a workable difference of opinion over the war.

Susan had never demanded that he get out of the army. She understood that he loved the people he worked with and felt he was doing something important. She knew the frustrations, too. She knew he was worried about his potential in the real world after the army if he got out and his potential for advancement if he stayed.

Hollister had felt the pressure to get to and through college as fast as possible. The difficulty involved going to night school when he was so often moved from station to station, overseas and back to the States. He had been moved to new assignments ten times since he had entered the army. At that rate, he had racked up eleven incompletes on his college transcript.

Her letters brought on more tension in the base of his neck, and he poured himself another drink without thinking about what he was doing.

Her words soon changed to how much she missed him. He knew she would be lonely in a big-city sense, moving back to New York, but she just couldn't bring herself to remain in Columbus, Georgia, after she was pushed out of army quarters with his departure.

He was beginning to realize how his attitude had changed about New York. He had loved it as a place to visit when he was on leave as an enlisted man. He had even enjoyed it when he and Susan had spent time in her flat in the Village and gone out on the town. But he felt different about her being there as his wife without him. God, how he missed her.

Over a particularly filling breakfast of creamed beef on toast, coffee, and very bitter grapefruit, Hollister looked at the roster the first sergeant had handed him.

"The Old Man wanted me to run it by you. It was the only thing we could do to keep the reassignments down," Morrison said, gnawing on a dry piece of unbuffered toast.

"Not thrilling," Hollister said.

"The toast or the roster?"

"The roster," Hollister said, looking up. He saw the dry toast and made a face. "I'll bet that wasn't what vaulted you out of bed this morning."

"No, sir. It pretty much screams for something like butter or jam." He leaned back and patted his stomach. "But I'm determined to get rid of my new call sign."

"What's that?"

"I got wind that the troops are calling me 'First Sergeant Heavy Drop.' I don't know how many pounds I've lost, but I'm making some serious progress on my web belt," Morrison said, pulling the tail of his belt out, displaying the crimp marks exposed on the free end.

"Looks to me like you're doing the job, Top," Hollister said.

"Thanks. I guess all that time in headquarters jobs got away from me. Never again!"

"The weight bother you?"

"No, sir—the morning runs do," Morrison said, breaking into a broad grin.

They both laughed, and Hollister slid the roster back to Morrison. "Well, it looks like you did what you had to here. How many people have been reassigned to different teams?"

"Moving six pretty much consolidated what we had and gave us the most full-strength teams. But three of those moved had only been with their old teams for less than a month."

"Okay. I'll see what I can do to make them feel more comfortable about the turbulence. It's a real confidence-buster for LRPs to be moved from team to team."

The area was as close as they could get to being totally secure and not being inside the wire of an American base camp. They needed to practice inserts and extractions as a full-dress rehearsal, complete with live fire. The Field Force, the ARVN district chief, and the local village chiefs had cleared the area for Hollister to use. Still, he wanted to recon it first before off-loading troops onto innocent civilians or waiting VC.

The ride out was a boyish thrill for Hollister. Jack Stanton wanted to fly the mission and had a Cobra that needed a maintenance check flight to confirm some blade-tracking error that had been adjusted earlier in the day.

Stanton and Hollister climbed into the Cobra on the Old Warrior Pad. "You can do everything from the front seat that I can do back here plus some," Stanton said as they spooled up to takeoff rpm.

"Kinda tight," Hollister said, having just compacted his six-foot frame into the copilot's narrow seat in front of and below Stanton's.

"It's an aviator's dream. Something tight that flies and shoots fire and brimstone."

"I've been in more comfortable places," Hollister said, trying to wiggle into a better position.

"Yeah, but you've never been in a more beautiful rotary-wing flying machine," Stanton said, reaching over to flip the radio to the control-tower frequency at the Cu Chi airfield. "Stand by, Jim. Let me clear us outa here."

Hollister clicked the mike button on the floor with his boot twice to let Stanton know he understood. He then adjusted his shoulder restraints, the chest protector he had strapped on before getting in, and the lip mike attached to his flight helmet.

While he made the adjustments, he heard Stanton talk to the local traffic controller, get clearance, and get wind and barometric readings.

"Okay, up there. Let's get this thing up to a cooler altitude," Stanton said.

"No shit," Hollister said over the intercom. "I never expected it to be this hot in here."

"You close up this Plexiglas with nothing to shade you and the temperature runs up faster than your tail rotor rpm. Don't worry about it. When we get in the air, it'll cool down a lot."

The initial sensation was much like being in the front car on a roller coaster. Hollister watched Stanton's control moves by noticing the changes on the cyclic and collective pitch controls up front. Whatever Stanton did with his in the backseat was mirrored on the controls inches from Hollister's fingertips.

It may have only been Hollister's perception, but nose-down altitude taking off in a Cobra seemed much more exaggerated than the same takeoff in a Huey. For a few seconds Hollister felt as if Stanton were going to turn the chopper over on its top. But as fast as Stanton dropped the nose and pulled up the collective, the chopper seemed to leap up off the ground and translate its upward motion into forward motion. "Jeeeeezus!" Hollister said, almost under his breath.

"You got a lot less drag with a three-foot-wide chopper than you do with a Huey that flies like a footlocker with skids."

"It sure seems to have more punch!"

"Three hundred more shaft horsepower than a slick."

The chopper skimmed over the concentric circles of concertina, double-apron barbed wire and neatly spaced perimeter bunkers. Troops on the ground looked up and waved at the Cobra.

"When was the last time you saw a grunt smile at a chopper like it's September and they just rolled out the new Corvettes?"

"I can see them. Is it the speed?"

"I think it's the look. A snake looks bad. But the fact is that we can hit at two hundred and twenty miles an hour while a slick is lucky to get near a hundred an' a half on a good day."

"This could sure make a grunt like me think about flight school."

"Hey, we don't want smelly old infantrymen falling in love with the magic of Cobra flying—just women, my friend. Just women," Stanton kidded.

As they headed out toward the training area, Stanton couldn't resist showing off his new toy for Hollister. He pushed the cyclic forward, causing Hollister's stomach to rise as the chopper sank toward the rice fields. Within seconds they were slamming along the ground barely inches over the highest paddy dikes. The dikes clicked by like muddy railroad ties.

It quickly became clear to Hollister as they screamed toward a stand of trees that Stanton would have to commit himself to a turn or more altitude—very soon. At a point where Hollister almost guessed it was too late to keep from crashing into the trees, Stanton jerked the nose up and started a climb that appeared to be almost straight up.

There were only a few things Hollister understood about flying, but the concept of stalling was one of them. As they gained altitude, the powerful turbine engine began to lose the battle against gravity. It was a very disconcerting feeling for Hollister. He was sure Stanton probably knew what he was doing. But what would happen at the top of the stall? Would they simply fall backward out of the sky? Tail down? What would it do to the rotor blades?

Not able to resist any longer, Hollister spoke up. "What happens now?"

"This!" Stanton said. Just as the aircraft seemed to come to a virtual standstill in the sky, Stanton kicked hard on the right pedal, spinning the chopper in a right yaw until it was suddenly facing straight down. And then the second half of the roller-coaster ride began. The chopper began to fall as it picked up speed; then it fell even faster.

As the chopper rocketed toward the rice fields, Hollister tried to gauge the time before Stanton would have to begin pulling out of the dive. In seconds they passed that point and Hollister again had to wonder what Stanton and the Cobra had in store for him. He glanced down at the airspeed indicator and had to look at it twice. The air rushing into the stingerlike pitot tube on the chopper's nose was pegging the hand on the ASI.

Hollister knew he was flying with a crazy man, and would surely die before the sweep second hand on his watch made another revolution.

At a point that just had to be too low, Stanton drew back the cyclic, corrected the pedal to compensate for the countertorque, and pulled the chopper out of the dive in a shuddering change of direction—from almost straight down to straight and level.

"This is where I get off!" Hollister teased Stanton, half serious.

"Aw hell, a little chopper ride couldn't scare an Airborne-Ranger-LRP, could it?"

"No . . . But that was not like any little chopper ride I've ever been on."

"The AH-IG Cobra is not any little chopper, either," Stanton countered.

"I'm a believer up here. But I feel like the front bumper in a demo derby."

They both laughed as Stanton snapped the chopper up on its side to thread it between two tall trees that were too close together for the forty-four-foot diameter rotor disk to squeeze between them.

"Man, this is some machine!"

"It's a sports car for aviators."

"I'm sold."

"Oh, wait until you see this thing shoot. I ain't the best shot in the west, but I can knock the chin whiskers off a frog at max range doing a couple hundred knots with anything onboard."

"What's *onboard*?" Hollister asked.

"This one's rigged with two six-barrel 7.62 miniguns in the chin turret—each firing four thousand rounds. And, on the little, stubby wing stations I've got rocket pods that'll fire one to nineteen pairs of rockets at a time."

"Pairs?" Hollister asked.

"Yep, pairs. One off each side. If I do it right, they converge out there ahead of us right where the bad guys are."

Hollister had decided that he liked Stanton and was growing confident in his flying, as well as getting comfortable with his sense of humor. "We sure are glad to have you guys on our team."

"Well, you better take care of us. You know what we had to give up back at Bien Hoa to come out here and live in the fuckin' boonies?" Stanton asked.

"I'll bet you're gonna tell me."

"I'll tell you now and remind you often. We had enough booze to swim in, women of all types and colors, clean sheets washed by hooch maids, and air conditioning. And that is only the beginning of the list. Back at Battalion we had a club with the fanciest card room in Vietnam, naked girls dancing on the bar, great stereo equipment, and transportation to houses of ill repute from Long Binh to Saigon. Hell, we even got regular trips to the R and R beach at Vung Tau."

"I'll bet you like it here better, huh?"

"I'd rather have hemorrhoids than be made to go back there."

They both laughed.

Stanton began a long, lazy descending left turn. "Well, here's your training area," he announced.

Hollister pulled his map up from its place, tightly tucked under his thigh against the seat. He looked out and generally oriented himself on the low profile of the Saigon skyline eighteen miles off to the east.

Cross-checking the chopper compass and then making a quick adjustment of his map, Hollister was sure he had himself oriented on the terrain.

His map had a black grease-pencil line that marked the limits of the area he had cleared, notes on the nearest friendly units, the training frequencies and call signs, and the proposed LZs and PZs he wanted to use.

"What do you say we have a closer look at the tree line near the landing zone?" Stanton asked.

"I'd like that. I don't need any surprises when we get in here," Hollister said.

Stanton rolled the Cobra over in a hard right turn, slipped from two hundred feet to treetop level, and ran down the length of the tree line closest to the fallow paddies they were planning on using.

As much as his shoulder harness would allow, Hollister leaned forward to look over the chopper's nose at the ground. Stanton eased back on the cyclic, slowed the airspeed to under five knots, and rolled it in a small circle, causing the rotor wash to blow the trees around. By doing that the tree branches moved in several directions, not allowing anything under them to be hidden from view.

"Man! You don't miss a thing doing this," Hollister said, surprised at the visibility.

"Yeah. And the lower and slower you get, the more it rattles anybody you flush out. You're more likely to get shot at by someone five hundred meters away than someone less than thirty feet below you."

They eased along the full length of the row of trees and looked over every piece of ground they revealed by blowing away the branches, bushes, and tall grasses. The ground showed plenty of evidence of use. There was a small trail, no more than a foot wide, that ran down the center of the windbreak. The lack of growth on it was an indication that it was used often. But Hollister knew use didn't necessarily mean that those walking the path were VC.

At one end of the trees was a small bunker that appeared to have one part of the overhead cover caved in. "Ho! You see that bunker?"

Stanton clicked his mike button twice and pulled the chopper off to the right and then back to the left, starting a slow left turn around the entire bunker. The maneuver gave him a better view out the left side of the chopper so he didn't have to look over the top of his instruments and Hollister's head at the spot on the ground.

The bunker had been built to house two to three soldiers. There was a small access hole on the back and a small six-inch firing aperture on the opposite side.

As they turned over the bunker, Hollister could see that the aperture had excellent observation of the football-field-sized paddy in front of it. With a simple light machine gun, an enemy soldier would level an entire LRP team stepping out of a chopper almost anywhere on the landing zone.

Even though the bunker was old and empty, it showed Hollister the awareness the local guerrillas had and the effort they would go to to kill Americans.

"Want me to fire it up?" Stanton asked.

"No. I think I want to leave it there for a training aid. Come left a little."

Stanton came to a hover and started to crab sideways over the bunker.

"There! See it?"

"What you got?"

"See the bottom?" Hollister asked.

Stanton slipped sideways a bit more and stopped at a solid hover. "Yeah, I got it. I can see the water and the weeds down in there. I guess it really hasn't been used in months."

"Let's leave it be and let the troops discover it."

"Okay with me. You're the boss here."

As Stanton rolled the chopper over to the right, Hollister made a note on the bunker's location and tried to estimate the fan of visibility and fire a gunner would have from inside. On the map he made a large V across the rice paddy with the apex at the bunker's firing aperture. As he checked outside the chopper for the orientation of the V, he was more impressed and surprised by the degree of vulnerability facing anyone standing in the large pie-shaped area.

They flew on and made the same low-level recon of all the terrain features in the immediate area that might present a threat to the safety of the troops who would use it starting that afternoon.

The other clumps and outcroppings offered no more indication of recent use than they had seen in the first stand of trees. That left only the landing zone itself.

"Can we take a closer look at the area between the touchdown point and the nearest cover?" Hollister asked.

"No problem," Stanton said. He eased the chopper over into a right turn and dropped down to an altitude only inches above the weed-filled field.

"This is it. Can we work from here to the trees—looking for anything unpleasant on the ground?"

"Make you a deal," Stanton said. "You check out the ground, and I'll keep my head up and watch our ass. At this speed and altitude I'm a juicy target. I'd just as soon be ready to render a ballsy gook gunner into smoking paste."

"Deal."

The inspection of the landing area turned up some bad cracks in the hard-baked mud that could easily reach out and grab an ankle, but nothing that looked like a booby trap or any signs of mines or other antipersonnel devices.

"I've seen all I need."

"Want to head home?"

Looking at his watch, Hollister thought of what was on the schedule for the remainder of the day and clicked the floor button twice. He then folded up his map and slid it into the cargo pocket on the side of his trousers.

"Lunch?"

"No, I want to get back for mail call," Hollister said.

"You expecting someone to write to you?"

"I always expect that, but mail call is the only place you can get a feel for what the troops are thinking."

Stanton reached a cruising altitude of fifteen hundred feet and leveled off for the trip back to Cu Chi. "What's that mean?"

"Means that when the troops are most themselves is waiting for mail call. Everyone shows up. There's little in the way of demands on them, and you can get a feel for their morale by looking at how they move, dress, talk. You get a feel for how much kidding around is happening. It's a better thermometer than a briefing, or a PT formation, or a reveille formation. They are more themselves there."

"How about at chow?"

"Uh-uh. Not all of them eat all meals. That gives you a bad picture. Nobody misses mail call, and nobody is worried about how they are going to perform at mail call."

"You worry about that kinda stuff, don't you, Hollister?"

"You bet, man. Without them, we'd be out of a job."

They both laughed. But they both knew what he meant.

Before the teams were launched, the team leaders were taken out to the training area to make an overflight recon of the landing zone.

Back at Cu Chi everything progressed as if it were the start of a real patrol. Each of the teams sat lined up at the side of the chopper pad with their gear grounded in front of them.

The team leaders went over the sequence of events while reinspecting the gear their teams would be taking with them.

Hollister and Sangean stood at the doorway looking out at the scene from inside Operations. "So we'll alternate supervising the inserts and then do the same thing with teams coming out," Major Sangean said.

"Yes, sir. That should allow each of us to get at least one look at each team."

"While you are up, I'll be here. And vice versa."

"Fine with me."

"In the event we make contact, we drop what we can in terms of training and go for the situation."

"In case we get someone hurt—without contact?"

"We'll handle it like a battle injury. We've alerted Dust-Off that we might have a need to call them."

"I've been over there . . . 'cross the perimeter to their operations office myself," Sergeant Kurzikowski added. "They know who we are, and I'm feelin' pretty good about them. They seem to act like they care if we have problems out there."

"Nice to hear. We square on freqs and call signs?"

"Yessir, and so are all the team leaders," Kurzikowski said.

A captain entered Operations. He was tall and wore a faded one-piece flight suit. He stopped, looked over Sangean and Hollister as his eyes adjusted to the dimmer light inside. He snapped his baseball cap, topped with Senior Aviator's wings, from his head and stuck his hand out to Major Sangean.

"Major, I'm Keith, Scott Keith. I'm the air mission commander for today."

Sangean took his hand and looked over his shoulder toward the choppers landing and shutting down. "You were at the briefing?"

"Yes, sir. I think I'm up on the mission, unless you folks have made any last-minute changes." He smiled. "And I'm pretty sure we can handle just about anything you need—as long as we don't exceed the fuel requirement I've laid on."

"Well, you're gonna have to go over the last-minute stuff with Hollister here. Your people eat lunch yet?" Sangean asked.

"Yes, sir. But we might be able to handle some coffee or cold drinks if you have 'em and if we have time."

Sangean looked at Hollister. "You call it."

"I don't think you're going to find any major changes, but let's go over it again," Hollister said, nodding at Sangean, then leading Keith back out the door toward the mess hall.

On the pad and in the open field behind it stood two sets of insert choppers—one set cranked and one waiting. Hollister was already inside the C&C for the first lift, checking out the commo, his headset, and his own personal gear.

He watched Team 1-5 load the insert slick, then he rechecked his notebook for an extra look at the call signs and frequencies. He knew he had the important ones written on his forearm in ballpoint pen, but didn't want to trust the longevity of the markings on his own skin.

He made one last-minute check of his own gear to be sure he had everything. He was wearing light web gear with ammo, first-aid packet, canteen, compass, and URC-10 radio. On the bench seat running the width of the chopper, he had secured his rifle with the seat belt. Under his jump seat he had wedged a PRC-77 radio and handset. He had learned never to trust his communications capability to a chopper. If it went down—so did his ability to get help beyond waving his arms at passing choppers.

The 1-5 team leader, a slim redheaded buck sergeant named Nessen, was doing a decent job of loading his six-man team and communicating his readiness to the chopper's peter pilot.

Behind the insert ship, an empty chase ship gently rocked at flight idle. Inside, Hollister could make out the shadowed outline of 1st Platoon's platoon sergeant, McCullen, who was riding as belly man.

Hollister looked back toward the teams that were still waiting. They were from the 1st Platoon, and Hollister searched for the platoon leader, who was going out as a patrol member to get some more experience. Hollister spotted him in the third chalk. He had an unfortunate name for an infantry officer—Patten—spelling notwithstanding. Almost no one could pass up making some comment about it when meeting him. Hollister was happy that he was able to resist.

Patten had spent six months in a rifle platoon with the 9th Infantry Division in the Mekong Delta, and while he had as little rank as an officer could have, he did have some field experience. Seeing him suited up and in war paint was enough to satisfy Hollister that his instructions about officer training were being followed.

"Clear?" Captain Keith, the command pilot, asked.

"Clear left—clear right," the door gunners replied, looking out their respective sides and to the rear.

"We ready back there?" Keith asked over the intercom.

Hollister raised his hand and waved affirmatively. He knew the copilot would see the signal and pass it to the aircraft commander.

"Roger that," Keith said over the intercom as he brought the fairly new Huey D model up to a point where the skids lost their spread and the chopper was barely exerting any weight onto the pad.

"Okay, people. We are on our way," Keith said as the chopper came up tail first and seemed to drag the nose forward and up—reluctantly.

The chopper made that predictable dip at the point where its forward motion fully replaced any upward motion. Hollister leaned forward and out to look at the choppers behind them. The insert and the chase lifted off simultaneously— the chase staggered to the left rear of the insert ship. He took his eyes off the slicks and looked out and above the C&C for any sign of the other choppers.

The copilot caught Hollister's search. "Sir," he said, "the guns are lifting off the arming area at the airstrip now. They will rendezvous with us as planned—just outside the wire, heading west."

Hollister raised his hand to the copilot, who was to his rear, and nodded his head to acknowledge the information. He had made the decision to leave the armed gunships at the airfield rather than park them near the Old Warrior Pad because so little parking space was available—most of it taken up by teams and extra lift choppers.

Making a quick check of the call sign on his arm, Hollister flipped a toggle switch in the small overhead switch box in order to transmit on only one frequency. "Falcon this is Houston Three. Over."

While he waited for a reply from the air force forward air controller, Hollister continued to scan the air around him.

"Houston Three, this is Falcon," the FAC pilot's voice responded over Hollister's helmet headset.

"What's your location?"

"I'm over the LZ, at thirty-five hundred feet, enjoying the view. Over."

"Good deal. We are en route. You should see us coming your way in a couple of minutes. What's the condition of the LZ? Over."

"Haven't seen anything that bothers me. There are some civilians about two klicks to the south, screwing with a Lambretta engine along the candy stripe. Over," the FAC replied.

"Well, keep an eye on them. They just might be LZ watchers."

"Roger that. Standing by here."

"Roger. Break. Reptile Six, Houston Three. Over," Hollister said into his mouthpiece, trying to establish communications with the gunship lead.

"Your ten o'clock, Three," Captain Stanton said from the backseat of his Cobra.

Hollister caught the full disk of the lead chopper two thousand meters in front of his C&C, making a hard right turn to keep from running away from the slick flight.

"Okay—got you. You set?"

Stanton clicked his mike button twice.

"Stand by," Hollister said as he leaned out again and looked back at the insert ship. He wanted to make one more check with the team leader. "Houston One-five, Three. Commo check. Over."

Hollister could hear the sounds of the buffeting inside Sergeant Nessen's chopper as soon as he keyed his mike. "This is One-five. Lima charlie. Over."

"Same here. You up?"

"We're ready, sir," Nessen said, a little false bravado in his voice.

"Good. We're going to put you and the chase in a short orbit while I make one last victor romeo of the LZ. I want to make sure we don't have a welcoming party."

"I can dig that. Over."

"Don't go anywhere," Hollister said, trying to lighten it up for Nessen a bit.

"You get that?" Hollister asked Keith over the intercom.

"Rog. We'll be there in zero four, and I'll hold everyone else in an orbit above us."

"Houston Control, we are zero four out for a reckie. If no problems, we will begin insert immediately after that. Over."

"Roger, Houston Three. Three Alpha Romeo standing by," the Operations radio operator said.

Hollister's headset was quiet for less than thirty seconds before Major Sangean's voice broke in. "Three, this is Six. We are at flight idle on the pad. Two-one is also standing by for you to take them in. Let me know when you are clear, and we will start our insert into LZ Bravo. Over."

"Roger, Six. Will notify you when One-five clears. Over."

"Understood. Out."

Captain Keith came up on the intercom for all to hear. "I got it," he said, taking control of the chopper from the copilot. The chopper immediately began to lose altitude. "Chief? You guys awake?" Keith asked the crew chief and door gunner.

"Cocked and locked," came the reply.

The door gunner next to Hollister had a tight grip on the M60 machine gun mounted on a pedestal welded to the chopper. He kept the muzzle up and slightly toward the approaching LZ as he scanned it with his eyes shielded by his aviator's sunglasses.

"We're here, folks," Keith said.

Hollister clicked his mike button twice. He leaned out as far as his seat belt would allow and surveyed the large open area dead ahead of them. "Let's look over the alternate LZ first and then check out the primary."

Keith raised his Nomex-gloved hand to signal Hollister, then laid the chopper over and then back to adjust the approach to cover the touchdown point on me alternate LZ.

At not much more than twenty feet off the tops of the weeds, Keith flashed across the LZ at seventy knots. No one inside the chopper spoke. All eyes were on the nearest tree lines and the pathways they had spotted earlier.

A flock of mud ducks feeding in a puddle of water near the far end of the clearing took wing in panic and followed a leader in the flock to a nearby field that had taller grasses.

At the far end of the open area, Keith pulled the nose up, slowing the chopper and easing it over the stand of brush and small trees. He laid the cyclic over toward his right knee and pushed a little right pedal to begin a lazy turn back toward the clearing—and toward the primary LZ. "Nothing up here."

"Clear. Nothing," the gunners said.

"Well, I sure didn't see anything. Let's hope the other one is clear, too," Hollister said.

The landing area they were about to use also appeared to be clear. Hollister made one final commo check with the FAC, guns, and Sergeant Nessen as the C&C took up its position above the insert chopper.

"Okay. Let's do it."

The insert ship broke out of the orbit and headed for a low-level approach to the LZ. The chase followed a hundred and fifty meters behind, while the Cobras shot forward with their greater speed to prowl the LZ before the arrival of the slicks.

Hollister swallowed hard and pressed the mike button on the drop cord that tied him into the chopper radios and intercom. "Houston, Houston Three. We are beginning first insert. Out."

CHAPTER 13

The Cobras bracketed the landing zone as they flew down the flanking tree lines, barely feet above the treetops. At the far end of the LZ, they turned, crossed over each other, and started back on the side opposite their first pass.

The insert chopper reached the last clump of vegetation before it would make its descent onto the paddy field. As it did, the pilot raised the nose of the aircraft, which slowed it measurably.

Above and behind the insert ship, Hollister watched the chopper's progress, checked the location of the chase ship, and looked around for a last check of the others. The Cobras, still searching the trees and hedges for VC, were targets for ground fire. The FAC was more than a mile to the west, making lazy figure eights in the sky.

Looking back at the insert ship, Hollister could see Nessen and his men moving closer to the open cargo doors, some stepping onto the right skid as they readied themselves to leap off.

The insert chopper reached a point just short of the desired touchdown point, and the pilot pulled back on the cyclic to stop forward momentum. The chopper halted, settled onto the ground with a rocking motion, and Nessen's team bolted from the right side of the chopper.

No sooner had the last man's feet hit the ground running than the pilot pulled pitch. As he did, he announced his intentions to advise the other choppers: "Comin' up and right."

The chopper completely cleared the LZ, and the chase ship followed the same path the insert ship had taken, though it failed to touch down. It, too, passed beyond the far end of the LZ and broke right and up.

As the two slicks gained altitude to fall into formation with the orbiting C&C, Hollister watched Nessen's team move from the touchdown point to the cluster of trees that would conceal them—for the time being.

The team members moved quickly, but were too close together, and no one was looking to their rear. All were watching the other three directions while moving to their rally point.

They disappeared into the trees, and Hollister checked his watch to give him a better idea of how long each insert and each extraction would take. He ran his fingers down the helmet cord and found the mike button. He moved the mike closer to his lips and pressed the button. "Houston Six, Three. Over."

"Six, go."

"You can launch now. Over."

"Any problems?" Sangean asked from Cu Chi.

"Negative. But One-five still hasn't reported the LZ condition yet."

"Roger," Sangean said as his C&C lifted off the Old Warrior Pad with a pickup flight ready to take Nessen's men out of the LZ.

"Roger. We'll be returning for the next lift as soon as I get an up from One-five."

"Roger. Out," Sangean said.

Dropping the mike cord, Hollister looked down at his watch, worried that Nessen hadn't reported in yet. He grabbed the mike button again. "Anybody see anything?" he asked the chopper crew.

"They're in trees all right. I haven't seen anything that looks hinky, though," Captain Keith said.

"Well, they're taking their sweet time." Unable to wait any longer, Hollister switched back to the Tactical frequency. "Houston One-five, this is Three. Over."

No answer.

He raised his voice, as if it would make any difference. "One—five . . . this is Three. Over."

A crackling sound came over Hollister's headset. It was broken up, but understandable. " . . . is One-five. We are in. LZ is cold. Handset trouble. Do you hear me? Over."

"This is Three. I understand you have commo problems. You are in and cold. Is that correct? Over."

"That's . . . 'firmative. Over."

"You able to fix the problem with commo?"

There was a long pause—no reply.

"Damnit, man, stay with me," Hollister said to himself out loud.

Suddenly, the quality of the transmission changed for the better, and Nessen's voice, though whispering, came through loud and clear. "New handset. How now? Over."

"Lima charlie. How me? Over."

"Same."

"Okay. Six is off Old Warrior and inbound to pick you up. We will be clearing out. Reptile Six is remaining on station. You have a problem, let him know. Out."

Nessen clicked his handset twice, and that ended their conversation.

"Let's go pick up another load," Hollister said to Keith.

The two flights of choppers crossed each other just west of Cu Chi. They exchanged waves, but no radio traffic. As Hollister's lift entered the approach pattern to land at Cu Chi, he began to monitor the cross talk between Sangean, his pilots, and Sergeant Nessen. The timing worked out so that as Hollister's choppers landed at the Old Warrior Pad to pick up Sergeant Glover's team to take them out, Sangean was picking up Nessen's team.

The pickup at Cu Chi took longer than the one in the field. First there was a warning light on in one of the slicks that needed attention. Once that was resolved, First Sergeant Morrison came out to Hollister's ship idling on the pad to ask him to hold up.

The first sergeant needed to find a soldier who had to be taken out of the training exercise to go home on emergency leave. His mother had been in a car accident and wasn't expected to live. Morrison's problem was that he wasn't able to track down the soldier and was afraid they were about to insert him into the training LZ. No sooner had he explained the situation to Hollister than Sergeant Dewey ran up to say they had found him.

Hollister's second lift got off twenty minutes late, and that bothered him. En route to the LZ again, he switched to the Admin frequency to talk to Sangean without tying up the Tactical frequency the pilots and the teams needed. "Six, Three. Over."

"What have you got?" Sangean replied.

"I'm more than a little concerned that I might have misjudged the turnaround time."

"Yeah, we might just be getting our root in a wringer here. Let's see how the next few teams go. We may have to break off and try this later on in the week."

"I don't want to take so long doing this that we're creating a target area for any hotshot VC looking to put a notch on his AK47 butt."

"I hear you. Let's see how it goes. Then I'll decide if we pull the plug."

"Roger that," Hollister said. He waited for Sangean to say anything else and heard no more transmissions. He flipped the toggle switch back to the Tactical frequency and took a look at his watch. It was taking too much time. He had been at it long enough to know when to worry. He decided to see what he could do to decrease the turnaround.

Sangean's lift had picked up Nessen's team without a hitch. The two flights crossed each other again at the Cu Chi base camp perimeter. That meant the alternating flights were lopsided and Hollister had to pick up the lost time. "We got any more speed in these babies?"

"I'll see what I can do. But know that next time back we have to go to the refueling point for some chopper juice," Keith replied.

The increased speed was almost unrecognizable.

Two more series of inserts and extractions plus a refueling stop went smoothly. During that time Hollister filled three pages of his notebook with cryptic notes he would use to critique the performances later.

As he made a note about the apparent lack of fitness of one of the soldiers on the LZ who couldn't keep up, he was interrupted by a call from Sangean.

"We have a monkey wrench from higher. If you haven't put your load into the LZ yet—hold up. I'll be right back to you. Stand by."

"Wilco. Standing by," Hollister replied. He looked down at the team he had just inserted and shook his head—too late. He then looked around the chopper, toward the copilot, with whom he could make eye contact. He shrugged as if questioning. He saw Keith raise his hand. "Pick up on guard."

Hollister flipped the toggle switch in the overhead box to allow him to monitor the aviation emergency frequency. It was a mess of overlapping conversations and excited messages. Somewhere to the north a battalion of the 1st Infantry Division had locked onto an NVA unit that was standing to fight. The division commander had requested that blocking forces be placed behind the enemy unit to prevent their escape. The problem was with air assets. There were not enough organic choppers available to move the blocking force.

"They're gonna yank us for sure," Keith said.

"Shit!" Hollister responded. "You sure?"

"We're the only slick platoon in the whole fucking corps area that isn't committed to combat ops today. Who else are they gonna pull?"

"Okay, then let's get ready to scoop up this team we just inserted. I'm going to give Sergeant Jackson a warning order, just in case we have to let you guys go."

Hollister flipped to the Tactical frequency. "Six, Three. I'm going to give One-two the word to stand by for our lift to extract him."

"This is Six. Roger that. I got the word. They want the slicks *and* the guns ASAP. Pull that team. I'm turning around with my load to head back to Old Warrior."

"Roger. Break. Houston One-two, this is Three. Have you monitored?"

Sergeant Jackson replied, in a hoarse whisper, "This is One-two. Roger. I copied. Understand—prepare for extraction immediately?"

"That's affirm. We're going to make a wide orbit and wait for you. Tell us when you're ready—but make it fast."

The sergeant promised his best, and Hollister looked over to the copilot for acknowledgment. He nodded.

As they made the first orbit, Hollister heard Keith groan over the intercom. "What?" he asked.

"Shit's getting ready to hit the fan. On the aviation freq there's a big flap about what constitutes ASAP. They want us *now* and not after your people are finished pulling this team," Keith said.

"No fucking way!" Hollister replied as Sangean's voice filled his headset. "Three, how long?"

"Stand by. Break. One-two, how close are you?"

Sergeant Jackson's voice was jerky and breathy, obviously on the move in the trees. "You can start in now. My guess is we are zero three from the tree line."

"Roger. Break. Six, we should be able to make this happen in under one zero mikes."

"Getting real heat. Higher wants us to leave the team and come back with these choppers or some other unit later in the day."

Out of reflex Hollister looked out at the horizon for any signs of bad weather. The memory of being left behind and switching chopper units, turning it all into a nightmare for him, was as fresh as the day it had happened on his first tour. "Neg-a-tive! Bad, bad move. We can pull them out and have these choppers back at your location in under two zero minutes."

"You firm on that?"

The fact that Sangean seemed to trust his recommendation felt good to Hollister. He wanted to make sure he was right. "Hold one."

He looked back to the copilot and asked over the intercom, "How are we on fuel? How soon can we be on the deck? Are my numbers realistic?"

Keith answered, "Good on fuel, we are zero two out. Everyone's on their toes. Numbers are good—if we don't run into any problems."

"Thanks," Hollister said and switched back to Sangean. "I *really* don't want to farm this pickup out. It's too long on the ground on a compromised PZ. Hell, who doesn't know where this team is? My guess is the only one who could fuck up their location is a new chopper crew. Over." He quickly keyed the intercom, "Sorry, no offense."

The copilot looked over and smiled, forgiving Hollister his remark.

"Okay. You go with what you got. I'll get them off our backs. Out," Sangean said without hesitation.

The insert chopper skimmed along the PZ as if it were gliding. The air was calm, and the winds were still. Sergeant Jackson's team burst from the trees and headed to the chopper—last man facing to the rear.

Then the order of march got screwed up. The soldier who was having trouble keeping up fell behind the one who was providing rear security. Jackson dropped back and tried to help the stumbling soldier, who was gasping for breath, his legs giving out under him. This created two groups on the PZ—one of four and one of two.

"Shit! We don't need this!" Hollister said. "Chase, you in position?" he asked because the chopper was directly behind and slightly below the C&C and Hollister couldn't see him.

"That's affirm," the belly man replied.

"Okay, stay sharp. Don't know where we're going here, but I got a feeling this could go sour. Let's not be asleep if it does."

The chase clicked back in acknowledgment.

The pickup ship sat on the PZ, light on its skids, waiting for the team to get on board. The first three LRPs jumped in and waited for Sergeant Jackson, the tail gunner, and the stumbling soldier to get to the chopper.

Within twenty meters of the chopper, the soldier began to vomit, buckling over and quickly emptying his stomach contents.

"Oh . . . shit," Keith remarked over the intercom. "He just puked all over one of his buddies."

"That's the least of his troubles. He's got to face those guys when they get back. He's gonna wish he'd stayed on the LZ," Hollister said.

After several more very long seconds of dragging the exhausted soldier to the chopper, the other half of the team got in and the pickup pilot announced, "Coming out."

Hollister looked around for any sign of a threat to the chopper's flight, then up and behind them to check on the chase, the FAC, and the gunships still orbiting the PZ. He looked back down to check on the progress of the pickup ship, which was gaining speed and some altitude as it reached the end of the large clearing.

Then Hollister saw the slight puff of smoke coming from a point across the landing zone, near the alternate landing site. He automatically drew a mental line from the firing point to the slick trying to get up and out of the landing zone. The fields of fire for the enemy marksmen was clear.

"Taking fire! I'm taking fire! Breaking right," the pilot of the pickup ship hollered over the radio.

"We got him," Captain Stanton said. "We're rolling in on 'em now."

Hollister looked over his shoulder and spotted the Cobras breaking out of their orbit and crossing under his chopper toward the source of the enemy fire.

"I'm in a trick!" the pickup pilot yelled. "Fucked-up pedals!"

"He's got some control linkage damage. He'll have to set it down. Hold on a sec," Keith said as he switched from the intercom to the pilot of the troubled ship.

The sun was starting to close in on the horizon—far beyond Cambodia. Hollister couldn't remember the light data he had read that morning, so he held his arm out full-length and bent his fingers ninety degrees to his palm. He counted four fingers plus between the horizon and the sun. With little quick math, twenty minutes per finger, he estimated that he had from eighty to a hundred minutes before dark made their life really miserable. He had a bad feeling about it all. He had to act fast.

"All right. Listen up. Chase—you get on them. If they go down, pick up the crew. We'll take the C and C in for the team. I don't want to mix loads. You got that? Chase?"

"Roger that."

"One-two?"

"Roger. Over."

"Up front?"

Keith waved his left hand so Hollister could see it above the armor-plated slide near his window.

"Okay. Break. Houston Control. We have a chopper going in. Have taken fire. Request additional gunships, security element, recovery aircraft, and replacement slicks. Details as soon as I can . . ."

Sangean's voice came up on the radio. "Okay. We got it. We are screwed on the backups. My complete flight has been released to refuel en route to Big Red One. I'm going to see if I can get them back. Do what you have to. Keep me advised."

The crippled chopper wobbled across a row of trees and found a large cluster of geometric rice paddies that would serve as a decent landing zone. At less than fifty feet off the ground, the chopper flew askew with its tail drifting out to the left.

"He's going to put it near the intersection of those two tree lines," Keith said.

"Fine. Tell him to get out, leave the chopper, and haul ass to the chase. Got it?"

Keith gave instructions to the aircraft commanders of the crippled ship and the chase ship and then came back to Hollister. "Okay, they got it."

"Any more fire coming out of that position?" Hollister asked.

Stanton came up on the radio at the end of his third firing pass. "I've put eight pairs of rockets in there, a couple dozen forty-mike grenades, and a shit-pot seven-six-two minigun ammo."

"And?"

"And it looks like to me that we've fucked up their sight picture. No firing for the last few minutes."

"Okay," Hollister said. "Let's widen your orbit to cover the two slicks and still be able to smoke the enemy position if they start some shit again."

Hollister looked back toward the chopper going in. It landed roughly, making rippling rings in the paddy water. Even before it came to rest, everyone bailed out. The crew went to the rear toward the spot they gauged the chase to be picking for a landing, and Jackson's team ran toward the tree line for concealment.

Hollister knew that no one wanted to be inside a downed chopper for several reasons, one of which was the likelihood of fire. He watched the chase ease into the spot behind the downed chopper and pick up the four-man crew. The chase wasn't on the ground for more than a few seconds before it lifted off again.

"Okay, One-two, we're inbound to pick you up. We are on final now. Stand by," Hollister said to Sergeant Jackson and his team in the trees as the C&C began to slide down the same slot the chase had just used.

"Houston Three, this is Six. Do not pick up One-two. I say again. Do not pick up One-two!" Sangean ordered.

"Go around. Break. One-two, stand by. We are going around. Break, go ahead, Six."

"They want us to secure the chopper until the recovery chopper can get there. Now I know what you're going to say. Don't. It won't do any good. Just pass the mission to One-two to secure the downed chopper. I have been promised that a hook is on the way to pluck it out."

"Roger. Understand. Give me a couple of minutes to get the gears shifted again here."

Sangean clicked twice.

Hollister dropped his head into his hand and let it all sink in for a minute. He was reaching for the mike button again when one of Jackson's men called him.

"Houston Three, this is Houston One-two alpha. I'm the alpha tango lima. The tango lima is buckled over with someone barfing his brains out. I'm taking over command of the team. We're secure for now, but I have two really sick troops down here."

"Jeezus!" Hollister said. "What else can go wrong?"

"You gotta ask," Keith said over the intercom.

"One-two alpha. You hold a sec. Let me work out a few things." Hollister remembered the young assistant patrol leader from their briefback. "Your new mission is to stay there, put out security, and don't let anyone screw with that chopper."

"Wilco. I'm kinda worried about my two pukers though."

"Stand by."

"Let's go over this," Hollister said over the intercom. "I've got a downed chopper, a team that's two-thirds effective and not able to run if it makes serious contact, and . . ."

"And you've got six minutes' more fuel before I have to go for more," Keith said.

"Sure. Why not?" Hollister said sarcastically. "Okay, here's the deal. I can't get a team in, can't pull these guys out, and can't leave them alone."

"Why not?" Keith asked.

"Because that assistant team leader is a PFC with less than a month in Juliet Company."

"So?" Keith asked.

"So drop me off."

"With them?" Keith asked.

"Yep. They need help, and they need someone who is more concerned with them than a fucking downed chopper. No offense."

"I buy that. You want it. You got it," Keith said, rolling over into a descending right turn, making a wide approach to the downed chopper.

In the seconds he had, Hollister unhooked his M16 from the belt on the empty seat next to him. He folded his map and stuffed it into his pocket, took a deep breath, and squeezed the mike button.

"Six, I've got two on the ground with something that sounds like food poisoning. But I'm no doctor. I think the best way to keep this from going bad quick is for me to get into it. So I'm going in and take up the sick tango lima's slack. The C and C is headed back for fuel and for you."

He heard Sangean key the handset back to Operations, but not speak. He must have been letting the information sink in. He let up and then pressed the button again.

"Okay. If that's your call, we'll support it. Give me your situation as soon as you are through eyeballing the team leader."

"Wilco."

"Don't do anything stupid."

"Promise."

Keith took the chopper to a point on the ground between the downed chopper and the trees that hid Team 1-2.

As they got closer to the ground, Hollister could feel his heartbeat picking up speed and his breathing getting shallower. He tried to take a deep breath to keep himself from getting nervous about the lone dash to the tree line. He knew that he needed all the wind he could get, and tension in his chest and a tight gut would be no help at all.

Hollister didn't wait for the forward motion to stop or the skids to touch down before he leaped out into the calf-deep paddy water. As soon as he hit bottom, he was less confident in the rubbery feeling in his legs.

As he ran, the water swirling from the chopper downwash and the water he was kicking splashed into his eyes. He tried to wipe the muddy wash from his face with his shirtsleeve, but was only partially successful.

As quickly as he got out from under the rotor disk, he looked up and saw one of the team members just inside the trees pop a signal panel. The momentary flash of international orange was all Hollister needed to set his course for the right spot in the tree line.

It never changed—crossing the open area from a chopper to any clump of trees was always difficult. A soldier making the dash had to believe that every VC in Giap's army was watching and was an expert marksman. The ground was never even or predictable. The equipment never rode right. The distance to the trees was always too far. And wind—you always ran out of wind.

A LRP had to put up with all this while trying to talk himself through it. *Don't panic. Watch your step. Head up, crouch low. Carry your weapon at the ready. Watch for puffs of smoke. Remember that you probably won't hear any shooting until you are away from the chopper. Run faster! Run lots faster!*

Hollister's dash to friendlies was complicated by his efforts to carry his rifle and a PRC-77 radio. He was no more than four long steps from the chopper when he lost his grip on the handset. It fell and went under the surface of the paddy water, bouncing back out as the coiled cord jerked it

Picking it up broke his stride and almost caused him to lose his footing. He promised to remember the difficulty of the unruly handset and cord and tie it down next time. He was just glad it was encased in a plastic battery bag. He guessed it would have a fairly good chance of surviving the dunking.

By the time he was halfway to the team, the C&C chopper had cleared the trees at the end of the landing zone and was climbing away, its blade and turbine noise fading rapidly.

The feeling of being naked came back to Hollister as he regained his stride, the handset secured.

The team had four effectives and two men who were totally wiped out by something that had turned them into pathetic victims. They had both suffered recurring bouts of vomiting and diarrhea, profuse sweating, nausea, and extreme weakness. One of the unaffected members was the team medic. He had talked to the medics back at Cu Chi, and they all had decided it was some type of food poisoning and what they needed was plenty of fluids until they could be taken out.

Both were asked about being medevaced, and they asked not to be taken out unless they got worse. By the time Hollister got to them, they were better than they had been and were at least conversational.

"We're in a bad spot. The downed chopper near us is a registration point for anybody with a rusty mortar, and no one can resist the temptation of coming our way to strip it out," Hollister reported to Sangean over a weak radio link.

"Well, I've got some more bad news for you."

"Okay?"

"They can't tear loose a Chinook to come out there and pick up that chopper before dark. You'll have to stay the night and keep an eye on it. All—I guess we have about half an hour till dark. So you have work to do. Let me know if you need anything, and I'll have someone fly it out."

"If we get hit?"

"We've organized a reaction force using all of three and four element. They'll be spending the night locked and cocked on the pad. You get a rustle in the weeds, and we'll send 'em," Sangean said.

"You gonna walk 'em out?"

"No, I raised enough hell that they gave me back the guns you released. When they broke the news about the Chinook, they coughed the slicks back up. They'll be parked here, too."

"That's good. I'd like some more work done on finding out what got these folks so sick out here. We don't need the whole outfit coming down with this crap."

"Roger. We're on it. Let me know what else you need."

Hollister had to treat the position as if it were a normal RON location and not the training site they had planned on leaving well before dark. He first took the time to find out what each man had brought and redistributed the two sick LRPs' equipment and ammo to the others. Then he got on the radio and plotted artillery and flares to be on call in the event they made contact that night.

Just after dark Hollister sent two of the team members out to the chopper to pick up the machine guns. They brought them back, set them up at the two most likely avenues of approach to the team position, and then went back for the long belts of ammo.

As a final measure, they set up a claymore mine under the fuel cell on the chopper. In the event they had to E&E they would want to blow and burn as much of the chopper as they could. Since they had not come in with any other explosives, they had to rely on the claymore.

After setting up for the night, Hollister made a second check of each man and then went back and made sure that PFC Curtis, the assistant patrol leader, had the radios working and enough batteries to get them through the night.

It only took half an hour for the temperature to drop enough for Hollister to feel the chill in his wet uniform. He had brought nothing with him to ward off the cold night air. He was also less than pleased that he had only brought six magazines of M16 ammo, which had to last him the whole night.

He made one more commo check and sent a SITREP back to Operations.

He began to shiver.

CHAPTER 14

Curtis tugged on Hollister's sleeve and pulled him back from a netherworld of distorted images and thoughts. He wasn't really asleep. He was in that margin where consciousness was on one side and sleep on the other. He tried to shake off the fog.

"We got movement on the other side of the paddies," Curtis whispered directly into Hollister's ear.

Shit, Hollister thought. He sat up and automatically tried to look more alert than he was. His chest hurt from too many cigarettes, and his joints ached from the damp ground. He looked in the direction of the trees on the far side of the downed chopper. His view was obscured by the brush that concealed him, and he had to move to a better vantage point.

Just eight feet from his original position, he was able to see across the paddies and beyond the chopper.

"We been pickin' up movement, but nothin' definite. Could be anything," Curtis said.

Hollister took the Starlight scope from Curtis and pointed it in the direction of the movement. He put his eye up to the eyepiece and steadied his hold on the clumsy night-vision device.

The green-on-green world of the Starlight scope was marred by the random spots of light that filled the sky and the ground all around them. Ambient light was necessary for the Starlight to have something to amplify. But when it picked up a source of light, it was amplified to the point where it washed out the fainter images that were painted in low light.

He handed the Starlight back to Curtis. "No use." He rolled over, leaned back to his original position, and pulled his binoculars out of the claymore bag that he carried things in.

Back in position, he looked at the trees again. He could make out shapes and trees and voids in the trees and lumps that could have been anything—even VC soldiers. "Handset," he whispered to Curtis.

"Houston, this is Three. Fire mission. Over."

"This is Houston. Send your mission. Over."

"Fire mission. Request illumination at five one niner, one one eight. Direction zero zero five degrees. Target troops in the open. Over."

"Roger, good copy, stand by," Base replied.

There was no telling who would be firing the mission since none of the artillery units in the area were tasked to be in direct support of the LRP mission. Operations would have to make the request and find out if the unit wanted to handle the fire mission by speaking directly with Hollister or through Operations.

Hollister had asked for a fire-support team to be attached to the company in his request to Major Fowler, but still hadn't received an answer. He was living the reason—coordination is communication, and communication is understanding.

"Standing by," Hollister replied, then turned to Curtis. "Tell everyone to get flat and check their camouflage again. If we get illum, it will give us away as fast as it will give the VC away."

Curtis simply balled up his fist and tapped Hollister's arm to let him know he understood and would follow through.

Pulling back his cuff, Hollister looked at the time. It was just after midnight. Inside he groaned. That meant there were far too many hours until dawn. He really didn't want to make contact at night and have to call in a reaction force that would have to link up in the dark.

Impatiently, Hollister cupped his hand around the mouthpiece of the handset and pushed the press-to-talk button. "Houston, Three. What's the holdup on the flares?"

"This is Houston. They're checking the availability of a flare ship. Over."

"Negative, negative. I don't want a flare ship. If I need one, I'll need one for more hours than it can stay on station. Just get me some redleg light, and it'll do for now."

"Roger . . . negative on flare ship. Stand by," Sergeant Kurzikowski replied from Cu Chi.

One of the LRPs made a slight noise with his weapon. Hollister turned to Curtis and pulled him close by tugging on his shirt collar. "You tell every man to ease back. We got as much chance of this being civilians looking to steal chopper parts as not. You got it?"

"Yessir," Curtis said. He then crawled to the first man and whispered the message to him.

The squelch broke on the handset. "Three, illumination on the way."

"On the way, wait," Hollister replied.

They heard the report of the howitzer that fired the flare round a split second before they heard the round slice through the sky near them and burst. The canister broke clear of the parachute flare as the flare blossomed and the parachute inflated. The canister made a woo-wooing sound as it tumbled toward the ground somewhere, hundreds of meters away.

The intense illumination of the flare round poured bright white light down on everything beneath it. The shadows it cast danced back and forth as the flare wobbled under the unstable parachute.

Before the flare reached its fullest brightness, Hollister made sure to shield his eyes in order not to lose his night vision. He closed one eye completely and held his hand over the brow of the other.

Raising his binoculars, he quickly scanned the trees for any movement. He thought he saw movement, but the flare quickly drifted toward him and made it harder to see the trees. He picked up the handset and whispered, "Houston, add two hundred, fire one. Over."

"Houston—roger, add two zero zero, fire one. Wait."

The first flare was getting very close to the ground and had already drifted over the top of the LRPs when it suddenly flared up a bit and then burned out. The flare's smoking remains drifted into a paddy behind Hollister's position, dropping sparks. It hit the water, making a hissing sound.

The second flare burst two hundred meters upwind and silhouetted the tree line that Hollister was trying to see. He raised his binos again and scanned the entire tree line. There were two lumps in it, about four hundred meters from him. They could be VC, civilians crouched down, or nothing. He looked at Curtis and handed him the binos.

Curtis took a look, dropped the binos, and leaned back toward Hollister. "Could be anything." He raised the handset again and spoke softly. "End of mission. Out."

"Okay, gimme your M79," Hollister said.

Curtis handed him his grenade launcher and took Hollister's M16.

"What's in it?"

"HE," Curtis answered.

"Good, give me a second round, and let the others know I'm going out toward the chopper. Disarm the claymore out there."

"What's up?" Curtis asked, unsure of Hollister's moves.

"Gonna lob one near the lumps in the trees. Don't want to kill 'em, just spook 'em—in case they are civilians," Hollister whispered.

"Why out there?"

"I don't want to give our position away if they are VC and don't already know our location. So cover my ass."

Curtis pulled a second HE round out of his grenade pouch and handed it to Hollister. "Wait zero two until I tell the others and unhook the claymore," he said.

While the second flare burned out and Curtis made contact with each man to let him know the plan, Hollister slipped the cravat from around his neck and tied the M79 round to its center. He then retied the cravat so that the round rode in the hollow of his throat and wouldn't be likely to get wet on the way out to the chopper.

He then dumped his gear, his map, and his hat. He handed the radio handset to Curtis and moved out of the tight LRP perimeter.

He half floated and half crawled in the water until he reached a point that placed the suspected VC on the far side of the chopper and concealed his movements from them.

He rolled over on his side and looked up to make sure he knew where the chopper blades were.

It occurred to him as he crawled out in the slippery paddy that he could fire the M79 grenade and hit the blade only a few feet from him. He knew it was a long shot, but he didn't like the odds regardless of what they were.

Able to distinguish the blades from the sky, he rolled back and twisted himself into a seated position. Aware that his breathing was labored, he tried to take a few deep breaths and get himself back to a normal rate. It took long enough to aggravate him. He thought about giving up smoking again. He then remembered he had a pack of cigarettes in his water-filled shirt pocket. To him this was a sure sign he had become a REMF—wet cigarettes.

Settled, he raised the M79 to his shoulder and took up a good firing position. He spot-welded the thumb around the stock to his right cheekbone and reminded himself to control his breathing. Using a peculiar tree formation as a reference point, he took aim at a point near the lumps in the tree line. The area he was aiming for was farther away than the bursting radius of the HE round, and on his side of the lumps. He hoped the burst would flush or scatter them.

He took a deep breath, let half of it out, and repeated to himself, "Squeeze, squeeze, squeeze" until the M79 jerked comfortably and hurled the grenade out its barrel. Hollister didn't wait to see where it hit. He broke the barrel of the launcher, pulled out the expended canister, and loaded the other round.

The grenade took its lazy lob and landed just outside the trees in the water. On impact it detonated with a small flash, plenty of water, and a loud explosion.

Hollister raised the launcher and fired again. The second round landed twenty-five meters right and ten meters short of the first round. As it impacted, Hollister was already moving back toward the team position. With each move forward, he strained to listen for any reaction from the other tree line. There was no return fire, and little else could have been heard over his splashing and labored breathing.

Curtis reached to help Hollister up out of the paddy water onto the slightly drier ground. As Hollister then stood, turned, and flopped down, Curtis grabbed him. "Shssh! Listen."

It was all Hollister could do to hold his breath and listen without crying out for air. His lungs burned, and water and mucus were running from his nose. But then he heard it, too. A motorbike! Someone had started a motorbike on the far side of the trees where the lumps were.

He grabbed the binoculars from Curtis and scanned the tree line. He couldn't find the lumps. They might have still been in the area, but he had enough confidence in the light level to know they had at least moved.

The motorbike's engine revved two times, putted, and then revved again. "Look!" Curtis said, pointing to a break in the trees.

Hollister swung the binoculars to the point and saw what Curtis saw—a headlight painting the dirt road behind and beyond the trees. He dropped the binoculars and let out his air to gasp for more. "Okay, okay. They're gone."

By three A.M. Hollister could hardly control his shivering. He decided to sit up and move around a little to generate some heat. He rubbed his arms and legs and looked around at the others.

The moon had reached a point almost straight up, and the others' features were easy to see. Though he was cold and very uncomfortable, Hollister was pleased to see that the four LRPs who were tagged to be alert and on watch were doing just that. The team leader and the other soldier who had been sick earlier were better, but sapped of all their strength.

Hollister had been impressed with Curtis's plan, which took the load off them, and he collected extra water from the others to try to rehydrate the two who had lost so much.

He might have drifted off or not, but the sounds were unmistakable. They were mortars. Hollister had to wonder if he was imagining them. He tried to clear his head. He was sure. Mortars! No doubt! He had heard the thunking of six mortar rounds leaving their tubes through the humming of the bugs and the mosquitoes and the frog opera that filled the night. "Incoming!" he yelled in a stage whisper.

The others didn't need to be told. The noise was close enough and clear enough that they all knew what was next.

The first round landed at least four hundred meters south of the team's position. It was a sixty-millimeter mortar. In rapid order the other five landed in a hundred-meter circle near the first. All were long, since the apparent location of the mortar tubes was somewhere to the north.

The handset pressed to his face, Hollister yelled into it, "Incoming! We are taking incoming. Gimme that flare ship now, and stand by for redleg request."

"Roger. Do you have ground contact?"

"Negative. SITREP in five. Out." He dropped the handset into his lap and listened, holding his breath, ready for any sound that would tell him the next move.

Shit, he thought. Again!

The first round of the second volley landed out in the paddy behind the chopper—just north of the team. They were bracketed! Someone was adjusting the fire—someone close enough to see the impacting rounds and sure enough to know where the team was.

The second and third rounds landed closer. The fourth and fifth landed on their position. One detonated in the trees and sprayed the team with shrapnel. Hollister felt something strike his head and at the same moment he heard someone cry out. It might have been him.

The last round landed in the paddy on the other side of their position and threw mud and water up and over the nearest team members.

He shrugged off the impact of what he was sure was only flying debris— rocks, twigs, or something. He began to crawl toward Curtis and the others when he realized he couldn't see out of his right eye. He was sure it was just mud and wiped his face with his sleeve. For a moment his vision cleared, then it blurred again.

He reached up with his hand and tried to make a better wipe when he realized the fluid was hot and thick—it was his blood. For a second he resisted the urge to try to feel where it was coming from. What if it was serious? What if he had really taken a serious head shot? He remembered all the crap he had heard about the brain not feeling any pain and chastised himself just to *do it!*

He stopped and leaned back on his heels. He thought to wipe his hand off on his shirt before touching his head. It could have made a difference, he thought.

His fingers found the ragged skin on his head just over his right eye and in his hairline. He had a jagged piece of metal stuck in his head. He had a horrible thought about it being iceberglike. That more of it could be in his brain than sticking out. He tried to calm himself and continued to feel his way around the wound. It felt no bigger than a quarter. The edges of the wound and the shrapnel were very jagged, and the blood was streaming out and running down his face and hand.

He tried to gather some composure and assess the situation. He listened for more mortar rounds leaving the tube and heard none. It angered him that he only had the general direction of the mortar tubes fixed in his mind and no real idea of the distance. It meant that the mortarmen who had lobbed the rounds on them were not only very good, but had certainly broken down and gone.

He squinted to try to keep the blood out of his eye, as well as to brace himself for a more detailed examination of his wound. He used his other hand to help pull the small patch of hair around the wound aside. As he did he felt the mortar fragment move. It wasn't lodged in his skull, but had slipped under the skin through the hole it had made on entry.

He wiped off his fingers on his shirt again and reached for the frag. With a good grip, he clenched his teeth and pulled. It came out in his hand, a jagged piece of dense metal no bigger than a thumbnail.

As soon as he removed the frag, the bleeding increased. He wondered if he had done the right thing. He knew that he had to slow the bleeding and that he couldn't do the things he had to do and hold his head at the same time.

He pulled his floppy LRP hat from his pocket and folded the brim in on one side of it. He then forced it down on his head so that the heavier material of the brim pressed up against the wound. The salt from his sweat immediately registered on the wound and reassured him that there was some feeling there after all.

He gave the hat one more tug and grabbed for the handset again. "Houston, Three. We are under sixty mortar fire. They have us bracketed. I need redleg flare support if that flare ship is going to take more than zero five to get here. Over."

Kurzikowski's voice responded immediately, "Roger. Calling for redleg now over lima lima. Have you taken any ground fire? Any casualties?"

"Negative on the ground fire yet. Not sure yet on casualties. Stand by."

Hollister reached Curtis and they spoke, though neither one looked at the other. Instead, they searched the opposite halves of the small perimeter and the surrounding area for signs of casualties and any sign of approaching enemy troops. "What you got?"

Calmly, Curtis said, "Nothing on this side. I've got everyone locked and cocked, but we haven't seen any movement yet. You suppose they'll drop some more mortar fire on us?"

"Plan on it," Hollister replied. "Okay, here's the deal. I've got flares on the way, and they're ready with a reaction force back at Cu Chi. Let's not fool ourselves. More people couldn't know where we are if it was in the *Stars and Stripes*."

"Ah . . . Captain, there's one other thing," Curtis said tentatively.

"What?"

"I'm hit. I don't think it's a big thing, and I don't want to be a problem. But I'm bleedin' pretty good."

Hollister spun his head around and looked more closely at Curtis. He sat there, both hands down between his legs, holding a spot just above his left knee. The mottled moonlight, shadows, and blood on Curtis's hands made it hard for Hollister to see just what was Curtis and what was shadow. "Let go. Let me see," Hollister said.

Without arguing, Curtis pulled his hands away and blood began to pump in strong arcs out and onto the ground beneath him. Hollister knew Curtis was in trouble if they didn't get the bleeding stopped. He reached over and pressed the heel of his hand against the slice in Curtis's leg. With the other hand, he reached over and felt for any exit wound or bone break. "Can you move it?"

"Yessir. I think it's all okay 'cept for the bleeding."

"Okay, let's get that stopped." Hollister slipped the combat dressing from the first aid pouch on Curtis's web gear and tore it open. He pulled the four long, folded ties loose and threw two of them on one side of Curtis's leg. He tucked the other two under his leg and tied the four ends firmly on the outside of it. "We're gonna have to put a tourniquet on it if this doesn't stop the bleeding. You got a cravat on?"

"Yessir."

"Okay, let's see how this works. How much blood you think you've lost?" Hollister asked.

"Not that much," Curtis replied.

Hollister didn't believe him. He wiped his hand on his trousers to get the blood off and then reached down to the ground under Curtis and felt the puddle of pooled blood. It was at least a quarter inch deep, thick, almost jellylike, and covered an area about a foot and a half across. He didn't really know what that meant, except "not that much" wasn't how he would describe it.

"Okay . . . sit here, and don't move around. Let me know if it keeps bleeding. You got that?"

"Yessir," Curtis said as he picked up his M79 and broke it. He pulled out the HE round and replaced it with a shotgun round—for close combat. "Hope I don't need this."

"You and me both," Hollister said as he wiped the trickle of blood from his face and checked his watch. It would be two more hours until first light.

He scooted back to his radio and picked it up angrily. "Houston, Three! I got one WIA that might be able to hold till first light. But I need some goddamn illumination before all shit breaks loose here."

"Three, Six. I'm going to bring up a pair of guns and alert the reaction force. Should be there in less than three zero," Major Sangean said.

"Negative, negative. There is nothing you can do right now. If you get out here and run short of fuel we're sure to need you when you're gone. We have it under control right now. Just stand by. But I need help with coordination and fire support more than I need a C and C."

"Understood," Sangean said flatly, taking no offense at the curt reply.

Less than five minutes later, three AK47 rounds shattered the calm and whipped through the trees just fifty meters west of where they were. "Hold your fire," Hollister whispered to the others.

He cupped the handset again. "Contact! We are taking ineffective small-arms fire. Stand by . . . for more . . . But get me that fucking illumination. Now!"

"Should be any second now," Kurzikowski said, the frustration in his voice matching Hollister's.

A second burst of enemy fire pounded into the dirt and cut down some bamboo in the same location. Hollister was sure the shooters didn't know the team's exact location, and their second burst gave away their position. They were shooting from beyond the downed chopper, using it to mask their location from where they thought the American patrol was.

Hollister grabbed the handset again. "Check fire. DO NOT FIRE ILLUM. Wait for my command. And launch those gunships—NOW!"

"Roger. They just called us, ready to fire. I understand you want to fire at your command," Kurzikowski asked. "And you request snakes?"

"That's affirm. Stand by," Hollister replied as he wiped more blood from his face and hooked his fingers under the U-shaped protective bar on the top of the PRC-77. He grabbed his gear and rifle with the other hand and scooted on his butt toward the perimeter's center.

"Listen up," he whispered for all of them to hear. "I think they're gonna make a move for the area where they think we are. Who has a good pitching arm?"

"I do, sir," said the only black face on the team. It was Sergeant Jackson, the team leader—a tall, long-limbed man who looked like a track star.

"You think you're up to hurling a rock or two in that direction?" Hollister asked.

Jackson looked over to where the incoming small-arms fire had hit. "Sir, if I don't do something to pull my weight, I'll never hear the end of this. You tell me what you want."

"I want you to drop a rock or a stick over there to make them think we're there and moving around. If they go for it, I want you to do it again."

Jackson sat up and started patting the ground around him looking for something to throw.

Many of the random light sources that had been north of them during the early evening had been put out—cook fires, lanterns, and headlights of far-off traffic. Hollister reached for the Starlight scope and scanned the trees on the far side of the chopper.

He could plainly see the outline of two enemy soldiers moving a light machine gun to a better firing position. They hadn't fired it yet, but he was now sure where it was.

Four other soldiers were moving on their bellies in the paddy water toward the chopper. His guess was that they were going to try to hit the team and get to the chopper at the same time. He dropped the Starlight and tapped the team members who were looking away from him. "Jackson, when I say so, throw that rock. Curtis, give me your M79."

"Sir, I'm really good with this."

"You think you can hit the chopper with an HE round? You only have one chance."

"Yessir."

"Okay, who has the clacker for the chopper claymore?"

A hand came up with the detonating device in it.

Hollister took it. "I want them to get the chopper, and then we'll take the initiative. Curtis, put a second round in the trees directly behind the chopper after you hit it."

He spoke into the handset. "Tell the snakes to hold south of my position and come loaded for troops in the open. Illum standing by?"

"Roger the snakes. Affirm on the ilium. The flare ship got diverted."

"Fuck!" Hollister said over the radio.

"We roger that!" Kurzikowski said.

"Okay, when I call for illum, I may want it for quite some time. Do you have HE capability with the same redleg, or is that too much to ask?" he said sarcastically.

"Affirm. They are confident they can provide HE and illum at the same time."

"Stand by," Hollister said.

He dropped the handset into his lap, wiped the blood from his eye, and raised the Starlight. He could see four, then five, enemy soldiers at the chopper. Three of them were inside.

Hollister grabbed the handset. "Fire the illum, NOW!" He didn't wait for the reply.

"Okay, Jackson—do it!"

Jackson sat up, grabbed a small tree for leverage with his left hand, and hurled a full canteen up and over the trees to the area the VC had fired into only moments before.

The canteen landed with a thud. Two AKs opened up from the trees, painting green lines across the tops of the rice plants.

Hollister grabbed the claymore clacker with both hands. "Okay, Curtis, NOW!" he said as he squeezed the detonating device.

The claymore went up immediately, momentarily rocking the chopper before igniting the fuel cell. Before the fireball reached its full size, Curtis's M79 round hit the fire wall behind the door gunner's seat. The combination of the explosives and the fire scattered burning chopper parts in all directions. The VC who were on board were lost in the fireball, and the two who had been standing by the chopper were already facedown in the water.

The artillery flare popped and blossomed to the east, bathing the area in near daylight.

The LRPs then opened up with rifle and machine-gun fire. The two M60s from the chopper, plus the one the team had brought, chewed up the dike and tree line that held the enemy machine-gun team.

"I got 'em," Curtis yelled as he saw the two-man machine-gun team stand to try to get away from the fires the LRPs were pouring into their position. Curtis calmly raised his M79 to point far above the machine-gun team, then kept lowering it until they were in his sights. The illumination gave him all the time he needed to aim and fire.

The M79 thumped, hurled the HE grenade accurately across the open field, and detonated in the trees just above the VC.

"All right!" Hollister yelled, unable to contain his excitement.

They all hesitated—waiting for more enemy fire. Nothing. It was silent, save the heavy breathing of the team members.

"Here," Curtis said, pushing the M79 into Hollister's hand. "I can't do any more right now, Captain. I'm sorry."

Hollister took the grenade launcher and looked back at Curtis, who had pulled his cravat off and was tying it around his thigh. The pool of blood under him had grown to the size of a card table and was an ugly, black-looking ooze under the flare light.

"Houston, give me continuous illumination," Hollister snapped into the mouthpiece before reaching over to help Curtis with his tourniquet.

They came to a grunting agreement over how tight the tourniquet should be. Hollister then turned to Jackson. "Medic?"

"Not on this team."

"Did you bring a first aid kit?"

Jackson pointed to a breadbox-size canvas bag wedged into the crotch of a bush to keep it up off the ground.

A second artillery flare popped, replacing the dying light of the first. Under the light from the flare and the burning magnesium in the chopper, Hollister could see that Curtis was starting to lose his color and that his eyes were starting to look bad. He knew if he didn't get some fluid into Curtis's bloodstream, he would die from shock. The wound itself was serious, but didn't need to cost him his life.

The bag was heavy and hard to maneuver while kneeling. Still, Hollister pulled it free from the bush that supported it and dragged it to his side. He quickly unzipped the top and searched around in the tightly packed contents. The kit was stuffed with advanced first aid needs, more than most field-trained medics could use.

He found it An OD can, not much larger than a soup can. He peeled the top back and dropped the contents into his hand—a bottle of albumin, a blood expander, and an IV tube and needle. He showed it to Curtis, who nodded his head. Hollister looked around and whispered over the sounds of the hissing flare and the burning chopper, "Anyone ever done this?"

No one offered so much as a reply.

Hollister shrugged. How tough could it be? He'd seen it done, but had never tried himself. He readied the tube and bottle and tried to find somewhere to hang the bottle high enough so gravity would move the fluid into Curtis instead of dripping Curtis's blood into the bottle. Finding nothing obvious, he picked up his M16 and shoved it, muzzle first, into the soft earth. He reached into the second first aid packet on his own web gear and pulled out his compass. The dummy cord, made of a boot lace, came free with a jerk at each end. He tied the bottle to the lower sling swivel on. his upturned rifle butt.

The easy part was behind him, and Hollister knew it. He pulled the belt off Curtis's trousers, wrapped it around his arm, and began to search for a vein. Finding one, he decided not to screw around and make it uncomfortable for Curtis—so he plunged the needle into it.

Curtis flinched, and nothing happened. The fluid failed to drip into him. Hollister apologized. "I'm going to have to try this again. Stay with me."

There was little recognition out of Curtis, who was beginning to get more distant. He made an effort to reply, but his lips only moved.

A second try was more successful. Immediately, blood began to flow out of Curtis's vein into the low spot on the IV tube, where it stopped.

Hollister raised the tube so that it was a straight shot from the bottle of blood expander to Curtis's arm without a loop lower than his arm. The orange-colored section of the fluid reversed itself, and the albumin began to run into Curtis. "Okay, man. Just relax. We'll have you out of here in no time. Let me know if you need anything," Hollister said, and then waited for some sign of recognition from Curtis.

Curtis looked up at Hollister and smiled.

The ground fog and the low-hanging smoke from the fire and the flares made it more difficult to see beyond twenty meters. That bothered Hollister. He called Operations and requested a medevac to pick up Curtis.

A cock crowed somewhere near the team. And the horizon made the transition from black to the slate color that often came just before dawn in Vietnam. With it came a slight breeze and a change in temperature. It warmed them for a few minutes, and then the breeze caused the wet uniforms to become colder. Hollister tried to suppress his shivering, but failed.

Jackson tapped Hollister on the arm and handed him the radio handset. "Six," he announced.

"This is Three. Over," Hollister whispered into the mouthpiece.

"We are seven minutes out of your location with a Dust-Off. Your WIA ready to be picked up?"

"That's affirm."

"We'll pick him up with the Dust-Off and then put the slick in to get the remainder of your element. Have you had any more movement or fire?"

"Negative. But I wouldn't trust them."

"I want to make very sure I have your location confirmed before we bring in the choppers. I'm going to have the snakes down in the treetops to give you the max support, but I don't want to make any mistakes."

"I sure can't argue with that. Roger, identification. We'll put out some panels and have flashbulbs standing by."

The Cobras were the first choppers to reach the team's location. As they began to circle, looking for any signs of the enemy that had made a feeble attempt to kill the LRPs and steal what they could, they found signs of the firefight. "Houston Three, Reptile One-three."

"Glad to hear the call," Hollister quickly answered. "This is Three. Is Dust-Off far behind you?" He motioned for Jackson to flash a signal panel at the chopper headed directly for them.

"Right on our tails. We're just gonna poke around in the brush here for anyone who might just be too stupid to live."

"Be our guest. You have a solid fix on our location?"

"Gotcha. Looks like you guys are kinda hard on Hueys. What's left of that one I could put in my watch pocket," the lead gunship pilot said, taking a slow pass over the remaining bits and pieces of the burned helicopter.

"We didn't want them taking it home to Hanoi," Hollister said, almost giddy with the promise their arrival signaled.

The Cobras made another pass over the VC's position. "Looks like you got at least two over here," they reported. "And there are some trails behind that work out of the trees and back toward the dirt road."

"I'm not as interested in the body count as I am in any remaining spectators," Hollister said, half asking for their assessment.

"Looks to me like the locals are just rolling out of their racks and scratching their asses. Doesn't look like any of them have any interest in moving toward your location, though. Don't sweat 'em. We'll keep an eye on them while we get you all out. How's your WIA doing?"

Curtis was sitting against a tree trunk. He was pale and exhausted, but alive. Hollister raised his voice enough for Curtis to hear him. He wanted Curtis to know that he wasn't too worried about his condition. Though he had no idea what Curtis's true condition was, he felt that speaking positively had to help him. "He's a rock. If we don't drop him in the paddy water, he'll be drinking some cold beer by noon."

Curtis gave another little smile.

The medevac chopper flared, throwing water up on the two LRPs who carried Curtis in a double fireman's carry. The other four LRPs and Hollister, took up firing positions with the three machine guns and the M79 to be able to respond to any incoming fire.

The medevac went off without a hitch, as did the team pickup. As his chopper lifted off, Hollister looked out across the fields. It always amazed him how the aerial view of the area where he had spent an intense night looked so different from the way his mind had organized it in the dark.

They took a shallow turn to the north, and Hollister could see the small, fresh craters the mortars had made and the outline of the burned chopper. Most of its ashes were submerged in the water, which was marked with a multicolored oily slick made up of lubricants and fuels that spilled from the chopper when it blew.

At about five hundred feet, the air began to smell clean, and the musty smell of the damp ground was. nearly blown away from Hollister's uniform. Many things ran through his mind, not the least of which was the recognition of how close they had come to being overrun. He was sure they were hit by a small, and probably under-strength, unit that had suffered losses in the Tet Offensive.

The contact had to have been a target of opportunity for the VC. If they'd had time, weapons, and manpower, they could have owned the chopper and seven LRPs.

The sun broke the low clouds out over the South China Sea like a dark orange ball. Hollister leaned against the fire wall in the chopper and said a little thank-you.

CHAPTER 15

The rest of the company was just returning from a PT run when the chopper landed. They broke from the formation and cheered the returning team.

Sergeant Kurzikowski stood in the doorway to Operations, a cup of coffee in his hand. When he saw Hollister step out of the chopper and make eye contact, he gave him a small thumbs-up.

First Sergeant Morrison yelled at the off-loading LRPs to remind them to drop their gear on the pad and head to the mess hall for something to eat. "Any man who takes any weapons into the chow hall doesn't eat!"

The reception was just not what Hollister thought it ought to be. He waved Morrison over. "How 'bout we come up with something else we can do for returning teams?"

"Like what, sir?"

"Like beer and soft drinks and someone to watch their gear while they chow down," Hollister said.

"I'll make it happen," Morrison said with a smile.

Morrison's response was what Hollister wanted to hear. He was tired of old NCOs who had reasons why things couldn't be done or why it was someone else's job. Hollister could tell that Morrison remembered being a lower-ranking EM, when little things meant a lot. He knew that Morrison would, in fact, *make it happen.*

As he slipped the magazine out of his rifle, cleared the round from the chamber, and started toward Operations, he couldn't help but remember the days when he used to come back from missions to find rowdy First Sergeant Easy with a jeep trailer full of iced-down beer for the troops. He liked the job Morrison was doing, but he missed Easy. He wondered how he was getting along on limited duty.

Hollister sat on a small stool at the 25th Division's clearing station. He had decided to go along with Sergeant Dewey to pick up Curtis's gear and to try to talk to him after his wound was dressed.

The meeting didn't happen. Curtis was asleep and Hollister had to get back to the company area for the team debriefing.

Still, he took a few moments to have his own wound looked at.

"It's a greater threat to you as an infection than anything else. There's no serious damage, but I'm going to slip a few stitches in to close it up and keep crap out of it," me doctor said. "How'd you do this, anyhow?"

Reaching into his shirt pocket, Hollister pulled out the mortar fragment and held it up for the doctor to see. "Mortar round."

"We didn't get mortared last night."

"I was on a patrol—west of here."

The doctor stood back and looked at Hollister. "What's a captain doing out on a LRP patrol?"

"What?" Hollister asked, unsure of the question.

"I thought those LRP patrols were just enlisted men."

The notion angered Hollister. "What's that mean? That it's okay for them to go out and get shot up? They're only enlisted swine?"

The doctor recoiled. "Well, excuse me, Captain," he said, angry at being challenged.

The doctor opened a packaged suture setup and moved the rolling tray toward Hollister.

Feeling the anger boiling up, Hollister stood up and squared off with the doctor-major. "I think I've had all the medical attention I need here." He started for the doorway at the end of the examining room.

"Hey, who is going to sew you up?"

"I'll have one of my *enlisted men* do it," Hollister said as he slammed the door.

By noon word had come down that Curtis would not only be okay, but that he would probably be back to duty within six weeks. They would evacuate him to Japan for treatment first. Hollister was determined to see him before he left, and the first sergeant helped him scrounge another ride to the hospital.

PFC Curtis sat up in the bunk, an IV in each arm. He smiled and managed a weak welcome. "Airborne, sir."

"How you feel, Curtis?"

"Been better. Sure want to thank you for tying me up out there. Coulda bled to death."

"I needed a good grenadier. Couldn't let that happen," said Hohlster— not entirely in jest. Curtis was one hell of a good grenadier.

"Well," said Curtis, "you're going to have to do without me for a while. They're sending me to Camp Drake. That's in Japan."

Hollister nodded.

"If you don't kill yourself on the Ginza, we'll be able to use you when you get back." He paused. "You know you could get some leg job in the rear if you want . . ."

"No, sir! I'm coming back to the LRPs. I couldn't face my kids and tell 'em I humped a typewriter during the war."

"You got kids?" Hollister asked, surprised at the soldier, barely nineteen.

"Oh, no, sir, not yet. But I got plans."

They both laughed.

"Okay, I've got to get back. You let us know if you need anything." He paused. "You did a great job out there."

"Thank you, sir. There is one thing."

"Name it."

"Sir, I'd sure like to have my own team when I get back. I know I'm young and I'm pretty junior, but I . . ."

Raising his hand to stop him, Hollister answered. "You get back, we'll find a team for you. I promise."

"Airborne!" Curtis said.

The jeep pulled into the company area and stopped next to the Orderly Room. Hollister stepped out of the jeep, his hat still held in his hand, unable to put it on over the laceration in his scalp. He thanked Dewey for the ride and walked across the company street toward Operations.

Sergeant First Class Rose was standing in front of the Company Aid Station. "Damn, sir! Word got back here before you did!"

Rose was the senior medic. He was wearing sterile gloves and holding his hands up away from himself.

"What are you talking about?" Hollister asked.

"Got a buddy over at the Clearing Station. Seems that leg doctor is some kind of pissed off at you, Captain."

Hollister frowned. "Oh . . . that . . . I guess he'll get over it."

"You're gonna be a long time before you wear a floppy hat again if I don't clean up that wound on your head, sir. Bound to get infected and make an awful mess." Rose bent at the waist and made a sweeping gesture of welcome to the Aid Station.

"You think so?"

"My guess is that at least a couple of APCs are in order." It tickled Hollister that Rose knew what kind of headache he had. He smiled at the tall, freckled soldier. "Okay, but you have to promise not to tell that major at the Division Hospital that I really did need some treatment."

Sergeant Rose finished swabbing the area with alcohol, then shaved a spot twice as big as the wound. "You're gonna have a scar no matter what I do to it. It's a pretty raggedy hole."

"I'm not going to worry much about it until I get old enough to start losing all my hair."

Rose filled a hypodermic needle with a local anesthetic and prepared Hollister. "This is going to sting a little, but after that I can hammer on you and you won't know it."

Hollister rolled his eyes up at Rose in a mock threatening expression.

"Okay, I know—no hammer!"

Rose injected the anesthetic in four locations. He put the hypodermic needle down, picked up a pair of surgical tweezers, and pulled the flap of skin at the edge of the wound.

"Hurt?"

"No. Are you finished?" Hollister asked.

"Only take a minute," Rose said, pulling the suture through the skin and drawing it taut. "I, ah, saw the job you did on Curtis, Captain. You ought to branch-transfer into the Medical Corps."

"You talk to your buddy about him?"

"Yessir. He's gonna be okay. They're either going to try to salvage that artery in his leg or replace it with one of those artificial ones. He was in more danger from shock than he was from losing the leg."

"I want to spend some time with you this afternoon," Hollister said.

"You mean more than this?"

"I mean talking about cross-training medics in each of the teams."

"I'm sure with you on that, sir! We are miserable sorry in the department. I need to have some time with the team medics if they are going to learn anything other than *stop the bleeding, clear the airway, treat for shock.*"

"You'll get it. That's the last time a team goes out with no one qualified to push some blood expander into a WIA," Hollister said, making eye contact with Rose. "I want the team medics up to where they can train the other men on their teams."

Rose put his forceps down and nodded his head. "You're covered, sir. You get 'em to me, and I'll train 'em."

Hollister knew he could trust Rose to get it done. The real work was his—making sure that a million and one things didn't compete for the troops' time to keep them from getting the training.

He smiled at Rose. "Okay, so what's the story on that leg major at the Division Hospital? Looked a little lightweight to me."

"You don't know the half of it. My buddy tells me they have contests seeing who can fuck with him the most. He seems to think anyone who is not a doctor is an errand boy. So they run all kinds of errands for him. Only thing is they never seem to find the right thing. He wants vanilla ice cream in their chow hall, and they pass the word until someone shows up with a manila envelope. He wants a prescription pad, and they find him a magazine subscription form. He gets furious, and they all play dumb. You know how us dumb enlisted men are, sir."

"Sounds like he asks for it," Hollister said.

Rose finished trimming the edges of the dressing and stood back to admire his work. "I think you are back for duty, sir."

"No profile, huh?"

"No, sir. Can't set the example for the troops if the officers are sick, lame, and lazy."

"Damn!" Hollister kidded. "Well, how about those aspirin?"

Rose filled a small envelope with a half-dozen crumbly army aspirin, folded it closed, and handed it to Hollister. "My unofficial prescription is to take two of these every four hours, with plenty of beer."

Hollister got up off the box he had been sitting on and started for the door. He took his hat out of his pocket and started to put it on—only to catch himself.

"You want me to write you a medical buck slip saying you don't have to wear your headgear?"

"If someone is stupid enough to give me shit over not wearing my hat, I'll ask him if he'd like it stuffed up his ass."

"Guess that means no," Rose said with a smile.

"Major Fowler, please, Captain Hollister calling from Cu Chi," Hollister said, the telephone cradled in the crook of his neck.

He lit a cigarette and waited. The other end cracked with static. He looked out the window of Operations back toward Long Binh. There was clearly an afternoon thunderstorm brewing out there.

"Fowler. What do you want now, Hollister?" Major Fowler said abruptly.

"Sir, I have to call you again about that request I left with you. Is there any word on any more of it?"

"You got your goddamn nerve, Captain! We give you slicks to train with, and you fucking go and blow one up."

"Sir," Hollister said, a clear tone of sarcasm in his voice. "We didn't blow it up. We got a body count in a firefight. Would you rather the team got shot up and the chopper stripped for equipment and radios?"

"Don't be fucking insubordinate with me, goddamnit! Now if you want any more choppers, I have to feel better about the likelihood that you aren't going to destroy them with some of your childish training. There's a war going on over here, Hollister. What we need is more contacts, more ambushes, and more body count. *Not* more training!"

"I'm pretty sure I don't need to be told about the war, *Major*," Hollister said, disrespect dripping from his voice.

"You show me some reason I should give you more assets, and I might consider it," said Fowler. "But you better goddamn work on your tone of voice with me, Mister."

Major Sangean stormed into Operations, having heard some of the conversation. He motioned for Hollister to give him the phone.

"Fowler—Sangean. This is the last time you give any of my people any shit. Now you get me the rest of the items on that list in forty-eight hours, or I'll be standing in front of your desk with a very bad attitude! You got that?"

Sangean didn't wait for Fowler to respond. He slammed the phone into the carrier, then took a deep breath, and looked at Hollister.

"Let's talk outside."

They walked over to the mess hall and found a place in the back. One of the cooks held up a coffee cup, and Sangean nodded. The cook filled two cups with hot coffee and brought them to the plywood table where Hollister and Sangean sat.

"You know what the problem is, don't you?" Sangean asked.

"Problem?"

"With Fowler."

"No, sir."

"Besides being the south end of a horse, he was one of the people who came up with the idea of creating a Field Force-level LRP company—Juliet Company."

Hollister frowned, and his wound hurt when he did. "I don't understand."

"Well, I got command of it—not him."

Hollister leaned back in the chair and let the news sink in.

"Oh . . . now I see. No wonder everything I say to him is a burr under his blanket."

"Fowler is a real slippery fuck," said Sangean. He took a sip of his coffee. "He almost convinced Colonel Downing to put him in this job."

"I can't understand that," said Hollister. "Why would Downing even consider him? He hasn't had his boots wet since Ranger School!"

"Some of us are soldiers," said Sangean. "And some of us are just officers."

Hollister nodded. He'd been an enlisted man. He didn't have to be told.

"Fowler is one of those guys that spends all of his time making himself look good to his boss, no matter whose face he has to step in to do it. For some reason I haven't figured out yet, it works more often than not."

"So, what do I do about it?" asked Hollister.

"Just watch your back. He's bad news."

"But if I tiptoe around him, we'll never be able to get any help around here. It's gettin' pretty old having to take the leftovers. Old and dangerous."

Sangean blew the steam rising from his coffee away from the surface and took another sip.

"You let me handle Fowler. It grinds his ass that when we butt heads, he comes in second."

"But . . ."

"I want you to spend your time working on manpower and training for now. We aren't getting enough bodies—or training them fast enough. At this rate we'll still be at fifty percent foxhole strength by summer."

"Okay, sir. I'm just as happy not to have to do any more business with Major Fowler."

Sangean stood and checked his watch. "Maybe he'll walk in front of a train or something."

Hollister didn't know whether to laugh or not. It was the closest to a joke that Sangean had ever come.

Inside Operations Hollister and Kurzikowski went over the training schedule.

"We could use a lot more time to get all this training done," said Hollister.

"We ain't gonna get it," said Kurzikowski, finishing a can of soda and crushing the can with the heels of his hands.

"You know something?" Hollister said, reacting to a suggestion in Kurzikowski's voice.

"Well, the NCO net has it that we're going to be getting a warning order tomorrow."

"Tomorrow? Where'd you hear that?"

"I was jawin' with Sergeant Allen at Two Field. He allowed as how we ought to be lookin' in our mailbox for it."

Hollister sat back and rubbed his eyes. "I guess I might have booted that up on the schedule by screwing with Fowler."

"Naw, wouldn't make any difference."

"What's that mean?" Hollister asked.

"If I can speak frankly, sir?"

Hollister laughed. "Sergeant Ski, where'd you get that shit? An old John Wayne frontier soldier movie?"

"Well, I just don't want to be bad-mouthing no field grader, sir, but . . ."

"But what?"

"I think that Fowler, ah, *Major* Fowler, would like to see us fall on our faces."

Hollister looked at Kurzikowski. "Well? How do we prove him wrong?"

Kurzikowski tapped the training schedule on the field desk. "By getting as much of this done as we can before we get back operational."

The field phone rang, and Kurzikowski answered it. He handed the phone to Hollister. "First Sergeant for you."

"Sir, I need to talk to you about a new body," the first sergeant said, using his official voice for someone in his office.

"First Sergeant, the only job I would imagine you would want to check out with me is my replacement," Hollister replied.

"Well, sir, I'll remember that when the time comes. But right now I got a young PFC named Cathcart standing in front of me. He tells me you were instrumental in getting him here."

"Well, you ask Mister Cathcart what he wants to do. I'm sure you can fit his wishes into your needs," Hollister said, kidding the first sergeant about the relative unimportance of the conversation. It was an experienced first sergeant's way of keeping from stepping on toes that just might be sensitive.

"Fine, sir. I'll do just that. Airborne."

Kurzikowski gave Hollister a questioning look.

"A kid from Two Field that I helped get reassigned here. First sergeant wants some input."

"Another warm body. Good."

"Yeah, I ought to thank the G-1 sergeant major. He made it happen." The phone was still in Hollister's hand. "I better do it now, or I'll never get around to it."

He cranked the ringer on the field phone and got the company switchboard. "Hey, Coots, Captain Hollister. Can you get through to Two Field for me? I need to talk to the G-1 sergeant major—Carey."

Coots told him it might take a while, end-of-the-day traffic being some of the busiest.

"I'll be in Operations," Hollister said, and hung up.

One of the radio operators came back into Operations from the mess hall with a stainless steel pitcher of coffee. Without asking, he topped off Hollister's and Kurzikowski's coffee and took the rest to the radio table. "Oh, Captain," he said. "I almost forgot—this came in for you." He put the pitcher down and pulled two letters out of his trouser pocket.

They were from Susan. Hollister looked at the postmarks—nine days old. Not too bad. He wanted to stop and read them, but had to finish the work with Kurzikowski, and it was a matter of setting the example and setting priorities. He had always disliked officers who dropped what they were doing for some personal item just because they could.

He stuffed the letters into his pocket. He looked forward to reading them later.

After considering several more plans to accomplish the training, Hollister and Kurzikowski decided that round-the-clock was the only way to do a decent job of covering the teaching points they felt were essential before running any more actual combat patrols.

They started that night. In the unused part of the abandoned area assigned to them, they established patrol RON positions. After establishing the RONs, the team leaders would call a mock E&E, as if the team had made contact, and move them to a simulated pickup zone. En route they practiced immediate-action drills against imaginary enemy forces.

The lack of vegetation to hide them made little difference. Each man got used to moving in the dark as part of a unit, got the feel for distance be-tween team members, and got a better perspective on how the team worked during movement and under contact.

After checking on the training, Hollister went back to his hooch to clean his rifle and get himself cleaned up. He had not stopped since landing earlier that morning. His head hurt, and his stomach was sour from taking too many aspirins and drinking too much coffee.

As he broke down his M16 to clean it, he remembered that he had the letters from Susan in his pocket. He decided he could probably do both at the same time. Putting the disassembled M16 on an old towel across his bunk, he opened his locker and pulled out his bottle of Scotch. He poured himself a strong drink—a mess-hall cup's worth—and placed it on his foot-locker. Then he opened the first letter from Susan.

She began by telling him how much she missed him, and after a little discussion of her day, she ended with the same notion. Hollister shared her feelings more than he had since he had been back in Vietnam. After being back in the field and coming close to death again, he realized how long the months ahead were and how much risk there was. For a moment he was angry and confused about why he had even bothered to come back to Vietnam. He wanted to be with her. He wanted to hold her. He wanted to be home.

He took a pull of the Scotch and promised himself that it would be his last tour. He would start writing to colleges next week for some hope of acceptance, even though he had nothing to offer but the GI Bill.

The second letter contained more information and less emotion. Susan seemed to have been in a hurry to get the letter in the mail and filled it up with encouraging news of her job, her family, and a plant she had managed to nurse back to health after it took ill on her apartment windowsill.

Hollister felt the effects of the booze and began to unwind a bit. His head stopped hurting, but he suddenly felt exhausted. More Scotch and a check of his watch, and he almost gave in to the urge just to go to bed. Instead, he finished cleaning and oiling his rifle and made one last walk to the end of the compound to watch the night training. It was important that the troops know the officers didn't send them to training to keep them busy.

When he turned the corner at the end of the empty tropical huts to look at the teams in the clearing off the chopper pad, he spotted Major Sangean already there. "Evening, sir," he said, saluting, even though Sangean had his back to him.

Sangean returned the salute. "Thought you were crapped out."

"No, sir. Wanted to make one more check on training."

"I thought it would be pretty much of a joke. But I have to admit they are doing a serious job. But then they always get serious after someone has been shot at in the bush."

"It's the best I could do with the time we think we have."

"We haven't got much. I just got off the phone with Colonel Downing. We have a warning order coming in tomorrow." Major Sangean looked down at the gravel and absentmindedly kicked it around with the toe of his boot, as officers have been doing in training areas for centuries. "You go on, get some rest," he said. "I'll keep an eye on things here."

"But what about the warning order?"

Sangean shrugged. "Don't know much. Wasn't a secure line. Guess we'll see what it is when it gets here. So, go on—get some sleep."

By first light all the medics were training at Sergeant Rose's Aid Station. Sergeant Kurzikowski had all the team leaders together for training on Operations and radio procedures. The platoon sergeants had all the other team members down at the firing range conducting circuit training. The large group was broken up into thirds. One third was firing and zeroing weapons, one third was practicing emplacing and retrieving claymores, and the third group was taking training in recognizing mines and booby traps.

All the officers, the Cobra pilots, and the Operations and Intelligence NCOs were assembled in one of the abandoned barracks, which they had turned into a classroom.

Hollister had removed a loosened piece of plywood flooring and propped it up against the wall to use as a blackboard. With a piece of crumbling limestone for chalk, he was able to draw diagrams and write numbers and call signs. He spent the first hour going over insert formations, extraction formations, communications networks, call signs, and required reports. Then he gave them a break.

He was followed by Sangean, who talked about mission capabilities. He was sure they were going to be committed to patrols along the border between the Angel's Wing and the Parrot's Beak.

"We are going to have to out-G the guerrillas out there. The conventional NVA units we can handle. They are a lot like the American units—big, loud, clumsy, and undisciplined."

The description raised a chuckle in the room. But it was nervousness. And they were waiting for him to explain his anxieties about the VC.

Sangean pulled a cigar out of his pocket and lit it He took a couple of puffs to get the end burning, and then he balanced it on the edge of the half wall that ended where the torn window screens started.

"The VC will be our undoing. If we can't tell the difference between the villagers and the VC, we are screwed. We can't keep people out of the area, but we can sure as hell worry that they are either full-time VC, part-time VC, or sympathizers. And there are some who just don't want to be part of anyone's war. We can't kill 'em all now and sort 'em out later. We've got to try something different."

"Something different than we're doing now?" Captain Stanton asked, toying with his aviator's sunglasses.

Sangean nodded. "Scouts."

"Scouts?" three voices asked together.

Sangean nodded again. "The program is called 'Kit Carson Scouts.' It's a spin-off of the Chieu Hoi Program—ralliers. Seems that some units are having good results using some of the Hoi Chanhs who have turned themselves in. And some of them were captured and then volunteered to work for us. Having them with U.S. units is giving some outfits the edge on the VC."

"Like the interpreters?" Hollister asked.

"No, the interpreter program is a washout. Seems that most of the Vietnamese that are interpreters got the jobs because their families had money or position, and it was a way to get their sons in uniform, but mostly out of combat."

A pilot made a face as if he didn't understand the problem. Sangean filled it in for him. "They were mostly educated and from the cities. Some were even educated overseas. They spoke English and French, and some even spoke German. But most of them wouldn't know a VC if he wore a sign.

"But the Chieu Hois are VC. They know VC. They know how it all works. And some of them would rather come to work for the Americans than spend the rest of the war locked up. They might sound shaky, but in Special Forces we had to put our trust in less reliable people than these sometimes. The program seems to be working."

"So we get a couple?" Hollister asked.

"We get one for each team."

The room went silent. No one needed to tell Sangean that the idea frightened every man who had ever been out on a five or six-man patrol. He took a couple of drags off his cigar to stoke the fire on its end and then leaned his weight on his hands on a tabletop.

"Don't worry. They will be good, and they will be reliable or they won't go with a team."

"How do we do that, sir?" Kurzikowski asked.

"We train them like we do the team members. Then we let them go out on a low-risk mission. When they return, each man on the team gets a vote. If one man blackballs him—he's gone."

Everyone started talking at once. The opinions varied widely, but no one was without one.

"How do we start?" Hollister asked.

"You and I are going to Long Binh tomorrow. We're going to have a showdown with Fowler, and then we'll go check out the prison."

"Okay with me," Hollister said.

"But for now, you take over here and continue. I have a few things to do. I'll catch up with you later."

Sangean put his cigar in his mouth and pulled his floppy hat out of his pocket. He started for the door, and everyone came to attention. He stopped, turned to the standing room, and barked, "Carry on," then took another step and turned back again.

He looked at Captain Stanton. "Stanton, I hate Nomex flight suits. You guys are gonna fly LRPs, you're gonna be LRPs. Get your people over to the supply room and draw cammies!"

Sangean left without allowing Stanton to reply.

The response from the others in the room was positive. They wanted the Cobras to be part of the team as much as the pilots wanted to be welcomed.

By late morning Hollister was bushed. He broke the training for coffee, then went to Operations to check in. He was quickly met with an air of anticipation. One of the NCOs jerked his thumb in the direction of Major Sangean.

Sangean looked up from the documents spread out on the field table in front of him. The cover sheet read: TOP SECRET–NOFORN.

"Op order?" Hollister asked.

"Warning order," Sangean said, not giving much away in his expression.

"How does it look?" Hollister asked.

"Looks like we are in the LRP business—full-time now."

"Good missions?"

"Could be better—or worse. We'll be okay. But it won't be a walk in the sun. We've got to be good, or they will hand us our asses."

"How much time do we have before the first team is on the ground?"

"A week. Can you use it?"

"You bet!" Hollister said.

"You got it. We need to be ready to go. When we run out of time, it becomes OJT."

"Even though we're still short of manpower and assets?"

"What work we can't do—we won't do."

"Where do you want me to start?"

"Get us a chopper. We're going to see Downing and Fowler."

CHAPTER 16

G ood mornin', sir. Airborne!"
      The words came from the doorway to one of the team hooches. Hollister turned to see PFC Cathcart standing on the step, beaming in his newly issued camouflage fatigues and floppy LRP hat.

"Well, how you getting along? You happy that you busted out of Long Binh or not?" Hollister asked.

"Yessir. This is where I want to be. I just wanted to thank you for helping me escape."

"Well, you may change your mind before it's over. You still have Recondo School ahead of you."

"I'm ready, sir."

Hollister remembered Nha Trang fondly. He had spent little time there on his first tour, but never forgot its beauty. He reached into his pocket, pulled out ten dollars in MPC, and handed it to Cathcart.

"Listen," he said, "if you get time while you're in Nha Trang—go get yourself a steak at The Nautique, on the beach road."

Cathcart was surprised by the gesture. "But I can't take your money."

"I owe you more than that for all the help you were to me at Long Binh. Just take it, and tell me how terrific the steak was. Okay?"

Cathcart smiled. "If'n that's an order—consider it done."

First Sergeant Morrison stuck his head out of the Orderly Room door and caught Hollister's eye. "Could I have a minute?"

Hollister waved back at Morrison, then stuck his hand out to Cathcart. "Welcome aboard. Just do a good job, and don't try to win the war by yourself."

"Sir, I got some good news for you. The new XO's in Long Binh—at Ninetieth Replacement Battalion. I just got the word from Sergeant Major Carey's office."

"Did you get through to him?"

"No, sir . . . just a message in the pouch that came in this morning."

"Let's try to get someone on the phone and tell them that the Old Man and I will be there today and we can pick up, ah . . . what's his name?"

Dewey had the message in his hand. He hurriedly looked through it and found the name. "Captain, ah, Vance. Captain Vance—that's him."

"*Peter* Vance?"

"Yessir, Peter A. Vance, Captain (P)," Dewey said.

Morrison made a face. "That bad?"

"No," Hollister said, breaking into a smile. "Peter A. Vance is good news. He was my Tactical officer in OCS, and I worked with him at the Ranger Department. If we had ten Peter Vances over here, we could wind up this war in no time."

Morrison rolled his eyes. "A snake-eating captain on the major's list? I was kinda hoping for someone with more of an administrative bent. I think we have plenty of warriors around here."

Hollister laughed. "Don't worry, Top. If there's anything Peter Vance can't do, I don't know what it is."

"If you say so, sir. What kind of trouble are we in with the new XO?"

"The one thing I'll never forget from OCS is that Peter Vance can out-run any man alive. He used to take our platoon on runs that never seemed to end. You two will enjoy the morning runs together."

The portly first sergeant patted his large gut and rolled his eyes again. "Just what I need—a Lamaze coach."

Sangean and Hollister sat on the leather couch in Colonel Downing's office while the colonel talked at length about the plans to deploy teams along the Cambodian border. Hollister took notes, and being the senior, Sangean did the talking for both of them.

"How many teams will you have ready by the time this operation starts?" asked the colonel.

"Twelve max," Sangean replied. "And I've got thirty new bodies going through Recondo School, or otherwise not deployable right now."

Downing made a face. "That seems awful short to me. I thought you had another thirty people?"

"They are on their way back to the Replacement Battalion for re-assignment."

"Why?" Downing asked, surprised.

"Seems like there were plenty of units that were ready to get rid of their sick, lame, and lazy by sending them to me. Half those folks never volun-teered to come to the LRPs. Some were legs, some were the wrong MOS, and

I even got a few that had less than a month left in-country. Some wanted in, but we didn't want them. All together, they're rejects."

Downing frowned. "You aren't being too picky, are you?"

Sangean didn't blink. "I'm being as picky as you'd be selecting the other five men you'd walk that border with, Colonel."

Downing let the answer sink in. "I see. Well, let's get the rest of the bodies you need—ASAP—and get you full strength."

"Colonel, I don't know if this is a good time for you, but I have to bring up the assets problem again. We—Hollister—has brought in our request, and all we have is a committed Cobra platoon. Now, we're very happy about *that*. But we simply can't do the job for you with odds and ends to support us."

"I know you need more responsive support," said Colonel Downing. "Believe me, we are working on it. Major Fowler has been trying to identify the units . . ."

A flush came over Sangean's face. "Sir, Major Fowler has been flat on his ass!"

Hollister was sure this would draw an angry response from Downing, but the colonel simply walked around his desk and opened the door. He crooked his finger at Major Fowler.

Fowler entered.

"Give us a rundown on the progress you've made on getting combat-support resources for the LRPs. Major Sangean seems to think there's a little too much delay in answering his request for support."

Fowler smiled as if he was fully prepared. "There's no problem, Colonel. We've identified a slick platoon, an FO party from Field Force Artillery, two full-time FACs, and I think I can almost guarantee a hundred-and-fifty-man reaction force."

Hollister hated the smug look on Fowler's face. He was sure Fowler had those resources available all along and was just screwing with the LRPs as his own little demonstration of frustration at not being given a field command. Hollister hated him for it and would not forget it.

"Good, good," Downing said. "How soon?"

"Should have everyone but the reaction force by the end of the week. The others will be confirmed by then, too, but not relocated to Cu Chi until the end of the next week. They're a ground troop from the Seventeenth Cav," Fowler said, matter-of-factly, as if he pulled off things like that every day.

"Well, I want the LRPs fully supported before the border operations begin. You understand?"

"Yessir," Fowler said. "Like I told Captain Hollister, none of this is a problem. We've been on it from the day he brought in the request. The only delay was in finding the right units and the right bodies. We don't want to give them support that is not up to their missions."

Hollister fought the urge to call Fowler a fucking liar. He knew he could never trust the man with anything important and would try never to need him for anything again.

"I know, I know," Sangean said. "Fowler is a lowlife. But there is nothing we can do about it except get mired down in a pissing match with a head-quarters puke. We can't afford the luxury. Now, you work off your steam by getting with Sergeant Major Carey on the personnel problem and finding out where Captain Vance is."

"Yes, sir. And you?"

"I've got to spend some time with the G-2 folks to get the situation along the border. I want to see the faces that are writing all these fairy tales about zillions of NVA soldiers still massing on the border after having their asses waxed during Tet."

"Okay with me. Where do we meet?"

"See you at the club at sixteen thirty."

"Airborne," Hollister said as he walked toward the G-1 Section and Sangean started toward G-2.

Sergeant Major Carey was drinking chalky fluid from a bottle of antacid when Hollister knocked on his door. "Got a minute, Sergeant Major?

He capped the bottle, wiped the antacid from the corner of his mouth, and waved Hollister in. "Sure. Come on in, Captain."

Hollister took the chair Carey pointed to and pulled his notes from his pocket.

Carey belched and raised his hand apologetically. "Sorry, that stuff is supposed to put the fire out in my gut, but it just seems to give me gas."

"Why do you drink it?"

"I been havin' ulcer trouble for almost eleven years now. The docs keep telling me to give up cigarettes and coffee and bourbon. Hell, what fun would that be?"

Carey was one of the real old-timers. His hair was thinning, and his skin was starting to liver-spot. He had been a two-stripe first sergeant in the Korean War and had seen the arrival of the supergrades of sergeant major and command sergeant major. Hollister had only spoken with him a few times, but he liked Carey and trusted him.

"You might as well hang it up if you have to give up all that," said Hollister.

"Well, I told the medics I would rather have the bellyaches. But I'm looking for a smoother bourbon. That's therapeutic, isn't it?"

Carey had a great smile, even though his mouth and eyes were surrounded by rows of parallel lines and wrinkles.

"If I come across some," said Hollister, "I'll let you know. Count on me to take point for you."

"So what can I do for you, sir?" the sergeant major asked.

"Bodies," Hollister said.

"Dead or alive?"

"Need more of the live ones and less of the dead-on-their-ass ones. We're still a bit short, and we have to throw some of them back in," Hollister said.

Carey made a face. "Hmmm, yeah, I heard from Morrison that some of my less-than-straight-shooting senior NCOs been using your place for a dump."

"That happens. I don't want to worry about who or why. I just need to move them out and get some more fresh faces."

"I talked with Morrison. We'll be shipping out some warm ones from the Replacement Battalion tomorrow, and I've got about a dozen more volunteers from the One hundred and first and the One hundred and seventy-third. It's kinda hard to get volunteers from leg units like the First Division, the Ninth, and the Twenty-fifth. But we'll get them for you."

"You get the word that your new XO is in?"

"Yeah, I need to find him to take him forward," Hollister said.

"He'll be here in a bit. I just sent a driver down there to find him. Where will you be?"

"You tell me where you want me, and I'll stand by to find him."

"Sir, I'll keep him here. You finish your business here, check in with me, and we'll link you two up."

"Good deal. Glad you and Morrison are talking."

"How's he doing?" Carey asked.

"Morrison?"

"Yes. He was a PFC in my platoon in Germany. He's really a good man who had some bad breaks. I think the LRPs and Morrison will be good for each other."

Hollister smiled. "I think you're right, Sergeant Major. I didn't think he was going to cut it when I first saw him. But I've changed my mind. He's thorough and competent. The troops give him a little shit about his weight, but he's losing it fast and the troops appreciate his efforts. He's got what I think a first sergeant needs."

"What's that, sir?"

"He's got the troops in mind whenever he does anything. Thanks for sending him our way."

Carey smiled.

The tangle of buildings, warehouses, hooches, latrines, and sheds that had grown up at Long Binh Post was a difficult maze to negotiate if you didn't work there. Hollister's efforts to make some other visits to the Signal office for new SOIs and to the motor pool to try to scrounge a jeep took longer than it would have if he knew the shortcuts. He wished Cathcart was with him.

The jeep he was assigned was in bad need of a new front end. It pulled to the left and took a constant tug on the wheel to keep it from driving into the oncoming lane. Still, it beat having to walk or hitch a ride everywhere.

Hollister found the Transit BOQ and made arrangements for him, Sangean, and Vance to stay the night. Sangean got a field-grade room, and Hollister and Vance took a small room with a double bunk.

Leaving the jeep at the BOQ since they wouldn't need it until morning, Hollister walked across the street to the MARS station. Like all MARS stations, it was packed with soldiers trying to make calls home to girlfriends, wives, and families.

The priority system surprised Hollister. He was put ahead of the troops who were waiting, but assigned to IIFFV Headquarters. Emergencies came first, then troops in from subordinate units, and then IIFFV Headquarters and Long Binh Post personnel. The good news was quickly marred by the fact that he had to give up after several tries. The operators were unable to patch a line through to New York. So he had to give up his chance in line to let another soldier try and call the woman in his dreams.

The PX was as crowded as the MARS station. Hollister had a list of things to get for himself and for others who had hit him up back at Cu Chi when they found out he was going to the rear.

For him it meant line after line. On a couple of occasions a soldier here or there would half offer his place in line either because Hollister was an officer or because of the uniform and the LRP arc on his shoulder. In each case Hollister declined. It was something he had promised himself not to do when he got his commission. He was proud that he had been pretty good at remembering the promise in the years since he had walked across that stage at Fort Benning and gotten his gold second lieutenant's bars.

He got a strange look from a young soldier who spotted the small shaved patch on his head. Hollister decided he didn't want to explain it and announced, "B-52 wound."

Toothpaste and cigars for Kurzikowski. Hollister himself needed razor blades, soap, stationery, and envelopes—all the PX had was the silly-looking stuff with the drawing of a soldier and an Asian wearing a conical hat in the corner of each sheet. Under the imprint it read: PROUDLY SERVING IN THE RE-PUBLIC OF VIETNAM. There was little choice, so Hollister took it. He needed a new watchband to replace the one he had broken on patrol, so he moved to yet another line at the watch counter.

And there was more: stacks of stereos, cameras, watches, jewelry, and use-less uniform items—useless, that is, unless you were stationed in the rear.

Hollister looked over a TEAC tape deck and remembered the one his hooch mate had had on his first tour. He remembered the fallen hooch-mate, too. It tugged at him and took away his enthusiasm for the stereo equipment.

He knew the flimsy paper bags the merchandise came in wouldn't make the trip back to Cu Chi, so he bought two zippered two-handled AWOL bags. After stuffing all the things he needed to get into one of them, he made one last pass around the single-room PX for anything else. Sure, there was plenty he wanted, but he resisted spending the money.

Across the dirt street from the PX was the Class VI Store. Class VI stores were the only places in Vietnam where soldiers could buy bottled booze and not pay the outrageous prices charged on the black market.

Inside, Hollister waited in another line to buy a few bottles of Scotch to take back to Cu Chi. He also bought a bottle of Wild Turkey to leave at Sergeant Major Carey's office.

He knew Carey had the job of putting the right people in the right places for over two hundred thousand slots in Vietnam. He felt that Carey had made the LRPs a special case. He wanted him to know he appreciated it.

Hollister pulled his ration card from his wallet and checked the number of bottles he was authorized to purchase. He was well within his limit since some of the booze he had back at Cu Chi had been bought by others for him when they had made similar trips to Long Binh and Saigon.

The water in the latrine that serviced the BOQ was clean enough, but smelled of some kind of petroleum product. Hollister didn't much care. All he wanted to do was wash some of the collected grime off his face and hands before meeting Sangean at the club.

Back in the BOQ he realized he had a few minutes before he had to meet his boss. He considered using the time to write, or at least start, a letter to Susan or his folks.

He decided to compromise, take some writing paper with him to the club, get some writing done, have a drink, and wait for Major Sangean.

At that hour—sixteen hundred—the club was like it had been on his last visit, almost empty. He knew how fast it would transform inside an hour—the end of the business day. That the troops assigned to the headquarters tasked with supporting the LRPs would call it a day at retreat and head for the clubs, of which there were several, and proceed to get shit-faced drunk angered him. All the while LRPs were out in the field worrying about the likelihood of being compromised and knowing the only hopes they had of evening out the score were reaction time and supporting fires. And these two things came from a headquarters that was overworked when people were at their duty stations.

The waitress came to his table at the corner of the plywood bar and took his order. He decided to try to keep it light, so he ordered a San Miguel.

"No hab," she said.

"How about Crown?"

"No hab," again.

"OB?"

"No."

"Aussie beer?"

"No."

"Thai?"

"No, Dai Uy. You mus' o'da what we hab," she said—frustrated.

"Okay, what do you *hab*?" He kidded her.

It went past her. She stared up at the ceiling and tried to remember. "We hab Carling, Blatz, Ba Mui Ba, Bier La Rue, and Bud-wai."

"Scotch, then."

"Scotch?" she answered, her voice raised in protest. "Why you may me tell you beaucoup beer an' then you o'da wi-key?"

"'Cause I don't like those brands of beer."

"Boo shid. They all da same kine. You jus' mess wid me. You dinky dau. All GI dinky dau."

"Okay, I'm crazy. Now get your little fanny over to the bar, and get me some Scotch. I hardly care what kind. You just get it. Biet?"

She harumphed, spun on the heel of her white plastic go-go boots, and wiggled her tiny behind all the way to the bar. He was sure it was for his benefit and that she was cocky enough to know he would be watching.

Hollister pulled out his writing paper. He apologized to his parents for being so long between letters and told them how much he missed the farm, but probably not the cold, windy Kansas winter. He talked about Susan, about the weather in Vietnam, and about missing them. He didn't mention the war. He didn't talk about the dead LRPs. He didn't talk about the Tet Offensive. He just wanted to tell them he loved them, was thinking about them, and missed them. He hated avoiding the war in his letters. But not as much as he hated the thought of seeing any more tears in his mother's eyes. To him there was no point in making her worry more than she already was. He didn't need to tell her anything about the war. She was a mother. If he died, she would know it before the army would.

The letter to Susan he had started before he left Cu Chi. He was eager to tell her that he had tried to call her, then stopped himself. What good would it do to tell her he couldn't get through? She would only get upset that they couldn't speak.

She had asked him about Tet. He decided to tell her that the stuff he had been picking up from the little news they got was a gross exaggeration of the truth. The NVA had not made a significant change in the course of the war—at least not his war.

The headlines that were in every major U.S. paper claiming that the NVA had inflicted heavy losses on the Americans and South Vietnamese were simply wrong. The only thing the NVA did accomplish was to attack simultaneously fifty-six provincial headquarters and embarrass the American Intelligence community to a point it had never experienced before. He wanted her not to worry, not to think the North Vietnamese had made the war even more lethal than she had already guessed it was.

The waitress came back and asked Hollister if he wanted another Scotch. He knew he had nothing important to do that night and not much scheduled for early the next morning. So he shoved the glass toward her and nodded yes.

Major Sangean caught her on the way to the bar and told her to bring three doubles. In trail he had Peter Vance—still in khakis from stateside.

Vance was unlike most of Hollister's peers. Though he was young to be on the major's list—only thirty—he looked older. His hairline had started failing him in high school, and his face and arms were weathered and taut from long days in an infantryman's sun. Vance had a look that set him apart, too. He had a crescent-shaped scar near his left eye, the result of a grenade fragment that had caught him standing upright adjusting an air strike in an attack on a Special Forces A camp on his first tour in 1964.

The scar, the slight squint, and his ever-present set jaw made him look as if he were in deep thought even when he wasn't.

Vance spotted Hollister and smiled broadly. "Well, I'll be a sack of shit! I thought I'd washed you out of OCS, and then you turned up at the Ranger Department. When I thought they'd kill you there—you show up here." He stuck his hand out and shook Hollister's vigorously, holding on to the captain's forearm with his other hand. His grip was as solid as his reputation.

Since Hollister had graduated from OCS, Vance had already pulled two tours in Vietnam and one in Laos—on loan to a government agency that he wouldn't be able to discuss in the club.

Vance's uniform read like a biography of his professional life. The Distinguished Service Cross topped four rows of combat ribbons sandwiched in between his CIB and his Master Parachutist wings.

He had earned the DSC, America's second highest award for valor, while serving as a company commander in the Airborne Brigade of the 1st Cavalry Division. It was the same campaign that had killed Hollister's OCS roommate—Kerry French. In it Vance had taken command of the remnants of a decimated infantry battalion and fought back a punishing attack launched by two North Vietnamese regiments just west of Pleiku. The battle was still being written about and would be studied in the years to come—a classic trap the Cav had walked into. Had it not been for Vance's efforts to reorganize and counterattack, the Cav would have suffered losses so great that the stain on its combat record would never have been overcome.

The trio moved to a corner table where they could talk and have fewer people close enough to overhear them. Hollister knew Vance would be eager to find out the whole story on Juliet Company and what he was getting himself into.

The waitress came with the drinks, and Vance told her not to leave. She made a face as if she had work to do.

"Dung lai, Co. We need another round," Vance said to stop her from leaving.

"You no need. I jus' bring," she said.

He raised his glass and challenged Sangean and Hollister to do the same. "Let this be the first of many and the beginning of a good year," he said, and then tossed the whole drink down in one gulp, slamming the glass back onto the shaky table for the waitress.

"Here, here," Hollister and Sangean repeated as they emptied their glasses.

Sangean pulled out twenty dollars and dropped the money in front of the waitress. "Keep 'em coming, and tell me when that runs out."

Vance put twenty more on the first, and Hollister matched the first two.

All three looked at each other knowing what was ahead of them. Vance bent over to look out the louvered screens that surrounded the room and squinted. "Looks bad out there!"

"How bad?" Hollister asked.

"Looks like a fucking drunk front moving in from the South China Sea!"

"Stand by for heavy rolls," Sangean added.

The waitress grabbed some of the bills and almost trotted to the bar for the refills.

It didn't take them long to brief Vance on the situation—or for them to get louder and drunker. It was the first time Hollister had seen Sangean really smile since he had been in Juliet Company. He just assumed the major was happy things were coming together—with Vance's arrival and the announcement that the assets had been committed to the LRPs.

Still, Hollister had a sinking feeling that he couldn't trust Fowler and that there would be some repercussions for the bad-mouthing Sangean had done in Downing's office.

Within less than half an hour, Vance, Hollister, and Sangean had every stiff paper napkin within reach on their table. They had made up lists of things that Sangean wanted Vance to get right on. Most of the company administration had been put off until the XO arrived. What did get done was the stuff that couldn't be postponed, and that was taken care of by First Sergeant Morrison.

There were also napkins that suggested changes in the organization, lines of responsibility, and logistical support for the expected pilots, airmen, cavalrymen, and replacements. And the Scotch kept coming. Hollister was starting to feel good about Juliet Company. He was starting to like the feel of the new team being formed, and he was glad that Vance seemed to respect Sangean.

The strippers came on about nine to a fully packed club. The LRPs were still deep in conversation about their plans and their priorities, while the others in the club were yelling and ogling the two tiny Korean strippers wearing stateside bikinis decorated with fringe and tassels.

The noise and the music continued to build to a level where there was just no point in trying to talk about Juliet Company. And the fact that they were coming close to depleting the money they had put on deposit for the drinks left them hardly capable of doing anything but joining in and cheering on the two strippers, who were doing their best to be seductive while wearing cheap and less-than-feminine platform shoes.

"Hey, Major!" a red-faced Signal Corps captain yelled.

Sangean didn't hear him or decided not to respond.

"Hey—you, I'm talking to you. What the fuck kinda outfit wears silly camouflage uniforms like that? You guys APs? 'Cause the last time I saw anything so fucking stupid, a puke air policeman was wearing it," the drunken captain yelled.

Hollister looked at Sangean and then at Vance. Neither one of them wanted to provoke the officer, who was obviously too drunk and too dumb to live. By silent and mutual consent, they tried to ignore him. But he wouldn't have it.

He raised his voice even louder. "Hey! You fuckers too good to talk to the rest of us Remington Raiders?" he said, a trace of jealousy still recognizable in spite of his slurred words.

"Well," he said, putting his hands on his hips. "I guess you guys must have some hearing problems. I know *I* have vision problems because I can't really see you fuckers in your no-see-me-suits."

Vance, Hollister, and Sangean exchanged glances again for another cross-check. Vance shook his head and stood up slowly.

Hollister looked at Sangean for a sign. Were they going to fight or what? Sangean gave him a look that he read as *just be ready.*

They watched Vance, who walked as if he hadn't seen the Signal Corps officer and was just heading toward the latrine. He got behind the captain, who kept on running his mouth, trying to get some of the others to harass the two in cammies. But they were all fixed on the tallest of the two strippers, who had removed her top and was showing off her tiny breasts, which were tipped with large brown, almost leathered nipples. It was the nipples that caused the room to explode in a concert of hooting and whistling. The stripper thought it was a sign of approval when it was really ridicule.

The captain tried again to goad Sangean and Hollister by hurling the standard line at them. It was obvious he knew who they were. "Only thing that falls out of the sky is bird shit and paratroopers."

With that Vance hooked the wrought-iron leg on the captain's chair with his jump boot, gave it a little shove as he twisted his torso, and caught the captain in the upper chest with a lightning-fast jab with his elbow. Vance was two steps away before the captain realized his chair was going over backward with him in it and the tableful of beer and filled ashtrays on its way down on top of him.

The others at his table saw the captain going over and turned to make fun of him as he collided with the concrete floor in a puddle of beer and light mud from the many dirty boots that had crossed the floor that evening.

The captain rolled out of his chair just as it hit the floor. He was on his feet and ready to fight, but found no one to challenge him. Vance was far enough away to cast some doubt on whether he had anything to do with upending the obnoxious captain.

He turned to look at Hollister and Sangean only to find them seated, laughing at him. Another officer made a remark about the captain's mouth making him top-heavy, and he struck out at him. In a matter of seconds, everyone within five feet of the captain's table was fighting—none of them knew why.

Some of the more sober officers in the room tried to break it up, but found themselves embroiled in the fight and quickly provoked to throw a punch.

The strippers were frightened and scrambled to collect their outfits and make a break for the door. The end of their striptease angered many near the dance floor who were not part of the fight, and they began to throw beer cans at those who were fighting.

Outside the club Vance, Sangean, and Hollister were doubled up with laughter.

"Fucking leg REMFs should all be taken out and shot. How the hell we supposed to win this fucking war with assholes like that running the headquarters?" Vance asked.

"Yeah, I hope I never need to talk to someone over the signal gear that that asshole is in charge of," Hollister said.

The trio tried to straighten up as they crossed the street to the Transit BOQ. But their line of march was ragged enough to give away just how much they had had to drink.

CHAPTER 17

The smell of the mess hall made Hollister's already uneasy stomach pitch. The smell was the same in every army mess hall. A mixture of grease, coffee, disinfectants, and the dominant food of the day. Today it was sausage.

Vance and Sangean didn't look much better than Hollister thought he looked. All three had very bad hangovers, but didn't want to admit how bad to each other. It was a matter of honor to be able to take it. Hollister was the first to suggest it: "I'd give a month's pay for one of those awful APCs that falls apart in your mouth before you can flush it down with something."

The comment brought sympathetic groans from the other two, but not much more. They were too busy eyeing the coffee level in the glass tube on the front of the huge stainless-steel coffee urn.

"So what do you suppose ever happened to that shithead Signal officer last night?" Sangean asked.

"I hope he drowned in his own puke. I was working on a really good hangover when he screwed it up for me," Vance said.

"Wish he'd been that successful with me," Sangean said.

Vance took some bacon and some unevenly cut toast. Hollister chose the SOS, and Sangean had the dry cereal and three big glasses of milk.

They took a table near the far end of the room, away from the wilting steam table. Even at six in the morning, the combination of the Vietnamese heat and the humidity of the steam table could sap the energy out of strong men without hangovers.

Over breakfast they tried to come up with a consensus on what they wanted to ask the Chieu Hois. They knew the first thing that would be in doubt was their loyalty and the second was their combat effectiveness. In teams of only six men, one that wasn't able or was unwilling to hold up his end was a significant loss in combat power.

They knew they would have to spend plenty of time training whomever they picked, and it was important that they not lose time on those who were just not up to it.

By the time they had finished breakfast, they knew what they wanted, but not how to find it. They decided just to wing it and see if their instincts were right.

They managed to get down, and hold down, the breakfast without embarrassing themselves. But the look of the three of them was enough to warn anyone not to mess with them until much later.

On his way to the jeep, Hollister lit his first cigarette of the day. It tasted awful, but satisfied some need to fill his lungs with smoke. The cigarette had swollen from the humidity in the mess hall and didn't burn normally. He didn't care. All he wanted was a cigarette.

The Interrogation Center was a large compound just off the road that connected the Long Binh and the Bien Hoa complexes. It was a prison, of sorts, that held up to thirteen hundred enemy POWs inside a combination of flimsy buildings and chain-link-fence enclosures.

On the four corners, Vietnamese soldiers stood guard in the gun towers that not only overlooked the yard, but had the responsibility to provide fire against any attacking force.

Mr. Pauley was one of the interrogators from the 500th MI Group. His job was to interview VC and NVA soldiers, day after day, to try to extract as much useful tactical information as he could. He was held by all the Americans who worked, at the Interrogation Center as the most experienced one there. If anyone had a question, they went to Mr. Pauley for the answer.

"Been here since nineteen sixty-three," the chief warrant officer said, pulling off his GI-issue glasses and rubbing the bridge of his nose. "Course then I wasn't with this place. I was a translator in the MAAG Mission Headquarters down in Saigon."

"You've sure been logging in some time over here," Hollister said.

"Oh, it wasn't so bad back early in the war. Saigon was a terrific place to be stationed before there were even five thousand Americans in the whole country. And it was a lot more peaceful in Saigon before Diem was assassinated. I worked for him for a few months."

"What was he like?" Vance asked.

"He was a regular asshole," Pauley said.

Hollister liked the fact that Pauley just spoke up and didn't worry about where anyone fell on the war or Diem. To Hollister that meant they would get straight answers out of him.

"So how do we do this?" Sangean asked.

"Easy," Pauley said. "It's like shopping."

"How's that?" Vance asked.

"You tell me what you're looking for in a Chieu Hoi, and I'll try and find him for you from the population."

"Well," Sangean said, "what would we be looking for? Young and healthy enough to survive on patrols. Ah, language would be lots of help. Combat experience would please the team members."

"We'd like him to know the area we're working in, but we can't discuss where we're working," Hollister said.

"I understand," Pauley said. "How about you let me guess where you might like them to be familiar with?" he said with a sort of wink.

It was common knowledge that the LRPs were working in the western end of the III Corps area and were based out of Cu Chi, so the only ones they were keeping the details from were other Americans. Still, operational security was desired whenever possible.

Pauley divided them into three different areas of the main building and set each one up with an interpreter, a desk, and a couple of chairs. Hollister was lucky enough to get a desk near a window that afforded some light and plenty of fresh air.

Pauley had detected that the three LRPs were in a bad way and had some coffee brought to them while they worked.

Sergeant Dinh was Hollister's interpreter. His English wasn't much better than Hollister's Vietnamese. Still, he was all that could be spared for the interviews. Pauley had to apologize that the better interpreters were being used to interrogate the new prisoners.

Pauley asked that they be patient with the interpreters, and said their efforts would go a long way in helping them improve then-skills. In return he promised to help them select the best Hoi Chanhs he could from the prison population.

The morning went slowly and was somewhat disappointing for all of them. They talked to VC after VC, most of whom promised to perform combat exploits they didn't even understand.

When Vance, Hollister, and Sangean broke to talk about their experiences, it became apparent to them that the prisoners had all cooked up their stories based on what they thought the Americans would want to hear.

It was clear that most of the prisoners they interviewed wanted to work with the Americans. According to Pauley, this was because they knew they would be treated better by the Americans than by the South Vietnamese and also because they were sure the Americans were going to win the war. And, of course, because they would be paid for their help.

The only thing the three LRPs were sure of was that there was no shortage of applicants. After the break, they went back to it. By midafternoon, they had narrowed it down to about four VC each. But they had decided not to accept more than ten in case the program was a complete waste.

As the questioning went on, Hollister was impressed with the savvy of some of the Hoi Chanhs. They knew quite a bit of American slang and seemed to project similar, or maybe even identical, can-do attitudes. By about the seventh Hoi Chanh who seemed to repeat the same phrases, Hollister held up Sergeant Dinh and asked him if he was using his own words to describe things or if he was translating the words the Hoi Chanhs were using. Dinh swore that he was giving Hollister the translations without any editorial comments.

At the opposite end of the room, Vance leaned on a table and questioned a Hoi Chanh. He looked up and caught Hollister's eye, then asked the next question: "Can you work for Americans?"

Vance's interpreter translated the question for the Hoi Chanh, who answered in Vietnamese.

Hollister spoke up just a moment before the interpreter translated the Hoi Chanh's response. "Let me guess. He's going to say, 'I can work for the Americans. I have never really been committed to the Communist goals.'"

The interpreter turned around and looked at Hollister, surprised. "How you know that?"

"We have to talk. Somebody has been coaching these guys," Hollister said to Vance.

"You know, I kinda got the feeling that the answers didn't fit the guys I was talking to, either," Vance said.

"Let's go talk to Pauley."

Pauley led the three LRPs to a large room where dozens of prisoners were squatting and listening to one who held their attention. The LRPs listened as Pauley translated the words of the squatting prisoner, who spoke with authority and punctuated his statements with a tin spoon that he rapped on the cement floor at appropriate points.

"He told them they could make fifty dollars U.S. a month if they took the jobs as Kit Carson Scouts," Pauley said.

"Why is that important to them? Where are they going to spend the money?" Hollister asked.

"For most of these guys there's a family somewhere that is starving to death because all the young men are gone. They have either been moved from them, or they are unable to get the most out of their fields. Money is the solution for most of their problems. These guys rarely got paid as VC or NVA, and, even if they did, it was so little money it was no help at home. Fifty bucks U.S. is a windfall."

"The guy coaching them sure seems animated," Vance observed.

"He is pretty enterprising. He speaks some English and some French, and he's a real character."

"How come he isn't pushing for the job?" Vance asked.

"He's got a bum leg, and the Viet guards told him he wouldn't be sent to the interviews. So he's making a buck coaching the others."

"He speak English?" Hollister asked.

"A little, and some French," Pauley repeated.

"We'll take him."

Hollister turned to Sangean. "That's if it's okay with you, sir."

"What are you thinking?"

"No matter who we pick, chances are he won't speak a word of English. We need our own interpreter who can be our head Hoi Chanh. We'll never get a regular interpreter out of Major Fowler after we burned him down in front of Colonel Downing. So I thought we'd just create our own."

"Good idea," Sangean said. "We'll take him."

"Wrap him up," Vance said.

Pauley called out to the enemy prisoner, "Bui, come over here."

Bui turned and was surprised to see he was being watched—and by the LRPs who were there for the interviews. He stood and tried unsuccessfully to straighten out his bad leg. He put the spoon in his shirt pocket and walked toward the four Americans.

No one spoke as they watched him take one regular step and then one halting step on the crooked leg that wouldn't lock at the knee. His stride was a one-sided waddle.

Under his breath, Hollister whispered, "It doesn't bother me. Walking is not what I want him for."

By dusk the trio was packed and waiting on the headquarters chopper pad. Bui was with them, wide-eyed and uncharacteristically quiet.

The chopper that landed was from the 145th Aviation Battalion in Bien Hoa. One slick platoon had been assigned to support all of the LRP operations. As they got into the chopper, the pilot, a warrant officer named Norton, told Sangean that the remainder of the platoon would be displacing to Cu Chi within twenty-four hours. This brought the second big smile that Hollister had seen on Sangean's face in as many days.

The chopper came to a hover check, then Bui watched the ground move about under the chopper. He still seemed shocked by the course his life had taken in a few short hours. He tightly gripped the edge of the bench seat and pressed his back to the transmission wall as Norton maneuvered the hover into a takeoff up and over the nearby one-story latrine that separated the chopper pad from the perimeter wire and the row of matching guard towers.

The sun was just setting when the chopper finally left the Bien Hoa traffic control space, headed for Cu Chi. Hollister, Vance, and Sangean were satisfied that they had accomplished much in their short stay in Long Binh. And Bui was still trying to get used to the phenomenon of flight.

The night was clear, and the thousands of tiny lights that marked life in the fields and paddies twinkled as Norton whisked the LRPs westward.

Not even close to Cu Chi, Hollister began making lists in his head

of the myriad things he had to do. Full operational status was rushing up
to meet him faster than he had guessed it could. He had endless lists of
training objectives that he might not get done before the first teams were
on the ground. And he had to add to his lists the coordinated training of
the new support elements. The burden would be to find the time, schedule
the training in the right sequence, and make sure the right people got to the
right training.

As he thought of the training requirements, he could feel the back of
his neck tighten up. Sure that he would never get it all done, he knew he
would have to settle for getting as much of it done as he could. It would
mean little sleep and virtually no wasted motion.

Vance and the pilot got into a conversation over the intercom about the
chopper support's routine. Vance's theory was that an organization as large
as the 145th Aviation Battalion would have a large number of flights as well
as ground-supported trips to make on any given day to support its own aircraft and crews scattered throughout the III Corps area. His suspicion was
that he might be able to take advantage of those missions when possible and
help increase the flexibility and response of Juliet Company's administrative
and logistical needs and solutions.

As the Juliet Company executive officer, Vance would not only be in
charge of administration, but logistical and supply needs and requests. He
knew it would do little good for him to requisition things for the company
if he didn't have a backup net of sources to move supplies when the supply
system itself bogged down with too much demand. One thing that was for
sure in Vietnam was that there was no shortage of supplies—just difficulty
getting them from where they arrived in-country to where they needed to
be to get the job done. Vance was not going to pass up any opportunities.

It was almost two in the morning when Hollister got to his hooch. He was
exhausted, still a little rubbery from the effects of the drinking and brawl
the night before, and he still had plenty to do before he could get to sleep.

Washing up in the dark at the outdoor shower point allowed him to
watch the sky. As he lathered up he felt, as always, a little vulnerable—naked
while choppers flew to and from missions, H&I fires went out to the margins
of the division's AO, and soldiers stood watch on the perimeter bunkers less
than a hundred meters from his shivering body.

He opened the spigot for a second time and let the cold water flush the
soapy film from his skin. For a moment he let himself miss the hot showers he
and Susan often took together. They would frequently use up all the hot water

in the small water heater in their quarters at Fort Benning. He glanced at his watch. It was nearly four in the afternoon in New York. She would probably be getting ready to knock off work. He hoped her day had been wonderful and she was not as worried about the months ahead as he was.

His mind switched from thoughts of Susan to worries about his responsibilities. He tried to tell himself that he was up to it, but he had done enough LRP work in Vietnam to know that every day turned out to be a surprise, no matter how hard he prepared for it. He knew that in training and planning he had to emphasize flexibility to adapt to the changes in the situation. Failing that meant filling body bags. He never wanted to see another one.

But he knew that was an impossible wish.

"We now have fourteen teams, full strength and deployable. We will be integrating the new Kit Carson Scouts after they finish company training and get some time to familiarize themselves with the teams," Sangean said to the mess hall full of LRPs, pilots, and artillerymen.

"They will not be brought into the company area until we finish the training. And even then, Lieutenant Potter—our new Intelligence officer, for those of you who haven't met him—will be setting some off-limits areas for them.

"But now we need to get on to operational matters. We have received orders to deploy LRP teams all along the Cambodian border from this point." He tapped the map taped on the wall behind him. "To this point." He tapped it again, at a point near the Plain of Reeds. He then held his hands up to stop any comments before they began.

"I know," he said. "It's like a fucking wet pool table out there. But it's where they want us and where we will work for now."

Even though silent, most of the men assembled exchanged knowing glances. They knew about the undesirability of the AO assigned to the teams.

"The patrols will be configured, inserted, and extracted to give them the maximum opportunity to survive without being compromised and to be able to bring the max smoke on enemy elements and positions in our AO. That means heavy with ammo and light on rations. In general that means the teams will take M60 machine guns and Starlights and stay in no longer than five days per mission."

Some of the LRPs nodded their approval at the mention of M60s.

"The G-2 has it that small parties are continuing to terminate their march from North Vietnam along the southern end of the Ho Chi Minh Trail complex and cross into South Vietnam in our sector."

Sangean paused and looked around the room for any questions or reactions.

A sergeant in the back raised his hand. "Will these be just interdiction missions, sir?"

"We will conduct combat patrols to eliminate infiltration where we find it, destroy roads, bridges, fords, and way stations. We'll direct artillery and air onto any encampments, training areas, or tunnel complexes we might turn up—on either side of the border. And we'll try for an occasional prisoner snatch where we can."

There were generally supportive grunts and noises from many in the room. They didn't like the AO, but they did like taking the initiative. Many had been misused before on patrols that were poorly supported because their mission was only reconnaissance. Somehow, when teams were sent into an area to look for something and report it, supporting headquarters failed to think about their making contact. It was as if they assumed teams that were just looking could avoid contact at their whim. That translated into little, very late, or no support when contact was made.

"We'll go in loaded for bear. We'll be full strength on air, choppers, and commo support, too. So we should be in good shape despite the unsatisfactory cover and concealment."

Sangean turned the briefing over to Lieutenant Potter, who introduced himself.

"I am here from the ARVN District Headquarters at Hiep Hoa. I've been in-country for ten months and have spent all of that time trying to get out of Hiep Hoa."

His comments got a laugh out of everyone in the room. They all knew how worthless the District Headquarters was in the small town between Cu Chi and the Cambodian border. They would send troops out in the daytime only to come up dry every time. One of the reasons was that they never left the highway. Each night they would pull back inside the wire at the District compound and wait for another day.

Potter had to have been a real standout in an ARVN unit. He stood six-foot-three and weighed in at about two hundred pounds. He had a large voice and a face full of teeth that flashed with his quick smile. Still, he was kind of a strange bird. He had been an infantry officer and an aviator, but he had developed a high-frequency hearing loss in one ear, and a flight surgeon had grounded him. Infantry Branch had wanted to profile him and restrict his assignments about the same time Military Intelligence Branch was desperately looking for quality officers to fill its ranks.

With a little salesmanship and lots of enthusiasm, Potter and MI convinced each other it was a marriage made in heaven, and he was branch-transferred into MI. So, though he wore the compass rose of MI on his collar, he also wore a CIB, with flight and parachute wings below them. The only dark spot in his transfer to MI was his eventual assignment to Hiep Hoa. That had been the end of the honeymoon.

Hollister remembered Potter from Ranger School. He had been a good student and an exemplary patrol leader. When Sangean had told him he was lobbying to get Potter from MACV, Hollister agreed that he would be an asset to Juliet Company.

Potter gave a thorough briefing, though he candidly disagreed about the size of the threat the higher command had suggested existed beyond the invisible border in the fields.

His assessment was that the infiltration was in fact taking place and being supported from way stations in the Ba Thu Corridor—inside the Parrot's Beak—and way stations inside western III Corps.

He felt the ARVN paranoia about another attack on Saigon made them overemphasize the need for interdiction along the routes from the end of the Ho Chi Minh Trail to the suburbs of Saigon.

Still, he did not want to play down the real danger to teams caught out in the AO. It would take very little for a team to be wiped out if it made contact with a lightly armed platoon-sized enemy unit—or if it was hit by a single RPG grenadier.

His briefing was solid and made plenty of sense. It was his first introduction to the company, and most felt that he inspired confidence in his judgment in spite of the bad reputation the Military Intelligence community had among the troops.

Potter's portion of the briefing was followed by Hollister's. He gave a general description of the schedule of deployments, the length of the patrols, and the priorities that would be in effect concerning contact and teams compromised in the AO. He finished with a reemphasis on the training that would take place before and between missions.

Captain Chris Edmonds followed Hollister and introduced himself. Edmonds was the platoon leader of the slick platoon, which would be with Juliet Company. His eight slicks, pilots, crew, mechanics, and ground-support personnel had displaced from Bien Hoa to Cu Chi and were busily refurbishing the old billets they were given.

"You know who we are. We're the guys who are trying to take those piece-of-shit barracks you-all gave us and turn them into a bit of heaven. When we're finished, you-all will be welcome to come down and spend some of your jump pay in our club. But—only after you have bathed. I've picked up LRP teams before." He made a face and got plenty of catcalls in return.

After settling the crowd back down, Edmonds wasted no time convincing all that he and his pilots were very pleased to be with Juliet Company and to be able to get a chance to know the people that they supported. They had several months of experience in what he called "bus driving." They were all tired of missed communications, wrong coordinates, bad messages, unhappy ground troops, and abused crews.

When Edmonds was finished, everyone was sure he meant business and was committed to Juliet Company.

The briefing went on for another hour as the FAC, the artillery forward observer, and the 25th Division liaison officer all spoke.

It soon became apparent to the leaders of Juliet Company that the company was coming together and that there was a consistent effort to coordinate support, reduce the time to get it, and let the parties involved get to know one another.

As the new Signal officer, Captain Newman, took his turn, Hollister looked over at Major Sangean. The confidence coming from the briefing was showing in a slight relaxation in the tension in his face. Hollister wouldn't have described Sangean as worried, but he might have used the words "seriously concerned" to describe him earlier.

Newman explained the post of commo officer and the duties of the company's Commo Section. The extended distances involved—border to Cu Chi and Cu Chi to Long Binh—brought the company several radio communications problems. Hollister's efforts to convince enough people of the need for constant and reliable communications had resulted in the creation and staffing of a commo element in Juliet Company. In a nutshell Operations was going to help them shoot, aviation was going to help them move, and Newman was going to allow them to communicate.

That brought a smile to every face in the room. To the man they all knew that survivability rested in the ability to tell people what they needed, and without reliable communications they were at great risk on the ground.

While training and mission prep continued for the next few days, Hollister, Sangean, and Potter made flight after flight out to the border area to get a better look at it. They tried to make the missions deceptive by flying in patterns that would indicate they were looking at things on the near side of the border, closer to Hiep Hoa than to the actual border. They brought binoculars, and while the choppers circled the Hiep Hoa area, they inspected the vegetation, trail patterns, old and new enemy position reports, and flight conditions at various times of the day.

Hollister was able to mix up the air support for the recons by getting rides with the air force FAC, Lieutenant MacNaughton. Mac was an F-4 pilot by training, but had been assigned to the forward air controller job after a hundred missions at the controls of a jet. During their flights along the border, Hollister learned more about the FAC business than he might ever have learned in normal infantry jobs in a twenty-year career. And the flights gave him a better perspective on what MacNaughton needed from a team to put in an effective and accurate close air strike.

Things seemed to be getting better and more complicated at the same time. Hollister's doubts about being able to direct the orchestration effectively nagged at him, and he spent longer hours poring over plans, maps, notes, and Intelligence Summaries. He spent a lot of time talking to his new source of information—*Sergeant* Bui. The officers had decided to make Bui an acting sergeant to give him some status with the Americans and the other Kit Carson Scouts.

Bui was as forthcoming as Hollister could have wished. He told Hollister about the AO, about the kind of guerrilla operations that had gone on there for years, and what he thought the Americans could expect.

Hollister listened and absorbed all he could, but kept in mind that Bui was a fast talker who might be handing Hollister a line of shit just to stay out of the prison and keep his job.

Bui's home was in the same type of terrain, although miles north of the AO that Juliet Company would be operating in. Hollister decided to ask Bui about his home area and not give away the actual area of interest for fear that he might go over the wire with the information and compromise the operations.

Two nights before the first team was to go in, Sangean dropped by Hollister's hooch with a bottle of bourbon and some last-minute questions.

Within an hour the others drifted in. By midnight an informal meeting of the company and support staffs had filled Hollister and Vance's small hooch.

The bourbon flowed freely, but there was a pregame anxiety in the air. Sangean said little, but the others talked about the operation like a football team on its way to a game. There were wide differences of opinion as to what they thought the enemy reaction would be to the deployment of several teams in their front yard. The vote went from avoidance to hell-bent destruction of the invaders.

By two A.M. the conversation had loosened up to cars, women, stereo equipment, and cameras.

Hollister liked his new team and didn't want to accept the fact that all of the same faces would not be around at the end of his tour. He had been at this war long enough to know that the casualties would happen and that he would make and lose more friends. The pull on his gut made him reach for another cupful of bourbon. Though it was not his favorite drink, it was what he started the evening with, and he subscribed to the taboo about not mixing drinks.

It made little difference. The morning run was just as difficult and his stomach was just as unsettled as if he had mixed bourbon, Scotch, and vodka, which some of those in his hooch had done.

The formation was much bigger now that the company was getting up to full strength, and they had embarrassed the pilots, air force, and artillerymen into joining them on the morning runs.

As Juliet Company ran through the narrow streets of the base camp, the thunder of their voices singing Airborne Jody cadences provoked insults from unseen soldiers still in their bunks. It was the kind of thing LRPs lived for—to embarrass the legs in their racks.

Running by the Division MP Company, Hollister recalled his morning runs on his first tour, in which the rivalry between his LRP detachment and the Brigade MPs was long-standing. He remembered some of the faces— and the morning was just as dark, and the day held just as many surprises. Not much had changed—except the losses and the pain.

The operational decision was to try to insert teams before first light to reduce the likelihood of discovery, but still allow them to use the coming daylight to support extractions if the team made contact.

The big worry was *Could they find the LZs in the dark?* The morning before the first insert, Hollister and the aircraft commanders took all the choppers out to an area similar to the AO, but forty miles south of it, and practiced flying to selected LZs in the dark.

Hawk Six, Captain Edmonds, was proud to boast that they didn't miss a single LZ except for one that had been misplotted by a pilot in Operations. Though they got to the LZ he had the coordinates for, it was not the LZ that Operations had intended. The object lesson was not lost on a single pilot in the debriefing held after the practice flights.

The night before the first insert, Hollister couldn't sleep. He got up twice and went back to Operations to recheck details that kept his mind running when he should have been sleeping.

At three A.M. he finally gave up. The liftoff time for the first insert was zero four one five hours. They would insert two teams that morning and two each day until they had ten on the ground. On the sixth day they would pull out the first two teams and insert two new teams somewhere else in the AO.

The plan would put a maximum of ten teams on the ground at once. But Hollister, Sangean, and the other old hands knew it was very unlikely that that many teams would stay in the full five days. Compromises, contacts, injuries, illnesses, and bad locations would reduce the number of teams on the ground.

The first policy was that a team stayed in unless compromised or in contact. If the team stayed in for five days, it would go to the bottom of the roster for a new mission.

If a team was pulled because it was compromised, or made minor contact, it would be reinserted the same day in an alternate LZ with an alternate mission. The policy seemed harsh, but it was a way to handle the human nature involved in thinking that a team was in more trouble than it was actually in.

Hollister and Sangean knew that if a team was considering declaring itself compromised, it would keep in mind that that would mean it would be extracted and reinserted into another possibly hot LZ. The policy would reduce the tendency to call wolf that had been so prevalent in LRP outfits that only worked recon missions.

The insert choppers stood ready at the pad. Sangean insisted on taking the first two teams in himself and wanted Hollister nailed to the radios in Operations in case anything went wrong.

He just couldn't do it. Hollister took a spare PRC-77 from Operations and walked out to the staging area. As the two teams were getting final inspections and the chopper crews were running through the ends of their checklists, Hollister rechecked every detail he could.

He talked to each team leader and the aircraft commanders just to make sure they had everything they needed and the last-minute things were right. While he stood on the pad, one of the choppers developed a problem with one of its FM radios, but was able to swap it for a spare without a delay in takeoff time.

Hollister watched the first team walk to the choppers under the heavy loads of their rucksacks. He stood by the waiting team and listened to the radio cross talk between the team leader and the Operations radio operator.

The team had a mission of moving to a small mangrove field and setting up an ambush on a very narrow trail that appeared to have been used in recent days.

Sergeant Rose crossed in front of Hollister and caught his eye. He walked over to one of the members of the waiting team, pulled open the neck of his shirt, and shined a flashlight on him. There, on his bare chest in indelible-marker ink, was the notation B POS/NO PEN.

This was evidence that the training was working. Rose had convinced the team medics to mark every man with his blood type and any allergy information so that any attending medic could save time when it was most needed. It felt good. Things were going well, and the insert ship was winding up from flight idle to full power for takeoff.

Hollister walked to a point where he could see Sangean in the pink glow of the chopper's panel lights. He knew Sangean couldn't see him, but he saluted the lifting chopper just the same.

Turning his back on the rotor wash to shield his eyes from the debris that swirled around the pad, Hollister allowed the buffeting of the wind to push him off a bit as he walked toward Operations.

The flight time to the first LZ was twenty-one minutes. During that time Hollister paced the stained and worn plywood floor of Operations just behind the radio consoles and listened to the five small speakers on different frequencies and nets.

They occasionally popped or crackled with a kind of static peculiar only to FM radios, and some limited cross talk took place between the pilots on the aviation frequency.

About ten minutes out, Sergeant Lopaka, the stocky little Hawaiian team leader of Team 3-1, called Operations for a commo check. The call was answered by PFC Cathcart, who was temporarily assigned to the Operations section as an RTO until he could get to and through Recondo School.

Cathcart calmly took the call and responded, letting Lopaka know he could hear him loud and clear.

Lopaka's voice was replaced by Sangean's in the C&C. "Houston Three, this is Six. We are five out of the LZ. Over."

Cathcart looked over to Kurzikowski for guidance—*Did anyone want to say anything to Sangean?*

Kurzikowski nodded. "Tell him you got it."

Cathcart put the pork-chop mike back to his lips and pressed the transmit button. "Six, this is Houston. Good copy."

The minutes ticked off slowly, and Hollister felt anxious. He walked over to the Operations map filling most of the wall next to the radio bench and looked at the spot that the team was approaching.

The radios were still silent.

He looked up at the flap of manila folder that had been pasted over a section of the map. It read: TODAY'S CHALLENGE AND PASSWORD. He lifted the flap, knowing he hadn't checked it out earlier. Underneath, in grease pencil, were the words GUEST/HEROIC.

CHAPTER 18

The radio broke the silence after a long pause. "Short final," the insert ship pilot said.

The announcement was made for the benefit of all those on the radio net who could not see what was going on. That included the entire staff of Operations.

Knowing what was happening didn't make it any easier for Hollister to wait it out. He mentally clicked off the time it was taking for the insert ship to descend over the leading edge of the landing zone he and the team leader had picked and get to the optimum touchdown point near the bamboo stand that bordered their initial rally point once off the LZ.

"They're down," Sangean said flatly over the radio.

Several more seconds went by, and Hollister spent them lighting a cigarette. He blew the smoke toward the ceiling and squared his Zippo up on top of the pack of Pall Malls he had placed on the edge of the radio bench.

"Coming up," the insert pilot said.

The silence before and after that was an indication that the insert was going uncontested and that they were not taking any fire or having any aircraft difficulties.

"So far, so good. Let's hope they're all like this," Kurzikowski said.

Nonetheless, it was taking too long for Lopaka to report that he was in and that the LZ was cold.

Hollister walked over to the map again and looked at the LZ. It was in the middle of an unusual cluster of vegetation in what was otherwise a flat, reed-covered wetland. The choppers landing there in the dark were probably not going to confuse anyone with the fake insert the chase ship had made only moments before and a thousand meters away. After the real insert, the insert chopper would make another fake one about two thousand meters north of the first fake one. Still, of the three touchdowns, the second, near all the wild growth of small trees and bamboo, was the most likely to end up holding Americans.

"Six, this is Three-one," Lopaka whispered into his handset, somewhere in the dense bamboo.

"Six, go."

"Lima Zulu cold. Over."

"Roger. Charlie Mike. Out," Sangean responded phonetically, telling Lopaka to continue the mission.

The transmission triggered a relaxation in Hollister's chest. He put out his cigarette and picked up the cup that held the remains of the coffee he had brought from the mess hall. Raising it to his lips, he realized it was cold and stopped just short of drinking.

Sangean called to let Operations know what they already knew. Lopaka's team was in, unopposed, the choppers were out of the LZ, they were moving to the last fake insert, and the insert package was then on the way back to Cu Chi to pick up the second team.

The minute hand on Hollister's watch was just touching the straight up—five A.M. There was enough time to get the second team in and get them to their rally point before first light.

The team—4-4, led by Sergeant Scott Decker, a bespectacled ex-fireman from Louisiana—would be going in near an abandoned ARVN outpost, which had been in use up until the end of 1966, when Saigon began relocating hamlets it couldn't protect. Once the hamlets in the vicinity were gone, there was no need for the two-hundred-man outpost.

Operating near an old outpost always had its problems. The minute one was abandoned, the VC would move in and strip it of all the usable military items that had been left behind. That always meant the minefield around the encampment had been dug up and the mines were probably replanted in areas that would protect the VC in the area, not the old outpost.

As he looked at the outpost—marked ABANDONED on the map—Hollister wondered again about its airstrip. Was it mined? If they needed to use it for reinforcement or for a medevac, would they find that the VC had mined the runway to prevent the Americans or the South Vietnamese from ever using it again?

When he stepped out to check the status of the waiting second team, he noticed that someone had repaired the broken screen door and attached a spring to it. He stopped at the bottom step and turned to look at the screen.

"Somethin' wrong?" Kurzikowski asked Hollister as he, too, stepped out to cross to the mess hall.

"How long has that door been like that?"

"Like what?"

"Like—fixed."

"Coupla days, sir."

Hollister stood there, bothered because he hadn't noticed it. He wondered what it meant.

"Something wrong with it?" Kurzikowski asked.

"No, I just didn't notice it," Hollister said, trying to play down how much it bothered him. Hell, he thought, if he could miss something that obvious, what else could he be missing?

"They're finished with the third LZ and are eleven minutes out for pickup," Cathcart said through the door for Kurzikowski and Hollister to hear.

Kurzikowski grunted something to Cathcart and turned toward the direction of the pad. Team 4-4 was there, somewhere in the dark. He put two fingers in his mouth and whistled once. "Decker? They're eleven mikes out. Stand by."

The only response was one word: "Airborne!"

It was still very dark when the slicks came back to pick up Decker's team. Hollister stood just outside the choppers' flight path and watched the team load and leave.

He wasn't sure what he was looking for while he watched Decker's team— maybe a small detail that could make a difference. It didn't escape him that he was as anxious as he would be if he were getting on the chopper himself.

But they were gone. He couldn't change fate, and he couldn't do anything more to protect them other than head back to Operations to be there if they needed anything. He knew he had to start drafting the contents of the daily operations summary to go to IIFFV. Somehow he had missed the paperwork end of the LRP business when he was a LRP platoon leader. But it wasn't giving him any slack in Juliet Company.

Staying behind and watching things unfold from Operations was very uncomfortable for Hollister. He was finding himself getting critical of every little detail. He wanted to know more than he could find out from the reports being radioed back. It was all he could do to keep from picking up a mike and asking for more details.

The only thing that stopped him was his dislike of higher headquarters bothering the hell out of troops in the field. He had experienced it as a platoon leader and as a LRP patrol leader. He had always promised himself to leave the troops alone. But now he was finding it very hard to do.

The second insert went as smoothly as the first, except Decker lost a handset to the paddy water in the first few minutes. He hauled out the spare and was up and back in commo in a minute or two.

It was almost seven A.M. before the choppers had refueled and returned to the Old Warrior Pad. Once they were all tied down, Hollister assembled everyone, including Sangean, in the makeshift classroom that doubled as their briefing room.

Each pilot, each door gunner, the FAC, the artillery FO, and Major Sangean took turns explaining what worked and what needed work from his point of view. Everyone had the same complaint—it seemed to take too long for the teams to get out and the insert choppers to get airborne again. They all admitted that the time complaint was only the product of not being able to see what was happening. In reality both inserts took less time than the dozens they had practiced in the daylight.

The conclusion was that the pilots would be better able to judge what was expected of them next if they had more information about the progress of the inserts. Sangean agreed to call out more progress reports as they happened.

First Lieutenant Lambert, the artillery FO assigned to Juliet Company, brought up the difficulty of being prepared to fire supporting artillery with the complete package of six aircraft circling the team. His concern was that if called upon to adjust fire for the team, he would need to designate a holding area for the aircraft so he could clear the area for the fire-direction center.

They had discussed it and even simulated it on the training inserts, but Lambert explained that he wasn't sure a holding area good for him would necessarily be good for the pilots and the C&C ship. It was all a matter of proximity.

This point spawned a lengthy debate about artillery and aviation needs. Hollister listened and occasionally made a note about something he wanted to follow up on. Suddenly, he looked up through the screening and noticed Sergeant Rose, across the company street, running fullbore from the Company Aid Station to the Orderly Room. *Was it a contact?*

A team under fire? No, Hollister calmed himself, they hadn't tripped the contact siren mounted on the Operations roof.

Still, something was wrong. Coots exploded out of the Orderly Room door and ran to Operations. He stuck his head inside, then pulled it back out, not finding whom he wanted. Hollister watched him race toward the classroom.

He burst into the building, half out of breath, half apologetic. "Ah . . . I'm sorry. But Sergeant Rose sent me." He gasped for a second breath. "The first sergeant had a heart attack. He's in bad shape."

Dewey and Rose were carrying First Sergeant Morrison to the jeep when Sangean and Hollister got there. Rose fired off a couple of short phrases between attending to Morrison and getting him into the jeep. From what he said, Hollister thought he understood they were going to the Division Hospital. What he knew was that there was nothing he or Sangean could do to help the first sergeant.

As Dewey and Rose drove off with the still-huge hulk of First Sergeant Morrison lying in the back, pale, sweating, and gasping for air, Hollister felt helpless. He had never felt so unable to influence things. His tools— weapons, choppers, manpower—were all useless. They couldn't push back the threat of death that hovered over the forty-three-year-old NCO. He was every bit as close to death as a soldier under enemy fire.

As the jeep turned the corner and faded out of sight, Hollister knew it was the last day for Morrison. Even if he lived, his days in Juliet Company ended when the pain crushed his chest.

By noon the teams due to go in five days hence had been briefed and the team leaders were out conducting aerial recons of possible LZs. Decker's and Lopaka's teams were laying up until dark to be able to make what moves they needed, and Rose had returned with the news: He found Vance, Sangean, and Hollister in the Orderly Room trying to figure out how to divide up Morrison's work.

"Well?"

"He's in intensive care. He's stable, and he's probably going to make it. The doctor thinks this is not his first one," Rose said.

"Not his first one? Heart attack? How can that be?" Sangean asked.

"He's been killing himself trying to lose weight, and he started having chest pains over three weeks ago. The doc thinks he had a smaller one a couple of weeks ago, and this one tried to eat him."

"Can we see him?" Sangean asked.

"Tomorrow, at the earliest, would be my guess. He's so doped up now he wouldn't know if Ann-Margret walked in naked."

"What'll they do with him?" Vance asked.

"They'll make sure the heart attack has passed, put him on some stuff to try to keep it from happening again, and ship him off to CONUS."

Hearing all this felt like a hot knife in Hollister's gut. He wanted to hear more about Morrison, but couldn't even find words to ask. He had seen men killed and crippled in war, but with Morrison it was somehow a different loss. He was an especially good man—a man who tried. He loved the troops and only had a problem with himself. Hollister knew he would miss Morrison and would remember that he had learned something about first impressions from him. At that moment he hated the army. He hated loss. He hated being angry.

The day got away from Hollister. He was involved in a blur of planning for upcoming teams, finding and recording grid coordinates in plans, reports, and notes. He talked at length with Kurzikowski and two of the platoon leaders about training and spent some time going over details that Dewey had inherited from First Sergeant Morrison. And during all that, he never stopped listening to the radios.

He had tried to work in the back end of the L-shaped building that housed Operations, but he couldn't. He just couldn't concentrate on what he was doing without wondering what was happening at the radios out in the AO. He finished the afternoon and announced that some of the other bodies who normally worked in Operations would be moved to his old space. The assistant operations sergeant, Quinn, got the word and moved that evening. After all, his job was ninety percent paperwork, reports and classified documents. He didn't need to be near the radios to do his job.

It was well after midnight when Hollister sat on the edge of his bunk. Vance was still in the CP trying to do some damage control. The loss of the first sergeant threw the brakes on several projects Vance was working on, and only more long hours would fix that.

Hollister thought about going over to help, but knew that as tired as he was, he would probably not be of any use. He looked at his watch and worried that he had to be up in just three hours to put in two teams before first light.

After an hour of trying to get to sleep, Hollister got up and turned on the light. The harder he tried to sleep, the more noise he heard in his head. He walked to the shelf that had once served as a perch for some supplies and grabbed the bottle of Scotch that stood at the ready.

He poured himself a few ounces of liquid sleeping pill and swallowed it with one gulp. The Scotch burned his throat, and he felt flush immediately. He wiped out the inside of his canteen cup with the corner of a damp OD towel. Wiping out the cup was a sign to himself that he did not intend to have another.

Hollister's first two inserts went well. He still felt uncomfortable with the darkness and flatness of the western III Corps area. He had learned that it took some real concentration to make sure the spot for the landing zone was the right one. It helped that he cross-checked his call with the pilots and the FAC, who had a better and more vertical picture of the ground. Hollister would have to become much more aware of and reliant on the rivers and streams running through the AO. Straight lines, larger dikes, and roadways were not as distinctive as the shapes of the rivers and were more likely to mislead him in his map reading. He missed the terrain features that were so obvious in northern South Vietnam.

That afternoon went like the first, and Hollister was beginning to see the operational complexities compound themselves. In two days the choppers had been in and out of the AO twelve times to insert teams and conduct recons for future teams. Already there was some problem with a radio in one chopper. Another one had developed a vibration that needed inspection and attention.

The four ground teams were having trouble with the necessity to lay up during the day and move only at night. Each team felt that the longer it stayed put, the greater the likelihood it would be discovered by any number of enemy, friendly, or in-between Vietnamese wandering around the AO.

But the biggest problem was keeping the airspace clear of uninvolved aircraft. The full force of the American and allied contingent in South Vietnam could be a threat to the safety and security of the ground teams.

The first aircraft that flew over a team only partially concealed from above and reported the presence of an unknown element caused three choppers to appear from nowhere. Sergeant Decker, the team leader of 4-4, spent several anxious minutes trying to convince a flight of navy gunships that they were friendlies and begged them please not to circle their position and give them away.

The flap generated several phone calls between Sangean and Fowler. All of them were angry, and none of them satisfied Sangean's demands that the area be closed off for LRP aircraft only. Fowler suggested that if the LRP team could be seen from the air, it was a training and camouflage discipline problem that was Sangean's to fix.

From the look on Sangean's face, the day was not going to be a pleasant one. But by late afternoon, things were quiet in the AO and Hollister's energy level was dropping from his lack of sleep and the demands on him.

Mail call came, and he felt guilty getting a letter from Susan. He was a couple of days behind in his writing, but not in his promises to get some letters written. Every time he had tried to write a letter, however, he had been interrupted with some little detail. It was becoming painfully obvious that the business of running a LRP company was many times more complex than being a platoon leader in a small LRP detachment.

Susan was already beginning to ask questions about their future—immediate and long-term. The immediate questions were about R&R. Before he left, Hollister had told her he thought that unless policy had changed they might be able to meet.

The long-term questions were general. What did he think about doing after Vietnam? She didn't ask directly, but it was clear she wanted to know what she had been asking him since they met: *Was he going to stay in the army or not?*

He put the letter down and lit a cigarette. The question had been nagging him as much as it had been chewing on her. When he first joined the army, there was no doubt that he was going to get out as soon as he could. But when it came time to get out, OCS seemed to be an option worth delaying his ETS for. Then the Gulf of Tonkin Resolution changed his plans. Instead of being able to get out after six months as a lieutenant, he was notified he would be on *indefinite* status until Vietnam was over. Since that day he had done well and made first lieutenant and captain. He knew if he could get some college in, there was a good chance he could make major in the next few years.

So getting out meant giving up a lot of professional accomplishments and starting over at whatever he went into. He knew what she knew. That was that each day he stayed in the army made it that much harder to get out and start over again.

He picked up the letter and wondered what he was going to say to Susan when he wrote back. At least he could offer some hope about R&R, if not any about getting out. He told himself to remember to get the latest on the R&R policy. The thought made him remember that they didn't have a first sergeant anymore.

He put down the letter and picked up the field phone. He cranked and got Coots in the CP. "Hey, Hollister here. Patch me through to Sergeant Major Carey at Two Field, will you?"

"You gonna be in Operations? It'll probably take a few minutes."

"Yeah. I'll be here," Hollister said, and hung up. He knew he had to do something about the first sergeant problem, even though Vance and Sangean were working on it, too.

The letter was filled with heart-tugging sentences that made him miss Susan more than ever. It was different from his first tour—before they were married.

"From Mama?" Kurzikowski asked.

Looking up from the page, Hollister smiled. "Yeah. She's making me feel pretty guilty about not writing as often as she does."

"Hey, get used to it, sir. Women make you feel like you're steppin' on your crank all the time."

"Shouldn't have married one that was smarter than I am," Hollister kidded.

"No. I married one that was dumber, and man, that was a real problem. She used to write me and ask questions about needing to change the air in the car tires when I was over here last tour."

"What did you tell her?"

"I told her to go ahead and do it. What harm could it do?"

"And?" Hollister asked.

"And she's married to some E-7 in Fort Belvoir now."

"Sorry," Hollister said.

"Oh, don't be sorry for me. Be sorry for that E-7 at Belvoir. He's her problem now."

They got a laugh out of the flip comment. Kurzikowski refilled his coffee cup and Hollister's from a mess-hall pitcher that someone brought over to Operations. Before he put the pitcher back on the side of the radio bench, the tactical radio net broke squelch and the sounds of hard breathing preceded the message. "Contact! This is Four-four, we have contact!"

In the background the sounds of Ml6s firing could be heard over the small radio speakers.

The room exploded into activity. Kurzikowski dropped the pitcher on the floor, reached up, and tripped the contact siren switch. The siren began to wind up to a high-pitched scream, spurring more activities all over the LRP area.

Pilots shot from the mess hall to their choppers. Crew chiefs rolled out from their slumbering positions on the bench seats of their slicks and began to untie their choppers' main rotors. Platoon Sergeant Krane, from the 4th Platoon, leaped from the steps of his hooch over the puddle that had collected after the night's light rain and ran to the slicks to be ready as belly man.

Inside Operations Hollister grabbed the pork-chop mike and replied, "This is Three. What do you have? Over."

"We just started taking fire from a tree line four hundred mikes to the northeast," Decker yelled over the outgoing small-arms fire.

Hollister turned to Cathcart, mouthed the letters "FO" and made a questioning face.

Cathcart reached for the land line and cranked it in an effort to track down Lieutenant Lambert.

"Do you have a target? Can you use arty or snakes? Over."

"Affirm. I have a fire mission going now on the redleg freq."

Angry, Hollister reached up and turned the dial on the side of the small speaker that was monitoring the artillery net. It immediately started spurting out the cross talk between Decker's senior RTO and the artillery-fire direction center at Duc Hue. He shot a look at the other two NCOs who were running the radios.

"You want us to launch a pickup?"

"However this ends up—we're compromised," Decker yelled.

"Rog. Stand by. Keep us informed."

He bent his knees and looked out at the chopper pad for the crews. Captain Edmonds was in the AC's seat on the C&C, running down the preflight checklist

"The Old Man back from division yet?"

"No, sir," Kurzikowski said. "Don't expect he'll be back for over an hour from what he told me before he left."

"Get a call into the Division TOC. They'll know where he is. Let him know what's going on. I'm going out with Edmonds and the C and C."

He hadn't even belted in when Edmonds pulled pitch and got the C&C airborne and out over the wire. Since the artillery was firing already, Hollister decided to leave the gunships back at Cu Chi until it was clear they would be needed. His worry was that he would get the guns out near the team in contact, not get to use them, leaving them in orbit, have to send them back to refuel, and then find that he needed them.

He told Decker he was keeping the Cobras back so that Decker would be able to manage the firepower resources available to him. It was the kind of thing that Hollister had always wanted someone to do for him when he was on the ground. He was conscious that too often the information ran one way—from the mud to the air-conditioned headquarters. Rarely the other way.

En route to Decker's position, Hollister waited until he was sure Decker wasn't tied up with adjusting the artillery fire and then called him. "What's your situation?"

"We're dropping redleg on the enemy position. We have one minor

WIA, and we are good and compromised. The small-arms fire we were getting has stopped. But I'm not sure we got them. Over."

"Roger. We are zero five out. Give me a panel, and we'll check out the area for you. How soon can you be ready to come out?" Hollister asked.

"We can be ready in one zero. The PZ is right in front of us."

"Rog, stand by."

Hollister called back to Operations and told Kurzikowski to launch the pickup ship, the chase, and the Cobras. He also asked the FAC to stand by to get airborne.

Edmonds took the C&C into a slow descending left-hand turn. The maneuver put Decker's team directly out the door that Hollister sat in, in the jump seat.

Below him, Hollister could see the long winding strip of green fed by a streambed. Inside the ribbon of trees and bamboo, Decker's team was trying to hide itself from any more incoming fire, but still make itself visible to the chopper.

Hollister strained to see the orange marker panels through the trees, but had no luck on the first orbit. At the same time he watched the area Decker had identified as the source of the ground fire. It was much easier to distinguish. The trees were splintered and some blown down by several 105mm artillery rounds. There were also three small craters already filling with paddy water.

As they flew over the enemy position, there was no sign of life—or death. So Hollister turned back to look for the team. A glint of sunlight immediately caught his attention. The sharp point of light kept flashing at the chopper—a signal mirror.

Edmonds saw it, too, and took the chopper into a tighter turn.

"Four-four, Three. You got your looking glass out?"

"Affirm."

"Roger. We have you. Ah . . . okay. I've got your panels now," Hollister said, finally seeing the markers stretched out in a break in the trees.

"Negative enemy fires since the redleg. You want to take a look-see?"

"Rog, stand by. We're gonna take a closer look," Hollister said.

Decker clicked twice.

"You up for a little low-level?" Hollister asked Edmonds over the intercom.

"I live for it!" Edmonds replied, dropping the collective and kicking the chopper into a tight right spiral heading first away from the enemy position and finally toward it.

With the chopper at just about treetop level, Edmonds stopped the descent and rolled the nose of the powerful Huey over to pick up some more airspeed. "Heads up back there. We're gook bait now."

"Just give me an okay. We're ready to go rock and roll," the door gunner volunteered from the other side of the chopper.

Hollister leaned forward in the jump seat to get a better view of what was coming up ahead and below the chopper. The trees were clipping by, some of them catching the skids of the chopper. It was all a blur of green until Hollister spotted what looked like a change in the color of the vegetation. A dead giveaway. The bushes had been moved, and someone had made an unsuccessful attempt at putting them back only to leave several branches twisted.

A twisted branch shows the texture of the leaves at an angle to the sun that is different from the way it normally grows. That difference in texture shows up in the sunlight as a different color.

Edmonds must have seen it at the same time because he quickly jerked up the chopper's nose, flaring and slowing its forward speed abruptly. At about the time the chopper lost most of its forward momentum, the disturbed bushes were just below it.

"Stay sharp back there," Edmonds cautioned the two door gunners, who were training their machine guns on the area around the spot they hovered over. They weren't as worried about someone shooting straight up at the chopper as they were about someone within range who could get off a few rounds and split before the gunners could spot him.

The downwash of the huge rotor disk blew the bushes violently, revealing the ground below them. The two pilots and Hollister scanned every piece of the area as it was revealed by the thrashing branches.

"Over here!" the copilot announced.

Edmonds slipped the chopper to the right in a skilled maneuver that arrested the forward motion while moving his door over the spot his copilot had pointed out.

"What you got?" Hollister asked.

"Looks like brass and some other packing or something," the copilot said.

"There, right next to that root outcropping," Edmonds announced.

There, just outside the left door, was a place under the small trees where someone had been waiting long enough to beat down all the ground cover and the grass growing against one side of a tree trunk.

"Bingo—blood trail!" Edmonds said. "Just to the east of that tangle of roots."

Hollister looked back at the reference point and let his eyes trace the ground in the direction that Edmonds had called out. Only a few meters from the roots was an area that looked as if someone had attended to a

wounded comrade. There was a pool of heavy organ blood and what looked
to be deep knee impressions. Bits of rag and a floppy hat were poking out
from under a branch felled by the artillery.

"Let's follow it."

"Goes this way," Edmonds said, slipping the chopper away from the
spot, down the tree line. As he did the wash peeled away more tree branches
and tall grasses revealing a trail of blood and footprints.

"Ho! Shit! Look!" someone yelled over the intercom.

There, standing over a body, was a soldier, hands raised, an AK47 on
the ground by his foot. The body appeared to be dead, an arm torn off just
above the elbow.

Hollister grabbed his M16 off his lap, spun it toward the VC, and flicked
the selector switch from safe to full automatic. He suddenly had to make
some decisions. What should he do about the team on the ground, the VC,
the flight approaching to pick up Decker's team?

"Keep him busy while I sort out a couple of things. Okay?"

"Rog. He's not going anywhere. Lemme ease on around here a bit to
make sure this is not an ambush," Edmonds said, pulling the cyclic over and
starting an ascending left turn, keeping the VC in sight.

"Find out the status on the pickup ships while I talk to Decker," Hollister said.

Edmonds nodded his head, telling Hollister that he had both hands
and both feet busy and was talking to someone else on a freq that Hollister
wasn't monitoring. Still, he got Hollister's message.

"Four-four, we got one in the trees here. What's your status?"

"We are packed and ready. Do what you gotta do, and we'll be here,"
Decker said.

"Rog. Stand by. Break. Houston, Three. You copy?"

"This is Six. I'm back in the saddle. Rog. You gonna pick up the VC?"
Sangean asked through a bit of radio interference from Cu Chi.

Hollister looked up for a signal from Edmonds. "What's your call? You
have any problem with that?" Hollister asked over the intercom.

"Hell, we've never captured a POW before. We need to stencil a gook
on the fuselage. Let's do it."

"Six, Three. We are going to try to pick up this VC, then pick up Four-
four and head back."

"Okay. Keep your head up," Sangean said, offering an unnecessary
caution. Landing a chopper to pick up a frightened VC was much more
dangerous than it looked.

"We'll keep you posted. Break. Four-four. You got this?" Hollister asked. Decker clicked twice.

"Okay," Hollister said over the intercom. "We good with the choppers?"

"Look out there by Duc Hue," Edmonds said, raising his hand and pointing out the windscreen.

There, at two thousand feet, were two Cobras, two slicks, and the FAC carving a wide, lazy circle over the ARVN outpost.

"Okay, let's get the Cobras over here to cover us, and we'll go down and get this guy. I'm going to get out and walk over to him. If the fucker blinks—drop him."

"Rog. Where do you want me to put it?"

"Land out there in the paddy where I can see him through the trees and he knows I can. Stay far enough away in case he's got a grenade. I don't want him to drop one in this jump seat—with me in it or not. I also want you outside the bursting radius in case I fuck up and step on something."

"Like a mine?" Edmonds asked, surprised at the thought.

"Yeah," Hollister said. "Just drop me. And come back in when I get him out of the trees. DO NOT WAIT."

"Okay, boss," Edmonds said. "Stand by a sec."

While Edmonds cleared the plan with the other choppers on another freq, Hollister pulled back on the charging handle of his M16 and ejected the round in the chamber, releasing the charger and seating a fresh round. He flipped it onto "safe" and dropped the rifle across his lap. He unbuckled the seat belts and laid them on the floor quietly. It was a habit he had picked up that grew from a bad experience on his first tour. A REMF colonel in a chopper popped his belt and let the metal buckles clatter to the decking, spooking two soldiers in the chopper into opening fire, nearly killing some friendlies on the ground.

He picked up the claymore bag that held his spare magazines, a couple of extra smoke grenades, and some other luxury items in case he had to spend some time on the ground.

"We're ready," Edmonds said. "Hold on. We're on the way in."

Hollister had a feeling the move was pretty stupid, but picking up a live prisoner was worth the risk. This guy could probably tell him much about the AO, the enemy units working there, and what they knew about the LRP teams. He swallowed hard as the chopper flared and touched down about thirty meters from the tree line that held the VC.

As he looked toward the tree line, he could see the VC soldier still standing there, his knees bent slightly and his hands folded on top of his head. The rifle was still on the ground.

The first step out was awkward, and Hollister tried to steel himself for the turbulence of the rotor wash.

He hit the ground running and tried to tell himself to relax and breathe. Instead, his chest tightened up and his pulse pounded in his temples as he crossed the open rice paddy, awash in a couple of inches of water. He tried to get the danger of a mine or booby trap out of his mind since there was almost nothing he could do about it.

The chopper lifted off behind him, and it got quieter.

As Hollister kept moving toward the VC, the man started to move his hands down. Hollister wasn't sure if it was a hostile move or just plain nervousness. He couldn't take a chance. He stopped, jerked the muzzle of the rifle upward, and yelled, "Up! Up! Keep 'em up!"

The VC began to bend at the waist, the same move he would make sitting down or going for the rifle. Hollister leveled the rifle and fired a burst of four rounds into the ground next to the VC, which straightened him up, made him jerk his hands back up on his head, and started him jabbering in Vietnamese.

The last few steps to the VC seemed to take forever to Hollister. He quickly looked around to see if there were any other VC in the area—ready to drop him. At that moment he realized if they were there he'd never see them until they opened up on him.

Reaching the VC, Hollister put the M16's flash suppressor in the center of his chest and applied a little pressure. With his left hand, he reached up and grabbed the VC's right wrist, which he brought down and around behind him. The move turned the soldier away from him.

Hollister raised his boot and tapped the soldier behind both knees, collapsing him to the ground. As he went down, Hollister pushed his torso forward until the VC was facedown.

He took one more look around for anything that didn't seem right. The other VC was dead—without a doubt. His arm was gone, and a large wound in the back of his neck most certainly had severed any connection between his brain and his body.

At that moment Hollister's stomach revolted at the sight and smell of the VC prisoner. He had forgotten how they smelled—of wood-fire smoke and cooking grease, with a large helping of body odor. The sensation caused Hollister to gag, involuntarily. He thought for a moment he was going to vomit, but got it under control.

His knee in the small of the VC's back, Hollister searched him with his free hand and found a chain and small carved Buddha in a metal setting

around his neck. Other than that, the soldier had only a rifle, a nearby
ammo pouch, and the flimsy pajamas he wore.

Hollister took off his web belt and tied the man's hands behind him by
slipping the belt around both elbows, VC-style, and tightening the buckle
until the VC's elbows almost touched behind his back.

Satisfied that his prisoner was not going anywhere, Hollister took a splintered tree branch and carefully lifted the corner of the ammo pouch. While
he did that, he made sure to watch the VC's response. If he had booby-
trapped the pouch, he would certainly do something to prepare himself for
a blast, even if he were going to sacrifice himself for his cause.

No expression change—no explosion.

CHAPTER 19

The prisoner was very frightened at the prospect of being hauled into a
chopper. As they approached the C&C, he resisted, and Hollister had
to force him into the aircraft.

Edmonds wasted no time getting the C&C back into the air. When
they leveled off at fifteen hundred feet, Hollister took his knee out of the
prisoner's back, and lifted him up off the deck of the cargo compartment.
He maneuvered him up to the center of the bench seat, and looked around
for some way to secure him better.

"Here you go, Cap'n," the door gunner said. He had unbuckled himself
from his gunner's well, scooted into the cargo compartment, and held up
the red-canvas tie-down strap.

It was perfect, Hollister thought. With it he and the door gunner tied
the prisoner's hands together and then slipped the seat belt between the
man's arms to lock him in place for the remainder of the extraction and the
flight back to Cu Chi.

Hollister was conscious of just how hard he was still breathing as he strapped
himself into the jump seat and slipped his headset back on. He cleared and
locked his rifle and placed it on the floor with his foot inside the sling to
keep it from going anywhere.

The VC's AK47 was in perfect shape, loaded, and recently fired. Hollister
cleared it and dropped the thirty-round magazine into his lap. He looked

around for a place to stow the rifle and decided to slip it under the short bench seat the door gunner sat on. It would travel well there and be within sight.

"So? You got yourself an AK?" the copilot asked.

"Nope. It's yours."

"Mine?" he asked.

"You spotted the blood trail. You deserve it."

"Hot damn!" the warrant officer said. "Never had a war trophy before."

"I promise you, you stay with Juliet Company and you'll be able to max out your hold baggage allowance going home."

"Don't you want it, sir?" the copilot asked. "No. I've got a warehouse full of this shit back home," Hollister lied. He had always felt a little uncomfortable explaining to others that he had never developed any interest in collecting enemy weapons or memorabilia. Anyway, it sounded better to say he had enough of it. Furthermore, an AK was worthless as a personal war trophy. It was an automatic weapon and couldn't be taken home, only sold to REMFs, who knew that.

"Damn, sir. Thanks."

"Believe me," said Hollister, "its no big thing. Stick around and you might get something better."

The extraction of Decker's team went without a hitch. While it was running from the tree line to the pickup ship, the prisoner had become comfortable enough flying to watch the extraction, amazed at American technology.

Hollister had considered putting a blindfold on the prisoner, but thought how frightening it would be just to be flying for what he was sure was the POW's first time. The blindfold seemed to be too much. He decided to hold off until they approached the base camp at Cu Chi, where it might be more appropriate.

Back at Cu Chi, Bui waited with Lieutenant Potter. As Intelligence officer Potter would do the initial interrogation of the prisoner to attempt to get any information of immediate tactical value to Juliet Company.

They met the choppers and quickly whisked the POW to one of the empty barracks to question him. Meanwhile, Hollister ran to Operations to give Kurzikowski and Sangean the details of the single-body count, the capture of the POW, and the contact and pickup.

As Hollister entered Operations, he was met with cheers and applause from the staff and three other LRPs. Capturing a prisoner didn't happen that often. And for the Operations officer to capture one was a real rarity.

"Okay, okay. You guys can get back to work. Next time I'll bring you a whole platoon of VC," Hollister said.

The group quieted down and got back to business. Diversions were rare in Operations and quickly passed when there were teams in the field. Everyone knew if a team called in a contact, anything less than immediate response was unacceptable.

Hollister dumped the VC ammo pouch on the field table near the door and cleared the AK47 again, then placed it across the ammo pouch. "The weapon belongs to Mister Farris."

"That one'll be worth a case of bourbon if he wants to trade it. I know a guy over at the Division Ration Breakdown Point that'll swap the booze for it right now," Kurzikowski said.

"You and Farris'll have to work that out. Right now I think he's pretty hot to keep it as a souvenir."

"We do this right around here, and he'll have a deuce and a half full of them," Kurzikowski said.

"Hope you're right," Hollister responded, taking off his hat and dropping his web gear over the back of a folding chair. "What's up with the other teams?"

"Quiet all the way around," Kurzikowski said.

Jerking his thumb toward the unseen prisoner, Hohlster said, "I hope we get some information out of this guy. He might be able to tell us just what the hell they were up to and why they fired on Decker's team. They had to know they'd get their dicks pounded into the dirt."

A cup of coffee, a cigarette, and a short walk to the abandoned barracks and Hollister was able to sit in on the interrogation.

"What's the deal?" Hollister asked Potter.

"Bui's been able to find out that the guy is new to South Vietnam. He was trained in Cambodia, after being drafted into the job from some village in the north."

"Ask him why they fired on the Americans. Didn't they know we'd find them out there in that terrain and run them down?"

Bui heard Hollister's request and began browbeating the POW with a rapid-fire rate of questions. Hollister couldn't tell for sure what he was asking, but his antics and exaggerated facial expressions told him a lot. Bui seemed to be embarrassing the prisoner over his stupidity.

The prisoner mumbled something. He was looking down dejectedly.

Bui turned to Hollister, surprise on his face. "He say he before been told that Americans almost all dead from Tet attacks, and he mus' clean up, ah . . . ah . . . strangers."

"Stragglers?"

"Yessir, *stragglers*." Bui made the correction.

"When did he leave Cambodia, and how did he find the team?"

Bui went after the prisoner again, thrusting his face into the prisoner's face. Bui looked angry and threatening.

"Whoa!" Hollister said, stopping Bui.

Bui looked up, puzzled.

"Let's try not to rattle him. He'll clam up, and we'll never get anything out of him." Hollister stepped over to the prisoner and took the blindfold off.

The prisoner timidly looked around the empty barracks, letting his eyes adjust to the light. Hollister pulled a cigarette out of his pocket, lit it, and stuck it between the soldier's lips. The VC took a drag, and nodded once to Hollister as a sign of thanks.

"Get him some water," Hollister said. "He's got to be dry."

Somewhat reluctantly, Bui stepped out to the "water buffalo," the trailer that stood in the middle of the compound. When he returned, the soldier had calmed down a little, apparently aware that he was not going to be tortured or shot.

"Ask him about the team. How did he know where they were?"

Bui fired the question at the POW. Hollister was standing behind the soldier and he silently signaled Bui to tone it down.

Bui tried a second time, in a little more moderate tone of voice, and the soldier responded.

Hollister looked to Bui for the translation.

"He say they don't know. He say they hear helicopt' early—dark. They go. They see trees to hide."

"Why did they fire on Decker's team?"

"No see Decker. They think good place to hide."

"You mean they reconned by fire? They were guessing?"

"Yes. Guess," Bui said.

"Shit!" Hollister said, throwing his hands up, frustrated.

"What?" Bui asked.

"If Decker hadn't returned fire, they might never have received any more fire."

"How you get prisoner?"

"Decker could have adjusted artillery or gunship fire on them."

Bui shrugged. "He talk like tell truth, but maybe he lie. Maybe just stupid, but can lie."

"What do you think?" asked Hollister.

Bui shrugged again. "I think he stupid, but also tell truth."

***

"How'd it go?" Sangean asked Hollister over lunch.

"We didn't need to compromise the team. They returned fire, and that developed the situation. If Decker had just used artillery, he might have avoided more fire."

"You really believe that?" Sangean asked.

"I wasn't there. There could be a lot more to it than that. My guess is that Decker really thought his root was in a wringer. He doesn't seem like the flappable kind to me," Hollister said.

"Well, I debriefed the team, and he said he never was sure they had him located, but the fire was too close to let it continue."

"I guess we know what that means," Hollister said.

Lieutenant Potter, sitting with them, looked up, puzzled. "What?"

"Means I'm picking locations for teams that might as well have a sign on them saying TEAM HERE!"

"All the blame isn't yours. We're just going to have to work harder at parking teams in spots that don't look like they would hold a team."

"I want to go out and do some more nosing around this afternoon. We can't keep putting teams in the obvious tufts of green out there," Hollister said.

"Okay. Say, did Bui get anything out of him about where they were going or what their mission was?"

Potter answered. "He found out they were heading to a rendezvous somewhere west of Saigon. He said he wasn't told exactly where for just this reason—case he got captured."

"Hmmm . . . Doesn't tell us much," Sangean said, stretching for the salt shaker, which was just out of reach.

"How big was the element?" Hollister asked, shoving the pepper shaker toward Sangean.

"Bui said that he admitted being with four other soldiers who were told to infiltrate from the Ba Thu Corridor to Saigon," Potter said.

Hollister reached into the side pocket of his trousers and pulled out his map case. With one hand he flipped it open and laid it on the table, next to his lunch.

"What?" Sangean asked, watching Hollister scan his map.

"There's no way that they can make it from Cambodia to Saigon in one night. They've got to be holding up somewhere."

"You'll never figure that out. They are probably holding up in dozens of places the VC and the sympathizers in the area have prepared for them."

"So, I say we look for where they've been and then track forward." Hollister wiped the corner of his mouth with one of the stiff GI napkins Sergeant Kendrick had scrounged.

"I'm not following you," Sangean said.

"Forget that look-see this afternoon. We have two teams going in north of Duc Hue tomorrow before first light."

"Right

"What do you say we drop them off and then try flying north to south through the reeds and look for some tracks of anyone who slipped across the border tonight."

Sangean and Potter smiled—the light going on.

"You're right. The grasses and reeds won't be up yet, and the trails will be easy to find," Sangean said.

"Sounds like the plan to me," Hollister said. "I'd like to take the guns and an FO with me."

"Let's try it."

"Hot dog!" Potter shouted. "Now we're talking. I can come along?" he asked, hopefully.

"Sure can."

"So you think you need an MI type out there with you?" Sangean asked.

"Nope. I just don't want to be out there before the roosters squawk knowing that he's back here in his fart-sack still stacking Zs," Hollister said.

Sangean and Hollister laughed at the expression on Potter's face. The poor guy looked stricken—but only for a moment. Then he grinned and said something about wanting to go out on a team sometime, maybe carrying one of the radios.

The next morning started with several problems. There was an engine problem in one of the slicks, then a weather hold over the LZ due to low-hanging clouds meeting a ground mist. Then the artillery battery that was tasked to support both teams going in got tied up with a fire mission in support of an RF/PF outpost and couldn't be relied on to be on standby while the team went in.

The delays put the team out forty minutes late. Fortunately, there was enough slack in the plan to allow for the delay and still get both teams in before first light—if neither team made contact on the way in.

By the time the second team was in and had reported that the LZ was cold, the C&C only had about forty minutes of fuel left. The gunships had even less.

Hollister decided to send the gunships back to refuel and use the C&C

to begin searching for trails in the wet grasses even before the sun started coming up.

Edmonds turned the chopper away from the more populated center and eastern part of Hau Nghia Province toward the Cambodian border.

"Why don't we swing down south toward the Parrot's Beak and then turn back north, putting the sunrise in their eyes and letting us fly at low level into the wind?" Hollister suggested.

"Zactly what I was thinking. You sure you haven't got aviator blood in your veins?" Edmonds replied playfully.

"You sure are chipper at this time of the morning," Hollister said.

"Hey, I got 'leven-hundred horsepower under my ass, two great door gunners, a peter pilot who can read a map with the best of them. What could possibly be the problem?"

Hollister looked at his watch. "My watch says it's still night out. Isn't that enough?"

"Naw. Every time I think of what life is like in a rifle company, an advisory job, or working in one of those fucked headquarters in Saigon, Long Binh, or Nha Trang, I get to likin' army aviation more and more."

"You guys must have to fail some kind of test to get into flight school," Hollister countered.

"Naw, we just have to be smarter than your average mud grunt."

Some giggling came over the intercom, and Hollister turned around to look at the door gunner, who suddenly made it look as if he were busy checking his M60.

Edmonds reached a point near the apex of the Parrot's Beak and made a hard turn back to the north. At the same time he dropped the collective, and the chopper seemed to fall as if it were floating toward the ground. At about two hundred feet, he pulled power back into the blade and leveled off.

"Heads up!" the copilot said, pointing off to the west out the left side of the windscreen.

"What the hell is that?" Edmonds said.

"Lights! No . . . vehicle lights . . . Jeezus! There must be a hundred of them!" Edmonds said.

Hollister pulled out his map and tried to find landmarks in the dark. The two small streams that ran near the border were too hard for him to pick out. He looked over his shoulder toward the glow of Saigon's lights on the horizon and then looked back down. He spotted the long, straight, and distinctive canal that ran parallel to the Cambodian border, just east of the village of Ba Thu.

"Looks like they are lined up north and west of Ba Thu itself," he said.

"That puts them just about a half a kilometer on the other side of the fence," Edmonds said.

"Shit!" Hollister said. "The fuckers are probably off-loading troops and supplies, telling them to walk toward Saigon."

The sun was starting to transform the blackness to a blue and pink dawn. The drivers were turning their lights off. "You suppose they're dumping their lights because of the chopper?" the copilot asked.

"No. They know we can't fire on them. They're probably just through using the lights now that it's almost sunup," Edmonds said.

Right in front of Hollister, about twenty meters out, two large puffs of black smoke appeared with muffled cracks. For a moment he didn't know what he was looking at. Each puff of smoke was half the size of the chopper and stood still in the sky once it appeared.

"Oh fuck! Triple A!" Edmonds yelled over the intercom as he nosed over the chopper, headed toward the rice paddies, and picked up airspeed.

"What?" Hollister asked.

Two more rounds burst next to and slightly behind the chopper.

"Thirty-seven-millimeter antiaircraft guns. We were told they had some out here. If they hit us, we're meat."

"Can you evade them?"

"I can outrun them. We can fly faster than they can track. Least that's the theory. If I can get the airspeed up, we can run out from under their reach."

Hollister held his breath and watched the 37mm rounds burst in the air just behind the chopper. Once Edmonds got the airspeed up to eighty-five knots, it seemed that the air bursts were shorter and shorter in their attempts to hit the chopper.

"I think you did it," Hollister said. He pinned his map to his seat by folding it once and tucking it under his hip. He reached into his claymore bag and pulled out his GI-issue binoculars. Putting them to his eyes, he scanned the horizon just inside the invisible Cambodian border, looking for the AAA site. "Did anyone get a location on the weapon?"

The two pilots and the two door gunners all said no.

"You think we can get some artillery or TacAir in there?" Edmonds asked.

"I doubt they'll clear it since we can't ID a target."

"The guns just checked in. They're in orbit over Hiep Hoa and want to know what the hell we're doing—trolling?" Edmonds said.

"Okay," Hollister said. "Let's get some ground searching done as soon as I call all this in. Guess we'll have to pick a stretch of open area a little farther from the border."

"You got that right," Edmonds said. "I'm gonna need a change of under-wear after that."

The emotion wasn't Edmonds's alone. Hollister still felt his heart beating up in his neck. He could only imagine what one of the 37mm rounds could do to the thin skin of a Huey if it burst close enough. There was no doubt that it would bring down a chopper with a half-lucky shot. He looked at his watch. It wasn't even sunup yet, and he had already pumped enough adrenaline on the two inserts and the 37mm to fill a bathtub. He reached into his shirt pocket for a cigarette.

Lighting a cigarette in the rotor-washed open cargo door of the Huey was a trick he had learned early on in his first tour. But smoking in a chopper was a routine more than a sensation. The wind was so pervasive that the smoke itself was dissipated as quickly as it left the smoker. So there was little evidence he was smoking except for the burning in his throat and lungs. Still, Hollister needed the cigarette.

Passing on the information about the trucks and the 37mm position took only a few minutes, but at that point it all came to a complete halt. None of this surprised Hollister. After only a short time in III Corps he had become accustomed to the NIH attitude—*not invented here.*

He had discovered that most supporting units and headquarters didn't think too many ideas, reports of targets of opportunities, or suggestions were any good unless they came from within. Anyone else's ideas or requests were looked upon as if they were more of an inconvenience than a chance to do something about the war.

So Hollister was not too surprised when the air force said that it would only fly a FAC out to the area to try to develop a target for fast movers and the artillery denied clearance to fire until an exact target was found. The air force added that it would have to find a FAC that was not already committed for the day since its day was just beginning and all flyable resources were put against known targets or operations. To Hollister that translated as *hold your breath.*

The politics involving the border always pissed him off. It wasn't the first time he had seen enemy units massed only meters on the other side of the Cambodian and Laotian borders just thumbing their noses at the Americans.

The search for new trails began late. Hollister braced himself for any un-known eventuality as Edmonds dropped out of the sky to a search altitude of a little more than a hundred feet. His path was still south to north, as they hoped to intersect the trail of trampled weeds, rice, and grasses any infiltrator would leave heading into South Vietnam.

All eyes in the chopper were on the reeds and grasses that were clipping by at over fifty knots. Birds were flushed from their nests, and random waterfowl elected to dive for safety or dash for the concealment the vegetation offered.

The search immediately got easier when the sun broke the horizon and cast long shadows from east to west, as this helped provide another dimension to the weeds, reeds, and grasses. With the sun throwing the shadows, the breaks in the texture were immediately visible. Most of the trails were from small animals and the occasional beaten-down pattern caused by flocks of cranes and egrets that had landed, fed, and flown away.

"We've only got about twenty minutes of go-juice left in this thing," Edmonds said.

"Gotcha," Hollister replied. "Let's stay with it and change our course to the northeast so we'll be searching while we're heading for the barn."

"Rog," Edmonds said as he gently changed the direction of flight, causing the chopper to bank slightly to the right.

Trees, intermittent streams, abandoned rice fields, clumps of trees, wild manioc growth, and endless vines and weeds snapped by beneath the skids. Hollister started to wonder if the idea of looking for trails was any good. Maybe the infiltrators were walking the streambeds, staying on the hard paths on top of the dikes, or using small skiffs to weave through the streams, canals, and deeply flooded paddies.

"Whoa! Live one," someone hollered over the intercom.

Immediately, Edmonds jerked the nose of the chopper up, almost stalling out. Then he laid it over to the right to make a hard one-eighty. The large rotor blades complained by giving out their distinctive *whop-whop-whop*.

Once they were turned around, headed south, Edmonds slipped the chopper to the right to see the most from his and Hollister's side.

"There's a narrow trail in the grass up over that next stand of trees. Looked like footprints in the mush to me," the copilot said.

No one said anything as the chopper cleared the small trees and the beaten path of grasses crossed under them from left to right.

"It's sure lookin' like real people tracks to me," Edmonds said as he pulled the nose up again, stopped the forward speed, and teased the chopper into a hover facing in the same direction as the footprints—east.

"Guns standing by?" Hollister asked over the Tactical radio frequency.

"We're locked and cocked," the lead gunship pilot replied from his orbit a mile and a half away and eighteen hundred feet above the C&C.

Edmonds slipped the chopper to the right, putting the trail out the left door and heading in the same direction. "Folks, let's each take our own quadrant of the chopper and search that area of the ground. Does us no good to all be looking at the trail up ahead of us," Edmonds announced to the other three crew members.

Hollister slipped the buckle on his seat belt to give him some more slack in order to get his head farther out the door. He watched new sections of the trail reveal themselves from just in front of the chopper's chin bubble. The footprints were clear. They were fresh, and the grass was still flattened down under an inch or so of water.

"We're getting real close," Hollister said.

"How so?" Edmonds asked.

"The water is turning muddy. It hasn't settled."

"Damn. Good eye, Cap'n H."

Two metallic *twaps* cut through the noise of the chopper turbine and the rotor blades.

"Taking fire! Bushes at ten o'clock," the left door gunner yelled just before he thumbed the butterfly trigger on the back end of his M60.

The tracers from the machine gun slashed by Hollister's face. He followed them to a stand of small trees at the end of the trail. Two more green tracers left the trees and went just over the chopper. Hollister had a horrifying thought: *What if they hit the blades?* He had no idea what kind of damage a direct hit with a rifle round would do.

Edmonds violently jerked the vehicle around to the right to put the long axis of the trees between the enemy fire and the chopper. At the same time, he dropped from under a hundred to almost ten feet off the ground.

For a split second Hollister thought the chopper's brutal motions meant they might have taken some main rotor damage and were going down. But it quickly became obvious that Edmonds was expertly using every trick he knew to reduce the chopper's vulnerability.

"Damage?" Edmonds asked, turning to look over his shoulder at the door gunner who shook his head—none that he could see.

The copilot did the same with the crew chief—seated on the opposite side of the chopper. He also shook his head.

"Well, something tagged us. It's still flying. So let's see how long the luck lasts. Keep your eyes open for damage back there," Edmonds said.

The door gunners kept their weapons trained on the source of the enemy fire and shot burst after burst of machine-gun fire into the trees.

Hollister leaned out and looked up and around for the gunships. He saw them rolling in on the target—one a hundred meters behind the other. He heard the lead gun pilot. "We've got the target. We're gonna lay a few rockets on their asses. Stay clear."

Edmonds answered, then put more distance between the C&C and the enemy position. As they pulled up and away, Hollister could see that the trail they had been following stopped in the clump of trees where the firing had come from.

The lead Cobra punched off two pairs of rockets. The four rockets erupted from the two large cylindrical pods hung on the stubby wings just outside the AC's position in the gunship.

As the four rockets passed the chopper's nose, the pilot broke right and announced his path to his wingman, who quickly reached the same spot in the sky and punched off two pairs of his rockets.

Just as the second pair of rockets picked up speed and stabilized, the first pair converged on the trees.

The enemy in the trees got a few rounds off—directed at the Cobras a fraction of a second before the first volley of rockets hit their target, turning the trees into shards and splinters in small puffs of gray-black smoke.

No one said anything, waiting for the second set of rockets to impact. Before the smoke from the first cleared, the second group hit lower on the target than the first.

"Shit!" Edmonds said.

"What?" Hollister asked.

"We have to break for the Texaco station. Or we can land this thing and walk home with a gas can."

"Guns? You got a plan?" Hollister asked.

The lead answered. "I'm going in for a look, and my wing is going to cover me. Couldn't be too much left in those bushes."

"Can we stay that long?" Hollister asked Edmonds.

"If we hurry. It's a real embarrassing thing to run out of fuel in a country that is damn near awash in aviation fuel."

"Okay, Reptile, make it fast," Hollister said.

The lead gunship pilot clicked twice, and rolled over and down out of his orbit. His wingman stayed high and ready to cover his partner's approach to the target.

Edmonds had taken the C&C to fifteen hundred feet and was on the opposite side of the orbit that the gunships had cut in the sky.

Every eye was on the lead gunship as he dropped to the deck and came toward the still smoking target from the east. With the sun to his back and flying a chopper barely three feet wide, he reduced the chance that any survivor in the target area could get a good sight picture on his approaching Cobra.

He took the gunship up and over the site in one moderately fast pass— no ground fire.

After a fast and tight turn, he did it again, only slower and lower. Still, no one spoke.

On the third pass the gunship came to a hover over the target. The pilot rolled the cyclic around in a small circle, and the rotor disk did a rotation like a spinning coin settling to a stop. The motion blew the loose debris in all directions and fanned the small branches of the trees. "We got two real dead bad guys here. There's a busted up AK, and the other guy either doesn't have a weapon or it's lost in the water somewhere."

The radio erupted in overlapping cross talk as the pilots cheered and congratulated the Cobra pilots.

"Anything left to go in for?" Hollister asked.

"Not much more than a grease spot. One of the rockets must have gone off just over their heads. The other three were close—but not in cigar territory," the lead Cobra pilot said.

"Okay, we're heading back. We'll see you there."

"You got time to take a pass over the site and give me a confirmation on the kills?"

Hollister switched to intercom. "Okay with the fuel situation?"

The copilot's left hand came up, making an O with his thumb and forefinger.

"Okay, we'll take a look for you," Hollister told the gunship leader.

Hovering over the spot from which they had taken fire only minutes before, Hollister looked down at the bodies. They were wearing simple pajamas and long-sleeved tops. One was wearing Ho Chi Minhs and the other was wearing lace-up Bata boots. The rucksack that had been scattered by the detonations contained another set of pajamas and a full set of cooking utensils—nothing more. The dead looked young. It struck Hollister that they died on their first day in the country. If you were going to go, that seemed as good a way as any.

"We have to go. This is real serious in the fuel business now," Edmonds said.

"Okay, take us home. We've earned a decent breakfast today."

"You got that shit right," Edmonds said.

Hollister sat back and reached for another cigarette as Edmonds nosed the chopper over and pulled in power to head back to Cu Chi.

"Two KBA," Hollister announced over the radio.

"Glad to be of service," the gunship lead replied. "Piece of cake."

"Thanks."

Hollister called in the action to Operations, which had monitored most of the short contact but still had many questions—most of which were coming from IIFFV. Unable to answer all the questions, Hollister told Operations they would have to wait until the debriefing to get all the details. He instructed them to tell IIFFV that they, too, would have to wait. He knew that message would not go over well.

Soon the chopper left the unpopulated western part of the province and reached the Vam Co Dong River. It was the north-south ribbon of water that divided the populated area from that which had been abandoned by years of war.

Lighting yet another cigarette and feeling the burn in his chest as he took a long drag, Hollister looked down at the activity passing beneath the C&C. The roads and side paths leading to them were filling up with peasants, farmers, merchants, and government employees, all heading out for their work. Hollister watched them pass beneath the chopper and wondered if any of them had heard or seen the killing that had just taken place only a few thousand meters west of them.

He remembered that there wasn't anyone on that ground who had ever known peace. So the sight of a couple of gunships and a slick rolling in on a small enemy target near their homes was nothing new for them.

They were just starting their day. Hollister was already four hours into his. And he could count on it not ending for at least sixteen more.

CHAPTER 20

The crew members and Hollister were joined by several curious LRPs at the Old Warrior Pad. They searched the Huey for damage. The AK rounds were not hard to find. One of them had sliced into the underbelly of the chopper and lodged itself somewhere in the fuel cell. The other one had glanced off the footpad on the forward edge of the skid and disappeared somewhere into the morning darkness.

"Whoa, boy! Check this out," the copilot said, standing on top of the chopper inspecting the rotor head.

Hollister and the others stepped back to see what he was pointing at. He tapped a portion of the complicated articulating control rods that changed the pitch on the rotor blades. One of them had three deep cuts in it.

"Looks like the frags from the thirty-seven mike mike came closer than we thought."

"That bad?" Hollister asked Edmonds.

"Coulda been. But we passed the basic aviation test."

"What's that?" Hollister asked.

"Equal number of takeoffs and landings. You get those numbers out of whack and your flying days are over. Gravity assumes control of your destiny at that point."

"If the thirty-seven had cut that rod?"

"We'd have assumed the flight characteristics of a spit-shined footlocker."

"No shit?"

"Hey, that's the risk of the stalwart aviator," Edmonds said. "That's why they give us all that fabulous flight pay."

"I don't get flight pay."

"You get passenger pay," Edmonds said.

"What the hell is passenger pay?"

"The mere joy of watching daring aviators do their magic. Money would be redundant."

"Get out of here," Hollister said, throwing a mock punch toward Edmonds.

"Seriously, we'll be out of business for a day or so while we make repairs. The fuel cell is iffy. Don't have any idea what else is damaged in this bird."

"Can we replace it?" Hollister asked. "We can't go without a C and C."

"I'll see what I can do. I've got a call in to maintenance in Bien Hoa. They're gonna pitch a bitch. But fuck 'em."

"Yessir, yessir. I understand. Yessir," Sangean said, finishing the phone conversation and hanging up.

Even though he came in on the tail end of it, the tone of the conversation caught Hollister's attention. He assumed that it was Colonel Downing and that he wasn't happy about something.

Sangean stood, looking at the phone for a moment and letting the conversation sink in. Then he turned to Hollister. "Where are we?"

"Guns are reloading, I have to brief two teams, Edmonds is going to replace the C and C, you have a recon this afternoon, we have to find out what else the prisoner gave us, and you and I need to talk about these early-morning flights."

"Hmmm, that ought to be enough to keep us out of trouble," Sangean said.

"Speaking of trouble. Are we in some with the head shed?"

"It's a cost-benefit thing. Some of the paper shufflers at Two Field are telling Colonel Downing that we are costing more in resources than we are bringing in on payday."

"Do you agree?"

"Fuck no!" Sangean snapped. He waved his hand across the twenty-by-thirty-kilometer AO marked on the map. "The information we bring out just by being there would take them a whole damn leg division. As an economy of force we're a bargain. But we're also bringing in prisoners, enemy intelligence, and KIAs." The frustration in Sangean's voice was unmistakable.

"You able to convince Colonel Downing of that?"

"I ran it by him for the fourth time. It sounds to me like he's being shown charts and stats. That shit kills any special unit operation. It's been chasing Special Forces for years."

"So what do we do differently?" Hollister asked.

"Huh?"

"What do we do to change their perception?"

"We talk louder," Sangean said, showing a hint of a sarcastic smile.

There was no doubt that Sangean was even more angry about what he was thinking than he let on. Hollister could only guess the pressure he must be feeling. And that meant pressure on Hollister to figure out how to do more, better—without adding to the considerable risk the teams were already exposed to.

One thing was the morning flights to look for small parties infiltrating into South Vietnam across the no-man's-land. He was convinced he could rack up some kills with a limited risk to the aircraft and crews—if he could stay away from the 37mm or knock it out. He made a note to talk to the FAC about it. There had to be a way to suck the gunners into shooting at something and then to pulverize them with fast movers.

"About the cost-benefit ratio of using the Cobras to search for infiltrators," he said to Sangean.

"What about 'em?"

"We are rotating the Cobra teams back to Bien Hoa every afternoon for maintenance and new crews."

"Yeah, so?" Sangean asked.

"Well, what if we rotate them in the mornings after they have made a run looking for trails—and after they have covered any insertions?"

"That way they'd already be out there, and if we ran late on any other essential operations we could scrub the trail searches."

"Yes, sir. We'd only run the searches when we had the blade time remaining, and by then they'd be on the way home."

"Good idea, but you tell Stanton. He's gonna have a small fit."

After a month of successful dawn patrols, Juliet Company had racked up twenty-four by body count and an estimate of six others that couldn't be confirmed—just by letting the Cobras prowl before going home.

The success was embarrassing the ARVNs and the 25th Division, who were normally responsible for the AO the LRPs were working. And it appeared to Hollister to be temporarily, frustrating Major Fowler's efforts to bad-mouth Juliet Company.

At the end of the sixth week of solid patrols, all of the Chieu Hois who were acceptable were integrated into teams. The others were transferred to a POW compound in northern South Vietnam to reduce the chance of their feeding information about the LRPs back to the VC/NVA.

As soon as the Chieu Hois were integrated into the teams, Bui became a TOC rat. He was kept around Operations in the event that there was a problem on a team and his language skills might be needed. On the few occasions when he had to speak with the Chieu Hois, Operations frequently erupted into laughter at his fractured radio procedure.

Hollister finally took him aside. "Sergeant Bui, we think you ought to get together with Captain Newman for some RTO procedure."

Bui made a sad face. "I do not good?"

Not wanting to destroy Bui's self-confidence, Hollister took it easy on him. "Let me put it this way . . . You are very good, but there is much for all of us to learn about using the radio and communicating well. It is so important that we even have a captain, like Newman, whose special job is communications. You understand that?"

"Yes, Dai Uy. I will see Newman," Bui said, standing stiffly at attention and saluting.

"And another thing, Bui. We don't need to salute all the time. Since we work together, it is only appropriate the first time we meet each other in the morning and at the end of the day—and only outdoors."

"Can do, easy," Bui said, resisting the urge to salute again.

"Good."

Bui left Operations to look for Newman. Hollister looked around at the others, who had tried to keep from laughing at the winsome Sergeant Bui.

"That bad leg never slows him down, does it?" Hollister asked.

"He's funny. But he's done a bang-up job with those Hoi Chanhs. I mean, he's just okay on tactical matters and patrolling techniques, but he has really been good at getting them comfortable with the Americans."

"The team leaders seem to be getting more confidence in the Hoi Chanhs. But we haven't had any real tough contacts yet," Hollister said.

"I don't think they'll bug out on us," Kurzikowski said.

"If they do?"

"Then we're in deep, deep shit. We'll have to change everything we do and assume that an AWOL Hoi Chanh has gone back to the VC and sold them all the information he's collected on us."

"We've tried pretty hard to keep them in the dark. I don't think I'd be happy to go on a patrol when no one is showing me the map, telling me the frequencies or call signs on the radios, or filling me in on the support available. Hell, the list of things they don't know is longer than they are tall."

"You know the troops are giving some of them money?" Kurzikowski asked.

"Money?"

"Yeah. They only make fifty bucks a month. But the team members found out that most of them have families somewhere that are hurting."

"Softhearted LRPs are giving some of these guys money to send to their families?"

"You got it," Kurzikowski said.

"I don't know why I'm surprised." Hollister smiled at the generosity and the complexity of the kids who had volunteered to be LRPs. He knew they were not the bloodthirsty killers people would make them out to be. They were kids who wanted to do their jobs, be proud of their combat service, and go home feeling good about it all. The rest was bravado, and no LRP would knock down the exaggerated stories that went around about them.

"Hope this doesn't backfire on us," Kurzikowski said.

"Keep your ear to the ground on this, will ya?"

"Yessir. I will. I'll add it to the list of thankless burdens we NCOs lift every day," Kurzikowski said, kidding.

"Must be tough being the backbone of the army," Hollister countered.

It was too late for Hollister to start a letter to Susan, but he hadn't written anything in days except a short one to his parents and another to his cousin Janet, which was almost a copy of the first one. He knew if he didn't carve out the time to write her, still another day would go by and he would feel worse. Especially if he got another letter from her first.

He kicked off his boots, but left them opened up and ready to slip on. He poured himself a very short Scotch since he was on call for any contact. Sangean was weathered in at IIFFV, so Hollister had the early and the late shift for the second day running. Before taking a drink of the Scotch, he finished the last few gulps of the coffee he had brought from the mess hall. It was cold, but he didn't care. He figured it just might help him snap out of the fog of fatigue he had been in all day.

He threw his shirt over the back of his chair and sat down at the makeshift desk in his hooch. Vance had been in his end of the hooch earlier, but had to go over to the CP for something. He still wasn't back.

Vance's radio was on. AFVN was playing a Zombies tune. It seemed to be one of the few popular songs that had cleared whoever okayed music because he played it at least once every hour or so.

A cigarette and a sip of the Scotch, and Hollister spread out the six letters he had received from Susan and had not completely answered. They showed her growing concern about the course of the war and the frustration that was becoming epidemic in the States. She tried not to thrust her feelings at Hollister, but just the fact that it was upsetting her hurt him.

He picked up his pen and began writing on the GI steno pad he had stolen from the desk that had been First Sergeant Morrison's. He began by trying to explain that the war from New York City and the war from Hau Nghia Province were two completely different wars. He agreed that there were many wrongs being done in the name of God and Country. Too many Americans coming home in metal boxes bothered him very much. But he tried to explain that there were innocent people who had been pressed into fighting for the VC. He accepted that there were terrible inequities and corruption in the government, but she had to understand that he had seen that the peasants and the simple farmers were not getting rich off the U.S.

He told her about Bui, who had had his entire family broken up and how he'd been drafted into fighting brother South Vietnamese, that he was crippled and still came to work for the Americans. He told her he was sure that if the VC or NVA found out he was a Hoi Chanh, his punishment would be the worst torture they could hand out.

He agreed with Susan that the war should end and that as long as it was going on there were going to be people killed and families destroyed. But pulling out and leaving South Vietnam to the North Vietnamese would mean the end for thousands and thousands of South Viets and their families—not to mention the complete Communist takeover of Vietnam.

He certainly didn't have all the answers, but he did know what would be the wrong thing to do. Walking away from the South Vietnamese would be wrong. Still, he wanted so badly to be home with her and not in that hooch. He could feel the dampness of his shirt against the middle of his back. His bare feet stuck to the grit on the plywood floor, but he was happy to be able to wiggle his toes after so many hours in boots. The front of his ankles were sore from the pressure of his laces.

It started to rain again.

He lit another a cigarette and considered having another shot of Scotch. No. Couldn't do it.

He heard Vance come in and stamp his boots on the floor to knock some of the water off them. Hollister went back to his letter.

He waffled and filled in some blank space talking about the weather and avoiding explaining that he didn't feel as if he had the same grip on things he had had on his first tour. Oh sure, he knew a lot more about war and the business of being an infantryman. But he didn't know the troops as well, and he had so damn many things to juggle at once that there were nights he couldn't sleep for worrying about details. He knew the difference between living and dying in Vietnam was often a matter of SLDs—shitty little details.

He was pissed about having Fowler in his hair all the time. He often thought Fowler was keeping him off his game by distracting him so much, but he considered that a copout.

He told her about the music on AFVN and how he picked her out of the lyrics of some of the popular tunes. He was writing, but he was lying by omission. God, how he wanted just one more drink.

On his first tour, he had had Lucas and Easy, and even Captain Michaelson, the CO, to lean on for advice and a friendly ear. He didn't have that yet in Juliet Company. They didn't get the time to talk that much, and Sangean was hard to get close to.

He told her how terrific it was to work for Sangean and how he felt comfortable with the pilots and the older NCOs. He hated lying to her. But what was the sense in telling her the truth only to have her worry more about him.

He reached for the bottle, and the field phone rattled.

"Hollister," he answered.

"Sir, One-three has movement."

He looked at his watch. It was almost two A.M. "Anybody tell the pilots?"

"Yessir."

"Where's the Old Man?"

"He's still grounded in Long Binh. Weather."

"Okay, I'm on the way." Hanging up the field phone, Hollister wrote across the bottom of his letter, *Can't finish now. Want to get in mail. I love you, J.*

Hollister was still buttoning his shirt and his boots were unlaced when he walked into Operations. It was still raining outside.

"So? What have we got?"

Lieutenant Patten, 1-3's platoon leader, was the duty officer, manning the radios with a PFC from the commo platoon.

"One-three is located on a marshy spot directly across from Ba Thu. They've seen nothing, but can hear movement to their north and west. They can't drop any arty or air on it because no one can confirm that it's bad guys," Patten reported.

The spot on the map that was marked with 1-3's unit symbol in blue grease pencil was only eighteen hundred meters from Cambodia. Hollister pulled out his notebook and cross-checked the coordinates with his notes. "Is that where we put them in?"

"No, sir. They moved after dark. The team leader wasn't happy with his location—too deep."

"Hell, for me any water for a whole night is too deep."

"You want we should do something now?" Patten asked.

"What's he hearing?"

"He said he thought they had heard voices and metallic clinking."

"Let's get the FO in here and work up a fire mission or two for the team to call. Get me a belly man. Your platoon sergeant, if he's available." Hollister looked at his watch. "What time are they due to check in next?"

The RTO scanned the duty log for the last entry. "They're due every hour on the half hour, but they just checked in six minutes ago with more movement."

That gave Hollister seven more minutes before the team would call in a scheduled SITREP, time for him to put together a list of yes or no questions the team leader could answer without talking.

He grabbed a piece of scrap paper on his desk and jotted down some questions. He motioned to Patten. "Watch this. You need to learn this."

"You wanted someone from the slicks?"

The voice was unmistakable—Captain Keith, one of the slick platoon's section leaders. Hollister turned and smiled. "You might have to earn some of that big-time flight pay tonight. Got a team on the border that's picking up lots of movement and has its ass hanging out. If they get compromised there will be no option—we jerk 'em immediately. They have nowhere to E and E to avoid contact. I want a pickup element ready to go on zero five minutes' warning. Can do?"

"Can do, easy, Dai Uy," Keith said, scratching himself and trying to let his eyes adjust to the lights in Operations.

"You flying the C and C?"

"Nope. I lost the last hand, and Edmonds is pulling rank. He's air mission commander, and I'm ACing on the pickup slick."

"Get a cup of coffee, and go secure all that money you won playing poker tonight so you can fly with a clear head and a clear conscience," Hollister kidded him.

Keith didn't respond. He just waved and stepped back out the doorway.

He was replaced in the door by Platoon Sergeant McCullen, 1st Platoon's senior NCO.

Hollister was glad to see him. He had known McCullen in Fort Benning. When Hollister was an officer candidate going through training, he had met McCullen on a live-fire exercise. He was impressed then with the newly promoted staff sergeant's cool and bearing.

There had been enough years in between for McCullen to make platoon sergeant and then be selected for promotion to master sergeant. He was due to sew on his new chevrons in a month.

His promotion had been a matter of much discussion around Juliet Company. Since they still had not received an acceptable replacement for First Sergeant Morrison, McCullen was being considered for the job. It was not something he particularly relished. He was a field soldier and bristled at the suggestion that he might ride a desk.

"Sergeant Mac," Hollister said. "We might have to pull One-three. You want to ride belly?"

"You ready to go?"

"Not yet. We need to make the decision here in a few minutes. If they're going to come out, we need to pull them in time to make the next two inserts before first light. If we get late on this, we will screw the two teams going in."

"Is it just movement or movement toward them?"

"They haven't said yet. You want to talk to them on their next SITREP? Here are some questions I need to know about," Hollister said, handing McCullen his list.

"Yessir," McCullen said, taking the list. "I'll get 'em squared away." He picked up the field phone and called one of the team hooches to get a team leader out of the sack to go and check the rigging on the chase ship while he made the radio contact with 1-3.

Lieutenant Lambert had entered while Hollister was talking to McCullen and was already on the land line to his battery, working up a fire mission and cross-checking the planned targets they had plotted in case the team needed to be pulled under fire.

Captain Stanton stood in the doorway, an unlit cigar stub in his mouth, wearing his Nomex trousers, a T-shirt, and a baseball cap with his bars and wings on it. His boots were in his hand. "Guess this means the guns are on the clock now, too. Huh?"

"Yeah," Hollister said, smiling at the always happy Stanton. "Why don't you hang out over at the mess hall, and I'll give you guys an update as soon as I get something from the team."

"Houston. One-three," the voice whispered over the small speaker in Operations.

McCullen grabbed the mike and replied. "This is One-six Alpha. Gimme your SITREP."

"We have more movement. Don't know if they know we're here. But they're so close their security might bump into us. If that happens we're in the shitter. Counted seventy-two figures moving west to east on canal road. Carrying small arms. Have called for arty—no fires yet. Can you do something?"

Hollister didn't wait to hear anymore. "Let's launch! Hit the horn!"

McCullen never needed to ask the questions on Hollister's list.

The RTO reached up and threw the toggle switch mounted on the wall to trip the contact siren. The siren hadn't even reached the top of its volume when Captain Vance jumped up on the step and entered Operations. He found Hollister talking to McCullen.

"You tell them gunships are on the way," Hollister said to McCullen. He looked at Lambert. "You get fucking arty in there for them. No—you get your radio and come with me!"

Turning to leave, Hollister scooped up his claymore bag and his M16 and almost ran into Vance. "You want me to take this one?" Vance asked.

"Naw. I know where they are, have to be out there in a couple hours to put in a pair of teams anyhow. No sense both of us fucking up a night made for sleeping."

"You sure?" Vance asked.

"I'm sure. If you want to do anything, stand by here and help these folks kick some ass. I got a feeling all the work is going to be done from here tonight—or not at all."

Vance tapped Hollister on the shoulder in a gesture of good luck, then turned to the radios.

The knot in Hollister's stomach couldn't have been tighter. He hated night contacts. They were the hardest to manage from a chopper. The confusion factor was as high as it could get. His worst fears were all built into a night contact. He could lose a team and not even have spotted their location on the ground. He could get a team split up and have to find a lost LRP. He could run into aircraft trouble and have to put a chopper crew down with a crippled ship.

The lights of the other choppers were about the only lights he could see. The rain reduced the visibility to about a mile, and the ceiling was not much more than two thousand feet.

Inside the chopper a spray of water soaked Hollister and Lambert to the skin as they crossed the wire on the far side of the base camp. Hollister grabbed a cigarette while he could, knowing that when they got to the team's location things would pick up to a pace that would surely not allow one. He offered one to Lambert.

Lambert shook his head. "The fire mission is being held up by the ARVNs," he yelled to Hollister, pulling his handset from his ear.

"Shit!" Hollister said. "Go up the chain. Tell your FDO that my troops have a visual on the target. If he can't get around the ARVNs, then get someone on it who can. Tell him the minute they take fire I want artillery— ARVNs or no fucking ARVNs!"

Lambert nodded and talked back into his handset.

"Guns are already there. One just took some ground fire and is rolling in on it," Edmonds said over the intercom.

"They have the team located?"

"Yeah. They were on the insert and knew the general location. The team leader and Stanton worked it out."

Hollister leaned out to try to see the contact up ahead of the C&C. Edmonds was flying to a point north and east of the team's location to clear airspace for the artillery to fire from the southeast.

"Gunships are gonna have to move out," Lambert yelled to Hollister.

"I know," Hollister said, looking out in front of them at the rotating beacons of the two Cobras on the black horizon.

"Contact! Contact! This is One-three, we have contact!"

Hollister's heart sunk a bit. He had a feeling that once the gun-ships started firing on the enemy troops, DeSouza's team would be sucked into it. He had hoped the C&C would have reached the contact site before the team got involved. "One-three, Three. Roger. What's your situation?"

"I'm still not sure if they know we're here, but we are taking ineffective fire."

"Have you returned fire yet?"

"Negative. We want to find out if they're reconning by fire or what."

Hollister was pleased to hear that the training was getting to the troops. "Okay, hold tight. We are inbound your location. Stand by for extraction. You have a PZ, don't you?"

"That's affirm—the primary we selected and plotted. Will hold fire. Will prep for extraction," DeSouza said.

Hollister looked at his map and the grease-penciled oval marked as De-Souza's PZ. He looked out again to confirm its location in respect to two distinctive terrain features—a very straight roadway running parallel to a canal and an intersecting intermittent stream.

The contact came into plain view for Hollister as Edmonds took up an orbit above the gun runs. The Cobras were rolling in without letting up on the long road-canal combination. The enemy troops had taken what little cover there was in the canal and on the embankment on the other side of the road.

Stanton and his wingman were rolling in on pass after pass, running parallel to the linear target, dumping pairs of rockets on each pass, and stitching the embankment with minigun fire.

Lambert had managed to get the artillery to fire flares. The first one made only a bright glow in the sky over the contact—the light diffused by the clouds and the steady rain.

"This is some bad shit to fly in. It's getting a little heavier, and the forecast is for more of the same," Edmonds said over the intercom.

"Rog. Stand by," Hollister replied. He flipped the toggle switch to transmit on the tactical frequency. "Reptile Six, you about out of ordnance?"

"We're about five minutes from having to go home. I have a backup team of guns en route now. Hold on . . ."

Hollister looked over at the lead gunship and saw that he was rolling in on still another pass. As he lifted his nose and broke right, trying to gain altitude, green tracers leaped up for the underbelly of the Cobra from a spot on the roadway that looked to be a culvert or some kind of lock for the canal.

Before anyone said anything else over the radio, the second Cobra rolled in on the culvert and quickly silenced the fire with his grenade launcher. Round after round puffed from the nose-mounted barrel, detonating on impact along the canal and the paddy next to it.

There were two large secondary explosions.

"Okay, I'm back," Stanton said. "Looks like we hit the demo man. Anyway, we have the other guns about zero three out."

"What do you think you got down there?"

"I don't think there's much of anyone left alive down there. Lots of them scattered and got away when they heard us coming. Guess we got about fifteen of them."

"Rog. Stand by. Break. One-three, can you see the damage?"

"This is One-three. Affirm. There doesn't seem to be much left."

"Okay, Reptile. You got enough time and ordnance left to cover the C and C if we go down and take a look? I can't pull that team if the ground is still crawling with bad guys."

"That's affirm. You can get a reckie out of me with no problem."

"Okay, you guys game up front?" Hollister asked Edmonds and the peter pilot.

"Let's go look."

Hollister turned to Lambert. "Can we get any fucking artillery in here this week?"

"Yessir. Now that we've had the contact, they are going to clear it."

"Tell them I'm going to clear someone's ass out when I get back!" Hollister said, clearly angry at the crap Lambert got requesting the fires. "Keep the illum going. We're going down for a look."

Lambert nodded.

Edmonds dropped out of the sky to treetop level, causing Hollister's stomach to feel flutter. Reaching a point just above the highest treetops, Edmonds sucked in enough power to arrest the descent and level the flight out at forty-five knots.

He had taken a long, sweeping path away from the target area while he was losing altitude, and now began a hard turn back toward the target.

Hollister steeled himself for the short flight into the target area. He patted his rifle to reassure himself that it was still in place on the bench seat next to him. He also slipped the sling from the claymore bag onto his shoulder. If he had to get out of the chopper, he didn't want to have to look for his bag or rifle.

He wasn't too worried about the spare PRC-77 he had with him. He had it on a backpack and had his right foot through one of the shoulder straps. If he got out, he could easily find and drag the radio with him.

Edmonds flipped on the chin light, and the ground below the chopper turned into a white-lit scene of mostly water and roadway.

"Comin' up on 'em," Edmonds announced over the intercom. Almost without taking another breath, he reacted to what he saw. "Jesus Christ! Will you look at this?"

There, beneath the chopper, were at least forty bodies on the left—against the road embankment—and an equal number on the other side, floating in the canal—out of Hollister's view.

"Let me go past them and come back, Jim," Edmonds said.

Hollister looked out and down at the carnage through the misty rain lit up by the searchlight. They were NVA. That took a load off his mind. He had a nagging worry that they might have mistaken farmers or other civilians for VC. But they were NVA. Most had pieces of uniforms on, while some wore black pajamas. Rifles and RPG rounds were the most recognizable military items. Some bits of clothing and hats were also floating in the paddy water. Hand-carried cargo was everywhere. Rice bags, ammo, medical supplies, papers—lots of papers. Some kind of dye or ink was evident in one corner of the paddy water, and on two of the bodies. Hollister guessed that it was either the pigment from a smoke grenade—or maybe just ink.

Edmonds came to a point beyond the bodies and made a hard turn, doubling back on his own line of flight. The maneuver put the canal outside the left side of the chopper, where Hollister could see it.

The dead there were almost identical to the others on the far side of the road. Splintered wood littered the banks of the canal. Some kind of boat or sled had been used to carry supplies. Some of the cargo could be seen under the water when the intense helicopter searchlight cut through it. The water was running with streaks of blood.

"New guns have reported on station," Edmonds said. "You got any plans to walk the team over here to have a look?"

"Negative. They're too far away to walk across open paddy fields. One live VC with a weapon would have their ass." Hollister looked at his watch. "We okay on fuel?"

"Yep. We still got pretty close to an hour left."

"Okay. I want to get that team out, then get someone in here to look through the debris for anyone or anything," Hollister said.

"Houston, Three. We got a pretty good body count out here. I need a ground element—large enough to provide its own security while they search the battle area."

"This is Five," Vance replied from Cu Chi. "Roger. We are on it."

"I also want you to launch the pickup ships to pull One-three," Hollister said.

"They are lifting off now," Vance said.

"I also need you to stand by to replace me in another slick in case this gets screwed up."

"Count on it."

Hollister took a deep breath to relax a bit. He really liked having Peter Vance on the other end of the radio.

It took the slicks twenty minutes to get to 1-3's PZ. The slicks, the C&C, and the new gunships got into a pickup formation and headed for DeSouza's team.

Hollister had released Stanton's guns to rearm and refuel at Cu Chi for the routine inserts that were scheduled to take place as soon as Hollister could get 1-3 out and refuel the C&C.

The radios got quiet. Hollister watched the new Cobras prowl the PZ as the pickup and chase ships slowed into the landing zone, only fifteen meters from the small tuft of weeds, bamboo, and trees that concealed DeSouza's team.

The lead pilot switched on his searchlight as he flared to put the chopper down. In the halo of light that spilled onto the wet paddy under the chopper's belly, Hollister could see the team running toward the left door in the chopper. He counted them, one, two, three, four, five—five. Shit! There was a man missing.

"What's going on?" Hollister yelled over the tactical freq. "There's a man missing!"

"He was right behind us!" a breathless DeSouza said from inside the pickup chopper, waiting dangerously on the PZ.

"Can you see him?"

"Negative," DeSouza said.

Just then the gunship on the far side of the PZ—out the right door of the pickup ship—spit a burst of minigun fire from its nose to a point in front of the pickup ship. The pickup pilot yelled, "We're taking fire! We're taking fire!"

"Get out of there!" Hollister yelled. "Don't wait!" he said to the pickup ship.

The pilot heard him, but didn't reply. From Hollister's position in a tight orbit, only a few hundred feet above the pickup chopper, he could see the pickup pilot dump his searchlight and roll forward for a full-power takeoff. As he did, he tried to get enough altitude and airspeed to be able to break hard right to keep from overflying the location the gunships were blistering with minigun fire.

The chase ship had passed over the pickup ship when it touched down and was already in a lower orbit than the C&C.

Hollister finally took a breath when the pickup ship had made the hard U-turn and was heading up and away from the enemy position—still taking occasional tracer fire.

"Okay?" Hollister half asked Edmonds.

"Seems to be. But he's still one man short. The crew told me that they think they saw him still inside the trees."

"How much time we got?"

"'Bout thirty minutes—then it's Texaco time."

"One-three, Three. Talk to me," Hollister told DeSouza over the radio.

From his place inside the orbiting pickup ship, DeSouza responded. "We got out of the trees. Made it across the paddies, and when I hit the skids I looked back and he wasn't there. I have no idea what happened to him."

"Okay. Does he have any commo or signal equipment?"

"Affirm. He's carrying a second fox mike radio."

"You try to call him?"

"Affirm. But I'm on a short antenna. No reply. Want me to try again?"

"Negative. Let me. Break. Houston One-three Bravo, this is Houston Three. Over."

Everyone held his breath again waiting for a reply. Finally, the silence in Hollister's headset was broken by two squelch breaks.

"One-three Bravo, this is Three. Did you just break squelch?"

Twice again.

"Okay. Are you *not* able to speak?"

Twice again—still affirmative.

"Are you wounded or injured?"

Twice again.

Shit! Hollister thought. One man on the ground by himself and wounded. "Can you move to the PZ?"

There was a long pause. Hollister repeated the question. Still, another long pause. Then a single word: "Maybe."

"Okay. Okay. You just hole up. We'll fire that area up around you and get you out of there. Can you give us a strobe?"

Twice again.

"Okay. First, give us the distance and direction to whatever you suspect is near you."

"Two zero zero break, three one five degrees. Troops," the weak LRP whispered in a shaky voice.

"You ready, guns?"

"Affirm," the gun lead replied.

"Good man. You relax. We got it. Keep your head down, and give us a strobe—now," Hollister said.

Everyone searched the clumps of trees for the flashing strobe light. After a very long wait, it popped once, then twice, not too far from the point in the tree line where DeSouza's team had broken out into the paddies for the pickup.

"There it is!" the door gunner yelled, pointing.

Hollister followed his finger to the spot.

"We got it," the gunship lead announced. "We're headin' on in with miniguns."

The lead Cobra rolled over on its side to set up a flight path that would pass right over the spot northwest of the strobe and two hundred meters away.

"Just hold on down there," Hollister said as much for reassurance as a wish for the success of the gun pass.

The Cobra started firing short of the target location by about fifty meters and burned up rice paddy until the tracers stitched their way into the clump of vegetation that held the enemy gunners. As the tracers entered the brush, the pilot-gunner wiggled the guns to scatter the impact points to either side of the line of flight.

As soon as his rounds burst through the back side of the brush, the wingman began his run and added M79 grenades to the mix. The grenades popped out of the nose turret and thumped their way to and through the small trees.

CHAPTER 21

Chase, you get in there and pick up One-three Bravo. We'll follow you in," Edmonds told the pilot of the chase ship.

"Okay, One-three Bravo. You ready?" Hollister asked the wounded LRP still sheltered in the trees.

He broke squelch twice.

"Let's do it now," Hollister said.

Edmonds fell into formation behind the newly designated pickup ship, and began the descent into the PZ.

Unbuckling his seat belt, Hollister got out of the jump seat and took up a kneeling position on the chopper floor. Riding in the new chase chopper, he wanted to be prepared to be the belly man in the event they had to go in and pick up survivors of the other chopper—if it was shot down.

The Cobras announced they were going to keep firing into all the likely targets near the PZ to suppress any enemy fire.

As the two choppers slid toward the spot on the PZ where they hoped to find the lost LRP, Hollister leaned out and watched the progress of the pickup ship. As it reached a point not more than fifty feet above, and a hundred and fifty feet short of, the touchdown point, the LRP broke out of the trees and started moving across the open paddy.

He seemed to be walking okay, but he was bent over a bit and held his face with one hand.

The chopper slid into the paddy ooze at a point less than twenty feet from the lone LRP. At that point the C&C overtook the pickup ship and Edmonds guided the chopper over its top with barely fifteen feet between them.

Looking straight down, Hollister could see McCullen reach out and pull the LRP into the chopper. But they weren't out of the woods yet. They still had to clear the PZ and get back up to a safe altitude.

The flash of light seemed to come without any noise as Hollister was thrown from his kneeling position up against the backs of the two pilots' seats. He didn't hear the explosion, but he did hear the high-pitched warning coming from the instrument panel, and he somehow caught a last glimpse of the RPM LIMIT light and the MASTER CAUTION light flashing on and off.

It was his nightmare! It was almost exactly the same as the dream that had brought him up from a deep sleep at least fifty times since his first tour in Vietnam.

This time it was real! They were going down! He had to get to something he could hold on to. He made an effort to reach for the legs of the jump seat and a red-hot bolt of lightning shot up his leg into his hip.

He saw the ground outside the left door, and knew the chopper was tipping over, slipping sideways, and going down fast.

The impact was a blur followed by darkness and silence.

***

It was cold and dark when Hollister heard the voice. "Captain? Captain Hollister?"

It hurt just to open his eyes. His head hurt from a point at the base of his neck across the top of his head to just above his eyes. He could smell aviation fuel and musty paddy water. He opened his eyes, and found Sergeant McCullen stretching out the tails of a combat dressing.

"What . . .?"

"RPG took you down. The chopper ended up in a ball in the bushes over there," McCullen said, nodding in the direction of the crumpled chopper carcass.

Realizing the situation, Hollister started to jerk himself up only to find he had almost no strength. "Edmonds? The crew?"

McCullen jabbed a thumb in the opposite direction. Hollister followed it with his eyes and turned his stiffened neck to see Edmonds seated on a nearby dike, his head hung, his flight helmet in the mud near his feet. Next to him was the body of Lambert and one of the door gunners. The other door gunner appeared to be unhurt and was still holding his dismounted machine gun and about two hundred rounds of linked ammunition.

"Oh, no! The pickup ship make it?"

"Sure! I'm here, ain't I?" McCullen said as he reached down and applied the dressing to the upper part of Hollister's leg.

The pain from the pressure made Hollister aware of his wound. He tried again to lift his head to look, but couldn't.

"You caught something in the upper thigh. I don't know what it was, but it ripped a pretty good hole in you."

"Real bad?" Hollister asked anxiously.

"I'm no doc, but I think you aren't gonna lose the leg or nothin'," McCullen said.

No one ever told a wounded soldier the truth when he couldn't see it himself. Hollister knew this and for a moment considered McCullen's words as a lie designed to comfort him. But then he tried to convince himself that McCullen was telling the truth.

"It doesn't hurt that much," Hollister said.

"Harumph," McCullen grunted. "I suppose a head shot wouldn't hurt either on that stuff," he said, reaching to flip up the empty morphine Syrette that had been pinned through the buttonhole on his shirt and bent over to stay there. It was routine to let the medics arriving later know the morphine had been administered in the field.

Hollister couldn't remember when he had been given the drug or who gave it. "Shouldn't I feel weird or something?"

"Don't rightly know, Captain. I've never had any of that shit."

The sounds of approaching choppers drowned out any further conversation. Hollister looked over toward the open paddy and saw Sergeant DeSouza standing in the middle holding a strobe light over his head for the approaching flight of the six slicks. Beyond him two other members of 1-3 were facing out, away from the LZ, providing some local security for the incoming choppers.

As they touched down, the troops from the reaction force fanned out to establish a perimeter around the downed chopper crew, the dead, the wounded, and the LRPs from DeSouza's team.

As the choppers lifted off, McCullen leaned over and yelled loud enough for Hollister to hear, "They're bringing in a Dust-Off for you. It's right behind them."

"What are they doing?" Hollister asked, a little confused by what was happening.

"They're going to secure the area, evac the wounded, and then do a BDA on all the folks in the canal."

"But I have two teams to put in before first light," Hollister said, even more confused.

McCullen calmed his fears. "Don't worry about it. The major's taking care of it."

The answer satisfied Hollister, who immediately slipped off into a dreamlike state of drowsiness.

The 12th Evac Hospital at Cu Chi was painted with the same red laterite dust that covered every item in the sprawling base camp.

Hollister's head pounded and his stomach was on the verge of vomiting, but his vision cleared enough for him to realize that he was not looking at a painting, but a view through a window to the outside of the hospital ward. It had stopped raining, and the sun was high and bright.

The brilliance of the scene outside hurt his eyes, and his first thought was that it was a bad hangover. But as his head cleared a bit, he realized he was in the recovery ward of an evacuation hospital.

He didn't remember anything from the chopper crash—not at first. But he knew he was hurt, and he quickly tried to sit up. He could see both his feet under the end of the sheets, even though they had been tented to stay just off his legs. He moved them, they reacted, but there was a dull throbbing in his right leg, in his upper thigh.

Determined to find out the extent of his injuries, Hollister tried to reach for the sheet, but found that his left arm was a mass of tape and tubing with two IVs converging into one needle inserted into the vein in the crook of his arm. He followed the tubes up and away from his body to an IV stand above his head that held a bottle of saline and one of dextrose something. He couldn't read the full label.

With his right hand, he lifted the sheet. Underneath he saw that he was bandaged from his right hipbone to his calf. The top of the dressing was marked by the oozing wound. It was orange and yellow, and was centered on the outside of his upper thigh. He reached down to touch it to see if there was a break or something and was interrupted.

"Checking it out?"

He turned to find Second Lieutenant Katherine O'Connell, K.O. to her friends. She stood not much more than five-three and had bright red hair, green eyes, and a great smile punctuated by a band of freckles that crossed her nose from cheek to cheek.

"How bad am I?"

"Wound-wise or just as a patient?" she asked, teasing him.

"What?"

"Well, the doctors will be around to give you the details, but you interrupted the path of some large piece of fragmentation with a body block."

"Bad?"

"You're going to be one sore LRP for a while. But my guess is that you'll keep the leg and have a scar that will be a conversation piece for a long time."

"And?" he asked.

"And as a patient you are a handful."

"What's that mean? And how long have I been here?"

"You were brought in yesterday, about noon. They operated on you right after that, and you slept like you were in a wrestling match most of the night. Around three I had to put you in restraints to keep you from flopping on the floor or ripping your tubes out."

He looked up at the two bottles of IV fluids and tried to conceal his embarrassment. "Must be some bad stuff in them."

"Naw," she said as she finished taking his pulse and slipped a thermometer under his tongue. "The anesthetic is a kick in the butt. Some guys sleep like the dead, some vomit their shorts up, and others have fistfights in their dreams. You went all twelve rounds last night."

"Thorry," he mumbled.

"Shush," she said, scowling. "Don't screw up my temp taking."

He liked her. There was no doubt that she was in complete charge of her ward, and that she made the rules. She gave him two pills. Then she came back and gave him two shots and fussed with his dressings and the drain tube that stuck through the dressings and emptied somewhere out of Hollister's sight. Within minutes after her visit, he was unable to stay awake and drifted off to a more restful sleep than the one the night before.

Around midnight Hollister awoke, again disoriented. The medications they were giving him were like a bad drunk. His head was foggy, and his stomach felt very tentative.

He tried to change his position so he could sit up. It was dark, and the only light in the room was the desk lamp at the nurses' station on the other side of the room, about twenty feet away. A nurse was hunched over some paperwork, flanked by two stacks of patient charts.

In the other direction were five beds, all of them filled. One of the figures was in a full-body wrap tethered to the bed by a complete complement of tubes and drains. He was unconscious. The others slept in various states of disrepair. One was an amputee. His legs stopped at the knees.

"These are for you," someone said.

He turned to find the nurse from the desk standing by his bedside. It wasn't K.O., but an equally attractive captain with a pageboy haircut and a stethoscope around her neck. She handed him a couple of notes. Her tone was cold in comparison to K.O.'s. She was all business.

He tried to read them, but the light was too bad. "Is there any light?"

She reached into the sleeve pocket of her fatigue shirt and pulled out a penlight, which she snapped on and held so he could read.

The first note was from Sangean. All it said was *Get some rest. See you in the A.M. Sangean.*

The second read: *Stopped in to see you, sir. But you were off somewhere. Be back when you land. And, I'm real sorry, sir.* It was signed, *PFC Cathcart.*

"Finished, huh?" She snapped off the light. "Got to save batteries until my folks send me some replacements. Hard to get these little ones from Sam."

"Parents! Oh shit," Hollister said. "No one notified my parents, did they?"

"I don't know. Why?" she replied.

"I'd just rather not upset them. I mean I'm in one piece." He nodded in the direction of the amputee. "I shouldn't even be in here with these guys. Should I?"

"You're in here to recover. Has nothing to do with damage. You need someone keeping an eye on you till the anesthetic wears off. Then we ship you out to a regular ward."

"Why?"

"Because we don't want you here. You mess up my sheets."

"No. Why do I need to be watched?"

"You watch a guy do parabolic vomiting from this stuff, and you'll know why."

He felt the uneasy response in his stomach. "Oh. I see. Yech!"

She repeated the checking and poking that K.O. had done earlier, then went back to her desk.

"Anything to eat around here?"

"Shssh!" she scolded. "You're eating." She poked her pencil toward the IVs.

"Bad stuff. My gut is keeping me awake making noise."

"Hold on," she said, getting up and going to a wall locker.

She extracted a teabag from the locker and dropped it into a cup on the medical table behind her desk. Next to the rolling table a hot plate was keeping a pot of water hot. She poured some of it over the teabag and dipped the bag a few times by its string. She brought the cup to Hollister. "Here," she said. "Live it up."

"Tea?"

"That's all you can have, except Jell-O, and I don't have any of that."

"This is the worst!"

"No, there's worse. And don't ask for it."

She walked back to her desk and got back to work. Hollister raised the tea to his lips and found it fairly pleasant, if weak. He leaned back and let things sink in. He inventoried his situation. He was wounded, but he didn't know exactly how bad. He guessed he would be okay. He was worried about whether Susan and his parents had been notified. He had elected not to have them notified when he in-processed at IIFFV Personnel. But that was no guarantee they hadn't already sent a TWX back to the States and scared the shit out of his family. He thought about the others in the chopper and wondered if anyone had died or if he had just dreamed it. So much was a blur of reality, fragments of memory, and a headache that wouldn't go away.

"Take these," the duty nurse said, handing him a tiny paper cup with four different capsules and two chalky-looking pills.

He took them and washed them down with the tea. "Shit!" he said.
"Hot, huh?"

"I'll say. That was pretty stupid of me."

"You'll do stupider things. It seems to be a pattern with you guys."

"Us guys?"

"LRPs. Don't you eat steel and spit out nails?" she asked.

"No, but we like folks to think that."

"According to your records, this is the third time you've been wounded."

It was the fourth, but he felt that telling her wasn't going to make her feel any better about him.

"Clumsy, I guess," he said.

She wasn't amused. She just grunted and walked away.

He knew that the LRP reputation was still bad and still rubbing the Cu Chi base camp commandos the wrong way. It just never occurred to him that it would piss off a nurse.

Breakfast was more of the same. It came at seven and consisted of Jell-O, weak tea, and a single soggy piece of toast—burned on one side, cold on the other.

After breakfast K.O. returned. "Hey there! You're getting a little color in your cheeks. How's that leg?"

"You tell me. I've been here two days, and I haven't seen a doctor."

"Oh, the doctors have seen you all right," she said while she attended to his IVs and took his vital signs. She made a few entries in his chart. "While you were snoozin' they were doctorin' and movin' on to other patients."

"They ever going to tell me anything?"

"Oh, it could happen. Some of them have even talked to the nurses."

She smiled and walked to the bed across the aisle. Hollister didn't miss the backside of her fatigues. *Cute butt,* he thought.

"Hey . . . Captain Hollister?"

Turning back from K.O.'s bottom to the other side of his bed, Hollister found PFC Cathcart standing there with a wire contraption sticking through his cheek. It wrapped over his head and around his neck and was attached to a leather straplike device that held tension into the wire.

"What the fuck happened to you?"

"Sir?" Cathcart said, confused by the question.

"How'd that happen?"

"Sir . . . I'm One-three Bravo," he said, dropping his head and his voice. "I'm real sorry I got you and the others fucked up."

"What? What are you talking about? You mean you were the lost team member?"

"Yessir, and if I hadn't gotten separated you might not be in here."

"I'm sorry, Cathcart. I've never heard you whisper before. I didn't recognize your voice."

"No sweat. I guess I fucked up."

"How'd it happen?"

Cathcart toyed with the floppy brim of his LRP hat and took a breath. "We busted out of the trees to get to the chopper. I fell behind just a bit and got parallel to the tail gunner. I tried to catch up, but instead I tripped on something and went down like a train wreck."

He pointed to the wiring on his face. "I hit my face on the top of my M16 and broke my jaw. It must have put me out because the next thing I know I'm laying in the tall grass and you're calling me on the horn."

"It's not your fault. Blow it off. You hear me? There never was till a LRP that didn't bust his ass about every other dash across a landing zone."

Cathcart didn't look up and didn't say anything.

"You did the right thing. Accidents happen. But you soldiered on out there, brought in the choppers, got yourself a couple of bad guys with some good instructions for the Cobras. Good work."

"Really?"

"Really. Now get it out of your head."

"Okay, sir. Thanks. I really been feelin' bad about this."

"Well, don't."

He smiled, reached out, shook Hollister's hand, and left quietly.

"Nice work, Captain," K.O. said, standing on the other side of Hollister's bed.

He turned and saw her walking away to attend to another patient. He leaned back and replayed the extraction in his head. Pieces started to come back—the RPG, the chopper crash. Then he remembered the bodies. He wanted a drink—bad.

"We have cleaned out the wound and debrided it. There was a lot of trash, dirt, and chopper fuel in and around the wound. There is a large amount of muscle tissue missing—that we cut out. And there's going to be some pain while you rebuild it," the doctor said, searching his pocket for a pen and putting his reading glasses on.

He never looked at Hollister while he spoke, only at the patient record he held open at waist level. His lips moved a bit while he read some of the nursing notations and flipped through the small lab slips snugged up under the file's spring clasp.

"So—is there any real permanent damage?"

The doctor looked up for the first time. "No. You might suffer a loss of strength that'll take some months to regain. But if you don't have any complications or nerve damage, you'll be ready for light duty in six to eight weeks."

"Can I go back to my unit till I get cleared?"

"No. I'm sending you to Japan for a month or so. You stay here with a wound that big, and you risk infection. You need some physical therapy and some rest. You're also anemic, and you have a slight respiratory infection. You go back to that stink hole you guys live in, and you'll rip my sutures out, tear the wound open, and give yourself a pile of grief. Japan," he said, snapping the lid of the file closed and walking abruptly away without another word.

Japan? Several thoughts rushed through Hollister's mind. He'd worked so hard since he'd been with Juliet Company—too hard to lose his job over a wound. But Japan? He could use a little time to get his head clear about a few things. The thought made him feel guilty. But *Japan?* It was still Japan, and he remembered it with mixed emotions from his first tour.

Things were suddenly crowding his head. If he could just go heal up and not lose his job. After all, they got along for a while without him. But the company was a mess when he arrived.

"Going to Japan, huh?" It was Major Sangean.

"Yessir. That's what they just told me."

"How are you feeling?"

"Okay. I haven't even been out of this bed yet. I don't really know how I feel. My leg throbs like a son of a bitch, and I'm really just now coming out of the fog."

"Good. We need you to get back to duty as soon as you're up to it."

"Can you hold my job, sir?"

"Vance and I will take up your slack."

"I'd like that," Hollister said, feeling some of the worry go out of his gut.

"We'll need you where we're going. We're moving."

"Moving? Where?"

"Well, the last couple of contacts have been large enough and turned enough intel for Two Field to move a brigade of the Twenty-fifth and the One hundred ninety-ninth Infantry Brigade into the AO."

"They think we've developed it enough to commit maneuver units back into the area to clean it out."

"That's great! We earned our keep?" Hollister asked.

"Seems so. Anyway, we're moving to War Zone D."

The words were chilling. War Zone D had gained a reputation for a great number of brutal battles and held many secrets of operations launched out of the forests and old plantations.

"I'm going to have to do some homework. I've never been there."

"Well, you know it is north and a little east of Bien Hoa—so we relocate back to our rear area. The terrain is much more forested and varied than that damn border."

"We have a mission yet?"

"Same old deal. They aren't sure just what is going on in there. They don't want to move a maneuver unit in there unless they're sure there are some bad guys worth going after. There's been some sightings of very small parties—probably couriers, bearers, and Admin types," Sangean said.

"Saturate the area with teams?"

"Yep. If they're in there, we should be able to find them."

"Can you have someone slip me some maps and keep me posted on the operations while I'm in Japan?"

"No problem," Sangean said as he pulled his hat out of his pocket and flipped it open. "I've got a couple of teams to debrief and a shitload of paperwork. You need anything?"

"I think I've got everything I need."

"Good. See you later," Sangean said as he turned to leave.

"Sir," Hollister said.

"Huh?"

"Thanks."

Sangean cracked the beginning of a smile. "You might be sorry you asked for the job back."

The next morning K.O. raised his bed, and he was able to watch her change the dressing. She cut the old blood-soaked dressings off and revealed a slightly withered and very purple and yellow upper thigh. Running from the outside of the knee to the bend at his hip was a long and jagged cut that was sewn closed with dozens of sutures. "What the hell is that?"

"What?" K.O. asked, swabbing the area down with some pHisohex.

"What kind of stitches are those?"

"Wire."

"Wire?" He reached down and touched them.

K.O. slapped his hand. "Hey! How the hell do you think you're going to heal up if you keep messing with it?"

"Why wire?"

"They had to cut away too much skin—raggedy edges. And when they tried to close it up, it meant they had to stretch the skin. Regular sutures would pull out or break. So they wired you up like a chain-link fence."

He thought for a moment about the removal, and it bothered him a bit. "Guess taking them out is going to be a real picnic."

"Nope. 'S'gonna hurt."

"Thanks. You're a lot of encouragement."

"I got an A in disingenuous encouragement in nursing school."

He watched as she continued to bathe his wound in disinfectant and then cleaned away the excess fluid from around the wires.

The touch of her tiny fingers was so soothing, even though the area was very tender. In the few months away from Susan, he had forgotten how it felt to have a woman's hands on his skin. He leaned back on his pillow and enjoyed her touch and the rich, clean smell of her hair.

The thump on his midsection startled him. He opened his eyes with a start and saw a large, stainless steel bedpan resting on his abdomen.

"Your turn to do some work," she said.

"Me?" he sputtered, feeling a flush of embarrassment come to his cheeks. "How do you expect me to, ah . . .?"

"I expect you to slip that under your butt and make it happen, Captain," K.O. said, half teasing him.

"But all I've been eating is Jell-O and tea. I'm not sure I can fill your order."

"You will, or it's enema time."

The thought brought cold fear to his chest. "Oh, no. I'll do . . . ah, something."

She threw the sheet back over his leg, patted him on the arm and smiled as she walked to the next bed. "I have complete confidence in you. Never met a LRP who couldn't fill a bedpan on a moment's notice."

It was not much different from the trip he had taken to Japan on his first tour. Cold, even though it was still hot and wet in Vietnam. But the trip was a medevac flight. The huge C-141 jet had been configured to hold patients. The full length of the cargo compartment was fitted with stacked stretchers, each holding a patient. The worse the condition, the closer to the front of the airplane you were. Up near the cockpit, a small seating area remained for the few ambulatory patients who didn't need stretchers.

The screaming jet engines prevented anything but hand-signal communications, and the air force flight nurses had to pantomime most of their messages to the patients. It finally got manageable when the large loading ramp was closed for taxi and takeoff.

Hollister was happy to see that he had been placed in a lower stretcher near the tailgate. That was a sign that he didn't need too much attention. But the dark lower rack was cold and drafty.

It was well after midnight before they were all loaded onto the aircraft. By takeoff time it was nearly three. His stitches itched, even though there was still a drain tube sewn into his thigh. He tried to scratch without scratching. He was sure if he scratched his leg too much it would only make the area itch that much more.

Bored, Hollister looked at his watch, moved the patient's ID band from its face, and checked the time. It was nearly five A.M., Saigon time, but he had no idea what time it was in Japan.

The nurse must have seen him check his watch because she came to his stretcher and kneeled down to be able to see his face.

"Here. The flight will dry you out."

She handed him a carton of orange juice that had an American brand name on it—Foremost. It looked familiar and felt icy cold as Hollister took it.

She then reached in the pocket of her flight suit and pulled out two red capsules, and put them in his other hand. "Take these. They will help you sleep."

"Thanks. I . . ." Hollister started to talk to her, but before he could, she had stood up, and was attending to the patient two stretchers above him.

He was groggy from the sleeping pills when he realized two American stretcher bearers were carrying him off the jet. The sudden blast of cold, rainy wind sobered Hollister up. He reached down and tried to tuck the single army blanket in around his hips to keep out the cold, only to get a face full of rain that dripped off the two-story-high tail of the large jet.

He got up on one elbow to see where he was and immediately recognized the air base at Tachikawa, Japan. He remembered the cold morning he had spent there picking up and escorting his brother platoon leader's body. Lucas had been a good friend. But the memory was not good.

The bearers carried Hollister up into a large American-made bus that had been converted into an ambulance of sorts. The seats were all gone, and poles had been installed with U-shaped devices that locked the stretcher handles in place, allowing patients to be stacked three high against the large windows.

Lucking out, Hollister got a slot that allowed him to look out. The air base quickly gave way to the streets of a suburban Japanese community. Men and women threaded through the narrow streets on bicycles that all seemed to have been made by the same manufacturer. Hollister found it curious that not one single bike rider was just riding a bike. They all seemed to have a purpose for their ride, carrying goods, parcels, briefcases, baskets of food, and one even had a bicycle strapped onto the back of his bicycle.

Schoolchildren in uniforms were everywhere. The girls wore white blouses and blue pleated skirts, while the boys wore black uniforms with high-buttoned collars. All of them carried briefcases for their books or wore leather backpacks. All were spotlessly neat and devoid of any signs of individuality. It amused Hollister—like being in the army.

After only twenty minutes of enjoying the clean, wet look and feel of Japan, Hollister drifted off again. The medications, sleeping pills, and strain of his healing had drained his energy to the point where he found himself in a constant state of drowsiness or sleep.

The smell of hospital filled Hollister's nostrils as he woke up. He was in a large, statesidelike hospital bed made up with rough, clean sheets. He found himself covered with a wool blanket and wearing heavier hospital pajamas than the ones he was wearing when he left Vietnam.

The ward had twenty-six beds—all filled with wounded GIs in various traction devices and plaster casts. He looked left and right and saw that the two patients in the adjoining beds were asleep. Everyone seemed to be asleep except him. He looked at his watch. Someone had changed the plastic and paper ID on his wrist. It had his name and GEN HOSP CAMP DRAKE USARJ, SURGICAL. His watch read 0200 or 1400. He guessed that both were wrong.

The sounds of a woman's footsteps came from the far end of the ward—out of his sight. Hollister watched and waited until a uniformed army captain wearing crisp whites, a nurse's cap, and a forest-green sweater came down the aisle in front of his bunk. He caught her eye.

"Ma'am."

"Well, good morning," she said as she stopped, stepped into the space beside his bed, and reached out for him. Hollister thought she was reaching to shake his hand and was embarrassed to find that she raised the other hand and looked at her watch to take his pulse.

"Morning," he said. "Is this the end of my trip? Or am I waiting for something else?"

"Like what?" she asked, plucking his chart off the hook at the foot of the bed.

"Like being moved again to another ward?"

"You are in a surgical ward at Camp Drake—near Tokyo."

"But these folks here seem to be a lot worse off than I am."

"You'll be here until they yank that drain tube, then they'll decide to put you in another ward if you're just mending and don't need monitoring."

He looked out the window at the spring blossoms on the dogwood trees. "Sure looks like a great place to be stationed."

She smiled broadly, and looked up at him as she was straightening the sheet she had lifted to check his wound. "Got that right."

"So?"

"So, what?"

"So, how am I doing?"

"You hurt?"

"No."

"You're lying."

"Yes."

"You are going to be one sore soldier until you get over most of the damage. What hit you—a tank round?"

"Not really sure. Piece of frag or some parts from a helicopter that was coming apart on the way to the ground."

"Well, it took a chunk of you with it. I'm glad I don't have to do your physical therapy."

"Bad?"

"Ranger School?"

"Yeah. I went through it," he said.

"You're gonna do it again," she said. She made a note in his chart and put it back at the foot of his bunk.

He let the news sink in. For a fleeting second he was dreading the healing, but then he smiled.

"What's so funny?"

"I'm real glad to be here. And real glad to have to go through this. I could be in a box somewhere."

"Guess that's one way to look at it."

"Yes, ma'am. I'm real glad," he said. It was the first time his head was clear enough really to absorb his situation.

"Can I call home?"

"After the doctors clear you for a wheelchair. Until then you belong to me and you are on the wagon."

"On the wagon?"

"You eat in bed, and you pee in a bottle."

"Guess that means more balancing on a bedpan, too."

"Got that right, too."

CHAPTER 22

An orderly brought Hollister back from the phones on the other side of the huge hospital complex. He hadn't minded the discomfort of being bounced along the corridors on a gurney since he had been able to talk to Susan.

He lied to her, just as he knew he would. He told her he had been slightly wounded and he was at Drake to let him heal up without excessive exposure to the chance of infection. He told her there were just a few stitches, and he would be up and around in no time.

It was the third day at Camp Drake, and Hollister found himself wide-awake at three in the morning. He had nothing to occupy his time or his mind, and he was not supposed to leave his bed. He tried to write a letter to Susan, but found he was filling the pages up with chatty talk about the weather and the dogwood trees. He had been promised another trip to the phone as soon as the doctors pulled his drain tube. The removal was scheduled for nine that morning.

He stopped the letter, rationalizing that he would talk to Susan again, and maybe his parents, before they could even get the letters he was trying to write. What he had written was full of lies and omissions. But why tell them? Why worry them?

"What's chances of getting out of bed?" Hollister asked the nurse who was working on a patient across the aisle that separated his row of hospital beds from the other half of the ward.

She raised her hand, without looking at him, and touched her tiny thumb to her forefinger, making a solid 0. A zero, a no-chance signal.

"What happens if I just up and get gone myself?" he asked, half kidding.

"You'll fall on your ass—Captain," the lieutenant said, emphasizing her pronunciation of Hollister's rank.

"Would I fall on my ass if I weren't a *captain?*"

She hesitated a long time before answering, and the two patients flanking Hollister's bed started laughing.

"Well?" he asked.

"Well"—she turned and looked at him—"if you were a field grader there might be a chance to waive gravity."

More laughing.

"Can't get any respect around here," Hollister grumbled to the CWO3 in the adjacent bed.

The CWO3 was propped up against the head of his bed. His left arm and entire shoulder were confined in a cast supported by a bar that extended from his hip to a point under his elbow. He had been blown out of his helicopter in Da Nang when 122mm rockets hit the runway. He had been trying to get his chopper off the ground, and he was happy to be alive. He was a great bedmate to have in the huge, cold, and impersonal ward. He and Hollister had become friendly in the short time Hollister had been there. He had a last name, but everyone in the ward, the doctors and the nurses included, just called him "Chief."

"Least you can consider getting out of the rack. I'm still looking forward to the day when I can wipe my own butt," the chief said.

"I guess I ought to count myself lucky," Hollister said. "How you doin' today?"

"What's it look like?"

The question referred to the plastic tube snaking out from under his blanket. It was filled with a pink- and rust-colored fluid and bubbles.

"Still isn't clear, Chief. But it's lighter."

"Nope—gotta be clear piss or I don't get any real food."

The chief had extensive internal injuries, and the drain from his bladder was still a warning flag of blood seeping into his system from the trauma he had experienced four weeks before.

"Maybe you need a beer to flush it out," Hollister said.

"Hey! Now that's an aviator's flush if I ever heard one."

He reached up with his free hand and grabbed onto the triangular grip that dangled from the framework that boxed his bed. He pulled himself up a fraction of an inch and raised his voice over the sound of a radio playing at the other end of the ward. "Lieutenant Honey Buns?"

The nurse turned to look at him, "Chief! For the last time—it's *Hunnicutt.*"

"Oh, yeah. I forgot. Anyhow, what's the deal? Will a beer be on my tray today?"

"You got a better chance of dancing on 'American Bandstand' today."

He turned back to Hollister. "Looks like we're shit outa luck."

"Maybe they want to keep all this stuff from us until we get well."

"No," Lieutenant Hunnicutt said, "we'd rather just deprive you of things. None of us cares if you ever get well."

"She hates us," the chief said. "We need to plan a break."

The chief's spirits were contagious. He kept everyone around him laughing, even though he was the only one of his four-man crew who survived the rocket attack.

Dozing off after breakfast and before the doctor's rounds was damn near unavoidable. Hollister tried to stay awake, but he had been in bed so long he was having trouble sleeping at night and staying awake in the daytime. Each day he promised himself he would not let himself drift off so he could sleep through the long nights. And each night he would doze off after lights-out only to find himself wide-awake within minutes. His nights would drag on while he tried to occupy his mind and coax himself to sleep.

After the tenth day at Camp Drake, Hollister gave in. He had declined the offer of sleeping pills from the nurses who came by with them each evening. It wasn't a matter of any one thing he could put his finger on. He just knew that taking sleeping pills had to be something he didn't want to do. So without any fanfare, Hollister simply shook his head each time the night nurse offered the pills—pills the others took freely and without comment.

Finally, one night he broke down and took the pills. He waited for something to happen to him. He knew he had been given pills on the plane ride from Vietnam, but he couldn't remember the effect they had had on him. He imagined all kinds of strange things. After all, it was 1969, and the horror stories about drugs and hallucinogenic madness were everywhere. The army was particularly alarmist about the abuse of drugs. To Hollister any line dividing sleeping pills from marijuana or LSD was not visible to him. He had grown up knowing that all drugs were bad and that they all had the potential for disastrous addiction. He steeled himself to be able to control the effects of the sleeping pills.

Early the next morning he woke up, unaware of when he had dropped off to sleep or of the effects of any of the pills. At that moment it seemed to him to be pretty much of a fuss about something he couldn't be convinced had any influence on him.

That night, and every night after that, Hollister accepted the offer of the two little red capsules. Each night he slept well and was able to take a nap during the day without any disruption of his sleep pattern.

Toward the end of his second week in Japan, Hollister was taken out of the bed and to a treatment room. No one explained to him the purpose of the visit. His drain tube had been removed more than a week before with very little fanfare.

A doctor whom he had never seen and a female medic came into the room. She motioned for Hollister to lie back on the treatment table while the doctor immediately went to Hollister's records and began flipping through the treatment pages. He finally stopped to look at a hand-drawn diagram of the wound and the surgery done by the original doctor who had operated on Hollister at the 12th Evac Hospital in Cu Chi.

The medic took a pair of surgical scissors and cut the dressing off Hollister's thigh.

Hollister raised his head and looked at the wound. It still looked bad. The skin was wrinkled from the constant heat and moisture under the dressings. The wire sutures had cut so deeply into his flesh that at each point where they disappeared into his skin there was a swollen pink spot. Some of the wire had been lost as the skin had swollen into place over it.

The doctor opened up a sealed package of surgical drape and revealed all the necessary equipment to remove the wire sutures. Without a word, he snapped on a pair of surgical gloves and picked up an expensive-looking set of wire cutters—all stainless steel.

"We going to pull these?" Hollister said lightheartedly, hoping to prod the doctor into saying something.

The doctor never looked up at Hollister, but replied flatly, "No. Not we. I am, though."

At that point Hollister decided just to shut up and let the cold fish of a doctor get it over with.

The doctor grabbed onto the first stitch of wire closest to Hollister's knee and jabbed the point of the pliers under it. The movement of the wire and the point of the cutters shot a lightning bolt of pain down to the bone in his leg. He winced.

"You get too uncomfortable, tell me. We'll just stop, give you some local anesthetic, and then finish this."

"No. I'm okay," Hollister said. He was determined not to give the shit of a doctor the satisfaction of seeing him ask for a painkiller.

The next morning the doctor who had been coming by on rounds for two weeks dropped by again and spoke to Hollister instead of about him. He was a balding lieutenant colonel with GI glasses that had been stained at the temples from repeated applications of aftershave lotion.

"Young man," he started. "We've done all we can do—surgically speaking. You will now be turned over to the physical therapists to get you back on your feet and walking again."

"Yes, sir," Hollister said, waiting for him to drop the other shoe.

"If you regain the use of your leg without any problem—we'll return you to duty."

"Picket fence?" Hollister asked.

"Yes. No medical profile if it goes like I think it will."

"How long?"

"About a month of PT, then a month of convalescent leave, and then duty."

It came as a surprise to Hollister that the doctor had already carved out what would be too much time away from Juliet Company. Hollister's heart sank. He knew that Sangean could never hold his job open that long. And if he got a clean release, he would be sent back into the manpower pool in Vietnam and might still end up in a shitty advisory job or some REMF job that would make him miserable. He knew he had to think of some way around it all.

Hollister started to ask the doctor about the schedule only to see him hand the chart to the nurse and walk to another patient.

"You'll be required to come in here every day for two hours in the morning, and we'll work on your leg. We expect you to work on it yourself each afternoon before the next morning's appointment. If we don't think you are holding up your end of the prescribed physical therapy, we will double your appointments and require you to come in morning *and* afternoon," the graying major, a physical therapist, said after she read Hollister's medical chart. She was in her late forties, severely manicured, lean, and business-like. She wore a white jacket with her rank and insignia on the collar and white trousers. Her nameplate said URBANIK.

"Yes, ma'am" was the only thing Hollister could think to say. He wondered if she was expecting him to say, *I promise.*

She looked up from the records and smiled. "Call me Connie. And you are . . ." She looked at his records again, and they both said "Jim" at the same time.

"Okay, Jim. First, let's get you to stand up."

He found a point of balance on the arms of the wheelchair he had ridden to Connie's office, and began to raise himself, most of the weight on his good leg.

She reached over and flipped on the brake that locked the wheels to his chair. "You gotta watch out for those machines. We've put more patients back into bed after wheelchair accidents than came in here with ambulatory complaints."

He smiled and nodded thanks as he raised himself to full height. His head spun, and he started to feel the pain shooting up his leg. He had not been on his feet since the day he was wounded, and the first sensation was one of complete lack of control over his leg.

Major Urbanik grabbed his hand and put it on her shoulder to steady him. "Hold on." She then kicked the wheelchair out from behind him.

He found himself standing in a shaky upright position with one hand on her shoulder as she stayed seated next to his bad leg.

"Okay, let's have a look," she said as she ripped the snaps loose that ran the full length of his orthopedic pajama leg.

The move caught Hollister by surprise, and he almost fell over trying to hide his nakedness as his pajama bottoms fell to the floor around his ankles. The only other thing he was wearing was the top to his pajamas, and it only reached to the top of his genitals.

"Easy. This is a hospital. I don't mean to embarrass you, but I have to look at this leg," she said as she reached over and traced the contour of his thigh muscle, feeling for the loss of mass he had suffered.

He didn't respond and didn't look down. Her touch on his leg was anything but unpleasant, and he was terribly afraid that he might be stimulated to respond to her slender fingers. He concentrated on not allowing it to happen.

"You have lost a considerable amount of muscle, but there is not much damage to bone or connecting tissues that attach the muscles to the bones."

"What's that mean?"

"Means work. You're going to the gym this morning and every day from here on out. After a workout you will go to the whirlpool and soak the leg, knee, and hip for an hour—each day."

"That it?"

"Nope. I want you to walk—anywhere, for an hour each afternoon, and a half hour each evening."

She took out a tape measure that was marked off in centimeters, slipped it around the top of his thigh, and took a measurement. She did the same to his midthigh and the area just above his knee. Each time she made a notation in his record of the circumference of the part of the leg she was measuring.

"Okay. Sounds like something I can do."

She got up, leaving him standing, and walked across the room, then looked at him from fifteen feet away. He self-consciously bent a bit, hoping the bottom of his shirt would cover him a little more.

"Stand up straight," she said, looking at his legs, knees, and feet.

He stood up.

She made no more remarks. After making a few further notes in his chart, she walked around behind him, then stepped out into the hallway where she could view his legs from the back.

Again, he was aware that his cheeks were exposed below the midline. He just stood there and waited for her to make some remark. She didn't.

He felt the wheelchair touch the back of his heel. She had returned from the hallway and pushed it to him.

"Sit," she said. "This is your last day in a wheelchair. You will go down to this room." She handed him a prescription with a number on it. "They'll give you a pair of crutches you'll use to get around for four days."

"Then what?"

"Then you turn them in, and get a cane. I just want you to use them for stability—so you won't bust your ass."

He was pulling his trousers up over his behind when she said that. He chose not to recognize her timing.

"I want you off the cane inside ten days."

"Great with me. I'd love to be able to walk."

"To the latrine," she finished his sentence.

"How'd you know?"

"Professional experience," she said. "And I broke a leg in three places skiing in Colorado a couple of years ago."

He smiled. He knew he and no-nonsense Connie were going to get on well.

As soon as Hollister got his crutches, he went to the phones instead of going back to his ward. He got one call through to Sangean even though the line was bad. Sangean's voice sounded up and eager to get Hollister back. Hollister dodged the question of when and let Sangean know he would get back as soon as he could get them to break him loose.

As soon as he was able to, he changed the subject to the troops and operations. Sangean gave him a quick overview. They were working War Zone D, and it was far superior to Cu Chi. Hollister asked Sangean to have someone send him whatever unclassified info they could on the mission and the AO.

Mobility was a sheer delight for Hollister. He took advantage of being able to leave his bed to make trips to the phone to call his family and Susan. He wandered over to the small PX and, after drawing partial pay from Finance, bought some flashlight batteries for the nurse captain with the pageboy back at 12th Evac. He went to the small post office and bought some stamps and envelopes to mail the batteries.

Back in his rack, Hollister wrote to Sangean and told him only part of the truth. He explained that he was ambulatory, sore, and working on getting the strength back into his leg. He said that the doctors told him he would be pretty close to healed up in a month and could expect to dodge any permanent profile that might restrict his duty. He promised to try to call Juliet Company if he could get through the maze of military connections.

He didn't tell Sangean the doctors were going to prescribe several weeks of convalescent leave after his therapy.

Connie Urbanik was a tough taskmaster. She checked on Hollister regularly, dropping in on the small physical therapy gym near her office.

She also checked up on him in the whirlpool. Soon he became used to her dropping in on him when he was naked. His response was mixed. It embarrassed him a bit and disappointed him that she didn't seem to care. He was aware that this was a sign of male ego.

His days were filled with exercise, whirlpooling, and walking. His mind was crammed with the conflicting demands on him. He missed Susan and wanted to get on with his life. "Getting on with his life" was every soldier's way of saying he wanted the war to be over—soon.

But he had unfinished business back at Juliet Company. He didn't want an endless stream of changing faces running the company, planning and supervising operations, and training the teams. He knew there was nothing more demoralizing in the life of a soldier than turbulence—both within and above. He knew he had to go back. He didn't know how he would explain the need to Susan.

It didn't take him long to find out what to do with his evenings. He found the small Officers Club in the hospital complex. Patients were allowed in the club if they could get there under their own power.

A small table was in the corner of the poorly lit room where a badly set light dribbled a pool of reading light. He staked the table out every evening and sat there drinking Scotch, listening to the reel-to-reel tape recorder playing popular music, and writing. He wrote letters to family and friends and made notes on training and operations.

It was the first real chance he had to catch his breath and think about what did and didn't work in Juliet Company. In short order he made another trip to the PX and bought his third lined notebook to capture his thoughts.

He would get back to his bunk after lights-out, a little drunk. He would take the sleeping pills the nurses had left for him and sleep without

dreaming. Each morning he awoke with a hangover and went to the gym
to work out the pain in his head and in his leg. By the time he got out of
the whirlpool, he would almost be recovered from the hangover. Each day
he decided that as long as he didn't have a drink until he got to the club
after dinner he had no problem.

But each night he would take his place in the corner, order a double
Scotch, and begin to write. He kept writing, and the Japanese waitress kept
refilling his glass. One night she asked him, after he had had several drinks,
"You hurt?"

He thought she was talking about his leg, as his limp was obvious.
"Yeah," he replied, and smiled. "But the Scotch is good medicine."

She wasn't talking about his leg.

"Tell me about convalescent leave," Hollister said as Connie Urbanik mea-
sured his leg again after three weeks of therapy.

"Good deal. Uncle Sam lets you have a month or so of free leave in Japan
after you get out of the hospital. You get to do nothing and finish mending."

Hollister made a face she couldn't miss.

"What's wrong with that?"

"I have to get back to Vietnam."

"Are you nuts?" she asked.

"I know it makes no sense to you. But I've got an important job—important to me. If I stay away much longer, I will lose the job and end up
being reassigned. My guess is it will be a job I will hate."

"I've never met a soldier who wanted to turn down leave."

"Do you have to take it?"

"Well, you have to come back off leave and get a release from the doctors or physical therapist."

"Oh," he said. He wasn't pleased to hear that. "You mean I have to take
the month, or whatever, and then come back to see you before I can be
cleared to go back to Vietnam?"

"You get the last week of this PT done as well as the previous weeks, and
I'll see what I can do to reduce your leave."

Hollister beamed. "Great. You're on." He got up to leave. "That all
for today?"

"Yeah. You're building muscle mass. Your range of motion is much improved, and my guess is that it'll continue. You have any complaints?"

"No, ma'am. I'm ready to go."

"Not so fast. Listen, you got a girl or a wife?"

"Yes, why?"

"Fly her over here, and spend some time with her. If you still want to cut your leave short, I'll make it happen for you."

She scribbled something on a pad, tore the sheet off, and handed it to him.

"Take this to Personnel. You are on leave effective a week from tomorrow. It authorizes you thirty days. Do what you want, and let me know."

"Thanks. I don't think I could ask for anything better."

"I could."

"What's that?" he asked.

"You could go a little easier on that booze."

Her words stuck in his head as he walked, with a slight limp, down the long corridor connecting two wings of the hospital. He shook it off as just a passing remark. She couldn't have meant anything serious about it. After all, he didn't drink during the day, and he never got sloppy drunk. It didn't mean anything. He was sure of that.

The phone call to Susan was a two-hour effort. He finally got her, waking her in the middle of the night. She shrieked with delight when he told her to get to Tokyo International for a week together. That was what he told her—that he had a week before he had to go back to Vietnam.

That part of the call cooled her, but she quickly returned to the exciting part. He promised to call her in twenty-four hours to find out her travel plans.

It was raining when the plane landed. Hollister stood up straight and waited just inside the terminal for her to get off the plane and walk across the concrete to the gate.

Susan looked wonderful, and Hollister was almost speechless when he saw her. Her hair was longer, she seemed to be more slender, and her face seemed narrower. She wore Levi's and a long coat.

She raised her head as she came through the door, caught a glimpse of him, and broke into her smile. Hollister was immediately aware that every man in the terminal was looking at her. It made him feel good—proud.

The crowd thinned a bit as she approached him. The last few steps she ran and almost threw herself at him. They embraced and kissed, and tried to talk, then kissed again. He laughed first. Then she got the giggles. When they got themselves under control enough to speak, they spoke at once. Then, careful not to interrupt one another, each paused to let the other speak. Then they did it again.

He couldn't contain his feelings and grabbed her, lifting her off the ground. She suddenly made a worried face and spoke. "Your leg. How's your leg? Shouldn't you put me down?"

"Never."

She slapped him playfully. "No! I'm serious. Am I hurting you?"

"Not a chance," he said as he spun her around and shook her playfully. "I'm not ever putting you down."

"You better, 'cause I have to pee!"

They both laughed, and he placed her gently on the floor and held her away from him so he could see her. "You look so wonderful."

"You look awful. You have bags under your eyes, your skin looks blotchy, and I haven't seen you walk yet."

"We can't all be beautiful," he said. And then he walked around— test-driving his leg. It was painful but he would never let her know that the skin was still so tight that it burned when he put weight on the leg. Each time the muscle expanded to take the weight, the skin stretched and he could feel at least four of the tight scars left by the wire sutures. "Look. I'm perfect. Little scar, and I got a Purple Heart."

"*Another* Purple Heart," she scolded.

"Enough. Let's go find your bags. I have a taxi outside and a terrific week planned."

The taxi took them to the tiny little hotel where he had rented them a room for the week. It was traditional Japanese, run by a family that spoke no English. The old couple stood at the front door and bowed deeply as Hollister and Susan got out of the car.

The driver took care of the baggage, and Hollister tried to explain to the couple that Susan was his wife and that he had not seen her for almost five months.

They didn't understand a word, but bowed and smiled and pretended they did,

The room was in the back of the hotel—ground level. Susan entered, shoeless, and took a breath of approval. "It's so neat and warm. How did you find this place?"

"There are plenty of guys at the hospital who are stationed here and know all the best places. They all told me this was the way to go. Okay?"

She turned, took him in her arms, and kissed him deeply for the first time. "Yes, honey. It's perfect."

The old man brought the bags and tried not to interrupt Susan and

Hollister, but was unsuccessful. They broke their embrace, a little embarrassed in the face of the old man's formal bow and traditional garb. Hollister thanked him, bowed, and tried to decide whether to tip him or not. Somehow, a man so dignified seemed above tipping. Hollister decided to deal with it later.

When the old man left, Hollister and Susan explored the rooms—three of them. Hollister had already seen them and knew where everything was, but he wanted to be with her while she discovered them.

She loved the tatami mats on the floor, the sliding shoji screens, and the hardwood trim that shined with years of care and polishing. It was an old building that surely went back to the turn of the century. A few Western conveniences had been put in—like a bathroom and better lighting. But the rest was traditional, sparse, Japanese decor.

"Oh, Jimmy! Look at this," Susan said as she opened the doors leading out into a private garden so manicured and so lush it took her breath away.

They walked out onto the narrow mahogany porch that looked over the small pool filled with Japanese carp. The pool was shaped in a double lobe, with a small concrete bridge crossing the narrow part.

A pagoda stood silently near the water, flanked by dwarf fruit trees anchored into a field of perfectly rounded pebbles that created a separation between the trees and the dark, rich grass.

As they stood there looking at the beautiful garden, Susan slid her hand up Hollister's back and dropped her head to his chest. "I missed you."

He looked at her and had no words to explain how far away the horror of the war had moved now that she was with him. He wrapped his arms around her, and for a long time they just stood there, silent and a little afraid.

There was an awkward moment when they realized the room had no bed. The bedding, to be rolled out on the floor, was put away in closets, and it would be conspicuous, if not embarrassing, to get it out in the middle of the day so they could make love.

They compromised and headed for the bathroom. It had a large Japanese tub that could hold four people. Susan made him leave while she undressed and fussed with herself. He spent the time finding space in the bedroom to put her things—most ended up in a closet with a few built-in drawers.

Susan emerged from the bathroom, her hair tied up with a ribbon, wearing the silk kimono that Hollister had bought and placed in there for her. She smiled and turned, showing off the beautiful pale blue floor-length robe. "I just love it. Where did you get it?"

"One of the nurses on my ward seems to know every shop in Tokyo. She sent me to the place where I bought it. It never occurred to me I would have to find a place for tall American women."

They both laughed. She was beautiful. He just stood there looking at her.

"Well," she said, waving toward the bathroom. "It's all yours."

Hollister called her. He had undressed and was already in the hot tub of steaming water—neck deep. He wasn't going to admit it, but he was putting off the time when she would see his scar as long as he could.

As soon as Susan entered the bathroom, she slid the shoji screen closed and dropped her kimono. Hollister groaned with delight. He hadn't seen her naked in so long. He reached out for her to join him.

As she stepped up on the small block to get into the tub, she intentionally paused long enough for Hollister to reach out and help her into the water.

She folded into his arms and leaned back against his chest. They didn't say a word or move for several minutes.

Then she spoke. "You gonna let me see that leg or what?"

"Oh, don't worry about it. It's just a scar. It's okay. I'm okay. Really."

She turned and looked at him, sternly. After a long pause she simply instructed him: "Stand—up!"

Hollister stood slowly. As the wound broke the water, she looked down at his leg. As he reached full height, his entire scar was above the water line in front of Susan's face.

She didn't say anything. She just reached out and gingerly touched the ugly scar that tracked down the outside of his thigh. After the healing, it had taken on an uneven thickness and the color ranged from red to blue-red.

As she ran her fingers down the scar, she started to sob—quietly. Hollister realized she was crying and started to reach for her. She refused to accept him; instead, she encircled his legs with her arms and placed her cheek against his wound—and kept sobbing quietly.

He let her be. Eventually, she let him hold her, and they stayed that way in the warm water until she calmed down. They didn't talk about it. He had no words for her, but he felt her pain over his confusing commitment to a war she didn't understand.

As the water cooled, they seemed to strike an unspoken agreement not to spoil their reunion with the war. That gave way to small talk, to more touching and more physical demonstrations of love.

They left the tub, and found the futon and bedclothes, and abandoned any worry about the old man. They didn't sleep that night.

The Japanese food was excellent. The weather allowed a postcard view of the city, and the on-and-off rain kept the streets sparkling clean.

They spent the entire day on the town in Tokyo doing all the touristy things. Even though he was in pain, Hollister worked very hard at concealing his limp. At lunch he had a few beers, and by the time they had finished dinner he had managed to stand off the pain with even more beer. He didn't want to provoke her into bringing up Vietnam.

The day turned into a wonderful night on the Ginza, then another passionate evening in the little hotel. By then they were over the awkwardness of being together again and had come to realize that they were quickly getting closer to being separated again. Their response was to become completely involved in each other and to avoid looking at clocks and watches.

It became a swirl of sightseeing, shopping, laughing, playing, and nights of intense intimacy. Finally, it was the night before she had to go home and he had to return to Vietnam.

They sat on the stone step leading down from the room to the little garden. "We going to talk about it or not?" she asked.

"About *it*?" he replied.

"Don't make this so hard for me. I want to know what we are doing. Is there an end to this? Do I have to go home and cry myself to sleep every night, scared shitless every time the phone rings?"

He dropped his head and remained silent.

"I just want to know when it will end. I want to know when this will be behind us and we get to live our life. Is that too much to ask?"

"No. It's not. But I don't know yet."

"When will you know? Are you going to keep putting it off until I have to bury you?"

Hollister snapped at her. "You think I want to be over there? You think I'd rather be in Vietnam than with you?"

"Jimmy, I don't know what you think. We have put off so many long-range decisions because of the short-range ones that I just don't know what we are doing."

"You're angry."

"Yes. No. I'm frustrated. I'm worried. I'm afraid. And I'm selfish. I want my husband. I want my life, and I want my future back."

He looked at her.

She continued. "I had a life before I met you. I had an idea what was possible and what I had to do to get there. Now I have no idea what is going on. You say you want to get out of the army, but I don't see it. You say that you want to do something else, but it's talk."

"I'll be home in a few months. Between now and then we can make plans. I don't want to come back here. But I . . ."

"But you what? You can't seem to break it off. You can't seem to get around to getting on with our lives."

"I will. I promise. I will," he said.

She looked at him with as serious an expression as he had ever seen. "Do it soon. I can't stay on this train much longer. Get this out of your system before it kills you or destroys us."

CHAPTER 23

"Well?" Major Urbanik asked.

"I'm ready for you to sign me out of here," Hollister said.

She took off her glasses and dropped them upside down on the medical forms on her desk. "You do understand that you can have another three weeks—and more—if you are having trouble with that leg?"

"Yes, ma'am."

She reached out and took the personnel form from Hollister's hand, then put her glasses back on. She scribbled her signature and checked some appropriate blocks. "This is wrong. You need more time. You need more distance from Vietnam. Listen, healing isn't just an end to bleeding and sharp pain."

"Yes, ma'am."

"No changing your mind?"

He shook his head.

It was called a "back-haul." Hollister was able to catch a ride back to Vietnam in an empty medical evacuation jet, like the one that brought him to Japan. The stanchions stood empty down the length of the C-141. Hollister knew they would strain under the load of all the patient-laden stretchers on the return trip.

He sat back in the seat and tried to get some sleep. It was the first night in weeks he hadn't had a drink or a sleeping pill to help him. He failed.

Brushing off his inability to sleep, he pulled out the maps and notes he had been studying. The handwritten letters announced his new preoccupation: WAR ZONE D.

The area outlined in marker ink wasn't much bigger than his hand—fingers spread. Still, it was over a hundred square kilometers. He sat and stared at the terrain. It had everything but mountains. There were bands of deforested terrain, stripped by air force Ranch Hand flights that dropped Agent Orange.

Trails crisscrossed everywhere. Streams meandered through abandoned rubber plantations. Roadways and abandoned hamlets dotted the clearings. Locks, canals, and irrigation ditches spanned the distance between small rivers and old paddy fields. And everywhere else there were trees, bushes, mangroves, and wild growth. All of this was a blessing—and a curse. The vegetation would hide LRP teams from immediate detection and conceal them when they needed it. But it would also conceal the enemy, who knew every single square meter of the area.

He continued studying the map. He wanted to know where all the major terrain features were and where they were in respect to one another. The more he knew about War Zone D, the less of an advantage it would be for the enemy.

The loadmaster brought Hollister a cup of coffee and then found himself a stack of soft emergency flotation equipment to use as a bed. Once the loadmaster was asleep, Hollister was alone again with his map in the cavernous jet.

The Juliet Company base camp at Bien Hoa was a palace compared to the broken-down and abandoned barracks back at Cu Chi.

It was dark when Hollister got out of the jeep that had given him a lift from the airfield to J Company. He stood by the roadway and looked at the compound. It was similiar to—only a lot better than—the one he had lived in on his first tour. Each of the team hooches was lit up with electric light, and scratchy music could be heard over the busy night sounds of the sprawling Bien Hoa complex.

Hollister picked up his small AWOL bag and entered the compound. He walked over to Operations, a large sandbagged building surrounded by a fifteen-foot concertina wire fence. The doorway was a zigzag entrance that obviated the need for a door. Light, fragmentation, and small-arms fire would not be able to make the turns to get from the outside to the inside.

He stepped into the small pool of light thrown by the low-wattage bulb over me doorway, then entered the maze, emerging inside Operations. He had not been there the only time he had visited the base camp.

Inside there were two rooms. The larger one held all the communications equipment and office space for the Operations officer and NCO and a similar setup for the Intelligence officer and NCO. The corner had a radio setup for air force radios, and the opposite corner was reserved for the Artillery LNO.

The smaller room, beyond the large one, was the briefing room. It held ten chairs, maps, easels, and a podium with a large LRP scroll painted on the front.

Kurzikowski spun around to reach for something on the field desk behind the radios and caught sight of Hollister.

"Well, I'll be damned! Look who came back from the dead."

The RTOs, Captain Vance, and Lieutenant Thurman, the new Artillery LNO, all turned, cheered, and then taunted Hollister for goofing off. Through all the heckling, Hollister could tell they were really very glad to have him back.

Things quieted down about ten P.M., and Vance turned the duty over to Lieutenant Thurman for the night. He let Thurman know where he could be reached and then led Hollister from Operations across the compound to the officers' billets.

The building was a combination of sleeping quarters, a club, and a dayroom of sorts. All the company's officers lived there, the lieutenants two to a room. The captains and Major Sangean each had their own room. Hollister was impressed.

Sangean was over at IIFFV for a late coordination meeting and was expected to make it back by midnight. Vance gave Hollister a few minutes to drop his gear in his new room.

The room was a pleasant surprise. It had a metal bunk, a desk, a sink, and a shower. At the opposite end was a window, and on the wall above the bed a Japanese electric fan whirred whisperlike as it oscillated.

Surprised by the comforts the room afforded, Hollister dropped his bag on the desk and opened the plywood door to the built-in closet. All his personal gear had been moved from Cu Chi, and his rifle and shredded claymore bag had even been recovered and brought back to Bien Hoa.

"Not bad, huh?" gunship commander Stanton said, stopping by the open doorway, a sweating can of soda in his hand.

"I'll say. Shouldn't I have to pay for a place like this?"

"This is the way you're supposed to live in aviation units. We're putting up with this place when we're away from our compound on the other side of Bien Hoa," Stanton said, teasing Hollister. He swapped the can to his free hand and wiped his wet one on his trousers. He stuck his hand out and took Hollister's. "Welcome back, buddy. You okay?"

"Yeah, thanks. I'm okay. Probably ended my track scholarship offers. But I'm okay."

"Good. We sure missed you around here." He jabbed his thumb toward the club. "Vance is damn near worn out. He'll never admit it, but he needs a break."

"Yeah. How's everything else?"

"Better—and not. Same shit with allies and regular units. Better AO. My pilots are getting good at this shit, and your guys are getting bigger balls."

"Okay. I can live with that. Where you headed now?"

He raised the soft drink. "Taking this out to my front-seater. I'm on tonight. I'll catch you later."

The shower was a shock to Hollister. The water was piped into the room, but it was at whatever temperature the sun had raised it to in the large black tank on the platform outside the building. Either it had been overcast in Vietnam that day or the engineers had just filled the tank.

After several tries, Hollister got used to the icy water and took his shower. Cold or not, he felt the miles of flying grime rinse off his tired frame and slide down the hole in the concrete floor of the shower stall.

Back in clean cammies, Hollister walked from his room down the short covered hallway to the very small Officers Club. The club was a cement-floored room, roofed and walled in corrugated aluminum. Four flimsy Vietnamese tables with chairs filled the center of the room, while an off-level Ping-Pong table filled one end. At the opposite end, a homemade bar stood a few feet from the wall. Seated on one of the four barstools was Captain Vance. He was leaning over some paperwork—no doubt from his executive officer duties. He held a mess-hall cup of coffee in one hand.

"You sure we're still in the army?"

Vance turned and smiled at Hollister. "Like being in the air force—ain't it?"

"I'll say."

"What's your poison? We have almost a full bar," Vance asked.

"Oh, ah . . . Scotch. Any kind as long as it will burn on the way down."

Vance turned and hollered out the open doorway behind the bar. "Hey, what does a guy have to do to get some service around here?"

A diminutive Vietnamese girl stepped behind the bar. She carried a plastic washtub filled with just-washed glasses and a few pieces of silverware.

"Yes?"

"This is Captain Hollister. He needs Scotch—right now."

"Who is this?" Hollister asked.

"This is Nguyen Te Tich. We can't seem to get her name right, so she is T.T. to us."

"Chao, co," Hollister said.

She nodded, and replied in unsteady English, "Hello, Cap-tan Hor, Horis . . ."

"Jim. Call me Jim. Can you do that?"

"Oh, yes. Can do."

She wiped her hands on the ragged dishrag she had over her shoulder, blew a stray strand of hair from her face, and quickly poured Hollister a Scotch over crushed ice from a small ice machine behind the bar.

"Where'd she come from?" Before he let Vance answer Hollister noticed the ice machine. "Damn! An ice machine, too?"

"You have to ask where an ice machine came from with Peter Vance on the job?"

He raised the Scotch, nodded to Vance and T.T., and took a long drink. He coughed at the startling taste and put down the glass. "And T.T.?"

"She's Hoi Chanh."

"A Hoi Chanh? We need an ex-VC bartender?"

"No," Vance said. "Bui got her for us from the ARVNs. He knows her. At first we used her to translate medical instructions to our team Hoi Chanhs, and then we found out that she had lots of useful skills. So we put her behind the bar, and we pay her like she's a local hire."

"What kind of *useful skills*?" Hollister asked suspiciously.

"Oh, no. It's nothing like you think," Vance said. "I think she and Bui are doing the thing on their own time."

T.T. looked up from the glass she was drying off. Her expression showed her dismay at what they were talking about. She may not have understood all the words, but she got the tone.

"Okay, okay," Hollister said to her. "Let me say I am glad to meet you. Maybe you can teach me some Vietnamese. Huh?"

She looked at Vance and then at Hollister. "Can do, easy, Dai Uy."

They had a good laugh, and she topped off Hollister's Scotch.

"So," Hollister said to Vance, "guess I have a lot of catching up to do?"

***

For the next week Hollister divided his time between catching up and getting on with his duties as Operations officer. He took double shifts on call to cover for Vance while he tried to catch up on the things that had fallen behind for him. The AO was different, the attitude in Juliet Company was different, and the level of combat effectiveness had improved with experience.

It was still obvious to Hollister that they could never fully count on other American or South Vietnamese units. There were too many conflicting demands on them, too many echelons involved in making rapid-mission changes to provide reliable assistance to the LRPs, and too many petty jealousies that tended to slow down reaction times.

He knew if he wanted to get support, he needed to set it up himself and make sure they were covered—and not just covered on paper.

Each day started for Hollister with a warm-up run before the company went out for their formation run. He found he needed it to get the stiffness out of his leg and reduce his tendency to limp. He would then join the company on its run. For him, the usual discomfort of the morning Airborne run was a much more painful experience than it had been before he was wounded.

Hardly a morning went by when he didn't remember Major Urbanik's words about healing. Neither could he avoid Susan's words and her pain. He didn't know what he was going to do. Just walking away from the army and the LRPs was easy to say—but not so easy to do.

He had been out over the new AO every day since he had been back, but he still wasn't comfortable with it. At altitude it wasn't real for him, and he felt kind of phony putting teams into an area he couldn't feel and see in his own mind.

Susan kept tugging at his thoughts. He kept trying to focus on the demands he could expect for the day. Still, she kept creeping into his thoughts with the gentle, but forceful, demands of her own. She had never been a nagging girlfriend or wife. But it was clear to Hollister that she wanted some stability, some future, and a family. He loved the fact that she was strong and independent. And he loved the fact that she was smart enough not to nag him to make decisions too soon.

He had to face facts. He would be finishing a second tour in Vietnam in less than five months, and his moves at that point might well set the course for his future. If he accepted orders to go to the Infantry Officer's Career Course he would be obligated for another year after that. That year could easily be a third tour in Vietnam—if the war dragged on that long.

The political football game that Vietnam had become put Hollister and a half million other Americans in a state of limbo that could end in death for any of them. He didn't believe the campaign promises he had read in the papers in Japan. He knew he had to make a worst-case decision—assuming that the war would drag on.

As Hollister approached the LRP compound after one of his warm-up runs, he met the rest of the company just leaving on its ran. One of the lieutenants led the run, the platoons following him and the guidon bearer. Hollister fell into the rear of the formation with Sangean and Vance.

"Mornin'," Hollister said as he slipped into the slot between them.

Vance grunted comically, indicating his unreadiness for the hour. Sangean waved his hand and kept his eye on the company stretched out ahead of him.

"This is a pretty good turnout," Hollister said.

"With only five teams on the ground and finally reaching ninety percent foxhole strength, they better be out here," Sangean growled.

"Glad we're filling up. New bodies from Recondo School are a good shot in the arm," Hollister said.

"Yes. Say, you got some time this morning?" Sangean asked.

"Yessir. I've got a team to brief after breakfast, and then I'm open—I think."

"Let's talk. G-2 is putting the heat on G-3 for a prisoner. They're confused about what we've been turning over in the AO."

Waving his hand and nodding as he reached for some air and tried to force down the pain growing in his leg, Hollister let Sangean know he would be there. He ran on for a few hundred yards thinking about the mission—a snatch.

Over breakfast Hollister read the Intelligence Summaries that had been sent down from IIFFV. The company had been in the AO almost two months. They had been successful at interdicting enemy movement of supplies, slowing down the infiltration of small units into the Saigon-Long Binh area, and interrupting the messenger communications between enemy units hidden in War Zone D and those they were supporting and reinforcing. But they didn't really have the big picture: Who was in the AO? What were they doing? Did they have a coordinated mission? Where were they getting their support? The questions went on. And for each one that was unanswered Hollister was uneasy. He still disliked planning patrols and giving the teams missions in an area he felt so unsure about.

***

The team briefing over, Hollister went across the compound to Sangean's office in the Orderly Room. Inside he bumped into the new first sergeant—McCullen. "Morning, First Sergeant. How's the paper war going?" Hollister asked, rubbing it in a bit. He knew how McCullen hated the new job and longed to be back in a platoon or a line job.

McCullen smiled at Hollister. "You really know how to hurt a guy, don't you, Cap'n?"

"Hey—nobody said it was easy, moving up the flagpole. The boss in?"

"Yessir. He's waiting for you."

"Come in here, Hollister," Sangean said from his office.

Pulling his notebook from his shirt pocket and his map from his trouser pocket, Hollister stepped into Sangean's small office and waited to be told to take a seat.

Sangean pointed at a chair while he cradled the phone in the crook of his neck. "Yes, I know. I'm sure your job is made infinitely more difficult by our existence, but I would guess that you wouldn't have much of a job if we didn't exist," Sangean said sarcastically.

There was little doubt that Sangean was talking to Major Fowler. Fowler seemed to be unrelenting in his continuing obnoxious behavior. It amazed Hollister that Sangean was able to spar with Fowler and not allow him really to get under his skin.

Sangean finished the call and hung up, showing a little frustration in the way he kicked his feet off his desk and snapped to an upright sitting position.

"More obstacles?"

"You gotta ask?"

"No," Hollister said. "I guess not. He got a new bee up his butt?"

"Not big enough to suit me," Sangean said. He leaned forward and interlaced his fingers. "Rang Rang."

"Rang Rang?" Hollister asked.

"I want to send a heavy team in there and snatch a prisoner—like I said this morning."

"Why Rang Rang?"

"Seems to me that there is more individual foot traffic in that area. All the spot reports, the photos, and agent reports tell us that the major messenger traffic through Zone D comes through those converging trails near the old abandoned airstrip at Rang Rang."

Hollister pulled his map out and looked at Rang Rang. The dirt airstrip probably had a history as interesting as the Vietnamese wars were long. He remembered using it as a reference point on his first recon flight over the AO. It was not very impressive, a rutted and sparsely overgrown red dirt runway with the stubble of old building foundations on the margin at its midline. Near the runway were several paths and trails that generally ran from north to south, converging and often crossing over at slight angles to other trails.

"You got a problem?" Sangean asked.

"No, sir. Just looking at it and trying to get a handle on where and how."

"We'll let the patrol leader come in with a plan."

"I want to take this one out."

"No."

"Sir," Hollister said, risking a butt chewing for arguing with Sangean, "I'm feeling pretty shaky about this AO. I've never been in there, don't know the real estate, and just want to get out on the ground for a quick one."

"Your leg?"

"It'll be fine. The terrain isn't that rough, and I'd probably do it some good by setting up a snatch and missing a few morning runs."

Sangean let go with as much of a smile as he ever displayed and nodded. "Okay. But I don't want any hot-dogging. I'm not going without an Ops officer again. You get tagged again, and I'm finding a replacement for you."

"I'll be careful. I promise."

"Good. There's one other thing."

"What's that, sir?"

"I want you to take Bui with you."

"Bui?" Hollister said, his voice rising in surprise. "He's not a field troop, and he's got a bum leg, and . . ."

"And he's been taking some shit from the other Hoi Chanhs about being a REMF. He's been bugging the shit out of me to go out. It's a face thing with them, and he was a field soldier when he was captured."

"What about his bum leg?"

"What about yours? You gonna hump so fast he'll slow you-all down, and you're not?" Sangean asked.

Hollister raised his hands in mock surrender.

"Anyway, it's a snatch. Either you are going to pluck some solitary zip off the trail or sit tight—no ambush, no long humps."

Sangean paused.

"Bui's really turned out to be a terrific resource around here. I'd hate to see him embarrassed in front of the others because he can't go to the field. And I think he thinks he needs to prove something to T.T."

Without saying so, Hollister made a face that questioned Sangean's judgment.

Sangean raised his hands. "Okay, I would never do this for an American to impress his friends and his girlfriend. But this is Vietnam, and nothing is like we would do it."

"That's for sure," Hollister said. He flipped open his notepad and waited for the details.

"Take the next two teams up on the roster, and make 'em a heavy. Find someone who is due for R and R, and let Bui replace him. Do what you want about the Hoi Chanhs if both teams have them. Don't know how you feel about taking them."

"I'll see how the team leaders feel."

"Good idea. Want you on the ground in seventy-two hours. You fill in the details. Just bring back a talker."

Standing, Hollister flipped his notebook closed and folded his map case, dumping it into his open trouser pocket. He waited for Sangean to dismiss him.

"You sure about that leg?"

"Yes, sir."

"Well, don't take forever on this one. You can't be a cowboy forever. There is lots of staff work that needs to be done, and you and I both know it is stacking up each day you're on the ground."

Walking back to his room, Hollister felt a slight twinge of guilt for being behind in his work. Sangean was right. It wasn't a captain's job. But Sangean was letting him go anyway. Hollister thought it just might be his last patrol or ground operation until the day he got to command his own rifle company.

Commanding a rifle company was every infantry officer's dream. The thought gripped Hollister in conflicting emotions. The thought of being a combat company commander was a prized job. But that assumed that he had already returned for yet another tour in Vietnam. He pictured Susan—crying at that Japanese hotel. He needed a drink.

The list of available teams turned up with 1-3 and 3-1 next to go. 1-3 was Sergeant DeSouza's team—short one American, but with a Hoi Chanh. Three-1 was Lopaka's team, which was full strength and also had a Hoi Chanh.

After lunch Hollister called Lopaka and DeSouza over to the mess hall to talk about the mission. They had already received a warning order from Kurzikowski and knew they were going out as a heavy team, but not much more than the liftoff time and that it was a snatch mission.

Lopaka and DeSouza couldn't have been more different. The stocky Hawaiian was high energy and conversational. DeSouza was thin to the point of near concern for his health and very self-contained. He was also tight with a word or a reaction.

Both team leaders had been in line units in the 173d Airborne Brigade before volunteering to come to Juliet Company. In the time they had been there, both had quickly become team leaders, and each had led more than a dozen patrols and had decent successes on almost all of them.

The two sat a little uncomfortably, so Hollister insisted they each get some coffee or something cold to drink in order to get them to loosen up.

He remembered what it was like being a sergeant and having to spend any time, one-on-one, with a captain. It just wasn't something that he had felt totally comfortable with, either. To a sergeant, captains were tolerable when they were busy—like in a training situation. But to sit and informally talk about an upcoming mission and how things were going to go would be awkward for Lopaka and DeSouza.

"Either one of you gone out on a heavy team before?"

"I have," DeSouza said, half raising his hand.

"And?"

"It was an ambush patrol. We set up on a pretty beaten down trail and got our brains baked for five days and six nights—nothing turned up."

"You got any idea why?" Hollister asked.

"I think we were busted going in. There had to be a couple hundred zips out there in the fields watching our choppers making the fake and the real inserts. Didn't take a Ph.D. to figure out what we were doing out there. Guess the word got passed not to use that trail. I'm just glad they didn't come looking for us."

"Both of you have Hoi Chanhs?"

"Xinh, the troops call him 'X-man,' is a former VC from down in the Delta. Good field troop. Doesn't say much, but understands everything I say. If you want my recommendation—I want to take him along," Lopaka said.

"We got one in my team, too. His name is Caps and he . . ."

Hollister interrupted DeSouza. "Caps? That's his Vietnamese name?"

DeSouza smiled briefly. "No, sir. He's got them gold things on his teeth with stuff carved in them—like stars and stuff. His real name is too hard to pronounce, and the team got to calling him Caps. It's cool with him."

"Okay. You want to bring him along?"

"I think he's getting pretty good. He wasn't a field troop before he was captured. He was a clerk of some type in a base camp just inside Cambodia.

He just put his tenth patrol knot on the string he wears around his neck. He's pretty proud of that."

"Language skills?"

"His English is just okay. He speaks Cambode, and Viet, of course. He's good at documents and stuff."

"We might be able to use that. So let's count him in on this one."

Both sergeants nodded.

"You know this is a prisoner snatch?" Hollister asked.

They both nodded again.

"Done one?"

"I have," Lopaka said. "We grabbed a guy last up on the Vam Co Dong. He was running rice to a tunnel complex. He fucked up. Only guy who was taking rice to the west."

"What?"

"We were watching a trail, and behind us there was a small canal, that the rear security spotted the guy using. He was buying rice from the farmers going to market and then heading back toward Cambodia with it in his boat."

"What happened?"

"We dropped the ambush mission and turned the patrol around. We moved into his area and snatched him coming down the canal. He ended up taking the Twenty-fifth Division tunnel rats to his unit."

"But it didn't start out as a snatch?"

"Nope. Lucky we were able to watch him for a couple of days—no other threat we could see."

"Yeah. Well, we're looking for one that easy. And we are taking Bui along."

"Bui?" Both team leaders looked surprised.

"He's a gimp, sir," said Lopaka. "No offense intended . . ."

Hollister smiled. "No offense taken, Sergeant Lopaka."

He leaned over to avoid being overheard by the others in the room. "Bui needs a little shot in the arm. All of his other people are working out fine. It's a face thing."

Both men nodded. They understood a man's need to show that he had whatever it took to be accepted by his peers.

"If he can keep up and keep quiet, it's okay with me," DeSouza finally said.

"Same here," Lopaka said.

"If he doesn't work out, we'll adios him," Hollister said. "It's not like we are expecting him to do something really critical."

DeSouza shrugged affirmatively. "Okay."

"I want you two to run your own teams. A team in each chopper, and on the ground we'll divide up into a security element and a snatch team. How's that sound?"

The men responded positively.

"I know what you're both thinking, but I have no intention of taking over your teams. Just let me honcho the mission, and you decide what your guys do. We'll just pass mission-type orders down the chain."

"Good for me, sir," DeSouza said.

"I'm happy. But who gets the extra, ah . . ."

"*Bodies?*" Hollister finished Lopaka's question.

"Yessir."

"Okay. Sergeant Lopaka, you make no changes." Hollister looked at DeSouza. "You got me and Bui on your chopper and in movement and security. If we get a live one, he goes out with Lopaka to even the loads."

"We know how long?"

"Five days—for now," Hollister replied. He put his coffee cup down and glanced at his watch. "How about the patrol order tomorrow morning at zero nine hundred?"

The sergeants wrote down the time.

That night Hollister stayed up until almost two finishing paperwork. He had grown to hate the large number of reports that were demanded of Operations by IIFFV, MACV, USARV, and the company's internal needs. He seemed to spend endless hours describing operations, reporting on numbers, and explaining successes and failures of patrols.

His problems with the growing paper demand began as soon as he got back from the hospital. Colonel Downing, the G-3, had been reassigned, and his replacement, Colonel Schneider, was demanding greater detail and more volume. Sangean had tried to explain it to Hollister but Hollister didn't much understand the army's new attitude about *quantifying* everything. Downing's replacement was just out of grad school at Harvard and had a shiny new degree in Operations research and systems analysis. It was shit, but it all rolled downhill.

It still got to him that every time he saw the same information consolidated into reports, the descriptions looked quite different. He decided not to worry about what he couldn't change.

The CQ knocked on Hollister's door to let him know it was four A.M. He thanked the unseen soldier and swung his feet over the bunk and onto the cool concrete floor. His head was foggy, and he wasn't sure if he really wanted to go run with a patrol coming up the next morning. He reached for his cigarettes and lit one.

Sitting there in the dark, Hollister tried to take the first quiet moment he could remember in days to get things organized in his head. He had things to do—simple things like getting his gear ready to go. He had to write to Susan—which meant he wouldn't tell her he was going out. Still, he wanted to get a letter off to her. He owed one to his parents, and he still had a whole day's work ahead of him before he could get ready to go out.

He had promised the two team leaders that he would go over immediate-action drills with their teams that afternoon, and he wanted to spend some time with Bui. He elected not to go on his morning run, but to take PT with the company when they fell out an hour later.

He grabbed his trousers, put them on, and searched in the dark for his shower shoes. Finding them, he headed for the shitter—twenty yards outside the officers' hooch.

Bui reported to Operations with his combat gear packed and ready to be inspected. Hollister had told him that he wanted to check him out before DeSouza did. What he really wanted to do was keep Bui from being embarrassed in front of X-man and Caps in the event he had something wrong.

He told Kurzikowski they would be in the briefing room and took Bui in for inspection. Once there, Bui stood at as much of a position of attention as he could with his damaged ankle.

Hollister started with Bui's rifle. He had drawn and cleaned an M16. Hollister took it, cleared it, and inspected it. Bui had done a good job of cleaning it and had even removed the sling and taped down the sling swivels for noise suppression.

"Ammo?"

Bui opened his two ammo pouches and showed Hollister the loaded magazines. Hollister looked at a couple of them and raised his eyebrows.

Bui took the gesture as a question and yanked the quick release on his rucksack shoulder strap. The ruck swung off his back, and he held it off the floor by catching it as it fell, while holding the strap in the crook of his other arm. He then lowered the ruck to the ground and started unbuckling the side pouch which held more magazines.

Hollister checked them, the others inside the ruck, and all of the other equipment. He was fairly well satisfied with Bui's preparations, and told him so. Still, it was just packing at that point. "You fire this rifle?"

"No, sir. Not yet I have not." Bui said. His English had improved considerably during his months with Juliet Company.

"Well, you better zero it," said Hollister. "Let's get some loose ammo and go over to the range."

Bui smiled and hoisted his ruck back up.

The compound had a large slash cut into the ground from a couple of side-by-side swipes of an engineer's D-9 Caterpillar tractor.

Someone had realized the shortage of suitable areas for a small rifle range. Due to the numerous villages surrounding the base and the density of the Bien Hoa complex, there hadn't been one. The solution was to cut a short range into the ground and pile up a very high berm on two sides and the back end. It was only twenty-five yards long and ten wide, but it allowed the LRPs to test-fire weapons and small demolitions without endangering anyone.

Bui finished placing ten empty M16 ammo cartons on the dirt, halfway up the berm, and walked back to Hollister at the firing point. He looked to Hollister for an okay.

Handing him his rifle, Hollister pointed down-range. "Go ahead."

Bui took the rifle, seated a magazine in the well, and tapped it with the heel of his hand. Raising it to his shoulder, he changed his footing to get a better alignment and sighted down the barrel. Flipping the selector switch off safe, he fired a round at the first small box. He missed it by three inches. The second round hit it on the top and knocked it over. He walked the rounds down the line and hit eight out of ten of the boxes the first round.

The marksmanship was certainly acceptable to Hollister, but he detected a kind of discomfort in Bui. He waited until Bui took the rifle down from his shoulder, then asked, "You like this rifle?"

Bui hesitated and then shook his head. "No. But it okay. I can shoot it."

"No," said Hollister. "You don't have to. What did you carry? AK47?"

"Sometime."

"You like it better?"

Bui smiled and nodded. "Sorry, but the AK better."

"Then let's get you one. We have plenty. Okay?"

Bui cleared his M16 and locked it on safe.

"Sure, it okay." He smiled. "AK better than the Bangalore torpedo."

Hollister frowned. "Bangalore torpedo?"

"Sure," said Bui. "You don't remember I was sapper before, Cap'n?"

"Well, Bui," said Hollister, "you keep up, and you'll be able to tell your grandchildren someday that you served with the best either side can offer—first the sappers, then the LRP."

The team leaders each ran the immediate-action drills with their teams, and then Hollister ran them with the combined patrol. Everyone watched Bui to see how fast he could move with his bad leg. He moved well enough, but with no grace or fluid movement. It was obvious to all that the movements were painful for him, and they began to respect him for his efforts.

Hollister could feel the pain caused by the extra weight of his own field gear. He wondered if he had bitten off too much. Bui's example told him he hadn't.

As they finished practicing for enemy contact and rehearsing movement formations, they called it a day. It was getting dark, and no one had eaten supper. Hollister suggested they eat together. DeSouza volunteered to make the arrangements with Sergeant Kendrick to set aside enough food to feed the two teams together.

As Hollister turned to walk to the officers' hooch, he caught sight of T.T. peeking out of the doorway behind the bar—watching Bui.

CHAPTER 24

It was late, and Hollister was still not caught up. He finished a cold, stale cup of coffee and lit the last cigarette in his pack. He finished proofreading yet another paper in the endless trail of papers that had come to be too big a part of his war.

For a fleeting second, he remembered how he almost never had to look at a full piece of paper when he was a platoon leader in an Airborne Battalion—first tour.

He felt the tension in the back of his neck, and tried to work it out with his hand. The effort was not completely successful. He gave up on it and reached for a cigarette, but remembered that he had one burning in the C ration can ashtray on his desk.

The radios were fairly quiet for nearly midnight. Four teams were on the ground—all in ambush positions. A fifth team was moving, having been compromised by an old woman moving through their position late in the day. She convinced the Hoi Chanh with the team that she was looking for roots to cure her aching joints. They let her go, but didn't trust her to keep her mouth shut. So after selecting an alternate ambush site and PZ, they plotted a route and moved out around nineteen hundred. The fact that they hadn't reached their new ambush site and reported in was another item nagging at the base of Hollister's neck.

Knowing he would be wearing his boots for days and already feeling the discomfort of the laces cutting into the tops of his feet, Hollister reached down and untied the knot. He then loosened the laces, pulling slack into each X that crossed the tongue.

A cook came into Operations with a mess tray loaded down with sandwiches. "Anybody hungry in here? If'n you-all don't eat this stuff, we'll have to give it to the garbage collectors in the morning."

Lopaka, who was copying down some information off the situation map, turned to the cook. "Oh, fucking great, brudda. You gonna eetha feed it to us or to the pigs."

There were a few laughs, but everyone in the room headed for the tray.

Putting out his cigarette, Hollister stood and walked to the tray. Without even thinking about it, he automatically waited for all the others to get a sandwich first. An old habit—officers eat last.

When he finally did grab a sandwich, it was a masterpiece that could only have come out of an army mess hall in Vietnam. It was two pieces of bread surrounding a three-quarter-inch slab of ham. The ham was cooked till almost dry, and the bread had been cut by an amateur. Some of the slices were a half inch thick, and others were thick only at one end and tapered to a paper thinness on the other end.

He didn't care. Food was food, and he was tired and hungry. Hollister took a bite, holding tight to avoid the possibility of the ham sliding out of his grasp, leaving him with a pair of bread slices.

Sandwich in hand, he returned to his paperwork.

It was just a little after three-thirty when the runner came to Hollister's room and rolled him out of the rack. He had an Operations Summary for the previous twenty-four hours for Hollister to sign. Signing the day's report that was typed up, unprofessionally, after midnight always meant that Hollister was awakened in the middle of the night so that it could be driven over to IIFFV and be there before zero five hundred. It was Fowler's requirement and an absolutely chickenshit one at that.

Hollister signed it, knowing that the report would probably be rewritten and distorted before first light.

His mouth tasted foul. The double shot of Scotch he'd had before sacking out was the cause. It had become his new sleeping pill. It worked for him, and he rationalized it by a self-declaration that without a drink it would take him too long to get to sleep. If that happened, he wouldn't get any rest at all.

It made no difference. He still woke up each morning feeling like shit. But he had no time to baby his sour stomach and dull, throbbing forehead. He had to get ready to launch.

The full patrol was on line—on time. Lopaka and DeSouza had their teams out at the chopper pad and were inspecting their gear when Hollister arrived. He found a spot at the end of DeSouza's team and dressed right.

DeSouza stepped in front of Hollister and was surprised to find him waiting for inspection. "Ah, good mornin', sir."

"Morning. You want to check me out?"

"You? Sure," DeSouza answered, a little uncomfortable with the thought of inspecting a captain.

"You are in charge of your chopper load of yahoos. If you were a jumpmaster on a jump—wouldn't you jumpmaster-inspect each man in your lift?"

"Yessir."

"Then get to it."

DeSouza straightened up, as if that were a statement of his official capacity, and began at Hollister's cap. He continued to check out his weapon and all of his combat gear, head to toe. When he was finished with the front, he walked around to Hollister's back and started at the top again.

Finally, satisfied with everything he could see and touch in the faint light coming from the bulb at Operations, he told Hollister to jump up and down.

The gear was noiseless, but there was an ammo pouch that had ripped through itself and had only one clip holding it to Hollister's rucksack webbing. It became obvious when Hollister jumped.

DeSouza reached down and pulled a piece of green tape off his trousers. He had pretorn several such strips and gently stuck them to his trouser leg for just such a need.

He used the tape to secure the ammo pouch to Hollister's rucksack, and thereby avoided having to look for a new pouch so close to liftoff time. "You need a new pouch back here. I got it nailed down for now. But you'll need to replace it, sir."

Finished with his inspection, DeSouza slapped Hollister's rucksack and gave him the traditional "Okay."

The teams loaded the two insert choppers before the pilots cranked. This gave everyone a chance to get settled in and to talk. Normally, there was so much chopper noise that the chatter stopped when they started to walk toward the idling choppers.

As the pilots began their preflight checklist routine, the conversation about girls and cars and the World faded.

They were all alike, Hollister thought. All were anxious and worried about how many patrols and how many chopper flights they could walk away from before the law of averages ate them up.

Bui was looking toward the officers' billets and the club's back door. There was a faint outline of a woman standing in the door. It was T.T.

Hollister didn't know how, but T.T. and Bui had somehow worked it out for her not to leave the base that night like all the other day laborers. Hollister was glad that Bui had T.T. back at the compound waiting for him. He wished he had Susan close.

The sky was starting to promise dawn when the choppers finally descended into the LZ. As they sank toward the clearing, fear of the unknown—and fear of the known—took hold of Hollister's chest and squeezed. There was no denying it. Bits and flashes of the shoot-down that had almost killed him before wouldn't go away.

DeSouza was efficiently warning and counting down the steps for the team. Hollister scooted out into the open doorway of the chopper and grabbed the corner of the door gunner's seat to give him some stability if the ship made a quick move.

"Go! Go! Go! Go!" DeSouza yelled as he leaped from the still-moving chopper just before touchdown. The other six team members leaped only fractions of a second behind him.

The impact with the ground sent sharp pain up Hollister's hip. It was all he could do to keep from crying out. His first step was faltering and awkward. He prayed that none of the others saw how unsteady he was.

Over his shoulder, Lopaka's team burst from the chopper that had landed to the left front of Hollister's. They were already half the distance from the chopper to the trees that would conceal them. DeSouza had taken the lead. He had his team oriented to cover the right side of the combined teams' route as Lopaka's people were watching left. Caps was bringing up the rear—and facing that way. Hollister was second in order of march as they sprinted across the open area There were three men behind him, with Bui and Caps in the rear. He took a quick look at Bui. Crippled, he still bounded across the ground in a hopping motion, putting most of his weight on his good leg. He was having no trouble keeping up, even though his movements looked painful and very awkward.

When they finally reached the concealment offered by the trees, Hollister's thigh was burning. The pain was so intense that he stuffed his cravat in his mouth and bit down on it to distract himself from the burn.

By the time the pain was gone and Hollister's breathing had returned to normal, the two sergeants had established a tight perimeter and were putting out claymore mines in all directions. Hollister called the C&C ship and reported that they were in and cold.

Major Sangean acknowledged the transmission and wished them luck. Then the choppers cleared the area entirely.

Daylight began to filter through the sparse single-canopy tree cover that concealed the LRPs. Hollister pulled his map out of his pocket and balanced it on his knee. He made a quick orientation, aligning the map's north with what he guessed was true north. In the trees he had no terrain features to use for terrain-association orientation, so he pulled out his compass and quickly got a solid indication of where magnetic north was.

Adjusting for the deviation indicated in the declination diagram on the map's margin, Hollister confirmed that he had north pegged where it should be.

The very broad and very gently sloping finger they would be heading out on was just to Hollister's left front. He was able to identify it because every other direction sloped off at a greater angle. The finger was almost level—at least from his limited point of view.

Using an intentional offset, Hollister instructed the patrol to move in a direction that would allow them to intersect the trail they would be watching well above the point they had picked by air and map recon.

He didn't want to miss the point or track it up with American-sized footprints. So he picked a point that was not only higher than their snatch site, but had more solid ground because it was exposed to more sunlight. It would allow them to work their way down to the snatch sight, rather than walk uphill to it. It also used the hardest, driest ground.

They moved toward their layup position for forty-five minutes and then ran out of darkness and adequate concealment. Hollister had been afraid they might have that problem, but couldn't find a better place to put the team in and not give away its direction of march to anyone watching or coming across them. It meant they had to find a place to hold up until dark fell again.

He held up the patrol, took Bui and Ayers—the RTO—and walked slowly up to a point off their route of march that looked like a dense stand of trees.

Once there they got down and crawled up to the knot of trees and peeked into it. It was perfect. It was a patch of a few tall saplings, spaced about five feet apart and densely undergrown with some kind of broad, flat leaf.

The inside of the stand of trees was unused and showed no signs of any foot or animal traffic. That would minimize the chance that someone would stumble on them while they laid up for the day.

The sun came up as if jerked over the horizon. The LRPs welcomed it for a few minutes and then cursed it, for it brought the flies and the noise of the day.

Finding a spot in the shade, Hollister pointed to his nose and then to DeSouza, who was on the other side of the half circle his team made up. DeSouza recognized that Hollister was letting him know their camouflage stick was fading and needed to be touched up.

Reaching into his shirt pocket, Hollister pulled out his signal mirror by its nylon string. He was careful not to handle it in such a way as to foolishly catch the sun and fire shafts of sunlight out of their position, giving them away.

He dropped it on the ground between his knees and leaned over it. His face was dirty from the remains of camouflage stick applied before liftoff, along with the dirt, sweat, and grime he had picked up since.

He was able to find his camouflage stick in his rucksack's outer pocket without any difficulty. He popped the tube's tin cap and pushed some of the lighter loam color out to apply to his face. He started at his throat—to lighten what was normally darker to break up facial features.

He made a lazy, kidney-shaped pattern under his jawline and then turned the tube around and did the same with the dark end of his chin.

The idea was to lighten things that were dark or receded on the face and darken the prominent features like cheekbones, nose, chin, and brows. The result was a confusing pattern as the eye tried to find a face in all the shadows and highlights.

By midday it began to rain again. Hollister had opened one of the dehydrated LRP rations they had recently been issued and checked it out for readiness. He had poured half a canteen of water into the brown plastic-wrapper container at around nine and refolded the packing, leaving it in a sunny spot on the ground. Until it had started raining, the sun had warmed it and the water had softened the contents—chili.

He took a white plastic spoon from his pocket and scooped up some of the mixture inside. The flavor was good, but some of the beans were still crunchy. He considered letting it go for another half hour, but decided that he was hungrier than he was picky. He ate the ration and washed it down with the remaining water in one of his canteens.

To Hollister the cost and inconvenience of the LRP rations were more trouble than they were worth. Sure, they were light and easy to pack, but it took a whole quart of water to eat one, half a quart to soften and dissolve the dehydrated contents and the other half just to wash it down.

The rations had almost unanimous appeal back in the base camp. With some doctoring, some added goodies like Vietnamese hot peppers and scallions, the meals were good. And heated and stirred in a larger container, they were even more appealing. But out in the field they were not getting rave reviews.

After lunch it was Hollister's turn on watch while others got some sleep. He looked around the perimeter and was pleased to see that four of the thirteen LRPs were alert and paying attention to the sectors of observation assigned to them. The others were dozing or sound asleep.

Bui should have been sleeping, but wasn't. Hollister assumed he was wired and trying to show the others how capable he was. It amused Hollister to remember the conversations he had had with Bui about being a field soldier. He had told Hollister that when he was a VC he hated being a soldier.

It was Hollister's guess that the complaining about his field duty as a VC soldier had to do with how well he had done it. Bui was very sensitive to criticism and jealously guarded his own self-image. What else could explain his pleas to Sangean to let him go along on a patrol?

Their eyes met, and Bui was quick to give Hollister a broad smile and a thumbs-up sign. Hollister returned the smile and the gesture and went back to scanning his piece of the perimeter's exterior.

The rain never let up. By nightfall the patrol was a sad-looking bunch. Every man was soaked and had picked up a dark mood, reflective of the weather. None of them wanted to go into the night wet and chilled. But with dark came the expectation that they would be moving out for their snatch site. The movement would warm them up and take some of the aches out of joints sore from sitting all day in the rain on cold ground.

Just after dark the rain started to pour down harder than it had all day, a mixed blessing. The extra noise the rain made would cover the noise of their movement. But it would also limit their ability to hear movement around them and severely cut their visibility.

The ceiling was no more than a hundred feet, and the visibility was less than that, which meant that if they needed choppers they were out of luck until the weather improved. Hollister said a little prayer and moved out behind Ayers.

As they moved, single file and five meters apart, Hollister heard the swishing of the fabric of his cammie trouser and the constant patter of the rain on the broadleaf vegetation.

Suddenly, the team stopped. It was not a stop because someone was hung up in the brush or to let the point man cautiously cross an open area. It was the kind of halt that was urgent, marked by the man in front rapidly dropping to his knee and taking up a firing position.

Fourth in the line of march, Hollister stepped around Ayers and moved to DeSouza, who was walking slack for Caps, who was walking point.

DeSouza grabbed Hollister by the sleeve and tugged him down to a squatting position. He stuck his arm out—straight, at shoulder level—and pointed off to their left front.

There, through a very small hole in the trees and shrubs, Hollister could see a flicker of flame. He stopped breathing long enough to listen for any voices—and heard none. He estimated the fire to be not more than forty meters away and slightly below their elevation.

Leaning over to get closer to DeSouza, Hollister whispered in his ear, "Pass the word—quiet!"

DeSouza nodded and gently rolled off his knees into a crouching walk, then stepped back to the next man in the file.

While he passed the word to the others, Hollister reached into his ruck and pulled out his binoculars. He raised them to his face and tried to find the small break in the trees in order to see the flame. The binos showed nothing but darker shades of tree branches, leaves, and tall bushy weeds. Then the flash of light filled the lenses and was as quickly gone. Hollister tried to find it again by scanning the area more slowly.

It worked. He was looking at a left knee, an elbow resting on it, and what appeared to be the back of the owner of the limbs. He steadied his grip on the binoculars and scanned in a small circle. It appeared to be a single Vietnamese male sitting next to a very small fire. He was either cooking something or stoking the fire. There was no sign of anyone else, but Hollister could see only a very small portion of the man's campsite. To assume he was alone could be a serious mistake.

Hollister widened his search of the area. He couldn't find any path or break in the vegetation the Vietnamese had used to get there. He handed DeSouza the binoculars, waited long enough for him to get a look, then motioned for him to fall back to the rear. Before following, Hollister reached forward and tapped Caps—letting him know to come back, too.

The entire patrol moved back another twenty-five meters—away from the lone Vietnamese figure. There, Hollister decided to take a scouting party forward to see what they had. It would be easy just to fire the area up and drop a lonely VC too stupid to put out a fire at night. But they were out there to grab a prisoner, and one might have just dropped into their lap.

He picked Caps and Ayers, figuring it was better to leave Lopaka's team intact and strip DeSouza than to take people from both teams. He instructed Lopaka to take charge of the patrol if the shit hit the fan.

The plan was for Hollister, Ayers, and Caps to move forward to get a better look at the man at the campsite. They would try to figure out a way to snatch him and come back for more firepower if they needed to. Hollister designated a rally point in the event the patrol got separated by contact and told Lopaka and DeSouza to give him an hour.

Caps needed almost no instruction. He took up a course that brought the three-man recon party downwind from the campsite and missed nearly all the noisy deadfall.

Walking just behind him, Hollister was impressed with the technique of movement and the path selections he made. He seemed to glide through the bush instead of getting it to submit. Inside twenty minutes, Caps had taken the trio to a point that looked down into the very small clearing that held the lone figure.

Stopping for another visual assessment, Hollister pulled out his binoculars. From the new vantage point, he could see that the man was alone and that there were two bags or rucksacks in the shadows near him. But nothing else. Hollister was looking for signs that would confirm him as a VC, or a bearer, or something else incriminating.

Standing behind the kneeling Hollister, Caps tapped him on the shoulder and pointed at something on the near side of the fire. Not able to see, Hollister had to get up and take a second look. There in the foreground was a small pile of strange, woven bamboo strips. Hollister couldn't make them out. He turned to Caps for some sign.

Caps pointed up at the tree branches. The signal meant nothing to Hollister. He shrugged.

Caps was frustrated, but didn't want to speak since they were so close. He finally put down his rifle, tucked his hands under his armpits, and flapped his elbows. He looked ridiculous, but it was clear to Hollister that he was trying to indicate something that had to do with flying or birds.

Hollister looked through his binoculars, and the Vietnamese leaned over to get something out of one of his bags. As he did, Hollister noticed that the other bag was uncovered.

Hollister watched for a long time, trying to recognize what was in the bag. It was very dark, and the dull flickering of the fire was no help in distinguishing outline or texture.

They were traps! Hollister thought. The bamboo devices were traps or snares. He looked at them and at the bag. Birds! The man was a bird hunter, not a VC. He was simply a hunter, sitting out the cold rain over a tiny fire.

The sinking sensation in Hollister's chest gave way to an almost audible groan. They had lost at least an hour of movement checking this guy out, and now he would have to get back to the others without letting the hunter know they were watching him. They would also have to change their route of march to avoid the hunter's campsite.

While the hunter posed no direct threat to the patrol, he was likely to be stopped by the VC and questioned. Hollister also worried about a trail they had left getting around the other side of him. The hunter now had tracks from the Americans on at least three sides of his position. If the rain didn't wipe out the tracks and cause the brush to spring back, he might discover the passing of the Americans in the morning.

Back with DeSouza and Lopaka, Hollister explained the disappointment and got on with plotting a new route to their snatch site. Hollister didn't much like to change plans in the dark and without an adequate reconnaissance of the new route.

The changes and the stop to check out the man at the fire had killed off nearly two hours. Again on the move, Hollister checked his watch. It was nearly midnight, and they had just about lost all hope of getting to their snatch site, setting up, and having a shot at catching someone on the trail at that hour.

They closed on their RON at just after two in the morning and quickly got the perimeter organized, security tied in, and claymores out. Hollister then called DeSouza and Lopaka into the center to make and change some plans they had left Bien Hoa with.

Lopaka and DeSouza were as tired as Hollister was. None of them had been able to log in more than a total of two hours sleep in the past twenty-four hours. Preparation for the patrol and the activities of the first day didn't allow for much rest. Their mood was dulled by the delay and the added knowledge that they had to worry about civilians. They didn't discuss it, but they all realized they could have made a serious mistake and grabbed the hunter, thinking he was a VC.

"We'll leave for the trail in one zero. Any problems?" Hollister whispered.

Lopaka looked at his watch. "Better get there before the rush hour," he said, a trace of sarcasm in his voice.

The comment didn't go by Hollister. He knew the most likely times of travel on the trail they had picked out were late evening and early morning—before dawn. There was a risk of compromising their presence, or even making a chance contact moving to the trail, but they had little choice. If they waited until early evening of the next day to recon the trail, make adjustments in the plan, and move the patrol into position, they would lose time and have less flexibility. Worse would be finding the trail site unacceptable. That would require a move to an alternate site. All of that would mean they might lose a full day.

Waiting to move on the recon, Hollister wondered what it meant—the hunter. He obviously wasn't concerned about enemy units being in the area. That meant he was a VC sympathizer or ignorant. Hollister wondered if he should have grabbed him and taken him back to question him. After a little more thought, he dismissed it as a bad move. Chances were that the interrogators would find out he had no useful information.

Ayers, Hollister, DeSouza, and Lopaka eased down the very slight hillside that led to the trail. The rain had stopped, and the wind had come up a bit. It chilled them and made them aware of the cold hours ahead once they returned from the recon. Lopaka, leading, stopped the foursome and got down on his stomach. The others came up alongside him and did the same. The trail ran across their front. It was a large trail, almost a roadway. It would support three or four men walking abreast and was hard-packed dirt. But that night it was a glazed clay and water mix. Footprints that had been left there were gone.

Getting up from his spot, Hollister moved to the left and motioned the others to follow him. He continued until he found what he was looking for—an easy bend in the trail.

He indicated for the others to take a look. Each stood in the same spot Hollister had selected and looked back up the trail. Then the other way. The spot gave the best observation of the trail in both directions. Anyone approaching, in either direction, could be seen from the vantage point Hollister had selected. It was better than waiting trailside, where the view up and down the trail required leaning out onto the trail to see what was coming in either direction.

He looked around at the site, as did the others. It was surrounded with thick head-high brush, bamboo, and small trees. It would conceal the snatch team. Everyone agreed, then set about to find a place for the security element to protect their backs.

They all turned away from the trail and looked behind the spot Hollister had selected. Off to the right, up the trail and about twenty meters behind, was the bed of an intermittent stream that had one bank higher than the other. It would provide cover for a security element and a second position for rear security.

Yet Hollister wasn't sure. He walked over to the streambed to check it out. The others dropped to one knee, facing in the cardinal directions, weapons at the ready and alert to any threat.

Hollister stepped into the streambed and squatted down. He found there was fairly adequate visibility of the trail going in both directions and good visibility of the clump of vegetation that would conceal the snatch team. It would need a little trimming of the undergrowth for some of the members of the security element, but it would work.

Back with the patrol, Hollister waited with the others. He realized just how tired he was at dawn. With dawn came a warming sun. Hollister took the opportunity to dry out a bit by finding a pool of light falling onto the floor of the small clearing where they would wait out the day. His first priority went to his butt. He was tired of sitting on wet ground in wet fatigue trousers. His buttocks were raw from the hostile ground. He mimicked the moves of two other LRPs who had rolled over on their stomachs, facing out. This served two purposes. It allowed them to continue to watch their assigned sectors of the perimeter, and it allowed the sun to dry out their trousers and butts. It seemed a little thing, but not to a wet LRP.

The day was a normal sort of day for a LRP team laying up. Security, some sleep, food, and whispered chalk talk. Hollister brought DeSouza and Lopaka into the center of the circle and almost silently adjusted the plan. Using a stick, he drew a diagram of the snatch site on the mud-packed ground. He assigned the ditch to Lopaka and the bend in the trail to DeSouza. Using hand signals to avoid speaking, he mouthed the words that he would be with DeSouza—at trailside.

The plan was as prepared in Bien Hoa. They would move the snatch element to the trail and position the security element to watch their backs and provide fire onto the trail if necessary. They were hoping to catch a single enemy soldier or courier walking down the trail and then overpower him.

If they got into trouble, the security element would lay down a strong base of fire and allow the snatch team to break contact and move back to them. Everything else would have to be played by ear. That made them all a bit nervous.

The afternoon brought more rain. Hollister wondered if there would be any chance of a letup. He looked at the sky and was unable to tell anything since the cloud cover was from horizon to horizon. It gave him no idea when, or if, it would clear. He tapped Ayers on the sleeve and handed him a note to ask for meteorological data on the next SITREP.

Word came back that the rain would continue through the night. Hollister passed the information to let everyone rig his gear accordingly, even though he knew that it would have a negative effect on their morale; they were already getting tired, bored, and anxious.

They moved out just as the hidden sun was going down. Hollister wanted to get to the snatch location quickly and get set up. The rain helped cover their movement, but didn't improve anyone's attitude. What started out as an optimistic group heading out for a snatch turned into a patrol that was showing fatigue and negative effects of the worsening weather.

Hollister hoped they would get into their duties and blow off their slipping attitudes. All missions were hard enough, but attitude often made the difference between success and failure, life and death.

CHAPTER 25

The brim on Hollister's floppy LRP hat began to droop so much that it was blocking part of his vision and allowing water to run down the back of his neck. The rain had finally saturated his hat. He took it off, rolled it, and stuffed it into his pocket. It was useless for the rest of the night. To keep some of the heat in and ward off the chill, he wrapped the cravat that had been around his neck around his head and tied it on.

Rain kept falling, yet the LRP team's movement went well. Hollister felt good about the efficient way the men moved. Maybe it was a sign that some of the training he had been such a pain about was working.

***

Caps held them up just a hundred meters from the trail. Hollister sent a small recon party forward to make sure the trail was clear before they moved in.

While the recon party was gone, Hollister got on the radio and double-checked the artillery targets he had planned and made sure he had established commo with fire-support personnel. He made sure Operations knew they were moving into position, and he double-checked to make sure they had the right location for the exact snatch site and pickup zones he had confirmed.

Lopaka came back and gave Hollister an *okay* sign. Time to do it.

The security team moved into position first. Hollister held the snatch team back behind them and let Lopaka place each man in a firing position that would cover the snatch team and protect the backs of both teams.

Once they were in, Hollister double-checked Lopaka's choices and made sure he knew where each man was and where he would be firing. He knew if he had to lead the snatch team out away from the trail, he had better know where the shooting was coming from and going to. Not to do so was to ask to get shot by your own people.

Moving the snatch team into position took twice as long as moving the security in. Hollister and DeSouza placed Ayers between them. They put Caps on the left end and Bui on the right end. The sixth man was a PFC named Quintana. He was a Mexican-American from Texas who was the second radio operator for the team and also carried an M79. He was posted to the rear of the team—facing away. Next to Quintana, PFC Montford completed the rear security for the snatch team. Montford was a medic and a rifleman. He and Quintana would provide early warning in the event someone—somehow—got behind them and posed a threat to the snatch team.

Snatch teams didn't work the way ambush elements worked. For one thing they couldn't stand back aways. They had to be right on the absolute edge of the trail to be effective. They couldn't surprise their prey if they had to move through the brush and get to the trail. They would certainly be heard if they tried that. Proximity to the trail, mobility, and expert camouflage were essential to their success.

Once they were in the snatch site, Hollister tapped two men at a time and signaled them to get their positions ready. This meant camouflage and ammo placement. It took a long time to get the men in position two at a time, but the alternative was too risky. Having all of them working on their

6

camouflage and putting out their weapons and ammo at once meant that no one would be paying attention to the trail.

They had talked about setting out claymores to use to break contact in the event that a large enemy element came down the trail and discovered them. But the claymores would increase the chance of their being discovered while putting them out. And they would slow them down as they had to be removed if the team silently snatched a prisoner and was ready to leave—fast. They elected to forgo the claymores and go heavier on hand grenades if they had to.

Each man had six grenades laid out in front of him and more in canteen covers on his web gear. They were all ready to throw grenades and break contact back toward the security element if things went sour.

The biggest fear was that they would grab a man on the trail only to find out there was a large element behind him. It was their nightmare, and if it happened, they could only respond with speed and return fire. For that reason they had rigged their rucksacks with C-4 and left them back with the security element. They'd blow up the rucksacks behind them if they had to break contact and run.

They would be able to move faster without the rucks anyway. If they were forced to go in a different direction than the security element, they didn't expect security to carry double rucks. So, the security element would blow them when they moved out.

They were in. Now the wait began. Now came the night, and the cold, and the boredom, and the worry, and the imagination, and the fight with the weight of sleep. Of all these, sleep was the hardest to fight. The men tried to get an hour's sleep each. That meant all were awake, except one man. But at zero four zero zero hours, they would all be alert because of the high likelihood of last-minute traffic on the trail before first light. First light was due at zero five four five hours.

Sliding his sleeve up, Hollister glanced at the dial on his wristwatch. It was only ten past ten. It was going to be a long night.

By midnight Hollister was ready to scream. None of the men could move for fear of giving away their position. They couldn't even sit up to get the blood circulating. The trailside was slippery and cold. Water dripped down the grasses and weeds onto their uniforms. There was no getting away from the rain. It rolled down their foreheads, and across their eyes. A constant drip of water fell from their noses and ears. Hollister was miserable, and he knew the others were, too.

Hollister's bad leg ached. He had overdone it. If a soldier working for him had done what he was doing, the man would be in for a real ass-chewing.

Another agonizing hour passed. Hollister started into the twilight world. Sleep tried to drag him under, and he fought to stay lucid. Things began to blur. His lids got incredibly heavy, and his mind began to mix reality with dreamlike images. He shifted his position slightly and twisted part of his loosened pistol belt buckle. He put its sharp end under his hipbone, then put his weight back on it. The discomfort the buckle caused woke him up a little. But that, too, was quickly overcome by the unrelenting demands of sleep. He bit his tongue, then wiped his face with the end of the wet rag he'd tied around his head. And still, he was really fighting to stay awake.

Hollister imagined someone pulling at his shirt. It happened again. He was sure it was his mind playing tricks on him. His eyes were open, but he stretched them even wider to convince himself he was still awake. But he wasn't. Sure, his eyes were open, but his mind was in the grasp of sleep.

"Sir!" someone whispered.

Hollister turned to find Ayers yanking on his sleeve. He looked at his face for some sign of what he wanted, but it was too dark.

Ayers pointed up the trail, to their right front. A figure was moving toward them.

The fact that he could see the figure surprised Hollister. The rain had stopped, and the moon had come out. The trail was a maze of moonlight and shadows. Splotches of light crawled up the man, then slid off his shoulders as he walked under the tears in the tree canopy overhead.

The man was carrying a rifle on his shoulder, his hand on the muzzle. Hollister thought it was a rather casual and unready posture for an enemy soldier to assume. That worried him. Could the man be so stupid as to think there was no threat to him? Or was he just walking out in front of a much larger unit that would come to his aid if he got into trouble? Hollister wished he knew the answer.

Hollister's head cleared. Checking to the left and right, he confirmed that the others were ready. He looked back up the trail at the soldier approaching. He was less than a hundred meters up the trail, and at his pace he wouldn't take much more than a minute to get abreast of the snatch team. The plan was for DeSouza and Caps to break out of the brush and physically overpower the guy once he came to the snatch team's position. Hollister was the backup. In the event they couldn't take him down, Hollister would assist.

Back at the base camp in Bien Hoa, all members of the snatch team had made two-man tackling runs at a heavy dummy made out of a worn-out lister bag and sandbags. Most were comfortable with the very American art of tackling, and even Caps caught on quickly.

Bui was totally baffled by the two-on-one concept, and the football tackle mystified him. It took a while for Caps to persuade him that he needed to use his body weight to overcome the dummy, not just try to reach out and hold it in place, but he seemed to enjoy it once he caught on.

Time seemed to slow down as they watched the lone figure walk toward them. Hollister pulled out his binoculars and scanned the area behind the soldier. He wanted to know if anyone was following him, so he could pass the word in enough time for all to let the enemy group pass.

With each step the man took toward the snatch team, Hollister could feel his breathing get shallower and his chest tightening. He raised his binoculars again and looked over his right shoulder toward Lopaka's team. He could see that every man in the security element was alert and watching the trail. He was happy to see that Lopaka was on his toes.

The figure got closer. Through the binoculars, Hollister could see that the man was wearing a shirt, pants, rubber-and-canvas boots, a floppy hat, and a shoulder-wide piece of plastic around his neck. The makeshift raincoat didn't seem to have been very effective since the soldier was plucking the wet fabric of his shirt from his skin.

Out of the corner of his eye, Hollister could see DeSouza putting his rifle down and sliding out of his harness. He cocked his right leg in kind of a modified, prone sprinter's starting stance, and Hollister thought he saw him grin.

Suddenly, the enemy soldier stopped. He froze in place, not taking his weapon off his shoulder, but obviously spooked by something.

DeSouza looked to Hollister. Hollister shrugged. Neither man knew what the problem was. Hollister looked around for something that might be giving away their presence. He could see nothing.

He looked back to the soldier. The man stood stone still for a moment longer, as if listening, and then he started backing up—very slowly. He looked as if he were trying not to make any noise.

Noise! That was it. There was *no* noise. The sounds of the bush at night was gone. *Shit!* The animal life, birds, insects, and all the other unseen life were silent, as if they sensed the tension.

Hollister had seen it happen before, on his first tour. It was a spooky phenomenon that all field soldiers experienced at one time or another. Everything had to be right for it to be detected, and the soldier—friendly or enemy—had to be experienced to pick up on it. Their quarry obviously was a field soldier—and a good one.

They all watched as he backed up the trail, picking up the speed of his steps until he finally turned and ran away.

The failure meant lots of work and more risk for the team. It would be light soon, so they would have to pull back and leave a small element to watch the snatch site and the security positions. They couldn't stay in position all day—that would be too risky. They had to assume that someone might use the trail during the day, and without the concealment the darkness afforded, they would be discovered long before they could pull off their snatch.

But leaving their sites unwatched was an invitation for them to be booby-trapped for their return if the VC discovered they had been there.

While everyone on the patrol knew the next move, no one looked forward to it. It meant moving away from the trail to another site, laying up for the day, and moving back in after dark. They had no option. Hollister reached over and tapped DeSouza, giving him the signal to start moving out.

The hole he had picked in a very thick stand of trees gave them the concealment they needed with internal room for movement inside their new perimeter, but it was filled with flies, and they wouldn't give Hollister a break. He tried to get some rest, but the flies wouldn't let him. They'd been silent back at the snatch site, but now the damn things were buzzing—and biting.

Hollister moved twice and even saturated his hat with insect repellent, but it did no good. Finally, he gave up all hope of sleep, and sat up.

The day was beautiful and full of sunshine, but the team looked awful. No one had shaved since the day before they left. Stubble, caked and smeared camouflage, and just plain field dirt made them a scroungy-looking lot.

Hollister laughed to himself as he remembered the time he had spent in OCS and Jump School picking stray threads off his fatigues and spit-shining his Corcoran jump boots. The tiny circle was more like Ranger School. Haircuts, shaves, polished insignia, and all that stuff had no priority. Hollister moved over to Lopaka to see if he had any suggestions about how they could avoid the spooking that had happened the night before.

Weather. Weather was Lopaka's solution to the problem, but he couldn't promise it. He was sure if they ran into another field-smart candidate for a snatch, bad weather would cover the sound of silence.

Lopaka's RTO called in for a weather forecast. Hollister was finishing a lunch of spaghetti LRPs when the RTO handed a note to Lopaka, who handed it on to him. It read: 1700 HRS TODAY TO 1700 TOMORROW—RAIN, WINDS OUT OF NE, 5-7 KNOTS. THNDR SHWRS POSSIBLE.

Hollister nodded and passed the note around. This was a break. Bad weather was good news. When the note came back to

Lopaka, he folded it and put it in his shirt pocket to make sure it wasn't left behind.

After moving back into it, Hollister felt as if he hadn't ever left his trailside position at the snatch site. His leg throbbed. The weather and lack of sleep were kicking his ass, but as patrol leader he had to set the example. He sucked up the misery and swallowed hard. At least the position had a homelike feel to it. That could be good, but it could just as easily be bad—very bad.

The rain came as predicted, and while it made them more miserable, the LRPs received it gratefully. They all were chilled after an hour at the side of the trail. Caps began shivering and reached down to rub his legs for some relief.

The night wore on, and the rain continued. Instead of the steady rain they had been getting for days, it was blowing in sheets that rolled over them, dumped lots of water, and then let up for a few seconds before doing it again. The trees and brush whipped steadily back and forth, setting up a level of noise that would surely mask the absence of natural night sounds but could just as easily mask the sound of companions coming behind a man they might choose to snatch. And what if they were compromised already? What if they hadn't left the site sterile and the enemy had come along and found some sign, then figured out their plan? Hollister tried not to worry. But it was hard sometimes.

The LRPs just watched and waited. It was almost midnight when the sleep demon tried to grab Hollister again. He fought for consciousness with every trick he could remember until he finally gave in and went to his pocket for relief.

Sergeant Rose had issued the teams pills to take if they couldn't stay awake. Some of the troops referred to them as *speed*, but Hollister thought that was just talk. Speed was some kind of illegal drug, and the army would never issue anything like that. In OCS they used to gulp down packets of No Doz to stay awake—but they were legal. Hollister was satisfied that the issue pills were similar to No Doz and probably worked as well as the sleeping pills they had given him at the hospital, or the No Doz at OCS.

He popped one into his mouth and swallowed it dry. Just the difficulty of trying to get it down without water was enough to wake him a bit.

He adjusted his position, trying to find a less comfortable one. It was the easiest thing he had done all day. As he shifted, his binoculars slid down off his hip, where he had been balancing them off the ground. He caught them just before they hit the mud. He decided to make another scan of the trail. He looked up the trail to the spot where the soldier had spooked and withdrawn the night before. He saw nothing.

At that moment he realized they were all watching the same spot. Half expecting the same soldier to return, he guessed. He spun the glasses around and looked down the leg of the trail that went off to his left front. Trying to be methodical, he started at the nearest point in focus and worked his way out and down the trail, moving the binos side to side in order to study every part of the trail as far out as he could see.

The rain clouds had blocked the moon, and the visibility was severely limited. He could see almost nothing beyond fifty meters. But he did see something. He took his face away from the binos, looked at the same point—at the limit of his visibility. Then he put the binos back to his face.

He was sure the night was playing tricks on him. He suspected that he was making up a figure on the trail out of the background colors and shapes. He remembered students in Ranger School hallucinating from lack of sleep and putting nickels in trees thinking they could get a cold drink out of them.

He pulled his binos away again and rubbed his eyes. He was sure he saw the outline of a standing man. He started to reach over and tap Ayers to pass the information to DeSouza, but thought how foolish he would feel if it turned out to be nothing but trees, large plants, and his imagination.

He looked again. Then he was sure. It *was* a VC with a weapon, and he was moving very, very slowly. Hollister tapped Ayers and Bui, who swung their attention to the other trail approach.

DeSouza turned to Hollister for instructions. Hollister pressed his index finger to his lips to reaffirm the need for silence.

They watched. The solo figure moved forward with his rifle at the ready—or at least at something approximating port arms. As he moved closer, it looked to Hollister as if the guy were wearing the same outfit as the man the night before. *Could he be the same one? Did he pass down the trail during the day, and was he on the way back?*

It made little difference, except that the man was spooky about the same area. He took a few more steps and stopped. He stepped off to the left of the trail, looked, and men came back. He did the same on the right side of the trail. He was as spooky as the VC the night before, but not as timid.

No one wanted to go through another blown snatch again. No one wanted to go through another day and another night of waiting.

Some slight rustling caught Hollister's attention. He looked over to his right and saw Bui moving around. He was naked from the waist up and was taking off his trousers. Before Hollister could reach out and stop him, Bui picked up his rifle and stepped out into the middle of the trail.

The other team members were caught totally off guard by Bui's move. They quickly looked down the trail to see the VC's reaction. He seemed to be aware that something was different and stopped—freezing in place.

Bui raised his rifle over his head and called out to the man in Vietnamese. Hollister was baffled. A sudden thought went through his mind. Bui was giving them away! He was going back over to the other side. *Should he shoot Bui?* The others looked to Hollister for some kind of signal.

Bui called out to the enemy soldier again and said several more words in Vietnamese.

They looked back down the trail. The soldier dropped his rifle from the ready but still wasn't sure who he was seeing.

Bui took a few steps toward him. His terrible limp was very evident. He hardly looked threatening. The soldier dropped his guard a bit more and started walking toward Bui.

Bui stopped, stood there a second or two, dropped his rifle barrel, a grip on the small of the stock, as the enemy soldier slung his rifle and walked toward him, talking.

The language was not a problem for Hollister. It was clear the soldier was complaining about the weather and the fear that someone else had been waiting in the area.

Bui laughed and squatted as if waiting for the approaching soldier to join him for a chat.

The others figured it out. Bui had taken the chance to suck the soldier into the snatch area. The VC reached a point where he needed only one more stride to be able to reach out and shake hands with Bui.

But before he could make that step, DeSouza and Caps hurled themselves from trailside in a two-man tackle. DeSouza hit him high, and Caps drove his shoulder into the soldier's upper thigh.

Before the soldier could react to what was happening, the two LRPs had shoved him across the trail, knocking him completely off his feet.

The three of them went down in a pile on the low side of the trail. Bui jumped up, spun his rifle around, and had it in the eye socket of the downed soldier before he could make any move to resist.

As quickly, DeSouza got the man in a headlock, his forearm across the man's mouth. Caps squirmed out of the pile and sat on the soldier, holding him down. He yanked one arm up behind the soldier to a point where any additional pressure would surely cause damage to the shoulder socket. The grip caused him to freeze up as if to say he would not fight.

It took only a minute for DeSouza and Caps to bind the man's wrists behind him and stuff a single rolled sock in his mouth. Once the soldier quit gagging on the sock, Caps tied a cravat around his face to keep it in place.

Quintana, Montford, Ayers, and Hollister had scrambled to their feet, picked up Caps's and DeSouza's weapons, and stood ready as the captors brought their prey back across the trail.

Handing the tacklers their weapons, Hollister motioned them to start back toward the security element. He and Ayers dropped to one knee and watched their backs, one looking in each direction for any sign of approaching enemy troops.

In less than ten minutes, the two teams had reached the rally point Hollister had selected. They stopped, set up a perimeter, and put out claymores. No matter what happened, it would be at least an hour before they moved out, so security was a high priority.

All were resisting the urge to cheer and pat themselves on the back for pulling it off. Everyone had known or heard of snatch missions that had gone sour or not come off at all.

Bui didn't display the same enthusiasm the others were trying to stifle. He slowly and tentatively held up the VC's rifle for Hollister to take. Hollister leaned over and whispered in Bui's ear. "You know I ought to kick your ass!"

Bui dropped his head in remorse. Then Hollister grabbed him and added, "But we wouldn't have him if you hadn't stuck your neck out." He shook Bui in mock anger. "We gotta talk when we get back to Bien Hoa. You understand?"

Bui nodded his head rapidly and sharply, showing understanding and obedience.

The weather caused them difficulty with the radios. One was wet and didn't work at all. Another had an intermittent short in the handset, and more swapping had to be done. All this delayed the full reporting of the successful prisoner snatch. Hollister was eager to get it called in, confirm the pickup time and place, and get on with an extraction.

While the RTOs were screwing around with the radios trying to get a combination of handset and radio that would work, Hollister began to worry about security.

If someone had seen or heard the snatch or if someone was already missing the captured soldier, time would be working against them. He looked at his watch. It was pushing two in the morning. That meant they would have enough time to move to the pickup zone, a thousand meters away, but they still had to kill the time until daylight.

The plan had been to wait until first light to pull out any prisoner—unless something else forced them to do a night extraction. Extractions were hard enough to pull off in the daytime. Night wasn't worth the risk if it wasn't necessary.

Hollister decided to send out a security party. He tapped Lopaka to pick three members of his team and make four shallow recons of the area just outside their perimeter. He wanted them to start from inside the perimeter and walk out and then back rather than walk around the perimeter. A team wandering around out in front of a perimeter became a liability to the perimeter in the event it took fire. The LRP within the perimeter would be reluctant to fire, not knowing the exact location of the team somewhere to their front.

By sending a small party out to look for anything that might threaten the entire heavy team and then having them come straight back in, the perimeter was ready to fire. Each man on either side of the departure point would know the recon party was going straight out and would know where they could fire and where it would be threatening to the recon party.

As the first shallow recon left the perimeter, Hollister felt a handset being pressed into his hand. Ayers whispered, "Six on the horn."

Sangean started by congratulating Hollister's team for the successful snatch. He confirmed the pickup and they set a time—zero seven zero zero hours. They had to insert one team before first light and would pick up Hollister's team on the back haul to Bien Hoa.

All they had to do was keep the prisoner alive and wait out the pickup. Hollister would move the team to the PZ at zero five three zero. That would give them time to make the move and some slack in the event that they were held up by an injury or something unexpected.

Time was available for a quick nap, but Hollister couldn't sleep. The pill he had taken had made him jumpy and wide-awake. His stomach felt sour, and he couldn't get comfortable leaning up against his rucksack.

The prisoner completely caved in on them. Hollister saw that he had quit fighting the rope on his wrists and was calmly leaning back against a tree with his knees drawn up under his chin. All Hollister had to do was get him and the team out, and they could chalk up a successful snatch.

The recon team came back into the perimeter after its third trip out. The leader of the party, Lopaka's assistant team leader, shook his head in an exaggerated manner to let Hollister and Lopaka know they had nothing threatening outside the perimeter. He then led the small party out of the perimeter again to check out the fourth side of the circle.

They had a little over an hour before they moved out.

"We better be going, sir," DeSouza said.

The words made Hollister realize he had been dozing lightly, thinking he was awake. "'Kay," he said. He looked at his watch. It was time to move. "Let's do it."

DeSouza passed the word to Lopaka, and the two teams stood and peeled off, straightening out the circle of tired soldiers.

The rain had stopped again, and the upper halves of the LRPs were drying out. Still, their trousers and boots stayed wet from the water on the brush they were threading their way through. The two team leaders were constantly reminding their people to keep alert and not move too fast. They knew it was normal for a team to want to rush the extraction when things were over. But they were still a long way from being out, and plenty could go wrong between War Zone D and the LRP compound.

As they moved, they heard the choppers heading north to insert another team. To the team members without maps, this meant they must be getting close to the pickup zone since the insert wouldn't take much longer.

Trying to form a schematic picture of the terrain's features in his mind, Hollister knew that before they reached the pickup zone they had to cross a small intermittent stream. He guessed that with the rain they'd had the stream would be anything but intermittent. Once they crossed it, it would be no more than two hundred meters to their PZ.

Ayers silently pressed the handset into Hollister's hand.

"Three. Over," Hollister spoke into the handset.

"Six. We are beginning our first insert. You on schedule?"

Sangean's voice in the chopper wasn't just a voice. To Hollister it was a sign that wheels were actually in motion—moving toward getting them out. "If you are not going to be here any sooner than three zero we are on schedule. Over."

"Rog. I'll be back to you. Keep your head up. Out."

Realizing that three nearby LRPs were looking at Hollister for some sign of a change, he shook his head to let them know there was nothing happening.

The file stopped. The word got passed back to Hollister, who was fourth in the line of march, that the point had reached the stream. He had instructed Lopaka to hold up and call him forward when they found the stream. Hollister wanted to take a look at the margin of the PZ and pick a point for the patrol to wait for the extraction. He signaled for Ayers to follow him, then started forward.

The recon of the far side of the stream took only a few minutes. Hollister, Ayers, and two other LRPs crossed the muddy, knee-deep stream and looked around the opposite bank.

Through the more widely spaced trees, Hollister could see the landing zone. There was room to call the team forward and set up a perimeter to wait for the pickup. He switched frequencies on Ayers's radio and called back to Lopaka to bring the rest of the patrol forward.

Less than five minutes later, Hollister spotted the movement of the lead man from Lopaka's team crossing the stream. Hollister and Ayers were up the stream bank a few meters to provide some security for the crossing patrol, and the other two from the recon party were downstream.

As the patrol's main body reached Hollister's side of the stream, he pointed them in the direction of the new perimeter. He then left his position and walked back to direct the establishment of the perimeter when he was stopped—cold.

The sound was unmistakable. A machine gun was firing on full tilt—long, twenty-round bursts. Then two explosions rocked the ground. Almost instantly, ten Ml6s were returning fire.

Someone was yelling, "Ambush! Ambush!"

The sounds of all the shooting pounding his ears while the rounds snapped by him in the trees made it clear he was in someone's sights.

Orientation was confusing Hollister. An ambush behind him? On the route they had just passed? How could that happen? Then it flashed through his head. They had waited until his patrol was split up—half on one side and half on the other side of the stream. He started back, toward the noise and the shooting.

As he did a LRP standing just a few feet from Hollister shuddered as a spray of dark matter exploded from the back of his head. The man collapsed as if all the muscle tone in his body had disappeared at the same moment.

Trying to turn off the burst of energy he had just sent to his legs so he could stop to help the fallen LRP made him start, stop, and start again once he realized he couldn't help. He leaped over the body of the dead man, quickly realizing that it was X-man, Lopaka's Hoi Chanh.

Looking back up the new trail he had just broken, Hollister could see parts of DeSouza's team on the ground returning fire off to his left at a furious pace. The incoming fire, generally going across his front, was chopping down the vegetation between the VC and the LRPs.

What? He had to do something. *Where was Ayers? Where was the radio?* Hollister spun around in a crouch and yelled, "Ayers!"

"Yo," Ayers replied, from a point not more than fifteen feet behind him and to the right.

"Call it in," Hollister yelled. "You *did* call it in?"

"Yes. They're on the way."

Trying to suck up the situation and retake the initiative, Hollister turned back around in the other direction. He could see three more members of Lopaka's team on the ground returning fire blindly, toward where they thought the enemy fire was coming from.

Hollister waved his arms and yelled, "Let's go. Up their flank!" He stepped back, helped Ayers to his feet, and started off in the direction of what he suspected was the enemy's right flank.

CHAPTER 26

Able to get himself, Lopaka, Ayers, and two others rallied and on line, Hollister led them toward the enemy ambush. They put out all the small-arms fire they could, only aiming down at the ground, hoping their fire would be effective and what wasn't would skip, low, through the enemy positions.

As they moved forward, they were unable to tell if they were taking any fire themselves or if their efforts were having any effect on the enemy gunners.

They had moved only fifteen meters when they ran into a solid wall of live bamboo. It was twenty feet high and ran off to the left far enough to go out of sight. At its right end was the path the entire patrol had taken toward the stream. It was obvious to Hollister that the ambushers had selected it to act as a barrier to just what he was doing—trying to roll up their flank.

In order for them to get around it, Hollister and his chargers would have to step out into the area that was the killing zone for the enemy riflemen.

He dropped to a prone firing position, and Ayers followed suit. "Get DeSouza!" Hollister yelled.

He was worried that DeSouza, only thirty meters away in the killing zone, would be dead or without a radio since Hollister had taken his other RTO, leaving him with one and no backup.

"Here!" Ayers yelled back, stuffing the handset into the crook of Hollister's arm.

"What's your situation?" Hollister yelled into the mouthpiece.

"I've got one KIA and some wounded—don't know how many now."

"Can you move? Toward me?"

"We can try. When?"

"We're gonna pick up the fire—you make your move. Stand by for my call."

"Roger," DeSouza said.

Dropping the handset, Hollister got up to his knees and started pulling hand grenades out of the canteen cover on his hip. He held two up to show the others, who recognized his signal. He picked up the handset again and pressed the mouthpiece to his lips. "Now! Now!" he yelled into it before he dropped it again. In one motion he raised his other hand, gripping a grenade. He pulled the pin, rocked back on his knees, and hurled it up and over the top of the bamboo stand.

The others did the same, and each man was soon throwing grenade after grenade. After the initial delay, the grenades starting going off as fast as they had been thrown. Hollister threw another and looked over to the right for signs of DeSouza's team, then threw another one.

"Sir! Hey!" Ayers yelled, trying to be heard over the shooting.

"Not now!" Hollister yelled.

"Gunships! Gunships!"

"Fucking great!" Hollister yelled back, throwing his last grenade. He took the handset again. "Keep firing! Don't stop! Shoot into the bamboo—low, low!"

Hollister watched DeSouza drag a body into view as he led his team to a position to the right of Hollister's element, making a straight line of LRPs facing what they assumed was the enemy flank, their backs to the stream.

Hollister yelled into the handset, "Where are you? How soon can you . . ." He stopped, hearing the choppers to his rear, near their pickup zone.

"Where do you want it?" gun leader Stanton asked in his normally calm voice.

"Let me mark. When I do—fire to the west of my mark, close. They're not more than two-five mikes away from my mark."

"Okay, partner," Stanton said.

Hollister unsnapped the single metal snap on the bottom of the nylon carrier that held his strobe light to his harness. It slid out into his muddy fingers. He tried to turn on the rubber-covered switch and found that his fingers slipped off the rubber.

The enemy fire had shifted. It was now coming through the bamboo. The riflemen would be coming around one end or the other of the bamboo hedgerow soon. "Shoot to the flanks—the flanks!" he yelled as he extended his arms and pointed left and right

He turned to Quintana, who was shooting an M79, and made a motion like he was shooting a free throw. "Keep dropping them over the bamboo."

The LRPs responded by shifting their fires, and the grenadier kept lobbing the HE rounds.

Hollister wiped his muddy hand across his shirt and tried the strobe again. It turned on and began to light up the area around him. *The sleeve was gone!* He had somehow dropped the oval tube that directed the high-intensity flashing light somewhere in the brush around his knees.

The flashing light marked his location for the enemy riflemen, and their fires came in even more accurately than before. Hollister quickly realized his mistake. He stood up, raised the strobe light behind his hip, and hurled it up and over the bamboo, hoping it would fall among the VC.

Grabbing the handset he yelled, "Forget my instructions . . . fire *on* the strobe. Fire *on* the strobe. It's in their position."

"Roger. You are to the east?"

"Affirm. Fire on the strobe before they put it out."

Hollister could hear the sounds of the gunships firing rockets and miniguns before he could see them. Stanton had started his firing run hundreds of meters out and came across the front of the LRP's position. In the dark the tracers and rocket motor flames looked much closer than they actually were, and the newer LRPs ducked from what they thought was certain death.

As soon as the first pair of rockets hit, Hollister corrected, "Long! Drop two zero meters from your last pair. I say again. Drop two zero. Over."

"Rog," Stanton said calmly.

Two explosions threw Hollister onto his face as if someone had hit him in the back with a full swing of a baseball bat.

He recovered and turned to see what it had been. Two enemy grenades had come over the bamboo and landed among them, wounding another man, whom he couldn't make out, and killing another.

The second gunship firing run came in right where Hollister wanted it—on the far side of the bamboo. The strobe went out. "Can you still ID the target?" Hollister yelled into the handset.

"Yeah, got enough dry stuff burnin' down there now to mark it," Stanton replied.

"Back up!" Hollister yelled to the LRPs around him. "Let's head toward the rally point on the other side of the stream!"

Those near him passed the word. Two figures stood and grabbed two bodies that lay dead behind their line and began dragging them toward the stream. Hollister wanted to tell them to leave the bodies, but knew better. A LRP who thinks he might be left behind is no good on any patrol. They had to take out their dead and wounded—it was their promise to each other.

He realized there was still another KIA to be carried out—X-man. He grabbed Xinh by the wrist, pulled it up and over his head, and lifted the small man's dead body up on his shoulders. The extra weight on his bad leg shot pains into his hip joint, making him bite his lip to keep from crying out.

The gun runs continued. Flares filled the skies, helping the gun-ships see their target. Sangean tried to get Hollister on the radio, and Hollister put him off, saying they were moving and he would give him a SITREP on the other side of the blue line. His only message, passed through Ayers, was for them to be ready to pick up the team.

RPGs—*grenades*! Hollister wondered what took the gunships so long to fire them if they had had them all along. The explosions were horrifying. Those standing threw themselves on the ground to avoid the fragmentation as the rockets detonated in the trees, mostly behind them.

Tracers continued to pierce the wall of bamboo, but were now coming down the trail with the RPGs. Hollister tried to gauge the distance to the landing zone in order to get the choppers in as fast as he could. He remembered the shape of the PZ from his chopper recon and the aerial photos he had studied before leaving Bien Hoa.

It was shaped like a dumbbell or a figure eight. The team was going to reach the PZ at nine o'clock on the lower lobe of the north-south figure eight. The two loosely connected landing zones were joined by an opening that was easily thirty meters wide, so choppers could enter the top lobe and fly through the narrow part to the lower lobe where the patrol would be waiting—if they all got there.

"Reptile, start walking your runs to the east. I say again, to the east— one hundred meters max. We have moved closer to the papa zulu, and you need to come my way. Over."

"Roger, your way, no more than a hundred. Keep your heads down," Stanton replied.

The lead chopper started pooping out grenades from its nose turret, thunking one every twenty feet as it crossed behind the assembling patrol. Each round landed on the far side of the stream bank, which the team had just left.

Hollister was sure the impact was either hitting the VC or was between them and the VC. Either way, it was suppressing the enemy fire and gave him time to consolidate his hasty perimeter and count heads. He put X-man's body down next to the other two.

"Lopaka," Hollister yelled at the top of his voice over the gun-ships. "Give me a count!" He then turned in the opposite direction and yelled the same to DeSouza.

Lopaka's RTO tapped Hollister again and passed him the handset.

"We are staged. You think you can get out in the clear for a pickup?" Sangean asked.

"Stand by," Hollister replied. Then he yelled again, "Well? Give me the fucking numbers, damnit!"

"I got one KIA, one WIA," Lopaka yelled from the nearby shadows.

"DeSouza! What is it?" Hollister yelled, the pressure mounting.

"Two KIA, two minor WIA. You got Ayers with you?" he yelled from a point out of Hollister's view.

Ayers? Hollister spun around. Ayers, where the hell was he? He had been behind Hollister crossing the stream. There was no sign of him. Security was shot anyway, so he yelled, "Ayers. Sound off!"

No reply.

He yelled for him again and looked over at Lopaka, shrugging in question. Lopaka shook his head, indicating he had not seen him.

No answer.

There was not much choice. He had to delay the pickup until he could account for Ayers. "Six, I got three kilo and three whiskey india alpha. But I'm still missing one. Stand by."

Sangean clicked twice.

For a fleeting second, Hollister recognized how happy he was to have Sangean as a boss. What he lacked in personality, he made up for in control under pressure.

"DeSouza! We got to find Ayers. Give me two men," Hollister yelled.

"Sir . . ." the other RTO said, holding up the handset. "Ayers. It's Ayers."

"What?"

"On the horn."

Hollister grabbed the handset and broke radio procedure. "Ayers?"

"Affirm" was the weak reply Hollister got over the radio.

"Where are you? Are you okay?"

"I don't know where I am."

"Are you lost?"

"No, sir . . . I'm blind," the soldier said. Hollister could hear the sobbing rising in the soldier's throat. "I been hit . . . rocket. I can't see, sir. I don't know where I am."

The report spun Hollister's brain. The choppers were orbiting, he had a blind man wandering around somewhere, and he was down to fifty percent effectives plus one prisoner and still hadn't even heard his ammo status.

He had to make a decision, and his options were poor. He could try to drag the wounded to the choppers. If he could find Ayers. And he still didn't know if his men and the gunships had been able to do any real damage to the damn VC, whom they had not even seen yet.

The gunships! The thought chilled Hollister. "Break. Reptile Six, check fire on the guns. We've got a man out there."

"Rog. We're breaking off," Stanton said. "You need us to look for you?"

"Maybe. Stand by. Thanks."

Just at that moment a single VC soldier stepped around the left side of the bamboo stand and leveled an RPG toward the LRP perimeter on the other bank of the swollen stream—just thirty meters away. Before Hollister could make a sound or even raise his rifle, the soldier took three hits in the chest and face and went down. The tracers that felled him were green. Hollister followed them back to a point only a few feet to his side and saw Bui standing there with his AK47 still at his shoulder.

"All right, Bui," someone yelled.

The enemy soldier's aggressiveness was the decision maker for Hollister. It told him the enemy wasn't backing off and would continue to be a real problem to a crippled team trying to get out. And then there was Ayers, wherever he was. Hollister grabbed the handset. "Six, we need someone to come in here. We can't safely get our own on the PZ and the choppers. I think we need the Sabers."

"Can you hold on till we get them out there?"

"Got no choice. Just keep me supplied with guns and some red-leg and I can make it—I think."

"You got it. Break. Houston, you copy?"

Vance's voice came over the radio handset from Operations. He had been at the radios since the first shot was fired and had the Cav troop reaction force on the pad waiting to be picked up. Hollister didn't need to hear any more now that the wheels were turning. But he needed the frequency.

He interrupted. "Six, I need this freq to find my missing man. Can you move to the alt freq?"

They cleared the net for Hollister.

"One-three Romeo, this is Three. Now, tell me what your situation is."

Ayers came on the radio, his tone hushed, his voice very shaky. "I don't know where they are. I don't know were I am."

"What can you hear?" Hollister asked.

"Gunships, gunfire, and I don't even know about that. My hearing is fucked in one ear, too."

Hollister swallowed hard and tried to give Ayers confidence: "Okay, pal. Now listen. We are okay. I want you to stand. Can you stand?"

"I am standing."

"Which way are your feet pointing?"

"What? . . . Straight ahead," Ayers said.

"No . . . now, take it easy. Remember basic night navigation? If your toes are pointing up, you are heading uphill. If they are pointing down, you are going downhill, and if your feet are on different levels, you are on the contour. Remember?"

"Oh, yeah. Up, they're pointing up. Up."

"Okay, turn around. You have to walk down to the stream. Toes pointing down. You want to walk down to the stream. It's the only low ground near us. Give it a try."

For some reason, the firing had stopped. The VC were either moving or waiting to see what Hollister had for them. Hollister hated the silence as much as the shooting. At least while they were shooting he had some idea where they were.

A single round rang out. Hollister snapped his head around to see that one of Lopaka's RTOs had dropped a VC soldier crawling toward them, not more than twenty meters away.

"Ayers? You moving?"

"Affirm. Down. Moving down."

The temptation to hurry Ayers crossed Hollister's mind, then he dismissed it. He had to assume that Ayers was moving as fast as a blind man could move. Pushing him would lay too much on him.

Hollister turned to Lopaka and held up an M16 magazine he had pulled from his own ammo pouch. Lopaka nodded his head. "Got at least two hundred rounds per man," he whispered. Looking to DeSouza, Hollister did the same. DeSouza's reply was "One hundred per man.".

"Good, get two mags per man from Lopaka," Hollister said. "And keep your eyes open for Ayers."

Quintana, the other RTO, stepped up behind Hollister. "Horse soldiers are off at Bien Hoa. Hang in there' was Captain Vance's message."

"Tell him we'll be ready," Hollister replied, but wasn't that convinced himself.

A splash off to the patrol's right combined with a muffled groan spun two of Lopaka's people at the ready. They waited.

Hollister heard it, too. He walked downstream and tried to see what had made the noise. He grabbed the radio handset from Quintana and looked at him. "Which freq?"

"The old tac freq," he replied.

"Good." He raised the handset. "Ayers? You still moving?"

"I found a stream," Ayers said.

The voice Hollister heard over the radio was echoed by a nearby voice. He dropped the handset and took two more steps downstream. "Ayers? You there?"

"Here. I'm over here," a figure said, trying to get up the mud-slippery bank.

The two soldiers on the right flank got up and ran down the stream to Ayers, grabbing him by the arms, dragging and lifting him out of the water.

As they carried him back to the patrol, Hollister wasted no time. "Okay, let's move back. To the PZ. Lopaka, you take the point and watch out for the fuckers. They could be behind us. They are if they're smart."

As they moved to the PZ, Hollister turned the gunships on again to cover their movement. The platoon of Cav reaction force troops landed in the top lobe of the PZ and started working their way down the tree line toward Hollister's position.

Lopaka sent two men up the tree line to make contact with the Cav troops and keep them from mistaking the LRPs for the enemy.

While they waited for the linkup, Hollister moved to the center of their new and tiny perimeter to check the casualties. The bodies of Xinh, Caps, and Doc Montford were laid out alongside the wounded Ayers.

Ayers sat up, allowing Lopaka's assistant team leader, Spec 4 Green, to tend to his wounds. Green was one of the team medics trained by Sergeant Rose.

"How you doing, Ayers?" Hollister asked. He could tell how he looked since daybreak had painted the perimeter with a heavy gray light, dissolving the shadows. Ayers's face around the dressing looked as if he had been hit with birdshot. He was a maze of tiny puncture wounds.

Dennis Foley

"It hurts like shit!"

"I'll bet," Hollister said, looking at Green for any sign of relief.

"I can't give him any morphine—never with a head or a belly wound."

"You got anything else?"

"I just gave him two Darvons with codeine."

Reaching over to reassure him, Hollister patted Ayers on the shoulder. "We'll get you out of here just as fast as we can. You gonna be able to hang in there?" He grabbed him by the upper arm and gave it a squeeze to punctuate his words.

"Yessir. Can do."

As he stood, Hollister looked at Green for any contrary assessment and got only a shrug, presumably a sign that he had no idea if Ayers would see again.

"Sir, Cav's here," someone said.

The lead element of the Cav troop reaction force was made up of a buck sergeant in regular fatigues and a steel pot. He was followed by two PFCs and a second lieutenant.

The lieutenant walked around the others and sought out Hollister. "Sir, where do you want us?"

"Stevens," Hollister said, recognizing the platoon leader who had attended briefing after briefing without ever being committed to bail out a team in trouble.

Pointing across the stream, Hollister swung his arm left and right. "They're over there—if you haven't scared them off. I'd act like they are staying. Can't go wrong that way."

He turned back to the lieutenant for a sign and caught him nodding. "You bring your people in here and relieve us. I've got to pull this team out, and I'm going to need at least a squad to cover our move to the choppers. That possible?"

"Sir, my orders are to help get you outa here and await further instructions. You want it that way. You got it."

"Good man."

Ayers and the other three wounded men went out on a medevac chopper. Hollister sat with his back to the transmission on one of the two pickup ships. The bodies of Montford, Caps, and X-man were wrapped in poncho liners and laid out just behind the pilots' seats.

The prisoner sat, tied and blindfolded in the center of the chopper, his feet touching Hollister's boots.

No one spoke.

Having reached a safer altitude, the door gunner locked down his machine gun and offered Hollister a cigarette.

Hollister, who was tired and getting angrier with each minute, took the cigarette to try to get his mind off the feeling of failure that was closing in on him. He looked at the prisoner. *Had he been a ploy? Had they been set up? Shit!* he thought. The word "suckered" kept going through his mind.

A strong urge came over him to reach across and smack the shit out of the prisoner, wiping the smug expression off his face. Hollister had never felt that before. To keep himself from getting angrier, he decided not to look at the prisoner or the dead LRPs again.

He put his head back against the insulation on the fire wall. After going so long without a cigarette, Hollister felt the smoke burn his throat and make his head swim a bit. He realized he had to do something. His time in III Corps, so far, seemed to have been a series of losses or draws.

He hated the fact that contacts never seemed to be theirs. It was always the VC who decided them—when they would happen and how long they would last. It seemed to him that the only thing he could control was the degree of response and the amount of lethality he could bring to the contact. And even that was spotty, depending upon the willingness of other U.S. and allied units to divert combat resources to his contacts, his battles, his needs. It sucked.

He knew one thing—if the rate of success was going to change at all, it would be up to him to make it change.

An unusually large crowd had assembled at the chopper pad to meet the team. Hollister guessed that some wanted to see what the prisoner looked like. He cleared and locked his rifle and stuffed the magazine into his pocket. The others followed suit.

The Hoi Chanhs came to the chopper to take off the bodies of their fallen comrades. The usual grab-ass and cross-chatter was gone. No one spoke.

Once the others got out of the chopper, Hollister stepped out and dragged his rucksack behind him. The lack of strength in his arms told him just how tired he was. And as he took a step toward the pilot's door to thank him, the pain in his bad leg shot bolts of fire through the muscle tissue to the thighbone.

Vance stood by the pad, silent.

"Hey, Peter. What's the word from the Cav?"

"Here, gimme your ruck," Vance said, reaching out to help Hollister.

"Naw. Don't want the troops to think it takes two captains to carry one rucksack."

Vance smiled. "They swept through the area where you had your contact and found a hasty ambush position set up. You guys racked a few up though. They counted four KIA and enough blood trails to guess you might have waxed another four."

Without answering, Hollister stopped long enough to watch the Hoi Chanhs carry the bodies of X-man and Caps to a three-quarter-ton truck. Somewhere in the compound the Zombies were singing "Time of the Season." He looked around for the source of the music and saw T.T. standing on the back step of the Officers Club wiping her hands on a dishrag. She was watching, too. But her attention was focused on Bui who, despite his difficulty walking, was carrying one of the bodies by himself.

"Wasn't worth it," Hollister said and continued toward Operations.

Vance didn't argue with him.

Vance and Hollister entered the briefing room. Most of the other team survivors were already there. Kurzikowski fished around in the cooler and found a beer for Hollister.

"There any for the troops?"

"Those that want 'em got 'em," Kurzikowski said.

"Thanks." Hollister spun a folding metal chair around and straddled it. He dropped his rucksack next to his left leg and balanced his M16 across the top of the webbing holding the ruck to its frame, the muzzle pointing toward the wall.

"We're still waiting on Sergeant DeSouza," Kurzikowski said.

"Where is he?" Hollister asked.

"Rose is pulling a piece of frag out of his back. He took some shit, I guess."

The news was just that much more depressing for Hollister. Another man wounded, wouldn't say anything about it, just kept doing his job. The feelings of pride and anger only served to confuse his mood more. He nodded at Kurzikowski to let him know they would wait and reached around and up under his cammie shirt skirt.

His fingers found his demo knife. He grabbed the braided nylon lacing attached to the loop on the end of the stainless steel knife and pulled it from the nylon carrier that held it to his web belt. He pulled out the can-opener blade and punched down into the top of the beer can. He left an angled slice not quite perpendicular to the rim of the can. He then made an intersection with the first by making a pie-shaped cut.

Pressing the tip of the hooked blade into the center of the V, he folded it down and away, making an opening every bit as good as a real church key would have made. He spun the can half around and did the same on the opposite side of the top.

The beer was cold, but it was Carling's Black Label. Like every can of beer he had tasted in Vietnam, it had that taste of spoiled beer. He didn't care. It was just another thing he had built up a tolerance for—or at least blocked out of his mind. Another in a lengthening list.

He lit a cigarette and looked around at the others. They were as exhausted as he was, chatty, superficial, and very glad they were there to talk about it and not in the back of the three-quarter on the way to Graves Registration.

"Where's Bui?" Hollister asked.

"He's with the prisoner. He and Lieutenant Potter are shaking him down," Kurzikowski said.

"Think they'll get anything out of him?" someone asked.

"I've never seen Bui that mad. I wouldn't want that little fucker sweating my shadow to the wall," Vance said.

They all laughed nervously.

A hissing noise came from the other half of the Ops building. Hollister jumped to his feet and stepped to the doorway that connected the two rooms. He stuck his head through the door and raised his voice: "Hey, quit spraying that shit now!"

The radio man spraying GI DDT didn't understand what the problem was. "Sir, I was just trying to kill the biggest fucking spider I've ever seen."

"Use a .45. That shit makes me puke."

No one said anything in the briefing room as Hollister stepped back in and sat down again. He quickly realized that he sounded like an asshole, but had no idea how to explain his behavior. He took another long sip of his beer and hoped they would start shooting the shit again.

"Tench-hut!" Kurzikowski yelled.

They all snapped to attention, thinking Kurzikowski was calling them to their feet for Major Sangean, but that was not Sangean's style.

Turning to see who had entered, Hollister saw Major Fowler and Colonel Schneider, the new G-3, and a brigadier general Hollister had never seen. He remembered Sangean's words about being back at Bien Hoa: *too close to the flagpole—the fuckers turn up for lunch and call it visiting the troops in the field.*

Fowler, as unctuous as ever, spoke as if the LRPs were familiar with him and his expectations. "How about some more chairs, Sergeant?"

Kurzikowski suppressed his contempt, stepped into the other room, and instructed the RTOs to bring three more chairs into the briefing room.

The general stepped around Fowler and Colonel Schneider. "Where's the patrol leader?"

"Sir, I'm the patrol leader," Hollister said.

The general stuffed his hand into Hollister's. "So you're Hollister. Good to meet you, son."

He knew that General Stone was the deputy commander of IIFFV. Hollister spotted the CIB and master blaster wings over his pocket and the 101st Airborne combat patch on his right shoulder and assumed that the man was probably an ex-infantry officer with some idea of what his patrol had just been through.

"Looks like you folks had a tough night."

"Yessir. We did," Hollister said flatly, not buying into the comment yet. He still wasn't sure where the man stood on LRPs.

"I'm very impressed with the work you folks have been doing. You're the Operations officer, aren't you?"

"Yessir. Just taking out this heavy team to get a feel for the new AO. I can't work an area I don't know," Hollister said, looking over at Fowler. He had made the statement for Fowler, not the general.

"Good. Good. Staff officers should spend more time on the ground."

The tendons on the sides of Fowler's jaw tightened as Hollister looked directly at him. He had to fight the urge to laugh at the major, who was wearing a pistol belt and harness, canteen, .45 and holster on his right hip, an ammo pouch and first aid packet. All the equipment was bright, clean, and new. But the thing that got to Hollister was the hunting knife taped upside down on his right harness strap. Hollister knew that no right-handed soldier would put his knife in the hollow of his shoulder if he had ever spent any time carrying a rifle in the field. The man was a joke and an embarrassment to Hollister.

Sangean popped through the door. "Sorry I'm late, but that prisoner is spitting up info faster than we can take it down." He nodded an acknowledgment to the general and his two staff officers, but didn't fawn over them. That pleased Hollister and seemed to irritate Fowler. And that pleased Hollister.

"What kind of stuff are you getting?" the general asked.

"Seems that he really wasn't a VC, but he was a sympathizer who lived near the site where he was snatched. The VC made a deal with him."

"Deal?" the general asked.

"Yessir. He was allowed to stay on his land and work if he would act as a guide for the new VC units moving into the area. But he didn't seem to be aware that he was being used as a setup for the ambush on Hollister's team.

"Before I got over there, he told Bui and Potter that the night before he was snatched he had noticed something wrong with the trail and told the VC. They told him not to worry about it, that they would check the area out.

"My guess is that the VC knew we were in the AO and let the prisoner get snatched, knowing the snatch team would surely move to a nearby PZ for extraction. They set up a hasty ambush and got lucky. They picked the right PZ."

The news hurt. Hollister began to wonder if they would have lost anyone if he had picked a different PZ or if they had let the guy go by and waited for another, less wary VC to snatch?

Sangean could read it on Hollister's face. "It was a lucky shot on their part. There are only so many PZs out there. If *we* had picked a less likely PZ, the team stood just as much chance of making contact by traveling the added distance." He didn't say it to Hollister, but he said it for him.

Like so many other visiting firemen Hollister had seen visit the LRPs, the staffers sat through the entire debriefing. He was sure they would sit around the Field Force Officers Club that night casually mentioning that they had "spent the day with the LRPs."

At the end of the briefing, Sangean asked General Stone if he had any questions or anything he wanted to say. This was expected.

The general got to his feet and walked to the front of the briefing room. Sangean moved from the podium to give him the floor when the general stopped him. "Don't go anywhere. I have an announcement to make."

He looked up at Fowler. "Major, please."

Fowler stood, pulled a set of orders out of his pocket, and stepped toward the general. He then reached back in his pocket and handed the general something else.

"Read 'em," the general instructed.

Fowler stood at attention and opened up the folded paperwork. "Attention to orders."

Everyone in the room stood and came to attention.

Fowler continued, "Headquarters, Department of the Army. Effective this date, Major George V. Sangean is promoted to the rank of lieutenant colonel in the Army of the United States."

The general reached up and pinned a silver oak leaf on Sangean's right shirt collar over the sewn-on, subdued major's insignia. Sangean smiled at the surprise.

"Congratulations. The Field Force commander wanted to do this himself, but he is at a meeting at USARPAC and didn't want you to have to wait until his return," the general said, still sounding very official.

The room broke out in cheers and applause for Sangean.

CHAPTER 27

In his room, Hollister dumped his gear on the floor, hung his rifle on the hook on the wall, sat down on the bunk, and dropped his head into his hands. He needed a few moments to get it all straight in his head. But even that was denied him by the tiny knock on his open door frame.

He looked up and saw T.T. standing there holding a double Scotch on the rocks in a cheap tumbler. "For you."

His initial instinct was to tell her it was too early in the day for a drink. But he knew better than to refuse the drink; it was obvious she had something on her mind.

He took the drink. "Thank you."

"Thank you, Cap'tan Jim."

"For what?"

"For my Bui. You bring back."

He could see how shaken she was. He had seen it in her face when they got off the choppers. "No sweat, T.T. He's a good man. He did a fine job."

"Please."

"Please what?"

"Please don' take he back to field again."

"It's important to you, isn't it?"

"Beaucoup importan' to me," she said, dropping her head—embarrassed. "I hab nobody. Only hab Bui."

Walking over to T.T, he reached down and took her two hands in his. She looked up at him. "No more. Bui's field days are over. I promise."

She smiled and then as quickly showed concern. "You no speak Bui. Please, Cap'tan Jim."

"I no speak," he said, squeezing her hands for emphasis. "Now you get back to the bar before he thinks you butterfly me."

"No, no," she said quickly. "Tich no butterfly."

He smiled, and she must have realized he was trying to tease her out of her mood. She returned his smile with her bright grin and ran down the hallway to the club.

Standing in the doorway watching her run away, Hollister realized again that there were other lives and other couples being ripped up by the war.

Weapons cleaned, rucksack repacked minus the things he carried in his claymore ready bag, Hollister stepped into the shower. He wiped the water drops off the small piece of broken mirror wedged into the support frame of the shower stall.

He let the water run down on the crown of his head and just stood there—trying to gather strength to go on with his day. He was nagged by the events of the morning as he leaned out of the shower to get the glass of Scotch on the window ledge only to find that T.T. had slipped in and brought him a refill.

A long sip of the drink burned but relaxed the tension he was feeling. He leaned against the shower wall, somewhat overwhelmed with a sense of futility, but knew that throwing up his hands was not the way to handle it.

He finished his drink and continued to scrub himself as he tried to make a mental list of things to do. He had to convince himself that he was doing everything he could to reduce the enemy's grip on the initiative. He knew there was still room for much more training, which he would insist on. Training would sharpen the troops, speed up their reflexes, increase the accuracy of their fire, and diminish their uncertainty in the event they were caught in other contacts.

Being smarter about operations and trying to outsmart the VC was something he, Potter, and Sangean had to work much harder on.

He also knew he had to get a handle on his mood swings. They had been troubling on his first tour, but this tour seemed even worse. He no sooner got the sense that things were getting manageable when combat losses, illnesses, and reassignments were ripping up the teams and the company headquarters—all causing backward steps.

A quick trip to Operations to check on the teams still out and a report on the team members who had gone to the hospital for treatment and Hollister was out again on his way to the mess hall. There he grabbed a thick slice of tough roast beef and some bread.

He worked his way over to the Orderly Room and checked on paperwork and then tried to track down Sangean, whom, he was told, was at the Officers Club.

The tape recorder they had all chipped in to buy was wailing "Bad Moon

Rising" as Hollister walked in. Sangean had given Captain Newman the job of morale officer. It was his responsibility, because he was the commo officer, to acquire the latest rock and roll music and have it copied to reels of tape for the club. Creedence Clearwater Revival was not the kind of music that could be heard on Armed Forces Network.

Sangean was sitting in the back of the room with a cold soft drink and a stack of papers spread out on a table. "Jim," Sangean said, rubbing his eyes at the bridge of his nose. "You get any rest?"

It struck Hollister that in spite of Sangean's low-key personality, he had never failed to ask about someone's welfare.

"Sit," Sangean said, picking up a handful of folders on the chair next to him. "You want something to drink?"

"No, sir. I ought to get back to Operations and get started on some plans for next week."

"Nope. You're off the clock until tomorrow. So have a drink, relax, and get back into gear without killing yourself."

"Okay, sir. I'll go for that." He waved to T.T. at the other end of the room and held his hands, one above the other, to indicate the size of the drink he wanted.

He turned back to Sangean. "Congrats on the promotion, sir. I didn't get a chance to tell you at the debriefing. Too many visiting firemen."

"Thanks," Sangean said. "It doesn't come without strings though."

Careful not to spill the drink, T.T. put the Scotch down in front of Hollister. It was just a little bit bigger than a normal double.

Behind the bar T.T. picked up the pencil on a string and made a check mark next to Hollister's name. They all settled up their bar bills at the end of the month; that way T.T. never had to handle any cash.

After a sip and a long pause, Hollister asked, "What strings?"

"They are putting my green beret back on me. I've been alerted to go to Fifth Group in Nha Trang. I sure hope they don't have any plans on leaving me at Group Headquarters. I'll lose my mind. Nha Trang's a place to visit, not to work."

"That's shitty. When?"

"Got to report to Group in a month. I'm going to spend a week in Hong Kong on the way. I haven't had any leave or R and R in twenty-two months."

"You'll be able to catch up there," Hollister said with a knowing smile.

"Yeah, I'm taking a sock full of piasters with me."

"Peter going to take command of J Company?"

"I doubt it," Sangean said.

"Tell me there's someone as good inbound, sir."

"I don't know. They don't tell me as much as you might think. Yesterday I had some seniority; right now I'm the junior lieutenant colonel in Vietnam. My guess is that damn near every infantry major who has picked up the rumor is hustling for this job."

"When will we know?"

Sangean shrugged. "The big green machine has its own way of doing things. I just hope it's after my promotion party."

The thought brought a smile to Hollister's face. "We sure aren't going to let you go without spending some of that new half-colonel money."

Sangean nodded and leaned back. "We need to talk a bit about you. I don't want to get snowed under nailing down last-minute details and get out of here without spending a few minutes with you. So let's get it over with now."

He was leading up to a traditional counseling session, something all commanders were expected to do, but not many did. The turnover in Vietnam rarely allowed the opportunity. Hollister pulled out his notebook.

"Let me tell you that I am going to give you a max on your OER and just tell you privately what I think you need to work on. I'd rather not put my critique in writing. The paper shufflers in Washington don't need to know our business.

"So know I am pleased with your performance and sorry I'm not going to be able to work with you for the rest of this tour. But that's this business. We'll cross paths again."

The words caused a mixed response in Hollister. He was pleased that Sangean was maxing him out on his efficiency report. He had learned in his few years as an officer that the system was way overinflated and that anything short of a maximum score and exaggerated words of praise were the same as a bad efficiency report. He had also learned not to let the praise on paper go to his head, but to listen to the rater for what he really meant. He knew it would be like Sangean to focus on what needed work and let his approval be assumed by his silence on other matters.

"You're a good field officer and working on becoming a pretty good staff officer. What you're missing in the staff business, you'll pick up in the Career Course. Your main failings are in getting too involved. You take every minor setback and every casualty personally. You work too hard and drive yourself too hard for your own good."

Hollister started to argue, and Sangean raised his hand to stop him. "I know what you're going to say. And you're right. These troops deserve all the time you can give them in training, supervision, and planning. But not when it's done with you a walking zombie. You need to learn to sidestep some of the things you can't change and not carry them around with you. I don't want to suggest that you not spend as much time with the troops, but you know the cost when you do. It makes it that much harder to accept the news when they get killed or wounded. Get a grip on this, Jim, or it'll eat you up."

He understood what Sangean was saying. He also understood that he wasn't advocating being more aloof. But this was something he would have to handle himself. There were no textbooks to give him the exact solution to the problem of familiarity and concern.

Sangean leaned back and pulled a cigar from his shirt pocket. He bit off the end and plucked it from his lips with his fingertips. He lit the cigar and leaned forward, arms on the table. "You decided if you want to stay with the army?"

"I don't know. My wife is expecting me to come home and hang it up. But as it gets closer, I'm just not sure. It's been good and bad and even with the war; I've met and worked with some terrific people. But I've never been a civilian, really. I have no idea what it would be like out there."

"I'm not asking for a decision. I had the same doubts when I was a new captain. So bank your bet. Make some moves like you're planning to stay, and it won't do any harm if you pull your rip cord and bail later.

"You want Infantry Branch to think you are in for the long haul. That'll give you the best chance of having your career development in place if it turns out to be true."

"Good plan. Thanks."

Sangean waved to T.T. for another round and quickly brought it to a head. "You're a good officer, Jim. I'd be happy to serve with you again, anytime. But you can fuck yourself up if you let this business eat a hole through you. You've got good instincts, and I have no problems with your judgment. Just keep listening to your gut. It'll steer you right."

"I will," Hollister said as he pushed the empty glass toward T.T.

"And watch out for that shit," Sangean said, meaning the booze. "It can jump up and bite you in the ass. I've seen plenty get dragged down by it. That's all I'm gonna say about that." He raised his cola can in a sort of salute to mark the end of the counseling session.

After several days of getting over the strain of the snatch mission, Hollister quickly got back into his job. The wounded were all coming back to duty, except Ayers, who would need more work on his eyes. He would see, but his tour was over.

The dead were remembered, and Sangean made quite a fuss over having Two Field accept a recommendation for medals for each Hoi Chanh.

Hollister had enough time to absorb the events and decide just what needed to be done to keep another patrol from being baited and ambushed as his was. He tried to make his decision based on the good of the teams, but knew that some of his own ego was tied up in having been had by the VC.

He was struck with mixed emotions when he read the Operations Summaries that were written at IIFFV Headquarters and distributed to all subordinate units. In them the description of the contact after the snatch was characterized as very successful, yielding plenty of intelligence as well as significant enemy casualties. Somehow, from the Cav's reported four casualties, the number had grown to an estimated added body count of twelve.

Hollister was angry about the account of the contact, but he was privately relieved to see that it was not described as a stupid move on his part. He tried not to let his emotions get him in trouble over his disagreement with the report, but he made sure Sangean knew how he felt.

Sangean made no secret of how angry he was when he called Major Fowler and dressed him down. Fowler was responsible for the reports and had to be accountable for the contents—even though he denied it.

Hollister tried to reduce his mail backlog while working on more Operations plans for War Zone D. He based them on the analysis of the enemy situation that came from the prisoner and the captured documents. As far as Field Force was concerned, there was a Main Force guerrilla battalion operating in War Zone D as a cadre, whose mission was to facilitate the passage and the concealment of NVA units moving through the area and those who needed to temporarily operate out of Zone D.

"You heard anything about any other friendlies moving into D Zone?" Hollister asked Kurzikowski, who had just returned from G-3 at Long Binh.

"They were dicking around with a brigade of the Hundred and first that was supposed to go in there. But there's some shit happening north of Ban Me Thout, and they're going to leave 'em up there for now."

"So it looks like we keep it, huh?"

"Looks that way to me. Problem?" Kurzikowski asked.

"We've been there long enough for the VC to pick up all of our tricks— at least the ones they didn't know when we first went in there. I want to start doing more to confuse them."

"Like?"

"I want to put some teams in on strings—no LZs. They have every damn landing zone in the AO covered by LZ watchers. I think if we rappel some teams in and even fake a few rope inserts, we'll throw them off. How's that sound to you?"

"Good. I've never felt we were getting away with anything they didn't know about anyway."

"Let's do it. But first . . ."

"I know, sir. *More training.* I hear you. We'll get the troops out on the rappelling tower right ricky-tick."

Night training was essential. Hollister was aware the troops were doing some grumbling about his increased training schedule that had the teams out night and day. But he had remembered Easy's words, "Careful you don't kill 'em with kindness." He was convinced that the more they trained at night, the more he would increase their survivability. So if he got some dirty looks and overheard some shots he'd just ignore it and keep up the training. It might mean someone getting home who might not otherwise.

Hollister stood on top of the rappelling tower watching soldier after soldier climb it, hook up, and rappel down. The night was so dark that it was even difficult to see the safety NCOs at the bottom of the ropes.

"Where are the Hoi Chanhs?"

"Over there," someone said. "By the shitter."

Looking across the compound toward one of the latrines, Hollister could make out the glow of two cigarettes. He couldn't see the smokers, but he assumed it was the Vietnamese.

"Sergeant Bui?" Hollister yelled from the top of the tower.

Bui's voice came back from the base of the tower, "Airbo'ne."

"Get those little people over here. This goddamn training isn't just for the Americans."

"Yessir," Bui said, then broke into excited Vietnamese as he chided the Hoi Chanhs for not being at training.

A voice called up from the base of the tower. "Cap'n Hollister up there?"

"Yo," Hollister replied.

"Sir . . . Captain Vance needs to see you in the Orderly Room—right now."

Walking to the back of the cramped mock-up at the top of the tower, Hollister picked a spare sling rope and a snap link off the wall. He flipped the gate on the snap link a couple of times to make sure the spring was still good and then slipped it into his mouth while he tied a Swiss seat around his hips with the sling rope.

Once the running ends of the Swiss seat were tied off in double half hitches, he fastened the snap link to the three passes of rope that intersected at his crotch. After seating the snap link, he looked over to the soldier next in line and motioned for a space in the doorway of the mock-up tower. "How 'bout letting me in there?"

The soldier stepped back and handed the double climbing ropes to Hollister, who dropped them down through the gate, came around, and dropped them through again. After checking to be sure that the gate was closed, he turned his back to the doorway, looked out and down, and yelled, "On rappel!"

With a forceful push of his legs, Hollister leaped up and away from the platform, allowing himself to fall twenty-five feet in the first bound. His feet then slammed against the wooden wall as his braking hand jerked him to a momentary stop, swinging his body back in toward the tower. He felt the impact in his bad leg, but shrugged it off.

Flexing his knees, he pushed off again and let some more slack into his breaking hand, behind his hip. He fell the last fifteen feet, his boots landing flat-footed on the ground. Without hesitation, he yanked some slack into the rappelling ropes and freed them from the gate of his snap link, yelling, "Off rappel."

The contact siren hadn't blown, so whatever Vance wanted couldn't be that earthshaking. After spending his hours in the darkness, the lights inside the Orderly Room seemed extraordinarily bright. As Hollister tried to adjust to the light, he found Sangean and Vance standing in the outer office—silent.

Hollister looked at the two of them and waited for someone to speak.

Vance went first. "Well, we have some shit coming down."

"What?"

Sangean waved a single piece of paper. "I've got a report date at the end of the week."

"Crap," Hollister said. "No chance of getting them to change their minds?"

"I'd have to take a bust back to major to stay," Sangean said with a smile.

There was a long pause which Hollister ended with the realization that without Sangean there would be no commander: "Who's your turtle?"

"Don't know. For now it's Peter here. He'll be acting CO until they find someone."

"No chance they'll make it permanent?"

"Sure, it'd happen if this were a mess-kit repair company. But there are too many eager beavers wanting my job," Sangean said.

"Well, we sure are gonna miss you."

Sangean stuck his hand out and took Hollister's.

Hollister wanted to tell Sangean what he really felt about him, but he felt a little awkward about saying it. He decided to put as much of it as he could into the firmness of his handshake and hope that Sangean understood.

"We ever going to have that promotion party?" Vance asked.

"It's going to have to be a promotion party and a going-away party combined."

"We can handle that," Hollister said.

The company had not had a break in weeks, and Sangean cleared it with G-3 to pull the remaining teams out of the AO and not replace them for forty-eight hours. The break would give Sangean a chance to throw his promotion party and let the troops get some downtime to recharge and even see each other. Too often they were taking turns out in the field on a schedule that didn't allow the members of a patrol platoon to ever see the other teams.

The platoon sergeants and platoon leaders also needed some time for the essential housekeeping chores that troops had to be around to accomplish. Equipment inventories, reassignments, billeting changes, maintenance, repairs, and cleanup all required bodies.

The time was also good for the aircrews. The pilots and crew members needed a break, too. Sangean made arrangements for the pilots to take all their aircraft back to their maintenance facilities and bring the crews back for the party.

The company area was filled with the aroma of steaks cooking on half-barrel barbeques that magically appeared. Sergeant Kendrick stood in the middle of the four barbeques flipping steaks and nudging hot dogs with a long two-tined fork.

It was the first time Hollister had seen all of J Company together since he had been with it and the first time he had seen so many of them in civilian clothes. Most didn't have complete outfits, so they filled out their ensembles with pieces of uniforms.

Shorts and shower shoes seemed to be the two items that each LRP had been able to bring over or get in the PX. The shirts were either T-shirts or no shirts. They all had a beer in each hand, and about half of them wore hats—boonie hats, patrolling caps, floppy hats, and the camouflage berets they had made in town.

By sundown the rock and roll music could be heard for several hundred meters in every direction. Ordinarily, that kind of racket would be considered a breach of noise discipline, but in the months since J Company had inherited the small base within a base, an engineer battalion and an Air Force Pedro rescue helicopter company had moved in on either side of the LRPs. Both units made more noise routinely than the LRPs were making on purpose. So the partying went on without fear of creating a bigger target than they already were.

Once it got full-on dark, some of the NCOs collected over by the mess-hall steps. Something was up. The beer flowed at a record pace, and the normally precise and well-coordinated LRPs began to get sloppy and clumsy. Hollister noticed it and caught Sangean's eye.

"That's what we promised 'em—a party."

"Glad I'm not paying for it," Hollister said.

"You'll get your chance—when you get those oak leaves," Sangean said.

The thought of being a major had hardly crossed Hollister's mind. He was just getting used to answering to the rank of captain. But *major* was an absurd thought. "Hell, I'll be lucky to keep these captain's tracks."

The gate at the front of the compound opened up, and a covered five-ton truck rolled in and headed for the motor pool.

"Then here's a way to keep 'em," Sangean said. "Round up the other commissioned types and report to the Officers Club ASAP."

Confused, Hollister turned and started looking for the other officers.

As Hollister found the last of the officers and headed to the club, he happened to glance over toward the motor pool, where one of the NCOs was unhooking the truck's tailgate. The action looked suspicious enough for Hollister to stop at the steps and watch.

As soon as the canvas drop was moved and the tailgate locked down, the NCO began helping Vietnamese bar girls and hookers out of the back of the truck, shushing them to try to stop their chatter and giggling.

It all became clear. It was best that the officers didn't know "unauthorized personnel" were in the compound after the curfew. Hollister stepped through the door to the club as the NCO hurried the women off to the team hooches for some partying.

Inside the club the aviators were trying to teach the LRP officers how to drink flaming Mimis, an invention of the 145th Aviation Battalion. It was a simple initiation to demonstrate manhood and unquestioned courage.

The drinker had to first select a beverage of his choice. There were only two requirements—it had to be booze, and it had to be flammable. Once the initiate had selected the booze, a shot glass was filled to the brim and the house lights were turned off. In the dark, the liquor was lit and the trial by fire began.

When Hollister arrived, Lieutenant Patten was being initiated into the 145th Aviation Battalion by Captain Stanton: "Now, at your command, grasp the shot glass, drink the contents, and hold the empty glass away from your face. When the glass is empty and away from your face, slowly turn it upside down. Once it is inverted, the flame must still be flickering in the glass and no remaining fluid may drip from it. If you blow out the flame, or if any liquid drips from the glass, we refill, relight, and try again. Any questions?"

"No, sir," Patten said as Stanton lit the rotgut bourbon the lieutenant had selected.

The lights went out, the room hushed, and Patten grabbed the glass.

"You've got it!" Stanton said.

Patten raised the glass, threw back the shot, pulled the still-burning glass from his lips, and inverted it. The crowd of officers watching started mumbling about his chances of doing it correctly when a single drop of burning booze leaped from the lip of the glass and hit the bar top.

"No! You failed the test!" Stanton yelled.

Patten hung his head as the others urged T.T. to refill the glass.

Hollister drank a couple of Scotches while Patten made eleven more attempts. The more he drank, the drunker he got and the less likely he was to complete the ritual correctly.

As he started to refill for his twelfth try, the phone rang. It was for Hollister.

Vance stood inside the Orderly Room, his back to the door.

"You really aren't going to like this," he said.

"So?"

"Sangean's replacement's been named."

"So? Who?" Hollister asked.

"Fowler."

"This is some kind of a joke, isn't it?"

"Nope. He's due in the day after tomorrow. And Sangean's due out the following day."

"Does Sangean know?"

"No, Sergeant Major Carey called me as soon as he saw the RFO come across his desk."

"Better tell Sangean. He's going to have a shit fit!"

"You can count on that."

Hollister dropped his head and stared at the scuffed plywood decking. He didn't have the words to express his rage.

The word got out immediately. Within a day it was all over the company, and the mood was down for everyone who knew Fowler's reputation.

As Hollister and Vance expected, Sangean went to Two Field to try to stop Fowler's reassignment to Juliet Company. Colonel Schneider, Downing's replacement, took offense at Sangean's suggestion that his recommendation was in error.

When Sangean tried to push it to General Stone, he was told that the reassignment of field-grade officers was a matter of the highest priority and that Fowler's service record was in direct conflict with Sangean's opinion. Still, Sangean promised Vance and Hollister that he would continue to work on the problem when the CG got back from a trip to CINCPAC for a conference.

Sangean reluctantly conducted a small change-of-command ceremony at the LRP compound. Despite his disagreement with Fowler's assignment, Sangean was professional enough not to make it a public issue at the risk of sabotaging the troops' morale and Fowler's chances to do a good job.

Hollister knew he had to get over his anger at the decision. That was one of the first things he had learned in OCS: Argue the decision until it is made, and then support it as if you had been for it all along. He knew he had to learn to get along with Fowler or jeopardize the safety of the troops by feeding his own emotions.

Fowler kept Vance and Hollister standing at attention in front of his desk while he hurled his opening remarks at them. It was all Hollister could do to keep from lashing out at him.

"Since the day I got wind of how you folks operate, I have been looking for a chance to put a little regular army in this pathetic group of prima donnas. And . . . as I have come to know more about Juliet Company, I can see that Sangean has let you two turn this place into a club for misfits and undisciplined children!"

"Major, I resent—"

Fowler cut Hollister off. "I didn't give you permission to speak. I'm doing the talking here, and I will decide when there is something I want to hear from you. And when that time comes, I will let you know. Have you got that?"

Hollister stood ramrod straight and didn't reply.

"Things are going to be quite different around here. We will do them my way and not *Mister* Sangean's way. He is gone, and *I* now command Juliet Company. And if either one of you has the slightest problem with that—you just speak up. I am sure I can find replacements for you within the hour.

"As it is, I'm not too sure how long either of you will last now that I am here. Your vacation is over. And there are plenty of *real* officers around who would jump at the chance to be here."

Hollister could only guess what kind of replacements he meant—staff rats, like Fowler, probably men who had never been with troops in combat and were more likely to get them killed than not.

"I will personally supervise all facets of Juliet Company's operations and will accept nothing but excellence. If I find you two are not carrying your load—"

"Major," Vance began.

"You can call me *sir*, Mister!"

Vance didn't stop to recognize the comment and sarcastically continued, "Just what is it you have trouble with? Is there something specific about Juliet Company you are unhappy with or are we going to have to guess?"

Fowler jumped up out of his chair and leaned toward Vance. "Don't press me, Mister Vance. 'Cause I'll have you out of here before the day is out."

The lecture went on for twenty more minutes with Fowler both angering Vance and Hollister and showing his lack of leadership and management skills by his description of how things would change. To follow Fowler's instructions, Juliet Company would have to turn itself into a perfect garrison unit. Formations, strict uniform regulations, Mickey Mouse procedures, and demeaning withdrawal of authority from the NCOs.

Hollister didn't have to look at Vance to know they wouldn't let it happen that way.

Team 1-5, headed by Sergeant Nessen, was due to be inserted into a wide spot in a dry streambed. The team would then move toward an area where there had been a report of enemy radio transmissions. The ASA guys could say there were transmissions coming out of the general area, but nothing more specific than that they were from an area the size of two side-by-side football fields.

Fowler insisted on supervising the insert himself. He declined Hollister's offer to ride along, saying that he wanted to get used to Juliet Company SOP on his own. He told Hollister that Juliet Company had better get used to the way he did things.

* * *

The morning of the insert, Hollister was in Operations when Fowler walked in. Kurzikowski was seated in Hollister's view, but not Fowler's. Hollister made a point of not making eye contact with Kurzikowski since the sergeant had already offered his unsolicited opinion, and Hollister was sure he would make faces of disapproval while Fowler talked.

Fowler was dressed like a real headquarters rat. He had on his cammie fatigues, all new web gear, complete with flashlight and hunting knife. But the ensemble was really topped off by a pair of army-issue sunglasses. He looked as if he were going to Hawaii instead of War Zone D.

"I'm going out and inspect the team before it loads the chopper," Fowler announced.

Hollister knew Fowler's attitude would not come across to Sergeant Nessen as a gesture of support but of oversupervision and distrust. He started to object, but Fowler cut him off. "Don't you have something to do, *Captain?*" Fowler said.

"I'll come along and see if I can be of any help out there."

"You will stay *here* and supervise this staff section." Fowler turned and left Operations, trying to juggle his map and his brand-new floppy LRP hat.

"His fucking oak leaf's in the back," Kurzikowski said as soon as Fowler was out of earshot.

"What?" Hollister asked.

"Got his fucking hat on backwards," Kurzikowski replied.

"You just don't know which way he's headed," Lieutenant Potter said.

Hollister glared at Kurzikowski and then at Potter.

Potter raised his hands in surrender. "I know. I'm sorry. That was disrespectful."

Hollister didn't respond. He had made his point. He walked through the light trap to the outside of the Operations bunker.

Hollister watched Fowler chewing out Sergeant Nessen for some infraction. Hollister couldn't hear his words, but he knew the major was making a fool of himself and committing one of the unforgivable sins—dressing down an NCO in front of his troops.

Nessen looked across the compound and caught Hollister's eye. There was no doubt that Nessen was as angry as Hollister had ever seen him. His complexion flared red.

As Fowler stepped into the C&C, Hollister noticed that Bui was getting in with him. Bui looked across the compound toward the officers' billets.

Hollister's guess was that he was looking for T.T., who should have been at work by then.

CHAPTER 28

"Six, this is Three. I noticed you took a senior member of little folks with you. I don't remember us going over that in any of the briefings," Hollister said.

"Remind me when I get back to explain to you that I *do not* have to check out everything I do with you. Out!"

Hollister put the pork-chop mike down and looked at Kurzikowski, who shook his head and mumbled, "You're right, Captain. I shouldn't be findin' fault with the new CO."

Hollister wanted to make a crack but realized there were six LRPs out there in the insert ship getting ready to be put into War Zone D. He had to focus on that and not his anger at Fowler or they would surely suffer while the officers squabbled like children.

Fowler did not stop talking from the moment he got into the chopper. He called in unnecessary reports, asked for commo checks, gabbed with the pilots, and issued long lists of instructions that should have been covered in or were contradictions to the instructions given at the briefback.

Each time Fowler's voice came up on the speaker on top of the radio bench, Kurzikowski groaned or made some comment.

"Not gonna make things better," Hollister said without trying to sound angry with Kurzikowski.

"Sir, if the captain wouldn't mind me saying so, I think the man's a friggin' idiot."

"Guess I didn't get a chance to object. Did I?"

The insert went well in spite of Fowler's oversupervision and constant radio traffic. The chopper pilots had worked together for so long that they knew how it should be done and just did it.

Inside Operations Hollister could tell that the pilots and the FAC were also very put off by Fowler's style. Their lack of chatter and light cross talk was evidence of that.

Out in War Zone D, Nessen got his team off the insert ship and into the thick bamboo margin of the streambed with no delays. No sooner had he moved them into the trees than Fowler started on him.

"One-five, this is Six. What is your situation?"

"One-five. Stand by, One," Nessen replied in hushed but strained tones.

"Don't give me that 'stand by' shit. When I ask you for a report, I expect it immediately!"

Hollister picked up the mike again and broke in.

"Six. This is Three. Procedure is for the inserted element to size up the situation and make a SITREP as soon as it is safe for him to do. It takes a little time to get a feel for the area and let the chopper noises die down."

"This is Six! Get off this net—now! When I want your opinion, I will damn well ask for it Out!"

Kurzikowski stood, pushed his metal chair back, pulled his floppy cap out of his pocket, and said, "Think we need some coffee around here."

Hollister let him leave without commenting. He knew it was Kurzikowski's way of letting him know he didn't want to be there while Fowler was jumping on him.

Several more minutes of silence went by.

"One-five, this is Six. I am still waiting!" Fowler yelled over the radio.

Hollister reached for the mike again and raised it to his lips. But before he could speak, Sergeant Nessen's voice cracked over the speaker in Operations: "Six. This is One-five. If you want to know the situation down here you are going to have to quit circling my position. I can't hear anything and where I am I can't see anything."

"Well, Mister, you better figure out a better spot than the inadequate one *you* selected."

Hollister raised the microphone again just as Kurzikowski entered with two cups and a mess-hall pitcher of coffee. "I wouldn't do that," he said.

"Oh? Just what would you do, Sergeant Kurzikowski?"

"Sir, this here is a rope thing."

"A *rope thing?*"

"Yeah. You give this new major just enough rope, and he is going to hang himself. No doubt about it."

"Well, what happens to Sergeant Nessen's people while all this is happening?"

"You won't have to worry about that. That's my guess. You jus' watch."

Fowler's voice boomed over the speaker again. "One-five? I'm still waiting for an answer."

"This is One-five. And I'm still waiting for you to move your orbit to somebody else's AO," Nessen responded.

"Don't get smart with me! Now I want you to get your element moving ASAP," Fowler screamed.

"Negative!" Nessen said. "That is not the routine."

"It is today," Fowler yelled back.

Hollister looked at Kurzikowski as he poured coffee, sat down, and put his feet up on the radio bench as if he were listening to a ball game.

"Yeah, that's gonna do it all right."

"What's gonna do what?"

"That's gonna make sure Nessen gets real serious about noise discipline."

Hollister knew what Kurzikowski was getting at. Both men looked at the radios for a long moment. They remained silent, even the aviation frequencies. The pilots, the FAC, and everyone else on the LRP frequency were waiting to see what Fowler's next move was going to be.

Finally, Fowler broke the silence. "One-five. This is Six. Over."

There was no answer.

He tried again, more forcefully and dripping with sarcasm. "One-five. This—is—Six. Over."

Still no answer.

Hollister and Kurzikowski exchanged glances.

"Yep," Kurzikowski said. "That's one terrific LRP out there. Ain't gonna get him to give away his team's location for some extra-ai-neous traffic that ain't SOP."

Fowler broke the silence again. This time his voice was more strained and his volume considerably louder. "One-five. Can you hear me? Over."

There was a long pause; then Nessen broke squelch twice.

Kurzikowski shook his head and grunted in approval. "Good man, that Nessen."

Hollister let it pass without comment.

Fowler's voice broke in again. "One-five. Is there some reason why you can't transmit voice?"

Nessen broke squelch two more times.

"Oh, Lordy. Shit's gonna happen. That sergeant's got some humongous gonads," Kurzikowski observed.

It was beginning to sound to Hollister as if Fowler were trying to cover his awkward situation when he broke squelch again and said, "Okay, One-five. I will assume you are concerned with security and that is the reason you cannot speak. I understand. So I want you to continue the mission and keep me advised. Out." He then shifted his tone and called Hollister. "Three. This is Six. We have completed the insert of One-five and are headed back to your location for the next element scheduled this morning."

Kurzikowski interrupted Hollister before he could reply: "Ask him if One-five had a cold LZ."

Hollister knew Kurzikowski wanted to screw with Fowler. He waved for him to be quiet and answered with a simple "Roger."

"I'm guessin' that at least a half-dozen prick 77s are monitoring the net out in the team hooches," Kurzikowski said after Hollister dropped the mike onto the bench.

"And?"

"And the new CO's *style* is not going to go over big."

Hollister didn't reply. He just let Kurzikowski's words sink in while he reached for a cigarette.

"You been doin' this long enough to know that them LRPs"—Kurzikowski jabbed his thumb toward the unseen team hooches—"will do just about anything for a straight-on boss—even if he's a nutcracker. But they'll lay down on an asshole in a heartbeat."

Hollister knew Kurzikowski was right. He was equally sure Fowler would come back to Bien Hoa with fire in his eyes.

Between inserts Fowler called a meeting in his office. He called in Vance and Hollister and made everyone else leave the Orderly Room.

Most of Fowler's remarks were meant for Vance, but he yelled at Hollister for several minutes for butting in on his radio transmissions. After generally dressing down both men, Fowler finished his speech: "And I want to see each of the platoon leaders before close of business today!"

Vance countered, "Just hold on. You won't be able to push these team leaders around by telling their platoon leaders to instruct them to behave. These kids have their asses flapping in the breeze every time they step out of this compound, and if you think any threat you make will impress them—I suggest you don't know what makes them tick."

"And *I* suggest you keep your goddamn leadership pointers to yourself, Mister. Now, you two are dismissed. Get the hell out of my office."

Vance and Hollister walked across the compound toward the officers' billets. "The guy's gonna get somebody killed," Hollister said.

"Don't be too sure he doesn't end up in someone's sight picture."

"Fragging? Yeah. Heard that somebody down in the Ninth Division got the ass at a platoon sergeant and slipped a grenade under the shithouse while he was in it," Hollister said.

"So we're going to have to do something about Fowler before somebody goes to Leavenworth for blowing his ass away."

"Any ideas?" Hollister asked.

"He's going to have to step on his dick before anyone up the chain of command thinks he's unfit for the job. He came down here because they thought he was a water walker, but what do we do with him in the meantime?"

"I don't know what we do. But we *don't* let him get between us. We're going to have to stand shoulder to shoulder and keep this guy confined to the minimum amount of space we can keep him in. We've got to get to the officers and NCOs in the company, the pilots and the RTOs, and make sure everything that happens from this day on is put in writing. Something tells me that if and when the shit does hit the fan, he'll turn on us and blame everyone but himself. So we have to document it all."

The next day Fowler caught Hollister coming out of the mess hall. "I want you to supervise the insertion of the two teams next up."

"Sir, that's not the best way to do this. Hell, I didn't issue those teams their operations order and wasn't there at their briefbacks or on the aerial recons."

"Again, Mister Hollister, I did not ask you for your opinion. Just get your ass over to Operations and get ready to keep those team leaders from screwing things up."

Before Hollister could reply, Fowler blew by him and into the mess hall.

At the same time, Kurzikowski came through the door, adjusting his headgear. "Oh, morning, Captain. Glad to see things are smoothin' out in the officer ranks."

"Now is not the time to fuck with me about a little friction, Sergeant K," Hollister said.

"Friction? That's a real interesting way to describe it. Guess I'll never understand officer stuff."

The inserts went well, and Fowler was not involved in any way. That was unusual since he had been involved in everything and had dominated the radio net since he arrived.

By the time Hollister returned to the compound, Fowler was driving in the front gate.

"Hollister," he yelled.

Hollister turned and rendered a less-than-enthusiastic salute. "Yessir?"

"I want to see you and Vance in my office—now."

It was getting to be a regular thing, Vance and Hollister standing in front of Fowler's desk while Fowler yelled.

"Why didn't you tell me that both of you were sending documents from this command to Field Force Headquarters without my approval?"

"Approval?" Hollister asked.

"Yes, you do know what the word means, don't you? From now on any scrap of paper or report of any kind that leaves here for Field Force Headquarters will go out *only* after it has my chop on it," Fowler said.

Only headquarters rats used the term "chop" to mean signature or initials.

"Sir, I don't understand what the problem is," Vance said.

"Mister—you better damn well learn that higher headquarters only knows what you send them and if it isn't perfect, then this unit will look less than perfect."

"On paper, you mean?" Vance added.

"Don't give me any of your shit," Fowler said.

"Whatever you say," Vance replied.

"From this day forward, anything—and I mean *anything*—that goes to higher goes by me first. You both got that?"

"Everything?" Hollister asked.

"Everything!"

For the next two days, each report Vance and Hollister drafted went to Fowler. He marked them up, revised them, and sent them back for the changes he wanted. For the most part, the changes were nitpicking. He sent one commo maintenance report back because it had two erasures on it. There was nothing in the report that could reflect badly on the company. Still, Fowler insisted that it be retyped, twice. Each time it took twenty minutes for a clerk to type it with the necessary carbon copies and another few minutes for Hollister to proofread and sign it.

There was plenty of grumbling going around about the administrative emphasis being placed on things in the company. It finally got to Hollister when he crossed the compound between the officers' billets and the Orderly Room and found Vietnamese laborers placing whitewashed rocks in straight lines down the borders of the footpath.

It was about midnight when Hollister finished his letter to Susan and began drafting the Daily Operations Summary that had to be in to Two Field before daylight. As he accounted for teams out, teams ready, and teams not deployable, the radio traffic started to pick up.

Team 1-5, Nessen's team, had found a stretch of commo wire just before dark and had set up to watch the area near it and to tap it, hoping to hear some voice traffic. If they were lucky, they would put their Hoi Chanh on to listen and translate. But by a little after nine, they found they were getting only evidence of battery power on the line, but no communications traffic.

Hollister told them to stick with it.

At four o'clock Hollister was called back to Operations. Nessen had called in movement, but said he was pretty sure it was not enemy. He had seemed pretty confident that it was wild boar or dogs, but he didn't want to take the chance of not reporting it at all.

While Hollister was drafting the report, Nessen called in a revision. He was hearing more noise and was now sure it was *not* animals.

Hollister grabbed the mike. "What do you think you got?"

"Voices, coming up the wire. Two hundred mikes away—north of my position," Nessen whispered.

Hollister turned to the RTO. "Go alert the pilots for a possible contact."

The RTO ran out of Operations, and Hollister continued talking to Nessen. "You think they're checking the wire? Maybe heard your tap?"

Nessen clicked the transmit button on his handset twice.

"Have you got a place to pull back to?" Hollister asked.

Nessen's voice came back on, hardly audible. "Affirm, but I'm afraid they'll hear me moving."

"If you stay there, will they definitely bump into you?"

Nessen clicked twice again.

"Then you haven't got much of a choice, do you?" Hollister asked.

"Negative," Nessen whispered into the handset.

"Roger. Keep me advised. We are prepping to give you what you need."

Stanton and Edmonds appeared in the doorway.

"We're going to have to pull a team. I'd bet money on it," Hollister said as he moved over to the situation map to look at Nessen's position again.

"They have a good PZ right behind them. I think we ought to lock and load. One way or another—they're coming out."

"We're on it," Stanton said as he bowed at the waist to Edmonds. "After you."

The pilots left and the Artillery FO came in, rubbing the sleep out of his eyes and buttoning his shirt.

"Should we wake up the major?" Kurzikowski asked.

"Naw," Hollister said, pulling his rifle off the hook on the wall and inspecting the chamber. "Wait till it gets serious. I'm going out to pull them. There's not much he can do from here."

"'Cept Monday-morning quarterback," Kurzikowski added.

During the flight to War Zone D, Hollister stowed his gear at arm's reach, made sure all the supporting aircraft were ready to pull Team 1-5, and cleared artillery plotted into the area.

Nessen kept reporting the voices getting closer to his location. But he hadn't moved away yet.

"You got any way to slow them down?" Hollister asked.

"I might be able to turn my claymores down the wire."

"If you feel that you can do it safely and that you have time—do it," Hollister said.

"Roger your last. Stand by one."

Hollister waited impatiently. He grabbed a cigarette and lit it. "You got a better feel for them yet?"

Nessen keyed the mike and whispered in an even lower voice, "Stand by."

Hollister looked over at the door gunner, who was listening in on the conversation. The gunner raised his fingers in a crossed good-luck symbol.

"Three. I can see nine—that's niner, victor Charlie's one zero zero mikes north of my position."

"Okay. Let's make this easy on you. Do you think you can engage? Yes or no only," Hollister asked.

Nessen clicked *no*.

"Okay . . . then get out of there. Can you mark them after you are gone?"

Nessen clicked *yes*.

"All right. At your discretion—make your move," Hollister said.

Nessen clicked an acknowledgment.

"Everyone ready?" Hollister asked over the intercom.

Banking slightly for a better view of the ground situation, Edmonds raised his gloved hand and gave Hollister an okay.

"Guns? You set?" he asked over the radio.

Hollister could hear the turbines and the blade noise of the lead gunship as Stanton keyed his mike and replied, "Ready."

"One-five, let us know, when you can, how much progress you are making so we can be there when you are ready."

Hollister switched frequencies and talked with the Artillery FO about placing steel on target just as soon as the gunships lifted their fire. He wanted to make absolutely sure the artillery didn't start too soon and wasn't delayed by some minor complication. Finishing, he went back to Nessen.

"One-five. When you are far enough away from the enemy element, say so and we will roll on your mark."

There was a long silence as the choppers loosely circled the landing zone that Nessen's team would use.

"Look!" the door gunner yelled, pointing at the heavily wooded area where they all assumed Nessen's team was moving.

Hollister looked and just caught the fading flash of an explosion.

"Three. One-five!" Nessen yelled over the radio. "We have blown our claymores. We might have dropped a few of them. But there are plenty more there. Request gun runs two five north of my mark."

No sooner had Nessen stopped talking when the small detonator of a grenade made enough of a flash for Hollister to see the grenade arc through the trees. The grenade landed, detonated, and shot a conical plume of luminous white phosphorous smoke and flame up through the trees.

"We got you, One-five. Inbound with minigun fire—first time. Please adjust," Stanton said as he laid over the lead Cobra and dropped to firing altitude.

As Hollister watched Stanton lead his flight into the target area, he keyed his mike. "One-five. Gimme a SITREP when you can."

"We are . . ." Nessen started, then stopped, then came back—very much out of breath, ". . . nearing papa zulu. Negative casualties. We'll be ready for pickup in . . .," he stopped and took another breath, "zero five."

"That's good. We're lining up now," Hollister replied as he looked back toward the gunships getting in position to make a second pass, the first having stitched up the area west of the mark.

"Negative! Negative!" Major Fowler's voice suddenly broke in on the radio net.

"*Negative* what?" Hollister asked, intentionally avoiding recognizing Fowler.

"Negative on the gun runs! Check fire! I want that team turned around."

"Oh shit!" Edmonds said from the front seat of the C&C.

"I do not understand your transmission," Hollister lied.

"This is *Six*. Don't jerk me around. I said for you to cease fire and send that team back to sweep through the area of the contact. NOW!"

"Six. Three," Hollister said. "Let's not discuss this on the Tactical freq. Can I meet you on the Admin?"

"Negative! You follow my damn orders, and do it right now. I am inbound to your location and will replace you on station. Do you understand that?"

Hollister declined to answer.

Fowler issued the instructions himself. "One-five. This is Six. You *will* turn your element around and engage any remaining members of the enemy element."

One-five also didn't respond.

The door gunner reached over and tapped Hollister. He pointed at the copilot. Hollister loosened his seat belt and looked back at the copilot.

"Sir," the nineteen-year-old copilot said, "Captain Vance just called me on our freq. He wants to talk to you on your alternate Admin push." He pointed at the chopper radios. "I just dialed it in for you," he said, raising his gloved fingers to indicate what toggle switch was pressed into service.

Hollister nodded and switched to the freq. "Five. Houston Three. Over."

"He's hot. Don't let him screw people up," Vance said, no pretense of radio-telephone procedure in his transmission. "When you get back here we'll figure out what to do. But I just don't have the answer yet."

"Start by keeping a very detailed record of all this . . ." Before Hollister could finish, Fowler's voice overpowered all other cross talk. "One-five. Do you hear me? I want you to move. Now!"

"This is One-five. Negative. I think that is unwise at this time. The size of remaining enemy element is too large for us to engage on the move, in the open. We do not have the firepower, and we are *not* prepared to engage."

"This is Six. I don't want any goddamn argument from you. Now you get those people moving, or turn your element over to your second in command. Do you understand me?"

After a long pause, Nessen responded flatly, "Understood."

"Good. Report to me when you are closing the earlier location. Break. Three. This is Six," Fowler called.

Hollister switched from the Admin frequency, where he had been talking to Vance and monitoring Fowler. "This is Three. Over."

"I am on station at your six o'clock. Take your chopper back to the rear, and get ready to send the horse element if we develop this contact into something," Fowler said.

"Three. I *strongly* recommend against this course of action," Hollister replied.

"And I did not ask for your appraisal. Now get off this net and get back to the base. Out!"

It was getting to be first light when Vance met Hollister's chopper. "He's fucking out of control!" Vance yelled over the chopper noise.

Hollister shouldered his gear and hustled toward Operations with Vance. "He's going to get someone killed. Look," Hollister said, pointing to clusters of teams sitting around radios outside their hooches listening to the traffic on the company radio net. "I'll be surprised if they don't all ask for a transfer out. They aren't stupid."

"One thing at a time. Right now we've got to worry about Nessen's people," Vance said.

Inside Operations the radios were still buzzing with cross talk. Hollister lit a cigarette as he scanned the radio operators' duty log for recent entries. Nessen had moved closer to the location where they had last spotted the approaching VC. Hollister put the pages back down in front of the RTO and tapped the top sheet. "Every word. You got it? I want every word of every transmission taken down."

The RTO gave him a solid "Yessir," and Hollister walked to the map. He looked at the greasy square that marked Nessen's team location. "The Cav been alerted?"

Kurzikowski swiveled around in the desk chair he had scrounged somewhere. "'Bout a half hour ago, sir. They're standing by. We can have them in the air as soon as the choppers wind up."

Vance tapped Hollister's shirt pocket, looking for a cigarette. Hollister pulled out his pack and handed it to Vance.

"He'll never last."

"Nessen?" Hollister asked.

"No," Vance replied. "Fowler."

"How do you figure?"

"I have faith that he'll be discovered like shit on a boot and removed."

"Hope you're right," Hollister said.

The radio broke the moment of silence. "Six. We have a problem." It was Nessen's voice.

"What? It better be a contact or you can just keep moving," Fowler said.

Kurzikowski didn't miss the look of disapproval on Hollister's and Vance's faces. "Think it's time for me to get some more coffee. Can't stay in here without a flak jacket," he said.

Neither Vance nor Hollister replied. They just stayed focused on the radio traffic.

"We seem to have stumbled onto something," Nessen said.

Fowler's strain was evident even before he replied. They could hear him key the mike and take a deep breath before speaking.

"Just tell me you are moving to contact!"

"Negative. We have stopped," Nessen said.

"Are you just stupid, or can't you understand English—Mister?"

"Probably a bit of both," Nessen said.

"Don't get smart with me. Now what the hell is your holdup?"

"We've lost a man into a hole or something. He's okay—just gonna take a bit to recover him," Nessen replied.

"What is it?" Fowler asked excitedly.

"Can't really tell. Lots of vegetation. Might be a well or a cistern or something."

"A tunnel? Is it a tunnel complex? Stop everything, and check it out. If they are around, they're bound to be in there," Fowler said.

"Oh, I don't know. I think that's a really bad idea. We have bad guys running around somewhere out here. They know where we are, and we're too damn light in the ass to stop and do an underground search."

"You *will* do as I say, and now. We'll talk about your insubordinate tone when you get back," Fowler snapped.

"Six, if we make contact—it will be their call. I'd rather not walk into an ambush. Could be really bad news," Nessen said.

There was a pause.

In Operations Hollister and Vance continued monitoring the radio cross talk. "He's getting rattled by Nessen's act."

"He hasn't got a clue, has he?"

"About?"

"About how Nessen can waltz him around until he runs out of fuel and needs to come back to top off."

"Yeah. Then he'll get back—get the runaround again, run short of light, and be forced to pull the team. Nessen's smarter on his worst day than Fowler's ever gonna be," Hollister said.

Nessen came back on with an interim report. "Six, this is One-five. Looks like it's an old tunnel all right."

"They could be in the tunnel," Fowler said, satisfaction in his voice.

Nessen took a long time to reply. "I don't think so. There don't seem to be any signs of recent use."

"That means they're in there for sure," Fowler said. "They are expert at camouflaging their traffic."

"Holy shit!" Vance said. "Now he knows more about it at fifteen hundred feet than an experienced team leader who's standing on the spot."

"Search it," Fowler said.

"For what?" Nessen asked.

"For VC—damnit!"

"We're not set up for tunnel searches. But I'll pitch some grenades and some smoke down into the tunnel."

"Negative! Negative!" Fowler said. "I want prisoners. Anybody can get a body count by throwing grenades into a tunnel."

Kurzikowski had returned and stood behind the two captains. Hollister turned to him. "The Cav?"

"They're ready, and the chopper crews are belted into their seats," Kurzikowski said.

"Crank 'em.".

"What are you thinking?" Vance asked.

"Got a feeling that things are going to get sour out there quickly."

Hollister turned to Vance. "You can hold things down here? I'm going with the Cav. If I let them go out there alone, Fowler'll have that platoon leader talking up his sleeve and then the troop commander will get involved, and it will be a fucking committee trying to decide what to do."

Vance made a painful face. "Fowler's gonna eat your shorts over this."

"He ain't getting no cherry," Hollister said. "Get the Cav Troop CO in here, so we can keep him up to speed. Okay?"

Vance patted Hollister on the shoulder. "You got it. We'll hold things down here."

Fowler's voice boomed over the speaker. "Three? I want the horse element out here to set up a cordon. One-five will be searching a tunnel, and I don't want to let any VC escape through other exits. Tell Saber Six to have his remaining forces standing by for deployment as well. And I don't want any screwups. You got that?"

Hollister reached for the handset, but Vance stopped him. "Let me handle this. You just get going."

Vance took a deep breath and then spoke. "Six. This is Five. Three is outside cranking the horse subelement right now. They should be skids up inside of zero five."

"Roger. Break. One-five. This is Six. Did you copy? Horse soldiers are inbound to give you some help. Have you made any progress?"

CHAPTER 29

S ix. This is One-five. We are following what looks like a horizontal section of tunnel shaft. We can't get down in it because it is too fragile. So
we are trying to trace it above the ground, probing with a cleaning rod,"
Nessen replied.

"Where is the wire?" Fowler asked from his circling chopper.

"The wire?"

"The commo wire. My guess is that it is probably going to end up
inside the same tunnel complex you are probing."

"I don't think so. The wire is a hundred mikes from here and parallel to
the direction of the tunnel. And this is not a complex. I just might have simply uncovered part of a very old tunnel or a large bunker," Nessen corrected.

"You just keep searching, and let me worry about what is going on."

The Cav platoon arrived at the landing zone nearest Nessen's team in six
sucks. Hollister rode with the third chopper in the formation while Lieutenant Boyce, the platoon leader, rode in the lead. Hollister had made it
clear to Boyce, at the chopper pad, that he was riding along to get out to the
site and that Boyce would be in command of his own platoon, not Hollister.

The copilot in Hollister's chopper turned to talk to him. Hollister got up
on his knees to get closer.

"Your CO's C and C is in trail with our flight. He wants to put down on
the LZ with us and drop off the interpreter. Then he's going back to refuel."

Hollister nodded that he understood. But he didn't. *Interpreter?* He
must have meant Bui. That was still another thing that upset Hollister.
Fowler still couldn't distinguish between Bui as the senior Hoi Chanh and
interpreters, which they didn't have.

Hollister was happy to hear that Fowler would be leaving the area for
a while. He might be able to get things sorted out and resolved before the
major returned.

The activity on the LZ was chaotic. It had been some time since Hollister
had made an airmobile assault with a full platoon. By the time the choppers had cleared the LZ, the squads had assembled in tactical formation
and Lieutenant Boyce had them moving toward Nessen's location. Hollister
found Bui. "Where's your weapon?"

Bui turned his palms skyward and shrugged. "No hab." Hollister was angry that Fowler had put Bui out of the chopper with no field gear and no weapon. He pulled his .45 out of its holster and gave it to Bui. "Try not to lose this. Okay?"

Bui smiled and nodded, then hobbled off to join the Cav troopers.

Movement to Nessen's position only took half an hour. And based on Nessen's recommendations, Boyce moved his squads out into a wide semicircle to watch for tunnel exits.

Hollister and Bui had joined Nessen's team, which was already searching the tunnel.

Hollister's first look confirmed what Nessen had been saying. It was not a new or even recently used tunnel. The floor of the exposed section showed light debris that had been deposited by rains and runoff. Any recent use would have disturbed the dead leaves and flushed most of them away. The tunnel walls, only a foot below the surface of the ground, were laced with a web of tiny roots that surely would have been disturbed by frequent VC use.

"Well, we can probably guess that no one's been using this section. How do you think the new major's gonna take it?" Nessen asked Hollister.

Hollister shook his head. "Not well. I think he believes that COSVN Headquarters is stashed in here."

"You want I should tell him, Cap'n?"

"Not yet. Let's just see where the ends of this thing go. There might be something yet. If we don't look . . ."

Nessen finished it for him. "I know, he'll want us to check it out anyhow."

"Well, I got my Hoi Chanh in there now," Nessen said.

"In the tunnel?"

"Yessir. We found another section of it just behind that clump of bushes," Nessen said, pointing to the other branch of the tunnel.

Hollister walked over to the second site and squatted down. He could see the first few feet of another abandoned tunnel shaft that went down, then turned, and then turned again, restricting his view. Near the opening a second LRP fed a length of commo wire into the hole. "Where'd you get the wire?"

"We found it near the landing zone . . . didn't seem to be connected at either end, and I wanted to be able to find Mister Loan if it gets shitty down there," Nessen said.

"Good idea," Hollister said. He realized what pressure Nessen had been under from Fowler since he had been on the ground. Not to let it get to him and still keep focused on his team was something that Hollister admired.

The tunnel search went on for an hour. Then the wire went slack, and the LRP started reeling it back up. Mr. Loan, as 1-5 called him because of his tendency to borrow money from the team members, was coming out.

"Get Bui over here," Hollister said.

"I am at here," Bui said, standing just behind Nessen.

Hollister grinned at Bui's fractured English and pointed him toward Mr. Loan's tunnel. Loan emerged, filthy and soaked with perspiration, a .45 in one hand and a GI flashlight in the other. He looked like something had shaken him up and started spewing Vietnamese even before he was out of the hole.

Nessen, Hollister, two LRPs, and the nearest Cav troopers watched as Loan and Bui talked excitedly.

"What?" Hollister asked.

Bui turned to Hollister and spoke rapidly. "He say he foun' dead man."

"What kind of dead man?"

"He don' know."

Hollister knew he wasn't going to get anywhere having Bui translate the excited jabbering of the frightened Hoi Chanh. "Give me that flashlight."

"Sir? Where you goin'?" Nessen asked.

Hollister looked over his shoulder and nodded toward the horizon. "We're going be out of light and shit out of luck if we don't get some answers so we can get all these people the hell out of here. This has turned into a fucking spectator sport. I doubt if any VC within ten thousand meters doesn't know how many of us are here and how far up our butts we have our thumbs."

Nessen agreed with Hollister and shook his head at the gaggle.

After dumping his gear and taking off his shirt, Hollister tied the wire to his web belt, turned on the flashlight, and grabbed Bui's pistol. Just before he stepped into the tunnel opening, he stopped long enough to check to see that there was a round in his chamber. There was.

The tunnel was built for men much smaller than Hollister. Each move, on his hands and knees, caused him to dislodge the earth above his head and it fell, sticking to the sweat on his back and neck.

The passageway continued to show a lack of use, except for the recent visit by Mr. Loan. Still, Hollister wasn't convinced that just because the passageway was unused that the entire tunnel was unused.

After twenty yards of zigzag horizontal movement, Hollister came to an air lock. It was a water trap, like under a sink. Normally, they were filled with water and a visitor would have to hold his breath and pass through the water-filled trap. But Hollister was lucky. Over time the water level had been neglected, and it only filled the bottom two feet of the trap. It would allow him passage, and he wouldn't have to hold his breath.

The water smelled of microscopic organisms and decaying root growth. Its color was almost black and a scum, broken by Mr. Loan, was trying to re-constitute itself. Hollister steeled himself for the entry and stepped into the trap. He wasn't sure what was in the water with him and really didn't want to know. He just moved as quickly as he could and stepped up on the other side. He realized the smell would be with him the rest of the day.

Continuing down the new passage, Hollister followed the scuff marks that Mr. Loan had left and stopped often to listen for any other movement in the tunnel. There was none.

At a turn, Hollister suddenly felt a small breeze. Somewhere, air was entering the tunnel and moving down the shaft he was in. The smell of the fresh air was a welcome experience, but he was concerned that there might be an opening up ahead guarded by one of the Cav troops, who might get spooked. He was as concerned about being shot by a VC in the tunnel as by an American. He had to hope that the Americans all got the word.

The tunnel turned again and began to slope downward. At the end of the slope, it spilled into a large room. Hollister noticed that Loan's marks stopped at the end of the shaft. He had obviously not gone beyond that point. Hollister could feel the anxiety gripping his chest like a fist. He tried to take a couple of deep breaths to calm himself. He then realized that the air was again foul and stagnant, which meant he had missed the fresh-air leak on his way down the shaft.

At the very end of the shaft, Hollister stopped and held his flashlight as high above his head as he could reach. He thought that if someone was going to take a shot at him, he wanted the shooter to be distracted by the location of the light and misjudge his aim.

The fractured circle of light played across a room that appeared to be not much more than twenty feet deep, fifteen wide, and eight high.

He started at the top and looked at the bristle of roots that had entan-gled themselves in the wooden shoring holding the ceiling in place. The walls were covered with a white, scaly, lichenlike growth that gave the room a whitewashed appearance.

He turned the light and began his search at the far end of the floor. The first thing he saw was one, then two, large mahogany logs running parallel to each other, about two feet apart. They were at least twenty inches in di-ameter and ran the length of the room.

Then he saw what had spooked Loan. Each log had heavy chains wrapped around it at every five feet. The chains stretched across the floor toward the walls. At the end of each of the six chains was a skeleton—clean, white, and old.

The sight shocked Hollister, too. It was some kind of prison. He played the light on the nearest skeleton. There was no sign of who it might have been. It was hard for him to gauge the age or size of the dead man. Not a single thread of clothing remained. The piles of rat droppings around the bones explained their cleanliness and the missing clothing. One ankle was still shackled to an end of the chain.

Hollister sank to a sitting position. The horror of the deaths of the six men hit him. *Had they been starved to death? Were they Vietnamese? What war were they from? Could they be French? Had their deaths been as horrible as he imagined?*

No one had been in that room for years, and Hollister didn't want to disturb the remains. As far as he was concerned—there was no reason to.

The air on the surface was fresh and clean and cool. Hollister took a few deep breaths and shook his head at what he had seen. He lit a cigarette, put his shirt back on, and explained what he had found to Nessen and Lieutenant Boyce.

"What now?" Nessen asked.

"I can't imagine we're going to make contact on our terms if we continue to press back toward where you saw those VC. This tunnel complex is older than dirt. Lemme report all this to Major Fowler and see if I can get us out of here," Hollister said.

"I could go for that," Nessen said.

"When you get back here, we'll get to the matter of what the hell you are doing out there when I specifically told you to get back to Operations!" Fowler screamed over the handset.

Hollister rolled his eyes and held the handset away from his ear while Fowler continued to scream. Finally, Fowler ended his transmission long enough to take a breath, and Hollister jumped in. "Roger all that, but we better get to extracting this lash-up before we run out of light. Over."

"Negative! Negative! Negative!" Fowler yelled. "I want you to send your senior little person back into that tunnel to see if he can identify the remains. We will have to make a complete report of what you found, and so far it is woefully incomplete!"

"Six, I don't recommend we send anyone back down there."

"Again . . . I didn't ask you your opinion. Now get that man down in that hole, and do what the hell I told you. Do you understand? We are about ready to land at the refueling point and should be at your location inside of four five. Now, get cracking, damnit!"

"Roger. Out," Hollister said.

Bui took Mr. Loan with him. They had been down in the tunnel for almost thirty minutes when Hollister began to worry about the time. It was getting late enough in the day so that if Fowler hadn't made arrangements to have the choppers standing by to pick up Nessen's team and Boyce's platoon it was almost too late to start. Hollister decided he had to influence things some other way and walked over to Nessen. "How 'bout getting Captain Vance on the Admin push for me?"

"Can you talk?" Hollister asked Vance, wanting to make sure Fowler wasn't somewhere near the radio or aware he and Vance were talking.

"Yeah . . . it's cool. What you got?"

"We got to get moving," Hollister said.

"I'm on it. Got the choppers ready. Instead of waiting for an okay from Six, I'm launching them when you say so."

"He'll hang you from the jump tower," Hollister cautioned.

"Won't be the first time. You just let me know if you need anything else."

"There's one other thing. Get ahold of Edmonds in the C and C on his push and tell him I think he should be *very, very* careful about his ship's maintenance status before they return to this location. Very careful."

"Got ya. I'll tell him how concerned you are about readiness. Let me handle it for you," Vance said.

"Roger. I knew I could count on you. Out."

Hollister checked his watch and worried some more about how long Bui and Mr. Loan were taking. He looked at the sun moving down on the horizon and reached for another cigarette. He was out. Nessen offered one from his crumpled pack. Hollister took it and was starting to thank Nessen when they heard a muffled noise. The first thing that came to Hollister's mind was the sound of the big wooden door closing at the icehouse in his hometown. It was heavy, but still muted. The two looked toward the tunnel shaft and saw a puff of dust and a gush of air come out of the small opening.

"Oh shit!" Hollister said. "A cave-in!"

As they reached the hole, Loan scrambled out, covered with dirt. He started jabbering so fast it didn't make any difference what language he was speaking—no one could understand him. It was clear that Bui was involved, and it wasn't good news.

Grabbing Nessen's arm, Hollister said, "Gimme someone who will fit down there."

He turned and waved at Boyce. "Send me the smallest man you have. It's a cave-in."

While Mr. Loan, a second LRP, and a small Hawaiian Cav trooper disappeared into the tunnel with an entrenching tool, Hollister got on the radio to crank up a medevac. Kurzikowski was taking down the information back at Operations when Fowler broke in again.

"Negative! Negative on a medevac request. You don't even know you have someone hurt. I don't want to risk a chopper sortie when we don't even know he needs medical attention," Fowler screamed. "Quit coddling those people, damnit."

"Listen . . . I am convinced that the man is hurt enough to scare the shit out of one of the other scouts. Now I don't want to risk his life by waiting until *I* pronounce him injured," Hollister snapped.

Fowler keyed his mike to respond and then stopped. There was a long silence while he rekeyed it. "I've been advised that there is a problem with this C and C, and we are going to have to swap it for another. You just get on with checking out that bunker complex, and get me some answers . . ." His voice trailed off.

Hollister assumed the chopper must have landed again, breaking off communications. He was just as happy to lose commo. He reached over and spun the dials on the radio to the Admin frequency.

"Five. This is Three."

Vance's voice came on immediately. "I'm here, partner. I've sent a medevac in spite of earlier instructions from Six."

When Vance didn't get an immediate answer, he called Hollister again. "Where'd you go? Problems?"

Hollister's tone had changed when he did reply. "Five, it's Bui. They're just dragging him out now. Fucking overhead collapsed on him. He's unconscious and spitting blood. Could be real bad!"

"You should be hearing from the medevac in less than five."

"Rog . . . I gotta run. Send me those pickup ships. We're getting the fuck out of here. Out."

＊＊

The sun had just slipped below the low tree line on the west end of the landing zone. The medevac picked up Bui only minutes after he was rescued by the trio of ad hoc tunnel rats. But it took another twenty minutes before the entire flight of choppers arrived to pick up the LRPs and the Cav platoon.

Hollister hated complete pullouts. Everyone around the area knew that once the troops were loaded into the choppers they would be most vulnerable. All the choppers and all the troops would be on the same small piece of real estate. Their only protection came from the gunships and the on-call artillery Hollister had plotted.

He waited until he saw the last man get into the last chopper before he stepped up onto the skid of his lift ship. As he did he slapped the peter pilot on the helmet and yelled, "Go! Go!"

It was too quiet for Hollister. They were only a few hundred meters away from where Nessen's team had spotted VC the night before, and that bothered him—plenty.

Hollister's chopper rolled forward as the pilots, both on the controls, pulled pitch and tried to get out and up at the same speed as the two choppers in front of it in the formation.

Hollister saw the first explosion on the PZ before he heard it. Then a second impact off to the right *Mortars!* He just knew it! The fuckers had waited and then dropped four mortar rounds onto the PZ. It was over as fast as it started. All four rounds must have been in the air at the same time. That meant that the VC who dropped the rounds down the tubes had already broken down the mortars and were running for cover before the first round impacted.

The cross talk over the radio was a confusing jumble of pilots and Operations all talking at once. Hollister stuck his finger in one ear while he tried to figure out what was going on by listening to Nessen's RTO's radio.

The chopper in front of his, one of six—in staggered trail formation—took some damage and was trying to limp back to Bien Hoa without putting down.

He spun around. The ships behind him seemed to be clearing the PZ without any trouble, and the gunships—four of them—were burning up the area where they thought the mortars had come from. He felt helpless. There was nothing he could do but hang on until they got to a safer altitude and then just ride back to the base camp.

Fowler still hadn't shown up at the LRP compound when Hollister got off the chopper with the other members of Nessen's team.

Vance ran out to meet Hollister halfway. "They just called from the

Clearing Station. I'm going up there to make sure our wounded are taken care of. You stay here and close out the details."

"Wounded? You mean Bui?" Hollister asked, yelling over the sounds of the choppers landing two at a time on the pad.

"Seems you took some casualties from the mortars. A door gunner got his shoulder separated when the concussion spun his machine gun around and clipped him. He'll be okay. But two of the Cav troops took some frags—doesn't seem to be critical. They'll be in overnight," Vance said as they walked toward the jeep parked outside Operations.

"And Bui?" Hollister asked, automatically looking toward the back door of the club for T.T.

"Not so good. He's pretty fucked up. They told Sergeant Rose that Bui's got three, maybe more, cracked ribs. Punctured both lungs. They also think he's fractured a vertebra in his neck. They're still waiting for the X rays to dry to make sure they got a handle on everything."

"What's that mean?" Hollister asked.

"Rose tells me everything should be fixable unless they find some more internal injuries. But even if they don't, he's a long way from being out of the woods."

Hollister saw T.T. as she stepped out of the club's back door. "I've got to go talk to her. How much does she know?"

"Rose told her what I know," Vance said.

"Fuck!"

"What?"

"I promised her he wouldn't be going to the field again. No damn wonder the fucking Viets don't trust us."

"Hey, go easy. Wasn't your idea," Vance said, offering Hollister a cigarette.

He waved off the smoke. "She won't understand that. And where the hell is Major Audie Murphy anyway?"

Vance smiled for the first time.

"What the hell is so funny?"

"Edmonds faked trouble with his chopper to ground the C and C at Two Field so he could keep Fowler out of our hair long enough for you to get that gaggle out of the AO."

Hollister laughed. "Well, I'll be damned. I'll be buying him drinks for the rest of my tour."

"So we better take stock of where we are and what damage has been done and get this ragbag operation back on its wheels—before Fowler gets back," Vance said.

***

It was almost midnight when Hollister and T.T. entered the Evac Hospital. Even before he stepped across the threshold a sergeant at the reception desk stood and started to hassle Hollister.

"Captain, if that woman isn't authorized personnel, she can't come in here," the medic said.

"Don't worry. She's an interpreter," Hollister lied.

"Oh. Okay, sir. Guess you're looking for the LRP casualties?"

Hollister nodded. The sergeant pointed toward the Recovery Ward and plopped back down in his chair.

The contraption that held Bui wasn't built for a man with a crooked leg. The doctors had had to pull the leg away from the board they had strapped him to. From the ankle of his good leg to his forehead, he was taped to the board to keep his body and his neck immobilized. A flexible tube was attached to the hole they had poked into his throat to help him breathe, and blood filled drain tubes that led from his torso to collection bags below his bed frame. His face was swollen and discolored. And his chin and nose were terribly scratched where he must have tried to force the earth away from his face to get some air while he was buried.

T.T. made no sound and gave away no expression as she walked to his side and knelt down next to him, taking his hand in hers. Hollister watched as she touched her cheek to the back of his hand, tears quietly slipping from the corners of her eyes. He knew she could hear better than he could the gurgling sounds coming from deep inside Bui's chest cavity as he strained to breathe.

It was almost four in the morning when they left. T.T. was silent, but Hollister knew she appreciated his efforts to get her in to see Bui. She wasn't even supposed to be on the Bien Hoa compound after ten-thirty at night. And at four A.M. it was too late to try to slip her out of any of the three gates that were still open. He would find a place for her to sleep.

As they crossed Bien Hoa Army Base, Hollister started to take inventory of what had happened. In a single day he'd been chewed out by his new boss, he'd disobeyed several orders, he'd been openly insubordinate, he'd lied, and he'd misused his authority to get around rules. It just wasn't like him. And he wasn't proud of his behavior.

He had also seen the worst demonstration of concern for the troops, poorest application of combat resources, riskiest maneuvering of manpower, and the most unwise splitting of forces and command responsibilities, as well as leadership blunders and willful suspension of established company SOPs. And it wasn't over yet.

***

At the compound Hollister took T.T. to his room. "You can sleep here," he told her. He looked at his watch. "It's easier than trying to get you out of the gate this late and then back in. You won't get any rest at all."

"Oh, no can do," she said with alarm. "This you room, Cap'tan Jim."

"No, for the next few hours it's your room. You've had a long night. Try to get some rest."

T.T. smiled at Hollister, and her eyes started to tear up. "My Bui? What you think happen to he?"

Hollister took her by the shoulders and gave her a slight squeeze. "I think that your Bui is a brave soldier and that he will be very sore. But he will be okay, and you two will be together again soon."

T.T. let out a small whimper and caught herself. "Thank you too much, Cap'tan Jim."

After checking into Operations and finding things out in the AO quiet, Hollister crossed the compound in the still-dark moments before dawn and entered the mess hall. Vance was already there, drinking coffee and jotting down notes on some scraps of paper.

Hollister grabbed a cup of coffee and walked up behind Vance. "You're up early, Ranger."

"Hey, Jim. How's Bui?"

"He's pretty broken up, but I think he's got a good chance of returning to duty in a few weeks. I just hope he wants to come back to work here."

"So where is he?" Hollister asked.

"Fowler? He got back after you left last night. He didn't say shit to me. Just went to his room and slammed the door."

"Where the hell was he?"

"Edmonds kept him tied up with that downed chopper until he finally blew his top and commandeered a quarter-ton to bring him back here," Vance said.

"So when does all hell break loose?"

Vance shrugged. "Got me. The fucker's probably writing up courts-martial charges that will have to be sent up the pipe in a footlocker."

"We're in big trouble, aren't we?"

"Could be. We could all be reassigned to the Disciplinary Barracks at Fort Levenworth for some of the stunts we pulled yesterday."

"Well . . . if he starts any more shit he's gonna have to explain his actions with Nessen's people and using the reaction force like a damn maneuver element and then sending Bui back down in that hole to get a fucking body count off of dead men from another war." Hollister collapsed a small milk carton and dropped it on his tray. "If we take it in the shorts on this, he's getting some on him."

"I'm not sure what our next move is right now. You think they'll get wind of this at Two Field?" Vance asked.

"I hope so."

"What if they don't?"

"I just don't have the stomach to go whine about Fowler. But he's gonna get someone killed, and I might have to get over my own principles. Pretty shitty options, if you ask me," Hollister said.

"If I go to General Stone and tell him—"

"No," Hollister interrupted. "That's a sure way to give Fowler an argument that you're just looking to get his job. If anyone has to blow the whistle, it can't be anyone who stands to gain anything by doing it. That'll only confuse the issues."

"So?"

"I don't know. Let's see what he's up to and do some damage assessment today. Maybe we're just a little too sensitive and overreacting to what is just an asshole for a boss."

"Yeah. Still, I don't expect Fowler went to his room last night and will wake up as a Sangean today. Nope, no bets there, partner," Vance said.

It was just getting light when they left the mess hall. "Oh shit!" Vance said.

"What?" Hollister asked as he stepped up next to Vance. "There," Vance said, pointing across the compound to an open area just outside Fowler's window.

During the night the LRPs had taken six Ml6s, fixed bayonets, and stuck them in the ground outside the BOQ. The message was clear. They had seen a team risked unnecessarily.

"Look," Vance said, pointing toward Fowler's window. "Seems like the troops are trying to tell him something."

Hollister caught the outline of Fowler stepping back from the window. "He saw it. Bet that isn't going to help his mood any."

By noon they had not heard or seen Fowler. Vance and Hollister met again and decided just to continue to march. Whatever was going to happen would happen. Their major concern was to get the company back on its feet and keep them too busy to stew in their anger at Fowler.

Hollister put priority on two things for the day, getting a letter written designating T.T. as the company interpreter so she could get in to visit Bui regularly and collecting notes on what had happened. If it came to a showdown, he wanted to have every move Fowler had made since taking over the company in writing.

On the morning of the second day, Bui had improved and Fowler had called the Orderly Room several times—from his room. He instructed the first sergeant to have paperwork sent over to his room and issued instructions for routine tasks that the NCOs in J Company had been handling without guidance from its commander.

The routine seemed to return to almost normal by the end of the week. Still, neither Vance nor Hollister had spoken to Fowler. He stayed cooped up in his room almost all the time, except when he left the compound with his driver to go to meetings at Field Force Headquarters.

Sergeant Major Carey told Vance that Fowler was attending meetings and submitting reports to the Field Force G-3 as if everything were running smoothly. But when he returned to the LRP compound, he closed himself up in his room and only went to the mess hall for something to eat well after the last regular meal was served. Around the company he became known as "The Ghost."

Hollister and Vance continued running the operations of the company with virtually no input from Fowler.

Early on the morning of the fifth day of self-exile, Vance sent a runner over to wake Hollister. Still half asleep, Hollister entered the Orderly Room. "Damn, it's two A.M. What's up? We got a contact about to pop?"

"No," Vance said, thrusting a document toward Hollister. "We have a mutiny about to happen."

Hollister rubbed his eyes and tried to read it. The letter was from Fowler to *All Members of the Command*. The subject was *New Tactical SOP*.

Hollister scanned the document. "What the hell is all this?"

"Let me save you the trouble," Vance said. "He's pissed about the performance and the lack of *aggressiveness* of the company and wants to change policy. Teams will stay on the ground until they make contact or run out of ammo, water, and rations. Air re-supply will be a method of *extending* patrols and increasing the likelihood of *successful* contacts. And in the future, all contacts will be pursued to insure every possible chance that they result in a body count."

"Yeah—ours!" Hollister said.

"He sent a copy of this to every man in the company late this afternoon, and the troops are hot."

"The troops? I'm pretty fucking hot myself," Hollister said.

"No, this time it's gonna be a showdown. Come take a look at this," Vance said.

They walked out the front entrance of the Orderly Room and found another sign from the troops. All the M16s in the company had been neatly placed in three-rifle, muzzle-up stacks—in army terms—they had stacked arms. They were through.

"Son of a bitch," Hollister said. "It's over, man. This'll fucking cripple Juliet Company. Let me take care of this," he said, not waiting for a reply from Vance.

Hollister didn't care whom he woke up as he slammed the screen door to the BOQ behind him. He quickly moved down the short hallway to his room and pulled out the sheaf of papers he had collected on Fowler. Tucking them under his arm, he went to the end of the hall and into the darkened Officers' Club. Behind the bar he found the stack of rock and roll tapes and picked one without a label on its clear plastic reel. Dumping it into his shirt pocket, he doubled back down the hallway and stopped at Fowler's door.

Hollister swallowed, straightened up, and kicked the door open. Hollister reached over and threw the light switch on. "Get the fuck out of that rack, Fowler," he yelled at the sleeping major.

Fowler jumped to his feet, wearing only his OD T-shirt and shorts. "What the hell is the meaning of this?"

"The meaning of this is that you are finished. You are leaving Juliet Company." He was rattled by his own anger and could feel himself losing control. As he looked at Fowler, he tried to calm himself, unsure as to what lengths he would go to rid the company of the major.

"Oh? Just who made that decision?"

"You are making it now," Hollister replied.

"Get out of my room, and report to my office at midday. I have had just about enough from you. Consider yourself relieved of duties."

"Shut up and pack," Hollister said.

"Do you realize the consequences of your actions, Captain?"

"Yes. Do you?" Hollister held up the thick packet of paperwork. "If you push it, I'll forward a complete report of *your* deplorable and dangerous behavior as a commander up the pipe. I've got chapter and verse on you, and General Stone won't have a problem seeing what a big mistake he made sending you here."

"Just your word against mine, Mister!"

Hollister pulled the tape from his pocket. "We've also taped all of your radio traffic."

The color drained from Fowler's flushed face. "You can't do that. Those transmissions are out of context. No one could understand the pressures of the situation. A commander has to be firm."

Hollister shrugged. "If you're right, they'll figure that out in an investigation. You ready to face the heat?"

"What choice do I have?"

"You can find a way to quit or I'm blowing the fucking whistle on you."

"You can be court-martialed for this," Fowler said.

"But I won't go down alone. Not much choice here. If I don't do this, you'll have some dead LRPs on your hands. But they seem to have quit on you anyhow. They'll refuse to go out as long as you're here." Hollister pointed to the window. "Look for yourself. You've lost them with your pompous little emperor act."

Fowler looked out the window. The sight of the stacked rifles made him collapse into a chair, speechless.

"You've got till noon tomorrow to do whatever you're going to do. Then I'm going to General Stone," Hollister said as he turned and walked out of Fowler's room, slamming the door behind him.

Every officer in the company was standing in the hallway. They all applauded as Hollister walked out the nearby exit and crossed the compound to tell Vance what he had done.

He felt uncomfortable with having instigated the entire showdown and for having lied. He knew he had crossed a line that he never, ever thought he'd even approach. He also knew that if it backfired he would be the one under charges.

Hollister drank Scotch as Vance nursed a cooling cup of mess-hall coffee. "What do you think?" Hollister asked.

"I called Carey at Two Field, and he said Fowler hasn't turned up there. He's been gone long enough to drive over there and back twice," Vance said.

"Well, it's his call."

T.T. took Hollister's empty glass without asking.

"No, I've had enough," Hollister said as she tried to pour him another

Scotch. She stopped, but pushed a glass with less than a quarter shot in it toward Hollister as if it would be a waste to throw it away.

He accepted the short drink and smiled at her. "You see Bui today?"

"Yes. He siddup."

"He what?"

She made a squatting, sitting gesture. "He sid. You know, sid."

"Oh, he sat up?"

"That what T.T. say."

Hollister laughed at her English. "You're right. That is what you said. I'm happy to hear he's feeling better. He ought to be back for duty in a few weeks. Yes?"

"Yes—but he no go wid patrol?"

Hollister turned to Vance and put on a serious face. "What do you say? Bui going to the field again?"

"Nope," Vance said, killing his drink and waving T.T. over for another. "I need him to do too much training of the new guys."

T.T. smiled and poured much too much Scotch in a glass for Vance. "Oh, sorry, Dai Uy."

"How's anyone supposed to drink that? It's filled to the damn rim."

"You can sip," she said.

"How come you can say 'sip' but not 'sit'?" Hollister asked.

She made a face at Hollister for poking fun at her.

"You better be nice to Dai Uy Jim. He's going to the land of the big PX soon," Vance kidded her.

"No. You no go."

"Got to. Getting short."

"When's your DEROS date?" Vance asked.

"Forty-two days and a wake-up."

"That's an estimate, huh?"

Hollister raised his arm and looked at his watch. "You want it in hours, minutes, and seconds?"

"No. But I'm starting to worry about what the hell I'm going to do around here with The Ghost locked up in his bunker and a new Operations officer."

"You'll be okay," Hollister said.

"Yeah. Right."

It was almost dark when the field phone rang in the club. T.T. answered it and handed the receiver to Vance. "For you, Dai Uy." Hollister was sitting at a table at the far end of the room finishing a letter to Susan. He put his pen down, lit a cigarette, and listened to Vance's side of the conversation. It was nothing more than a series of "yessirs" and "right away, sirs." He hung up and turned to Hollister and four other officers in the room. "Don't ask me. I don't know what's going on. But General Stone and Colonel Schneider want me at Two Field, ten minutes ago."

Hollister and Vance were alone in the Orderly Room.

"He went over to the Field Hospital and convinced some doctor that he had seriously hurt his back and that he's in constant pain," Vance said.

"What happened then?"

"Seems that the doctor took pity on him and put him on a limited-duty profile for six months. He took that to Colonel Schneider and cried the blues about how disappointed he was that he couldn't carry out the duties as Juliet Company commander."

"And?"

"And Schneider went to General Stone, and they both decided to replace Fowler with a new CO," Vance said.

"Great! So what happens to Fowler?"

"Fowler's been put on bed rest in a BOQ at Long Binh Post for a week and will be reassigned as a special projects officer in the G-5 Shop. But he's out of the way and won't get anybody hurt again.

"And then he dropped the bomb."

"What? You're making this tough," Hollister said.

"He told me to assume command of Juliet Company and continue the mission."

Hollister broke out in a wide grin. "Beautiful!" But Vance wasn't smiling. "Okay, what?"

"You can tell me no, and I'll understand."

"What are you getting at?" Hollister asked.

"I can't be CO, XO, and Operations officer all at once. Hell, I can't even take over and break in a new XO *and* a new S-3 at the same time—if I had 'em."

Hollister could feel it coming. He pulled out a cigarette and tapped it on the face of his watch.

"Jim, I gotta ask you to extend," Vance said.

"Oh shit, Peter! You really know how to lay it on," Hollister said.

"You understand the bind I'm in. What we need around here is stability. We play fucking musical chairs with the top three players and it's gonna spook the troops worse than they already are."

Hollister raised his hand. "Listen, you're preachin' to the choir. I know what you mean, and I understand it. But I'm scheduled for the Career Course just after New Year's and . . . and . . ." He threw the cigarette at a trash can across the room and missed. He looked at Vance again and took a deep breath. "Okay. How long do you need me, and when do you need to know?"

"Four more months. Just give me that much time to get this company back on its feet."

The letter to Susan was the most difficult one Hollister had ever written her. How could he explain what was happening and why he had to stay the extra months? She didn't understand the delicate balance of confidence that creates teamwork and keeps LRPs alive in the bush.

He started the letter three times and tore each one up, only to start again. He had another Scotch and then another and still another while he wrestled with his explanation. She had been so patient with him, and the news would just set them back.

He knew she was waiting for him to come home and tell her he was ready to get out of the army. He wondered if she would be more angry or just more disappointed. Would she see it as just another postponement of his decision?

And what if he did stay the extra months? It would be almost another half year before he would be able to see her. He made a note on the corner of a piece of scrap paper to suggest that they meet halfway on his way home. They could have a second honeymoon; maybe in Hong Kong or Paris. It smelled like a bribe to him—he scratched it out.

He decided that the only thing to do was to tell her everything and make her understand how important his extension would be to so many people. He would just have to ask her to trust his judgment and be patient.

He loved her very much. But the ache in his gut over the decision to extend wouldn't go away. He remembered First Sergeant Easy's words: "You're in this now. Don't walk away." Words from a man who gave his leg to save a fellow LRP.

The letter took him all night to write.

GLOSSARY

AC—AIRCRAFT commander

ACL—Allowable cargo load

Advanced Course—The second level of training for infantry officers after the basic course. Also called the Career Course, conducted at Fort Benning

Alpha—The first letter in the military phonetic alphabet to reduce the chance of misunderstanding the letter alone. When used with a radio call sign it indicates the assistant, i.e., Rattler Three Alpha would be the assistant operations officer

AO—Area of Operations. The geographical area assigned to a unit by specific boundaries

APCs—Army abbreviation for aspirin

APL—Assistant patrol leader

arty—Shorthand for artillery. Indirect fires provided by howitzers and cannons

ARVN—Army of the Republic of Vietnam. The South Vietnamese army

ASA—Army Security Agency

AWOL bag—A small, zippered, canvas bag used by soldiers to carry the essentials for a short trip away from a unit or station: shaving gear, underwear, and socks. For sale at just about every post exchange. The term AWOL became attached to it out of the assumption that anyone going absent without leave would only take what he needed, not every thing he owned

BDA—Bomb-damage assessment

belly man—An experienced LRP or Ranger who flew to an insert or extraction landing zone in the chase helicopter to be of assistance to anyone needing help getting into the chopper. The other members of the chopper crew already had duties that would not allow them to assist

Big Red One—Nickname for the First Infantry Division

BOQ—Bachelor officers quarters

briefback—Having received an order, subordinate leaders analyze the mission and verbally give the order back to higher headquarters to insure understanding

C&C—Command and Control. Term applied to a field commander's headquarters or his helicopter

cammies—Camouflage fatigue uniforms

CG—Commanding General

chalk—One aircraft load of passengers

CIB—Combat Infantryman's Badge. A blue enameled badge with a rifle
on it, surrounded by a silver wreath. The badge is only awarded
to infantrymen who have served in combat and under enemy fire.
During Vietnam the duration had to be at least thirty days

CINCPAC—Commander in Chief, Pacific, headquartered in Hawaii

claymore—Directional, command-detonated antipersonnel mine. Set up
above the ground

commo—Short for communications

CONUS—Continental United States

cross talk—Listening to cross talk is hearing two or more conversing
stations or parties on a radio or telephone network

DEROS—Date of estimated return from overseas

dai uy—The Vietnamese term for captain

DR—Delinquency report

Dust-Off—Original call sign for all medevac choppers

E&E—Escape and evade

ETS—Estimated time of separation (from the army)

FAC—Air Force Forward Air Controller. Controls tactical air support

FO—Forward observer. Adjusts indirect fires

FOB—Forward operating base

G-1—The designation for the administration and personnel section of a
division headquarters or higher

G-2—Intelligence section of division and higher-level headquarters

G-3—The designation for the operations section of a division headquarters
or higher

G-5—The designation for the civic affairs section of a division headquarters
or higher

H&I—Harassing and interdicting fires

HE—High-explosive ordnance

Hoi Chanh—North Vietnamese and Viet Cong soldiers who surrendered
under the Chieu Hoi (Open Arms) Program were called Hoi Chanhs

IFFV—First Field Force, Vietnam

jumpmaster—NCO or officer in charge of parachutists and the execution
of a parachute jump

KIA—Killed in action

klicks—Kilometers—map/ground measurement

leg—A derogatory term used by parachute-qualified soldiers to refer to nonqualified ones

LZ—Helicopter landing zone

mad minute—Fort Benning's traditional VIP live fire demonstration of the lethality of combined arms weapons firing simultaneously. It is usually reserved for VIPs because it is an expensive and dangerous display

MARS—Military Affiliate Radio Station

medevac—Chopper evacuation of a casualty for medical attention. Sometimes applied liberally to any mode of transportation to more comprehensive medical facilities

mikes—Meters or minutes, depending on the context

MTO&E—Modified Table of Organization and Equipment

NVA—North Vietnamese Army

OCS—Officer Candidate School

OER—Officer Efficiency Report

OJT—On-the-job training

old man—Affectionate term used to refer to the commanding officer. Never used in his presence

Operations—The staff/headquarters section responsible for the tactical employment and planning of maneuver units (S-3, G-3)

papa zulu—Helicopter pickup zone

PCS—Permanent change of station

peter pilot—Helicopter copilot

point—The lead man in a combat patrol is called the point man, and the position in the file is known as point

pork chop—A radio microphone separate from the receiver. Similar in function to a police-car microphone

POV—Privately owned vehicle

prick 77—Slang for AN/PRC 77, squad FM radio

profile—Medical condition limiting types of duty

prop blast—The violent turbulence behind airplane props and even jet engine turbines. Also parties to celebrate first parachute jumps in an Airborne unit

PT—Physical training

push—Slang for frequency

PZ—Helicopter pickup zone

redleg—Nickname for the artillery

REMF—Rear echelon motherfucker

Republican—Communist Vietnamese term for the South Vietnamese

RF/PF—Regional Forces/Popular Forces. The local military militia established by the ARVN. Similar, but not nearly as well equipped or trained, as the American National Guard and Reserves

RFO—Request for orders

RON—Remain overnight

RTO—Radio telephone operator

S-2—Staff section at Battalion or Brigade that handles all battlefield intelligence

sapper—Specially trained VC soldiers who conducted infiltration, obstacle breaching, and demolition operations

SITREP—Situation report. A scheduled or spontaneous report of the tactical situation sent or transmitted to the next higher headquarters

slicks—Troop- and cargo-carrying helicopters

SOI—Signal operating instructions, code words, and frequencies—classified information

SOP—Standard operating procedure

sortie—One aircraft flight of a takeoff and return

spoons—Cooks

Starlight—Night vision scope that uses ambient light

the Cav—The First Cavalry Division (Airmobile)

the World—The United States, from the term "the real world."

TOC—Tactical Operations Center

turtle—A soldier's replacement—because he takes so long to get there

Two Field—Slang for II Field Force, Vietnam

URC-10—Small survival radio that emits a signal and can be used for voice transmission

USARV—United States Army, Vietnam. The headquarters in Vietnam that directed all U.S. Army operations and organizational matters. As distinguished from the MACV—Military Assistance Command, Vietnam, which controlled all advisory efforts

Victor Romeo—Phonetic for visual reconnaissance

warning order—Early operations order issued, minus all the details, so planning and preparation can start

WD-1—Double-strand communications wire

web gear—Term applied to the load-bearing equipment carried by the combat soldier. His ammo pouches, canteens, grenades, first-aid packet, and the like would be attached to his web gear—belt and shoulder harness

XO—Executive officer. The second ranking officer in most units

ABOUT THE AUTHOR

Dennis Foley retired from the army as a lieutenant colonel after several tours in Southeast Asia. He served as a Long Range Patrol platoon leader, an Airborne Infantry company commander, a Ranger company commander, and a Special Forces "A" Detachment commander. He holds two Silver Stars, four Bronze Stars, and two Purple Hearts. In addition to his novels, he has written and produced for television and film. He lives in Whitefish, Montana.

THE JIM HOLLISTER TRILOGY

FROM OPEN ROAD MEDIA

OPEN ROAD

INTEGRATED MEDIA